ENDGAME

Cover: Image of the arms of the Russian Federation fixed on a monument to Peter the Great at the Mikhailovsky Palace in St.-Petersburg. Courtesy Shutterstock.

This book is a work of fiction. Any resemblance to actual events or persons, living or dead, is entirely coincidental.

"Endgame," by Douglas Clark. ISBN 978-1-949756-40-1 (softcover); 978-1-949756-41-8 (hardcover); 978-1-949756-42-5 (ebook).

Published 2019 by Virtualbookworm.com Publishing Inc., P.O. Box 9949, College Station, TX 77842, US.

BY DOUGLAS CLARK

BELFAST
TAKE FIVE
SHELL GAME
EVERMORE
CRITICAL MASS
FAULT LINES
PROVOKE THE DEVIL
THE IRISH SPY
ENDGAME

To Josie

Endgame

A Novel

Douglas Clark

The winner of the game is the player who makes the next-to-last mistake.

Quote by chess grandmaster
Savielly Tartakower

CHAPTER 1

PARIS, FRANCE

Victoria Prescott woke from a restless sleep. Outside the Air France Boeing 777 it was early morning as the aircraft approached over the British Isles for the final leg of the overnight flight from San Francisco into Paris Charles de Gaulle Airport. Her first time back to Paris in years. This hurried trip unexpected following a telephone call just two days earlier.

That morning in her office at Stanford University in Palo Alto, California the caller identified himself in Russian launching a flood of emotions. She had not spoken to Anton Grigoryev for twenty years. Fluent in Russian although with an Anglicized accent, she fumbled with what to say.

"Anton, is this really you?"

"Have you forgotten my voice after all these years, Victoria?"

"Of course not. My god how are you?"

Of course she had not forgotten him or those ten days in Moscow so long ago. With his assistance her academic career catapulted. Considering their short but intimate relationship, a sense of guilt flooded back for never having reached out to him. Must he not think of her as ungrateful after all he did for her?

"I have followed your career all these years, Victoria. According to your online photograph, still as uncommonly attractive as that first time we met. Age has been more than kind. No one would mistake you for an esteemed professor of history and twentieth century Russian scholar."

What was this about? Why was he reconnecting now after all these years?

"Still the charmer I see, Anton. So good to hear your voice. I want you to know that I regretted not …well, remaining in contact after …

"No need for recriminations, Victoria. I did nothing either. Complicated circumstances for both of us. But we can explore all that when we see each other. At least I hope that can be arranged.'

"See each other? What do you mean?"

"Listen, Victoria. I need to ask for your help. Can you come to Paris?"

"Paris? What is this about? We haven't spoken for twenty years now you want me to fly to Paris?"

"Victoria, please listen to what I have to tell you. Not just for me but … but let's just say for reasons of world security. That is not exaggeration. I have absolutely vital information for the United States. Your father was formerly with your State Department. He will know the right people to contact."

"Contact for what, Anton? You're scaring me."

"Victoria, I can't discuss this on the telephone. Understand what I'm saying. I am still in the Russian Foreign Security Service. Now the first deputy director with a general's rank. I'm defecting, Victoria. What I have to offer will scare Western intelligence. Will you help me?"

"Defecting!"

The shock of hearing from him now compounded with this bizarre and admittedly frightening implication of what he was saying. Was this some elaborate Russian hoax? The current autocratic regime nothing like the Yeltsin era when they met. Was he the same person? Might he be playing on their brief intimacy twenty years ago? To accomplish what?

"I've so many questions, Anton. Aside from why you are doing this, why me? Can't you just go to the U.S. embassy in Paris?"

"Too risky. I suspect my colleagues by now suspect I have already left Russia. What I possess is too dangerous to the current regime to allow me to go over to the other side. My business is Russian intelligence. I would never trust American intelligence to handle this without incident. And of course your current president's close ties to Putin. Your foreign service is in disarray with no qualified senior people. I need to negotiate a deal before begging for asylum on terms drafted by some bureaucrat."

"But I'm an academic, Anton. A historian. I know nothing about your world of espionage."

"You're an expert on Russia. The Stalin and Cold War eras. Of course you know something of espionage. You uncovered that World War Two Soviet spy decades later. According to your website you are currently pursuing research to explain modern Russia following the collapse of the Soviet Union. Fluent in Russian, you can immediately translate and appreciate what I have to offer the West. Personally you'll have a wealth of exclusive confidential material for your research. And your father will know how to go about this.

"You're the perfect intermediary because I can trust you. Defection is a delicate mating dance. It takes time. I need to go underground while the Americans make the necessary security preparations. Putin's thugs have a long reach. I don't intend to end up like the defector Alexander Litvinenko murdered in London years ago."

Prescott did not know what to say.

"Trust me, Victoria. You will not regret the adventure. Paris is so much more appealing than Moscow."

She remained silent for several moments. It was the summer break at Stanford so she had no teaching commitments for the next three months. Recalling those days in Moscow with Grigoryev brought forth a flood of images. No denying the thrill of revisiting that past great adventure now wrapped in this new mystery. Assuming it was as it seemed. But if she said no, she would forever regret her timidity.

"Okay, Anton. Because of our time those years ago, I'll trust this isn't some elaborate Russian spy thing. So where in Paris do I meet you?"

"For security reasons let's discuss that when you arrive. Text me at the number I'll give you of your schedule and again when you arrive at Charles de Gaulle. Sorry I can't offer to meet you there. I'll take care of getting you a room. Can you come right away, Victoria?"

"Yes. I'll try to get a flight no later than a day after tomorrow."

While waiting for her bag at the airport carrousel, she received a text message. *You have a room booked at the Relais Christine on the Left bank. I will meet you at 6:00pm in the lobby. Anton.*

The Hotel Christine turned out to be a charming luxury boutique hotel occupying a 17th century former abbey in the Saint-Germain-des-Pres district on the Left Bank. Tucked away on a secluded street with the River Seine only a couple of blocks to the north, she decided on a walk along the Seine, stopping for a light lunch. With a few hours to kill before meeting Grigoryev, a nap and shower shook the jet lag. This was certainly a time to be at her most alert. Meeting a defecting Russian spymaster of all bizarre circumstances.

Beyond the intrigue was the excitement of meeting Anton after all these years. Attractive at fifty-two, vanity dictated she take particular pains with her makeup. The black knit dress flattered her physical assets. It felt like first-date expectation nervousness. And why not when reuniting with a former lover from twenty years ago?

Promptly at six o'clock, she descended the lift exiting into the hotel lobby.

Anton Grigoryev walked over immediately. Still as handsome and fit as she remembered. Dressed in a fashionable sport coat with open-collar shirt, together they looked a trendy attractive mature couple. Anything but an American academic and Russian spy chief.

He greeted her in English, "Victoria, you look lovely," embracing her and kissing each cheek in the French style.

"My god, Anton, hard to believe it's been so long. It is so good to see you."

"So much to talk about, Victoria, but first I must explain the circumstances that compelled me to drag you to Paris. Once you hear the whole story I'm sure you will not regret coming. A wonderful evening so let us go out into the garden. I'll explain everything over a bottle of good Bordeaux then we'll have dinner."

The elegant Parisian setting stood in sharp contrast to the reason for this Paris rendezvous. For Grigoryev, defection meant an extreme altering of his life. Leaving his country forever. Obviously dangerous given his official position. The thought provoked a flicker of concern for her own safety.

Once seated in the interior garden patio, Grigoryev briefly discussed wine in excellent French with the waiter.

"Are you in danger, Anton?"

"Well of course. Senior Russian intelligence officers defect at great risk. The Putin regime doesn't shy from killing journalists and certainly not intelligence officials that possess damaging information. Had I remained in Russia I would now be in some undisclosed prison."

"And here in Paris?"

"You mean are you in any danger? No. You will not be here long enough. Nor will I. They are of course looking for me but I have taken precautions. After all, espionage is my profession."

"Who are *they*, Anton?"

"The SVR, the foreign intelligence service of course. My superior the Director of the SVR General Dubrovsky, is now in a career-compromising position. Then of course the Federal Security Service, the FSB, the equivalent to your FBI will take the lead in trying to locate me. Now outside Russia, I pose a serious counterintelligence threat."

"But what you are asking me to do might take time to arrange. What will you do to remain safe?"

"Victoria, trust me. I've planned this for some time. I have a false passport and credit cards. I speak French and English fluently enough to fit those carefully created identities. I'll be fine long enough to negotiate terms with the Americans."

The waiter brought the wine and after the ritual of examining the label, opening the bottle and inspecting the cork followed by tasting a sip, Grigoryev pronounced it excellent.

Once the waiter finished pouring and left, Prescott said, "Okay, Anton, tell me why you're doing this."

"A long time in the making," he said speaking in Russian. "I don't need to convince you what Russia has become under Putin. Any thoughts of a democratic governmental structure evaporated long ago starting with Putin in 2000. Imagine the disillusionment of being on the inside and witnessing the disintegration. As dysfunctional as the Yeltsin era appeared to be, it was a start. Even those of us having started our careers in the KGB did not embrace life in a police state. I spent much time in the West. Life there clearly preferable to Russian circumstances.

"Progressively Russia has descended into a state criminal enterprise. Even a ranking insider could never feel secure. Once you look at what I will give you will understand just how far things have degenerated."

"And something happened I'd guess that made you take the leap now?"

Grigoryev's face darkens as he nodded affirmatively.

"They attempted to arrest my brother-in-law five days ago."

"Oh no. What for?"

"My brother-in-law was a senior Federal Security official. He was deputy head of the Economic Security Department. Ostensibly, his department investigated financial crimes. In reality, a corrupt process rigged to charge or threaten opponents of the current regime with financial crimes as a means to control any opposition to the Putin regime. Beyond that, he was intimately involved in covering up for a vast illegal financial empire controlled by Putin.

"I'll go into greater detail later, but suffice it to say that Stepka Lytkin and I conspired for a long time. What I'll turn over is a well-documented dossier of covert investments of individuals in the Putin regime. How state-owned assets and public funds financed personal investments. Corruption on an industrial scale. The material reveals the mechanisms of Russia as a state operated criminal enterprise."

"What will happen to your brother-in-law?"

Grigoryev shook his head.

"I said they tried to arrest him. He prepared for something going wrong. Knew he would be tortured to reveal everything. Shot himself in his apartment when they came for him."

"Oh my god!"

"Did it to save his wife and two daughters from being used as leverage. He made sure there was never any incriminating material in his office or apartment. Never shared anything with them about his subversion. Nevertheless, he shared everything with me. By agreement, I kept electronic files well hidden. If ever discovered in my possession, he and his family might possibly escape arrest, or least have some warning. As for me, my only family is Stepka's wife, my sister Ursula and her two daughters. Therefore, without the material, the government probably does not yet know the extent of what Stepka uncovered."

Grigoryev's account left Prescott visibly shaken. This evoked the horrors of the Stalin era. In her research, she read countless firsthand accounts of decades of brutal NKVD reprisals. However, this was today's ugly reality with a personal connection.

"I'm so sorry, Anton. Will your sister and your nieces be okay?"

"If you mean will they be imprisoned, probably not. As I said, Stepka was careful. But they will still suffer greatly."

"Such a terrible tragedy. But I don't understand what you meant on the phone about what you were offering would scare

Western intelligence. I would think this evidence of widespread corruption of the Putin regime your brother-in-law documented would delight rather than scare the West?"

"You're correct, but it is the other thing that both my brother-in-law and I discovered that is of immediate international concern. Bred from the same corrupt Russian environment but with far different ramifications than financial corruption. Remember we were both high-ranking security officers. Both former KGB. Just like Putin and a good many others now in all sorts of positions within the government. Russia is a police state. Not exactly Stalinist era repression but moving closer to the worse of the Third World dictatorships. The security services leak information internally in their own form of corruption. Both of us could access the most confidential material even if often outside our principal areas of responsibilities. A true den of thieves.

"You recall that great scandal causing the fall of the American corporation, Martinelli Global a few years ago?"

"Of course. The journalist responsible also published a book. I read it since the corporation was intimately connected with a Russian oligarch. Revealed a lot about modern day Russian corruption between the public and private sectors."

"Then you know the involvement of that oligarch's tangle of corporations with the Russian nuclear industry."

"And the author made this allegation that someone senior in one of those Russian corporations was involved with the theft of Russian nuclear bombs. Nothing ever came of that obviously. Even the United States denied such a thing took place. Sounded wildly preposterous."

Grigoryev set down his glass and leaned in toward Prescott.

"To be precise, the theft of three fully operational thermonuclear warheads each with a 400- kiloton yield. I have evidence proving theft did in fact occur."

"Oh no! And what happened to them? Who has them?"

"Iran."

"Jesus Christ. You're sure of this?"

"Both the internal and foreign security organs investigated. I'll be handing over the full transcripts of those investigations. There is no doubt it happened. The reports are thorough. Including what happened to the perpetrators. Makes for chilling reading."

"Why has Russia kept silent?"

"My dear Victoria, being a scholar of Russia you should know the answer to that. Russia would never admit to such gross negligence. Worse yet, possibly accused of complicity with the Iranians. Given both Iranian and Russian support to the Assad regime in Syria, an admission that advanced thermonuclear warheads found their way to Iran would surely provoke destabilizing Western sanctions on Russia."

"Those few senior officials that know the truth may see the weapons as another strategic problem for the United States."

"So what are the Iranians intend to do with these weapons?"

"That remains unknown. Personally, I believe the Iranians are waiting to develop the necessary missile capability before exerting political advantage. Might be something more complicated such as factional disagreement within the leadership. This theft happened before Iran concluded the 2015 agreement to limit Iranian nuclear weapons related technology in exchange for lifting sanctions. Since the United States has recently pulled out of that agreement perhaps they are rethinking their options.

"Of course they are studying the Russian advanced design for their own weapons program. Whatever they do they must exercise extreme caution not to alert the Israelis. That could invite an Israeli military response. Perhaps even a Saudi response given their new leadership's muscle-flexing in the region."

"So your information confirming the theft is disastrous for both the Russians and Iranians."

"More than that, it will upset international equilibrium. All the world powers and the entire Middle East must eventually confront the situation. Impossible to anticipate the range of possible reactions."

Prescott staggered under the scope of what Grigoryev was saying. If he possessed documented evidence this was world shaking.

"I have so many questions I hardly know where to start, Anton."

"Of course. I will go into greater detail tomorrow. Better yet, I'll show you the raw documentation. But right now let's take just a few hours to be human. We have twenty years to catch up on, Victoria. Let's do that over dinner. I've a favorite small bistro not far, near the Sorbonne."

Prescott could see why Grigoryev liked this restaurant. Small and cozy. Although close to the university, the other patrons were locals rather than students. Everyone speaking only French. She felt sorry for Grigoryev. Undoubtedly this would be his last time in Paris. At best, he could only hope for a new identity provided by the witness protection program while living out an alien existence in obscurity in some boring U.S. city.

She would do everything she could to help him escape to safety although hardly knowing him. Their very brief romantic relationship was twenty years ago. Yet she connected with him in a way eluding her since then. In addition, she owed him professionally. His assistance in accessing Soviet-era intelligence archives proved led to her spectacular academic success. The information she obtained in Moscow identified a previously unknown Soviet spy within the ultra-secret Manhattan Project during World War Two. A trusted U.S. Army officer on General Groves' staff with access to every aspect of the scientific project to create an atomic bomb. Perhaps as instrumental to Soviet nuclear development as the infamous spy Klaus Fuchs.

Grigoryev provided access and guidance into Soviet intelligence archives under the openness of the new Yeltsin presidency. This was 1998 just seven years after the collapse of the Soviet Union. That brief period where Russia attempted to embrace democratic governess and the West suddenly seemed no longer the great enemy.

Settled at a back table in the garden patio of the Christine with a bottle of wine, Grigoryev suggested they converse in English since she did not speak French. No point in arousing unwelcomed curiosity by speaking Russian.

She laid her hand over his on the table and said, "When you called, it brought back an old guilt. Something never really forgotten but buried in the recesses of memory."

"Guilt? Over what?" he said genuinely surprised.

"Over us. I guess is how I'd put it. It was more than just a brief affair yet that is what I made it out to be. I never attempted to contact you. Never even properly thanked you for the professional help much less the ... emotional connection I experienced."

He clutched her hand, "You should dispel any such recriminations, Victoria. We did make a deep emotional connection. We were perhaps both vulnerable but it was still something profound. Neither of us expressed what we both knew. There could be no future together.

"An American academic and a Russian spy? Living where? We both had careers on opposite sides of the world. Our identities shaped by our careers and history. What would a retired Russian spymaster do in America? You could never live in Moscow. Our very lives, our cultures were worlds apart.

"Your leaving was very ... difficult, Victoria. I realized I would probably never see you again. I reconciled to each of us proceeding down separate paths. Had to be that way. The situation back then left no practical personal choices."

Tears ran down her cheeks as she dabbed them with the table napkin.

"Damn, I told myself I wasn't going to do this," she said. To redirect the conversation to him, "And what happened in your life these last twenty years, Anton?"

"Well I eventually married. Over ten years ago. A brainy woman like you. A medical researcher."

"And?"

"Natasha died four years ago of cancer. An ugly death."

"Oh no. I'm so sorry."

"With Russia visibly reverting to a new form of Soviet-like repression, her death drove me deeper into an already developing depression. Rather than opting out of life, I chose to resist this criminal regime. No defined objective at first but not long before my anger turned to specific means of sabotage.

"My sister is the only family I have. She made a great effort to return me to the living after Natasha's death. It proved difficult to withdraw into depression around her two precocious teenage daughters. In addition, I liked her husband Stepka. We shared high positions in the security organs."

"And you soon learned that your brother-in-law shared a common loathing of what was happening in Russia?"

"Exactly. Our conspiracy quickly developed. If caught, the first suspicion would be a foreign intelligence penetration. We would disappear but not before enduring severe unpleasantness."

"If caught? But you were caught. At least your brother-in-law."

He smiled. "Obviously. And if I had not left Russia immediately, I would also have been arrested. Not only being connected to Stepka since he was married to my sister, but other indicators caused me to suspicion I was out of favor professionally. In today's Russia that alone is dangerous."

"And with no personal ties in Russia you planned your defection? How did you learn of your brother-in-law's death? How did you manage to get out of Russia? Aren't they probably looking for you all over Europe?"

"Most certainly they are looking for me. But I am safe temporarily. Tomorrow I'll explain everything in more detail. How I escaped and how I intend to elude my former comrades. And of course, I'll show you what I have to offer the Americans. But now you must tell me about your life these past years. I resisted researching you more thoroughly to avoid leaving any trail to you. All I know is what the Stanford University website says in your biography.

"I never asked if I was complicating your life by asking you to come to Paris."

"You mean if I'm in a relationship? The answer is no. No one to be accountable to."

Never a serious relationship over these many years. Might never be although she felt an unidentifiable emptiness. Intelligent enough to know it was her rather than poor choices in men. Something amiss within her makeup, or a combination of factors always ending in disappointment.

By her tone, Grigoryev chose not to pursue the obviously uncomfortable subject.

"I did read your book *Critical Mass.* Good writing. Reads like a suspense novel. And you actually met this old Soviet spy?"

"Yes. Thanks to your help, Anton."

"And that unusual period of Russian glasnost. Would not happen today. Not since Putin came to power in 2000. What I have to give you now will top that Soviet Stalinist era history, Victoria. This is about today. The post-Soviet Russia of today. Make sure you keep copies of everything. Don't trust your government. They will cut you out of the picture invoking reasons of national security. Might just bury the material if it suits the objectives of the current U.S. administration. You will understand tomorrow when I show you the material. Now let's enjoy the evening."

CHAPTER 2

PARIS, FRANCE

The following morning, Prescott found Grigoryev seated in the same garden area of the Hotel Christine. With a clear sky the temperature this early suggested a warm summer day. As he departed from her the previous night, he told her he was not staying at the hotel. For security reasons.

A feeling of disappointment? Did she harbor some thought of reprising that long ago romantic adventure in Moscow? This was literally life or death for Anton. For security he said. Her security. Get your head straight Victoria.

"Sleep well?" He said bending down to kiss her on the cheek as he joined her for morning coffee in the hotel lobby.

"Not especially. Too much wine, and worry over how ill-equipped I feel to help you."

"You'll be fine, Victoria. Once you see what I have, you will understand why U.S. Intelligence will jump at the chance to debrief me. With all that's gone on involving your last election, I can connect the dots. Your father will know how the process works and who best to contact."

"And because of what you have to offer, you're in great danger aren't you?"

He placed his hand over hers. "Of course, especially given my level of access to Russian state secrets. Defecting is a dangerous act of rebellion. That's why I am using you as a back door rather than attempting direct arrangements. That would involve contacting some low-level U.S. intelligence functionary at an embassy. Far too dangerous if my intentions become known to many levels in your bureaucracy before reaching safety.

"Your NSA's capabilities prevent using electronic communications to make contact with someone in Washington. You and your father represent a much more secure conduit."

"But that might take time. Are you safe here in France?"

Grigoryev smiled, "Safe enough, Victoria. I have been planning this for some time. I know the tradecraft. That's my profession."

Time however was critical. Russian intelligence was as good or better than any in the West. Grigoryev's own foreign intelligence service had its own special forces unit. Outside the senior leadership of the SVR, little was known about the shadowy unit known as Zaslon. Grigoryev however was intimately familiar with their capabilities and operations. These were the operatives tasked with sanctioned assassinations outside Russia. If he is located, a Zaslon team will likely be dispatched to kill him. If they didn't fear the blowback from another high profile Russian assassination in a Western country. Probably a secondary consideration given the sensitivity of his foreign intelligence service rank and Putin's increasingly aggressive posture internationally.

"Without revealing details, here in Paris I am not Anton Grigoryev. I am not even Russian. I have a French residence visa. I speak French and English. I am a foreign national with solid credentials to support an alternative identity. A valid passport, not forged, that allows me to travel freely as that other identity."

This elaborate construction of an alternative identity began not long after the death of his wife. That dark period proved a pivotal point. Self-reflection concluded his dedication to country had blinded him to the tortured political arc that once again was consuming Russia.

With the fall of the Soviet Union, he realized the failure of that absurd system to which he once served. Joining the First Directive of the KGB following graduating from the University of Moscow, he applied himself to excel professionally without regard for the legitimacy of what he was doing. Born after the death of Stalin, the repressive uncertainty of life during those times was a thing of history replaced with the nationalistic climate of the Cold War.

Life for the average Russian in the last three decades of the USSR increasingly became a struggle for just the necessities of a decent life. Not of course for a promising KGB officer. The vast security organ took care of its own. He only recognized this during the final years before the rotten mess collapsed as economic circumstances in Russia progressively deteriorated during the 1980s. The ill-conceived Soviet-Afghan War lasting nine years during the decade added to his disillusionment. His foreign postings including Paris and Ottawa starkly contrasted the quality of life in the West compared to the Soviet Union.

He secretly embraced the new possibilities offered by the prospects of democratized Russia with the fall of the Soviet Union in 1991. Although he was KGB, his duties never involved the dark specter cast by the enforcers of a police state. The internal policing and counter intelligence functions of the former KGB now fell under a newly formed Federal Security Service, the FSB. Foreign intelligence functions split off to a separate Foreign Intelligence Service, the SVR.

So Grigoryev felt unburdened with any guilt associated with his past as a part of a feared secret police. He was in the spy business. Every country maintained a foreign intelligence service. A necessary state function. An honorable patriotic profession no different than service in the military.

However, the transition to democratic institutions along with a market driven economy proved too much for Russia. A country that bypassed those evolutionary processes of the last two hundred years experienced in the West. The Romanoff Dynasty of absolute monarchy rule collapsed in 1917 after 300 years. During that time, much of Russia remained nearly feudal. A vast agrarian society largely bypassed by the Industrial Revolution.

Seventy years of Communist rule left no foundation of democratic institutions. The radical transition to a market economy after the economic failure of the Soviet autocratic state economy was doomed to failure and corruption from the start.

Grigoryev said, "Planning to leave Russia began after the death of my wife. I could not abide being part of Putin's kleptocractic regime. Russia is little better than some postcolonial African country ruled by a greedy despot. I was angry that criminals betrayed all hope for my country. What I was about could only end in imprisonment or death unless I chose to defect to the West. I may love Russia but not enough to martyr myself for a criminal regime."

"How did you learn of your brother-in-law's death?"

"Days later. Only after leaving Russia. You see Stepka and I prepared for such an eventuality. Each of us carried a burn phone, a prepaid untraceable phone. Only for use should arrest appear imminent.

"So you spoke to your brother-in-law before he ... shot himself?"

"No. The call disconnected after just several seconds. He had little time I assume."

Prescott shook her head. "Jesus. I guess I understand your precautions. So what's the plan for today?"

"After breakfast we shall spend the rest of the morning here in the garden. I will present you with the electronic files and provide you an overview. There is a directory identifying each file and the subject matter. Everything is further organized into broader categories. Not possible to review everything in detail while here in Paris. Simply too much material. As it is, you will still have endless questions, Victoria."

An incongruous setting. Coffee and croissants in the garden of a five-star Parisian hotel on a sunny summer day. Within an hour, they found themselves alone in the garden patio. Grigoryev informed the waiter that he and the lady wished privacy to enjoy this gorgeous day outdoors. He tipped the waiter generously.

Once Prescott returned with her notebook computer, Grigoryev removed two USB drives from his jacket pocket.

"These two USB drives contain the files associated with the FSB and SVR investigations into the theft of nuclear warheads over three years ago as alleged by that journalist. Keep one and turn the other one over to your father to hand over to the U.S. government. Ample payment for my asylum."

"And it conclusively confirms these nuclear weapons are missing?"

"Yes. And you will agree after I show you the documentation and sources."

"But why did it take the Russian's so long to confirm the theft?"

"My dear, it didn't. The investigations concluded over three years ago. The results sealed. The archives and databases purged under Putin's direct orders. My bother-in-law accessed the FSB files on the investigation before the effort shut down. I did the same for the foreign intelligence investigation results of the SVR."

"Too embarrassing for Putin to admit such gross incompetence I imagine. But how did Russia hide this from international scrutiny? I thought there were onsite internationally supervised physical verifications of nuclear arms inventories to validate treaty commitments?"

"There are. When you read the details of the theft, you will see how the West has been kept in the dark. A complicated process managing all the varied components of nuclear weapons. Like anything else, governed by paperwork. That's what made the theft elegant. Even though Russia publicly refuted the journalist's evidence, U.S. intelligence has never stopped investigating. To your CIA, NSA, your Energy Department's OICI, and the IAEA, I suspect the journalist's uncorroborated evidence has always been troubling."

"And you know these warheads to be in Iran?"

"No question, although Iran has kept them well hidden. But Iran engineered the theft as implausible as that seems. This could only happen in the corrupt environment of today's Russia, as you will see when you understand the details. Still an extraordinary feat. The Iranian mastermind behind the operation is to be admired."

"And this other financial corruption stuff your brother-in-law obtained?"

Grigoryev retrieved another USB drive from his pocket.

"Right here on this drive. Copy it to your hard drive and hide the USB in a secure place as backup. You will have to sort through a lot of material. Complicated financial manipulations. Illegal dealings on a truly grand scale. The Russian state operates solely for the preservation of the Putin regime. Vast sums of illegal money insure his hold on power. You should work with this material as an academic endeavor. Be careful however, Victoria. Many fortunes will be lost. Lives probably lost too. These are people as bad as it gets. I do not fully understand the scope of what is contained in Stepka's stolen files. However, he was at the center of this shadow financial empire. Your government would like to get their hands on this material as well. Don't trust them either. "

"Okay. Let's stay with the nuclear weapons. Show me how the theft was accomplished," Prescott said.

For the next two hours, Grigoryev walked Prescott through his summary of the 2014 theft at Trekhgornyy in the Chelyabinsk Oblast of Russia east of the Ural Mountains. He punctuated his narrative by citing various supporting documents from the Russian investigation.

Prescott asked question after question, riveted to the seemingly unbelievable event. Yet here was real evidence. Unsettling to think the Russian nuclear arsenal could be so vulnerable.

She said, "So these army officers thought they were participating in a high-level mission ordered by Putin himself to falsify decommissioning of warheads? But they were also being well paid. Wouldn't that make them suspicious?"

Grigoryev shook his head. "Hard for someone from America to understand how things work in Russia. Every senior official in some way participates in the underground economy. If one doesn't then they are clearly not part of the power structure."

"And you, Anton?"

"Did I receive special financial benefits? Of course. So did my brother-in-law. In our positons as senior intelligence officials, refusal would have cost us our positions by arousing suspicion. In my case it allowed me to amass a modest sum of money secreted away in a Swiss account."

"So how it is that Russian intelligence identified this Iranian named Savi as the one behind this? Why not the Russian Garnitsky? You're saying it was his rogue operation apparently."

"Look at this. This is a transcript of a detailed confession of Garnitsky's subordinate Yuri Dratshev, the person running the operation on the ground. His brother is an Orthodox monk living in seclusion in a monastery on Mount Athos, Greece.

"It was Dratshev's written details of the operation that provided the evidence linking this to the Iranians. Written in anticipation of his possible liquidation by Garnitsky. He worked closely with Colonel Farzard Savi of the Iranian Ministry of intelligence. So he knew this was being funded by Iran. Knew it was a Garnitsky off-the-books operation. Garnitsky's boss the oligarch Krasin would never engage in anything so foolish. Dratshev surmised Garnitsky was getting a vast sum of money that made the risk acceptable. That was never confirmed."

"Probably a Swiss account like you," she said with a raised eyebrow.

Grigoryev smiled. "Well you'll learn far more sophisticated financial schemes than Swiss bank accounts to secretly enrich those that run Russia. Garnitsky was never more than a former KGB officer turned criminal. But his boss Nikolai Krasin was one of the new breed of entrepreneurs that combined their business expertise with collusion of state officials."

To Prescott, Grigoryev seemed to characterize his KGB background as something quite different from others like Garnitsky or Vladimir Putin. Being from the KGB First Directorate with postings in Western Europe embassies seemed a legitimate undertaking contrasted with the darker stigma of the vast Soviet secret police organ and the even darker past of the KGB predecessor agencies under Stalin.

He continued, "Dratshev knew Garnitsky would eliminate all those involved. Knew he could not rely on being spared, yet there was nowhere to turn. Garnitsky maintained links with the largest Russian criminal syndicate, Solntsevskaya Bratva. You will see their filthy fingerprints throughout all these documents.

"After the safe smuggling of the warheads into Iran, Dratshev immediately paid a visit to his estranged older brother. According to Brother Fyodor Dratshev, his brother Yuri confessed to him of committing a great sin that would probably cost him his life. He said nothing more then handed his brother a sealed envelope. Told his brother to make the contents public should anything happen to him.

"Yuri Dratshev accurately foretold the dangerous position in which he found himself. Later inquiries led to a Moscow police report citing witness statements of his possible abduction at gunpoint from a restaurant. The matter dropped after uncovering no further information, nor his body ever turning up.

"The envelope contained a detailed written account of the entire operation. Brother Fyodor knew nothing of his brother's disappearance until one of our agents turned up at the monastery. The document tied everything together. From Dratshev's description of the Iranian, we concluded it was a senior foreign intelligence officer named Colonel Farzard Savi. Also known as, Farhad Sattari, his working identity outside of Iran is a trade specialist for the Iranian Ministry of Economic Affairs and Finance. Dratshev's document is of course included in the digital files I gave you."

As an expert on Russia, Prescott said, "Something I don't understand, Anton. Russian nuclear weapons fall under military control. You haven't mentioned the GRU. Why weren't they all over this once that journalist Reynolds published his allegations?"

The GRU, the Russian acronym for the Main Intelligence Directorate of the Russian military, is the largest Russian foreign intelligence agency with six times the number of foreign agents as Grigoryev's rival SVR agency. The investigation of allegations affecting nuclear warhead security would seemingly fall to their responsibility.

Grigoryev smiled. "They were. The suspicious deaths of those army officers involved alone raised concerns. They immediately launched an investigation. Once the SVR interviewed Brother Fyodor and uncovered the complicity of the murdered army officers involved, the GRU shared their results with the FSB and SVR.

"Putin went into a rage on learning that army officers could be so easily duped."

"Duped?"

"You'll read all the details when you dig into the files. However, the core element of the scheme turned on a general named Ryndenko. A morally corrupt obscenity deeply compromised by Garnitsky. Remember, Garnitsky worked for the oligarch Krasin. He was Krasin's link to Russian organized crime as well as being a former KGB officer. Ex-KGB spread into positions throughout the post-Soviet government representing a loose fraternity of shared background.

"Already deeply compromised, Garnitsky apparently had incriminating photographs linking Ryndenko to the murder of a call girl. With that threat and the inducement of a large amount of money, Garnitsky forced Ryndenko's cooperation. It was Ryndenko that enlisted the necessary subordinate army officers to perpetrate the theft under the pretext it was an ultra-secret military mission. A theft accomplished principally by manipulation of documentation. More like embezzlement than stealing something as tangible as thermonuclear weapons."

"So what did Putin do?"

"First, he wasn't about to rely on the GRU to investigate the military's incompetence. That is why he directed the FSB and

SVR to initiate separate investigations where he could exert more direct control.

"Putin forced the GRU to share everything they had with the FSB and SVR. Putin is as ruthless as Stalin and just as clever. Someone must pay for this monumental failure. Never of course would he acknowledge his part in involving Krasin's businesses in the Russian nuclear sector as a means to obscure decades of Soviet incompetence.

"Putin however cannot write off the affair. Someone must be held accountable. He knows Western intelligence is intensely trying to assess the credibility of the journalist's allegations. If he lops off the heads of senior Army generals, it will only raise red flags. Therefore, since the theft over four years ago, he has quietly but systematically purged by reassignment the former chain of command of the 12th Chief Directorate of the Ministry of Defense responsible for nuclear weapons."

Grigoryev suggested they take a walk then have lunch. Slightly overcast yet still a glorious summer day in Paris. He directed her west into the 7th Arrondissement. A particular bistro she would like. One he knew well. A semi-outside area with the large doors thrown open looked out unto a quiet street.

It was close to his apartment registered under the name Byron Laurent. His alternate identity he chose to conceal from Prescott for security reasons. Not that he did not trust her, but it was his last line of defense to remain hidden from Russian intelligence should events take an unexpected turn.

After ordering lunch with the ubiquitous bottle of red wine, Prescott said, "From what you say, this evidence will shake the world. First, the North Korean nuclear threat now Iran in possession of advanced nuclear weapons. There is no predicting what Washington will do. Or the Israelis or the Saudis for that matter."

"Or the Russians. Putin is not the type to back down. He'll spin this as another assault on Russia by the United States."

"And speaking of Putin, you said your brother-in-law was intimately involved in an illegal financial empire controlled by the Putin regime."

"Far more than just a financial empire. Stepka was expert at this since he participated in its creation. He once described it to me as the Russian state turned into the world's largest criminal enterprise. With Putin as the ultimate despot. Every opportunity for illicit gain utilized. Banking, natural resources, trade agreements, public spending manipulated to maximize control and returns to the stakeholders, the Putin regime.

"Both Stepka and I enriched ourselves as well. Necessary in our senior positions or fall under suspicion. Can't very well be part of a gang of thieves while refusing to steal?"

Prescott raised an eyebrow.

"Guess that sounds self-serving," he said. "Probably a rationalization of the end justifying the means."

"I'm sorry. I'm in no position to judge."

"Well, like everything in life, it seemed more complicated. Both of us wanted to damage the regime. At some point, we both intended to defect. That planning fell to me. Stepka had never been outside Russia. We needed to accept the economic benefits thrown at us to both stay involved then fund our escape."

"So how did you receive this ... shall I call it *supplemental* income?"

"Like most beneficiaries at our level in the regime, it came in the form of periodic financial options. Options on everything from investments in stocks, commodity futures, or derivatives. Always sharply discounted from the current trading prices. The difference realized in the sale of the options then deposited in a bank account under your name.

"In our case it was obviously necessary to find a means of transferring our money out of Russia. Stepka set up his own Cayman Islands shell corporation then moved the money into a Cayman bank. No different from what he did for many senior government officials. I declined his offer to do the same for me. The audit trail seemed too obvious. I told Stepka he was underestimating his own agency's capabilities in response once he defected.

"As I told you, my plan was to establish an alternative identity. An identity that was in every sense real to Western governmental authorities. To fund that alternative identity I needed to move money out of Russia to avoid any suspicions, and then disconnect from its Russian origin."

"Launder the illicit money you mean?" Prescott said.

"Precisely. Just like the other criminals. When I left Russia, I immediately assumed my alternative identity. Anton Grigoryev disappeared."

"So if you have a solid new identity and money, why defect to the United States?"

"Victoria. I have been in the spy business for almost forty years. I created an elaborate room of mirrors to facilitate my escape. Elaborate equates to complicated. Therefore, there are always subtle vulnerabilities. My intelligence service has enormous resources with a long reach. Defecting into the fold of the United States improves my odds of survival. I will disappear into your effective witness protection program."

"So who did you become?"

"For security, better you don't know, Victoria. Once I'm secure in the United States I'll tell you the whole story."

He was now Byron Laurent, Canadian citizen with all the necessary documentation to back it up. Actual government issued documents not forgeries; passport, driver's license, Quebec health card, physical residences maintained in Montreal and Paris, tax returns with his stated profession as an art broker, and a bank account with supporting deposits and withdrawals. The real Byron Laurent died as a teenager in an auto accident with his parents in 1958. Grigoryev's passport as Laurent supported a photo with glasses and theatrical mustache. The Canadian passport carried actual exit and entry stamps between Canada and France for the last several years. The trips served as test runs as well as building his legend. Consistent with his business cover as an art broker, he possessed a French *visa commerçant* allowing him to conduct business in France.

The birth certificate of the deceased eight-year old Laurent provided the foundation by which to claim Canadian citizenship. The over-arching cover story of living with relatives in France for most of his life. With a passport, all other forms of identity proved easily obtained.

The cover would hold up to scrutiny within Canadian government databases and even a cursory probing. Closer examination would reveal his history in Canada went back no more than a couple of years. If questioned, his response as to living most of his life in France therefore applying for a Canadian passport just a few years ago would quickly fall apart on the French end. But the whole construct was far more secure than the forgeries of the SVR. With this passport he could travel openly.

Better to conceal his carefully constructed alternative identity as a Canadian citizen. He trusted Prescott but not American intelligence or their bureaucracy. If they set him up with a new identity in exchange for his cooperation, why not continue to maintain his Canadian identity? Geographically so close to the United States. Just in case.

His comment brought Prescott back to the more immediate circumstances. Tomorrow she would leave Paris for New York. Carrying evidence of missing Russian thermonuclear weapons that would precipitate an international crisis. While also carrying the offer of defection from a high-ranking Russian intelligence official. A disorienting cascade of staggering circumstances.

"Might it still be possible for your sister and nieces to leave Russia?"

His expression changed. "Not likely. Maybe someday if Putin is brought down, but ..."

"But that's a very long shot isn't it, Anton?"

"I don't know. The nuclear weapons incident will be a problem for Putin but will not topple him. Within Russia, his control is just too complete. He will just tighten the repression if necessary. Russia today is already more like the Stalin era than the final Soviet years of Gorbachev. Putin has already instituted show trials against political opponents. The only thing missing are the Siberian gulags."

"And this other financial dirt you have on Putin? Is that bad enough for the Russian people to rise up?"

"Who can say? The Trump administration has its own corruption problem with continuing criminal investigations. Trump is systematically destroying America's international alliances. And he clearly suffers from multiple mental disorders. What does it take for the American people to remove him from power?"

They took a break to enjoy lunch and each other's company. She pleasantly experienced the same attraction that led to their affair so long ago.

While overwhelming and alien, the excitement of all this was admittedly intoxicating for Prescott. It came at a down period in her life. A measure of academic ennui, the onset of midlife internal reflection, and the long absence of a fulfilling relationship.

She should harbor some sense of fear. Grigoryev was already in great danger. No matter how clever his planning he was stuck out in the cold in tradecraft jargon. She too might even now be in danger. Grigoryev more than once brought up the FSB defector Alexander Litvinenko's murder in London by radioactive poisoning. That alone should scare the shit out of her.

Yet right now, she wanted to enjoy the fantasy element. A summer day in Paris with this handsome Russian spymaster with which she shared a romantic past. Her last day before thrusting herself into the reality of this unfolding adventure.

"Anton, can we enjoy the rest of the day? Just two special friends meeting after so many years, enjoying Paris? I expect to find the next few days dominated by ... anxiety. So many unknowns for both of us."

He smiled, cocking his head with an expression of why not.

"Well I think I have covered about everything. You understand the broad pieces. Your government will be wary when your father approaches them. But I can assure you, once they see the digital files they will be jump at the opportunity to bring me in."

"Won't they maybe think this is some elaborate Russian intelligence gambit? Like the old KGB days which you were a part of?"

He laughed. "Of course they will. My debriefing will last months. But the Russians would never give over the kind of stuff I am offering as disinformation. Certainly I have no value as a double agent. I am confident the Americans will quickly come to that view. With nothing to hide, I cannot be tripped up in some lie.

"So how about we go to my two favorite places in Paris. Just down the street is the Musée Rodin. Ever been there?"

"No," she said.

"Wonderful. It is quiet and elegant. The great sculptor's mansion with a beautiful surrounding garden. Then perhaps the Musée d'Orsay? I can never get enough of their collection of Impressionist art."

"Yes. I'd like that. Perhaps a drink after that? Could we go to the famous Bar Hemmingway at the Ritz?"

A downturned expression came over Grigoryev's face.

"Afraid that would not be a good idea, Victoria. Remember, I am now on the run. My agency knows my connection to Paris so they undoubtedly will search for me here. When I visit Paris on official business, I am of course under surveillance by the French and probably by Russian intelligence. I have occasionally gone to the Ritz's Bar Hemingway. Generally, I frequented the Right Bank during those official visits. Therefore, we should keep to the other side of the river. Sorry. But I know a cozy bar. Nothing fancy. A favorite of the Sorbonne faculty."

Prescott sipped her martini, Grigoryev a good single malt Scotch. Everything became more surreal as the day wound to conclusion. The bar stood off from the small restaurant in an intimate walnut paneled alcove giving the feel of an English or Irish pub. The mixed ages and dress of the clientele suggested this was a favored water hole of the nearby university academics.

Tomorrow was not only a return to reality but the start of unpredictable unknowns. An adventure spiked with danger. While Anton's danger was obvious, she could not put her finger on her own jeopardy, yet it felt palpable. He had drawn her into something totally foreign. The stuff of novels. She felt like a female agent in a Bond movie.

"So what's the pitch to the Americans, Anton?"

"Your pitch is to your father. You are to remain my point of contact but let your father deal with your government. He knows how they operate and as his daughter he will look out for your welfare."

"What do you mean?"

"Listen, Victoria. The functionaries in your government are just as bad as in Russia. They will be distrustful at first then offended that some outsider is interceding in negotiating terms for an enemy spy. Always keep in mind that you have something they want. I know you. You can be tough. Push back hard. Remember always, they cannot be trusted. In Russia, we would try to intimidate a defector. Historically Russians pursue such matters aggressively by employing fear. Why should American intelligence be any different?"

"I get your point, Anton. What should I demand?"

"Very simply, asylum and a secure life. You give them my reasons for defecting as I have described to you. They know who I am. You as an intermediary became an obvious choice because of our past connection. Using you through your father is safer than me personally approaching someone at a foreign U.S. consulate. Especially since Russian intelligence must be franticly searching for me. U.S. intelligence may already know something unusual is going on if they have good sources. Tell them I am willing to cooperate fully, disclosing everything I know on any subject. But the clincher is the details confirming the theft of the thermonuclear warheads."

"And what are you demanding in return?"

"Asylum and a new identity in the United States."

"And if they don't agree?"

"They will. Nevertheless, if some bureaucrat wants to exercise his or her stupidity, threaten that I will shop the deal instead to their European allies. And tell them if they cannot exfiltrate me according to my instructions, I will deal elsewhere."

Grigoryev's tone conveyed his agitation. Prescott marked it as a sign of his stress and undoubtedly conflicted emotions. Defecting to what had been the enemy all his professional life a wrenching decision. No less difficult even though this was about betraying Putin not Russia.

"Tell American intelligence I can expand on Russian cyber warfare strategy, the 2016 American election interference, and Russian Middle East strategy. I can provide names and incriminating information on Americans with business interests closely aligned with Russia.

"Remember to keep the financial stuff to yourself for the time being. That is an even more powerful weapon against Putin. But I am not sure how your government would use it given your President's relationship with Putin."

"What makes it so damaging? Won't Putin just shake it off calling it Western propaganda? He'll prevent publication of the material in Russia by what you've said."

"The threat will personally damage the regime from the top financially. Their shadow financial empire extends outside Russia. Billions in illegal funds hidden in foreign accounts and laundered investments. The West can freeze or even seize these assets. The axiom to follow the money applies here as well. Disclosure could badly cripple the Putin regime by destroying their wealth. Despots can only survive if their lieutenants see them as necessary to their own interests. Putin cannot contain damage inflicted from outside Russia."

"How are the Americans to contact you?"

"They won't, you will, at least initially. Here, take this phone."

After handing her a cellphone retrieved from inside his jacket he said, "This is what's known as a *burn phone.* Prepaid minutes paid in cash. The number has no connection to a name. I have inserted one contact. I thought *Deep Throat* an appropriate name. The number is to a burn phone I will carry.

"After making the arrangements and you and your father are convinced the matter is in the right hands, turn the phone over to them. From there I'll work out the specifics for my extraction directly."

"I'm still worried how long this will take. You said yourself this might take time."

"France is a big country, Victoria. I speak the language and blend in. I told you I have a solid alternative identity. The SVR might be good but so am I. I have planned this for a long time. I will be fine."

For Victoria Prescott an overwhelming desire surged through her. The martini may have fueled the mood but the arousal came from being again with Anton. Seeing him for the first time brought back vivid memories of their brief affair. She had not been with a man much less one she felt fondness for in months. When she might see him again after leaving Paris tomorrow remained an uncertainty. Once successfully in the United States, effectively placed him out of reach. Witness protection meant severing all previous ties including her.

Recalling the first time they made love brought a smile to her face. She made that first move enticing him up to her Moscow hotel room.

He noticed her expression. "What seems funny?"

She reached her hand to touch his face.

"Remember that first night together, Anton? That's how I feel right now. Let's go back to the hotel?"

He smiled in return than wiped a tear from his eye.

Sun streaming into the room woke them early in the morning. Grigoryev was fully awake when Prescott stirred.

She looked at him gazing at her. Turning to reach out to him, the sheet fell away exposing her bare breasts. As she kissed him her left hand slide down to find his cock. It took only light fondling with her hand to bring him fully erect.

Climbing on top, she vigorously worked him back and forth as tears streamed down her face.

As her climax brought on his release, she collapsed on his chest sobbing.

He said nothing while just holding her.

Rolling off, she said, "I didn't mean to turn all weepy, Anton. That was so beautiful. And yet so sad."

"Why sad?"

"Because I don't know how this is going to turn out. When I'll see you again."

"I understand. I cannot tell you how grateful I am for your help, Victoria. I perhaps should not have drawn you into this. Selfishly, I am glad I did.

"But time is short. You must make your plane. You shower while I order breakfast from room service."

An hour later he said, "I'm afraid it is time, Victoria."

He reached into his wallet and counted out a wad of large denomination Euros, "Take this to settle your hotel bill."

She quipped to lighten the encroaching goodbye, "For last night?"

"And for much more, Victoria" He responded with his own forced smile. "Pay the hotel bill in cash. Probably being overly cautious but no need to leave any trail of your involvement."

A short time later a final embrace and kiss then Grigoryev left Prescott's hotel room. "See you in the United States, Victoria."

"Be careful, Anton." She understood he could not accompany her to the airport yet it could not stop her tears as he left.

CHAPTER 3

BAKU, AZERBAIJAN – 2014

Feliks Garnitsky was sitting in the lounge at the Park Hyatt Hotel in Baku, Azerbaijan. The capital of Azerbaijan located on the Western side of the Caspian Sea is a city of mixed impressions. The old walled section is a picturesque collection of medieval buildings that could be anywhere in Western Europe. South of the old city is the architecture of the early twentieth century. The fine old mansions now housing museums were the product of the early oil boom of that time. Beyond the old walls, the city spreads outward with typical Soviet era planning. The new oil industry of the twenty-first century funded a skyline of modern-ugly high-rise structures.

Baku is petroleum. At the turn of the twentieth century, half of the world's oil came from Baku. The World War Two Battle of Stalingrad to the north was a strategic struggle for control of the Baku oil fields. Petroleum brought Garnitsky to Baku as well. At the beginning of the twenty-first century, the Caspian Sea has the largest undeveloped petroleum reserves in the world.

Garnitsky worked for the prominent oligarch, Nikolai Krasin. Ostensibly he held an executive position in Krasin's Moscow Capital Partners, the holding company for a vast business empire. Garnitsky stuck out as an archetypical Russian shady character in a landscape of questionable but more sophisticated businesspeople. As ex-KGB, he easily transitioned to the criminal underworld following the collapse of the Soviet Union. Turtle necks with leather jackets his typical attire.

Garnitsky's criminal past provided the basis for his recruitment into the burgeoning Russian entrepreneurial environment of the 1990s. Nikolai Krasin's vision for acquiring wealth went well beyond applying legitimate mechanisms of market economics. Garnitsky proved the perfect facilitator for Krasin's bold illicit schemes.

Garnitsky was in Baku establishing business relationships for a Krasin Caspian Sea project. The two other men having drinks with Garnitsky were executives of an oil extraction equipment manufacturer. It was late in the afternoon in the spacious hotel bar lounge.

Sitting on the other side of the sparely populated lounge a familiar face made eye contact with Garnitsky. Only an imperceptible flicker of Garnitsky's eyes betrayed any surprise.

The slender, dark-skinned man across the room stood and walked to where Garnitsky assumed the toilets might be. Taking the cue, Garnitsky excused himself from his two guests for the same reason and followed the man into the toilet.

A brief inspection by both men confirmed they were alone in the toilet. They embraced and kissed each other on both cheeks.

"My dear, Feliks. I must say you are looking well," the dark-skinned man with a close-cropped beard said in accented Russian.

"And you as well, Farzard. What brings you here?"

"I have something of importance to discuss, my friend. I preferred meeting somewhere away from Moscow. When I learned you would be in Baku I seized the opportunity."

"I do not advertise my travel plans. Your intelligence is excellent."

Farzard Savi smiled. "Since you must return to your guests, could we agree to meet tomorrow perhaps?"

"Of course. Where do you have in mind?"

"There is a small café in the old town section called The Azeri Cafe. Two blocks north of the Boulevard, just behind the Maiden's Tower. Perhaps noon would be a suitable time?"

"I shall see you tomorrow, Farzard," Garnitsky said, then left the toilet.

Farzard Savi was now a colonel in the Iranian Ministry of Intelligence and Security, or MOIS. Garnitsky knew him from his earlier time with the KGB. Their respective intelligence agencies had cooperated in trying to assess the extent of the nuclear technology proliferation of Pakistan's A. Q. Khan. Iraq's Suddam Hussein had been a recipient of Khan's sharing of nuclear technology among Muslim nations. Iran and Iraq then fell into a protracted war lasting most of the 1980s.The Soviets had their own concerns about an Iraq with nuclear weapons. Cooperation therefore developed between the KGB and the Iranian MOIS for intelligence sharing on Iraq.

Garnitsky had gotten along well with the Iranian. Savi was not a wild-eyed revolutionary, nor an Islamic fanatic. He instead was a shrewd pragmatist able to navigate successfully within the Iranian theocracy. From a secular professional family, an older brother was an unusual holdover from the former regime's repressive secret police, SAVAK. During the Iraq-Iran War in the 1980s, the brother secured him a position in the new government's successor security agency, the Ministry of Intelligence and Security. Savi related this to Garnitsky one night in Moscow after too much vodka.

Savi was a talented intelligence professional. He was smart and resourceful in adapting to all manner of circumstances. Apolitical and pragmatic, Savi was a chameleon who thrived in the clandestine world of espionage. Under the cloak of his profession, he could indulge himself in behavior otherwise prohibited under the religious fervor of the Iranian post-revolutionary Islamic state. Savi held no religious feelings. Since he predominately worked outside Iran in his role heading the foreign intelligence department of the Ministry of intelligence, he was free to indulge in a worldlier secular non-Islamic lifestyle.

Garnitsky liked Savi. Both were intelligence professionals. Both enjoyed their pleasures. Garnitsky saw fundamentalist Islam as untrustworthy as Soviet Communism. Ideologues could never be trusted. Garnitsky trusted to human greed and the utilitarian social order of thieves. In Savi he saw a clever opportunist with ambition. Someone he could do business with.

Garnitsky's curiosity was aroused. What could Savi want after all these years?

Arriving at the Azeri thirty minutes early, Garnitsky stood some distance away from the café outside a small art gallery. Ostensibly looking at the paintings displayed in the window, his purpose was to observe the arrival of his old acquaintance. Would Savi have operatives with him? Old cautions died hard.

Farzard Savi arrived alone at five minutes before the hour. He took a small table outside. If someone was with Savi, they were not obvious even to Garnitsky's trained eye.

"Are you alone?" Garnitsky asked as he approached the table.

Savi smiled. "You took up a surveillance I presume?"

"Of course. I have not spotted anyone. So that means you are alone or he or she is very good."

Savi laughed. "Over there. The one selling theater tickets."

Garnitsky turned to look at the person in period custom. He had been hawking tickets when Garnitsky had first arrived to take up his own surveillance.

"Very good. Why is he needed for this meeting?"

"Only to make sure you are not being watched, my old friend. You are a very important man, Feliks Alekseev. Who knows who might have interest in your movements? It is best if we are not connected."

Savi ordered cheese, olives, and bread along with a bottle of wine. While they waited, they each lit cigarettes.

"You have done very well my friend," Savi said. "You are perhaps rich by now?"

"I am doing well. Not sure I would consider myself rich. Besides, you can never be rich enough."

"Exactly. I have followed your career with some interest over the years. Now you are a trusted associate of the billionaire, Nikolai Krasin who is close to the Kremlin."

"Do you have a dossier on me, Farzard?"

Savi smiled broadly. "But of course. I am in the intelligence business. We have dossiers on everyone of importance."

The waiter brought the food and wine. Once the ritual of opening the wine and tasting concluded, they resumed their conversation.

"And what interest does the Iranian MOIS have in me?"

"Your talents. Your organization. Your connections. And most importantly, your access to certain places of interest."

"Sounds as if you want to steal something, Farzard."

"That is precisely what I want. Something so valuable that I am prepared to pay an enormous sum to get it. So much money that even someone of means such as you will be interested."

"How much?"

Savi paused to light another cigarette. After taking a sip of wine, he said in not much more than a whisper, "600 million Euros."

Garnitsky said nothing for several moments while he also lit a cigarette. It was a staggering sum.

"To steal what?"

"Nuclear weapons."

Garnitsky registered an expression of distaste at the absurdity. A screwball idea from the religious fanatics running Iran. Savi should know better. However, for such a sum of money, he would hear Savi out.

"You are not seriously suggesting Russian weapons?"

"Of course."

"You're fucking mad. We Russians are not some half-assed nuclear state like Pakistan. You work for religious lunatics, Farzard. I would have thought you had better sense. No one could pull off such a theft. Even if they could, they would never get away with such a thing. The Russians and every Western intelligence agency would be after you."

Farzard expected Garnitsky's reaction. "Come my friend, you know me better than that. I admit it is bold beyond all imagination. But I assure you, it can be done. It was my idea in fact. I have worked out the details. An elegantly simple magician's illusion."

"And what would be my part be in all of this?"

"You have access to a certain Krasin subsidiary, Rusatomic. Among other work for the Ministry of Atomic Energy, Rusatomic dismantles Russian nuclear weapons for maintenance. It stores nuclear materials and reprocesses fissionable fuels. You have unique access to these facilities as a senior executive for Krasin's holding company, Moscow Capital Partners. You also have strong ties with your former associates in the KGB. Ex-KGB people now control Russia. Even Putin is ex-KGB. This new FSB is nothing more than a new name for the old KGB."

Savi was correct. The post-Soviet Russian security service the FSB and their business partners such as Nikolai Krasin and Feliks Garnitsky controlled the Russian economic sector. The Soviet era KGB transitioned into a shadow state within a state. Economic control now replaced the Soviet style police-state control.

Foreign intelligence and internal counterintelligence became secondary priorities with the collapse of the former Soviet state. Fifty years of contesting with the United States changed overnight. Putin now replaced Soviet-style Communist Party rule with his brand of kleptocracy.

"No, no, Farzard. Rusatomic only operates the facilities. The Ministry of Defense maintains security. The highest level security. Military guards with high-tech security measures. The security protocols are not sloppy."

"I am aware of the details of the security arrangements. But any security system involving people can be breached. "

"I am guessing you have informants within Rusatomic, perhaps even the Army? So what do you need of my services, Farzard?"

"My friend, before I go into greater detail, I must understand your interest in this venture."

"Venture? It is the theft of all time! It will change world politics. Are you saying if you tell me more and I refuse, you will have me killed by your agents? Would you not do that anyway with what you have already revealed?"

"You exaggerate our capabilities. I do not suppose that killing Feliks Garnitsky would be easy. However, this undertaking is not possible without your special contributions. If you do not join with me in this then the project will be abandoned."

"Then tell me more of the details, Farzard. It will depend on how good your plan is."

"Very well. The general plan is this. I have two Russian Army officers that work at two different Rusatomic facilities. They are well paid. They have provided details on procedures and security. Including photographs. Without going into all the fine points, the plan is to hijack the fully operational core of several nuclear warheads. This is carried out between Rusatomic's Ozyorsk reprocessing plant following disassembly at the Trekhgornyy facility."

Garnitsky interrupted, "I know the transportation between the facilities is done by the Military in specially secured trucks. If you hijack the truck you'll never get far."

"Of course not. I used the term hijacked only as a metaphor. The Military will transport the intact warheads to the reprocessing facility. Normally this would only be the fissionable material cores, but these will be the intact operational warhead assemblies. The transport personnel will not know that of course.

"Your services are required after that. We need you to arrange for your own people to impersonate soldiers and to establish a false military installation. Again, with forged orders, the Military will transport the warheads from the reprocessing plant to your sham facility. All this is necessary because the security is much less at the reprocessing plant. It will also add to the complexity of the audit trail of these warheads.

"Your people will need full security documents. The sham military facility must be convincing. I have an abandoned location perfect for our use. These are all details we are contracting for you to provide. You have access to these Rusatomic facilities, and you have special relationships with high-ranking military. For that, we are paying 600 million Euros for the delivery of three warheads to Iran. 200 million each."

"Farzard, I believe you are oversimplifying these tasks."

"Bear with me, Feliks. I can explain down to the smallest detail how this theft is possible. But let me first expand the full scenario. Once your people have the warheads, you will smuggle them through the high country into Northern Iran. I am well aware that you have extensive connections among Kurdish smugglers. Guns, drugs. Even Iranian oil. You already have indirect relationships with Iranian Republican Guard factions."

"I have seen these bombs at the Trekhgornyy Plant. They're too large to easily smuggle, especially through the mountains."

"You will not be smuggling the bombs, only the operational part. Placed in secure boxes, each will weigh less than 200 kilos. Possible to lift by as few as four men. We are seeking only modestly sized warheads." Savi chuckled at his own black humor.

"All right. So let us say all of this is successful. First, the Russian Military will discover the theft. They are not incompetent. That puts me at risk. Second, the theft will be tracked to Iran. Who else? Too sophisticated for terrorists. Next thing, Israel bombs the shit out of Iran before you can reassemble these warheads into deliverable missiles or bombs. The Israelis would have no other option. If not the Israelis then the Saudis. Sunni Muslims consider Iran a threat."

"You are right. Secrecy is absolutely essential. Yet that is not the full extent of the plan. We have devised a way to account for the missing material by falsifying past records. When they take their next semi-annual inventory and discover the discrepancy, it will be reconciled when they dig back through the records and discover the prior *errors*. Our key asset is a senior Russian Army officer, a full colonel who heads the auditing team. He is paid very well."

"Well that all sounds interesting, Farzard, but there's still a major problem. There are too many people involved. Why are they spying for you? If you pay them some great sum of money, they will spend it and become targets of suspicion. There are no cutouts. Everything leads back to theft of Russian nuclear weapons and the whole world goes fucking crazy."

"All these people think they're working outside the normal chain of command under orders from some high-ranking general. They think that because our Russian Army colonel will show them *secret orders*. These officers believe they are working under direct orders from the High Command, and the President himself. The ploy being that the Russian President wants to circumvent U.S. monitoring of Russian nuclear weapons inventories.

"These lesser officers also receive monies to make their deceit more palatable. The Colonel understands he his spying and paid well for the information. Uncommonly corrupt, he asks no questions why he is paid so well for seemingly mundane procedural intelligence. I am his only point of contact. He believes I am a Muslim from the Caucus region but does not know who I work for. He likely expects a terrorist group but expresses no concerns. His female companion is also one of our assets. We monitor his reliability closely."

"That is not very reassuring with so much at stake, Farzard."

"Therefore, we need your other special services, Feliks. There's surprisingly few people needed for the plan to work. Once concluded, we need all of these functionaries eliminated quickly. Their deaths accomplished in such a manner as to avoid any connection with their work. That is why you are vital to this operation. You have associates that can remove these liabilities under some contrived pretext. That is an important piece to this. Also necessary to insulate yourself from personal involvement therefore I'm confident you will manage it professionally under a plausible cover."

"Why is Iran willing to take the risk of this failing? Your government is in serious negotiations to curtail your nuclear weapons program in exchange for dropping Western sanctions. Playing a double game?"

Savi said, "Of course, aren't we all? Any Iranian nuclear program that advances to any significant degree of achievement would undoubtedly provoke an Israeli attack. Therefore pursuing those aspirations must proceed differently. The negotiations with the major world powers center on curtailing fuel enrichment in exchange for relief on sanctions. Other aspects of nuclear weapons development continues. The genie is long out of the bottle. The physics universally known. What remains are engineering refinements, and of course methods of delivery.

"Acquiring Russian thermonuclear warheads might provide the means to pursue a forced rapprochement with the West while still moving to achieve a weapons program. Possession of functioning warheads will deny the Americans and Israelis a preemptive military option. It will change the political dynamics in the Middle East. These weapons are much more advanced than any Iranian program could ever hope to produce. This is not Pakistani level technology. These are weapon designs of the most advanced type. The yields of these weapons will rival anything the Israelis have."

Savi did not share the more far-reaching and frightening Iranian nuclear weapons strategy involving possible partnership with North Korea.

"Let us assume everything goes according to plan. The theft never discovered. Iran assembles the warheads into operational weapons. At some point, you have to make the threat known to the rest of the World. To make that threat credible, you have to suggest the origin of the weapons. Might that not put me at risk?" Garnitsky said.

Savi smiled. "That is why I came to you Feliks. You are a master at hiding and smuggling, at bribing and getting around legal obstacles. I would assume that you could devise a plan isolating you from personal suspicion. The Military is ill paid and therefore corrupt. Your enterprises have taken advantage of that corruption. You designed that part of Krasin's business empire. Perhaps this might be blamed on Chechen separatists? Putin blamed them for all the bombings in Russia. For this kind of money I'm sure you can be creative, my old friend."

"I must give this considerable thought. I will only agree if I can devise a way to insulate myself. Once this becomes known, it would be the end for anyone involved. Might even be the end of Iran. Have you thought about, Farzard?"

Savi uttered a laugh. "I would then have to find another country."

Garnitsky said, "I shall contact you in one week. How do I do that?"

"Here is a cellphone number. Untraceable. Simply say agreed or declined." Savi wrote a number on a fake business card.

Garnitsky rose to leave. Savi rose also and embraced him.

"If I do accept, Farzard, the price is 900 million Euros. There will be certain large expenses."

Savi shrugged. "Life is a negotiation. I believe that we can agree to that figure."

CHAPTER 4

MOSCOW, RUSSIA - 2014

Garnitsky accepted the deal after giving much thought on how he could insulate himself. Savi's plan for stealing the warheads was deceptively simple. With the level of poor military pay and limited availability of advanced security hardware, it was a wonder that a dangerous security breach had not already occurred. As it was, hundreds of pounds of Russian weapons-grade fissionable material already remained missing whether physically or by records errors. The real task was insuring he remained insulated from complicity once the Iranians made their move to leverage their new assets. When that occurred, the obvious origin meant either Russia or North Korea, ruling out predominately Sunni Pakistan.

To accomplish that, he must limit direct connections to the operation. There must also be a plausible alternative group on which to shift suspicion. The basic plan inherently got rid of the active participants with the killings blamed on the same group ultimately accused in the theft. Who better than Chechen separatists as Savi suggested? Their last major attack came in 2011 with the Domodedovo International Airport bombing. A logical escalation in scope. They were also Sunni Muslims casting suspicion away from Shiite Muslim Iran. Disinformation might further suggest the Chechens to be in league with the like-minded fundamentalist Sunni terrorist groups of Al-Qaeda or ISIS.

That left only who would remain to connect him to the event. Farzard Savi would know, but he was Iranian with no motivation to reveal Garnitsky's participation. Obviously, Garnitsky needed to co-opt a high-ranking army officer in the 12th Chief Directorate to issue false orders for the bogus transfer of the warheads. In addition, one more person was essential. Someone must direct the operation in the field. That would clearly be Garnitsky's right-hand man, Yuri Antonovich Dratshev.

Dratshev was only in his early thirties but a proven asset. His rapid rise among Garnitsky's staff was a result of his exceptional organizational abilities. Not only could he assimilate complex variables into a plan, but proved adept at making adaptations to changing circumstances.

The son of a midlevel bureaucrat, Yuri Dratshev received a good education, receiving an advanced degree in mathematics. With his father regularly took bribes from Garnitsky, Dratshev quickly saw a faster career path to success by association with the criminal-business elite represented by people like Garnitsky.

As former KGB, Feliks Garnitsky realized he must seek a new career following the collapse of the Soviet Union. Trained in the shadowy brutality of KGB's Second Chief Directorate responsible for counter-intelligence and internal political control, Garnitsky sought to enrich himself in the unbridled economic turmoil of post-Soviet Russia. He quickly found opportunities to enhance his questionable business enterprises by partnering with Russian organized crime. Years later, Garnitsky's successful smuggling ventures and connections led to his elevation to a powerful position in the shady business empire of the oligarch Nikolai Krasin.

"Yuri Antonovich, you have proven to be an outstanding asset to me," Garnitsky said to Dratshev. Seated in a secluded corner of a small Moscow restaurant, after finishing a traditional Russian meal, Garnitsky poured another round of vodka.

"Thank you, Feliks Alekseev. I appreciate your confidence."

"I have something of great importance to share with you. An opportunity of a lifetime. A private matter. Not something to do with our work with Moscow Capital or Smolensk Logistics. You have the opportunity to make a great deal of money, a very great deal of money. There is only one catch to the offer."

"And that is what?"

"Once I tell you, you become committed. It would not be possible to back out."

"I think I understand. How much money is involved?"

"10 million Euros."

Dratshev's eyes widened. "How much would I personally get?"

"10 million. That is your commission for managing the project."

Dratshev was silent for a moment as he digested what he had just heard. An unbelievable fortune. For something commensurately difficult and dangerous. But if he refused to accept the offer, it would be career limiting and therefore likely life limiting. You cannot turn down an assignment from someone like Garnitsky. It was no *offer*.

"I thank you for your confidence in me, Feliks Alekseev. For such a sum you can count on me to do whatever is required."

"Excellent. I never thought otherwise."

Dratshev speculated on what Garnitsky wanted him to do for such a sum. Eliminate another oligarch? Assassinate a foreign official? Start a war somewhere?

"We are going to steal three nuclear weapons," Garnitsky said.

Stunned, Dratshev could not imagine something so unbelievable. Starting a war may not be that farfetched. "Do you know this to be even remotely possible?"

"Very much so. I will tell you the broad outline of the plan. I shall rely on you to develop the necessary operational details and then direct the actual operation. Only you, Yuri. No one else must know what this actually about. Anyone you use must believe it to be something else. "

Garnitsky explained the plan. Dratshev interrupted only occasionally to ask questions. He concluded the plan was indeed workable, but the implications were still staggering. Yet, internally he shuddered at the implications of a nuclear-armed Iran.

"One final thing, Yuri. Do not commit anything to paper. Do not use emails. Keep this deep and dark. You will have to supervise this first-hand from the Urals. No trail of any kind must lead back to either of us. As much as I hate to, we will have to communicate by cellphone. We must be cautious there as well. Mindful of signals intelligence intercepts whether Russian or American. Make no direct references to the project."

"When is this to take place?"

"That depends on my convincing General Ryndenko for his participation," Garnitsky said. "I would think we could put this together over the next 90 days if I am successful there."

Oleg Ryndenko was a major general in the 12th Main Directorate of the Ministry of Defense, officially named Glavnoye Upravleniye Ministerstvo Oborony. The 12th GUMO was the directorate responsible for Russian nuclear weapons. Ryndenko had been the liaison between Krasin's Rusatomic and the Ministry of Defense from inception. He was the one who arranged the agreed on offsets that made Krasin's investment in the Russian nuclear industry highly profitable. Another Krasin enterprise, Advanced Technologies, received non-bid contracts and preferential government business. A clever bureaucrat, Ryndenko assembled the deals then fixed documentation to obscure the audit trails.

As the chief of all nuclear weapons programs for the Ministry of Defense, General Sobolev appointed Ryndenko to the position after arranging the Putin-approved deal with Nikolai Krasin years before. These illicit deals with the Government were Garnitsky's principal area of involvement with Rusatomic and Advanced Technologies. Ryndenko's association with sanctioned corruption made him a prime target of Garnitsky. What better way to get an even better deal than to bribe the fixer. Garnitsky simply paid much better than the Military.

Ryndenko had fallen so deeply under Garnitsky's control over the last several years that his lifestyle was one of dependency. A better apartment, newly remodeled with western furnishings. A cook. Expensive wines and liquors. Jewelry for his wife. Black Sea vacations. Education for his daughter in Paris. Dining at the best Moscow restaurants. And the ubiquitous status symbol of a mistress with her own apartment. All provided by Garnitsky.

Then of course, there was the matter related to the death of Leysa Varvarinski. Garnitsky covered up the incident, saving Ryndenko's career by avoiding prosecution for manslaughter after a night of sex gone wrong. Garnitsky showed him incriminating photographs.

Ryndenko was the reason Garnitsky accepted Savi's proposal. Ryndenko had the means to institute the necessary false orders then alter the paper trail. And Garnitsky held absolute control over Ryndenko. Ryndenko could hardly refuse. If he did refuse, he had no recourse other than his own ruin. More compelling was the staggering sum of money therefore, expecting avarice to win out over fear.

"What if Ryndenko balks? Maybe he might not have the balls," Dratshev said.

"In that event, Yuri, the General will be a liability that will need to be removed. But I do not think he will refuse. Let's remain positive."

"For now I need you go to Trekhgornyy and Ozersk right away. I need you to become familiar with all of the physical aspects of the warhead disassembly and the reprocessing. We need a full understanding of the security measures at both locations. Most of all, get a look at these warheads. What do they look like? How big are they? I will get you the necessary access."

Farzard Savi arrived in Moscow two days after Garnitsky dispatched Dratshev to the Urals. They met at the same café.

"Let us not haggle about running this operation. It is of too great importance," Savi said.

"I am not haggling, my friend. I need to have control. I need to understand all the players. Can they be relied on? Will they keep quiet? It is my neck on the line if this should fail."

"I fully understand. Obviously you need to know of these officers to set up the remaining details of the plan. Yet I believe that my intelligence penetration has provided me with a better understanding of the internal security mechanisms. Even though these are Rusatomic plants, it would take you some time and at some risk to gain the same knowledge. You have been in intelligence. You know that it is risky to change control of operatives."

"I was not planning to exclude you, Farzard. However, there must be no misunderstanding that I shall dictate the operation. You will work with my key man, Yuri Dratshev. He will be the one in operational control, under my orders."

"And I shall be kept informed on all details by Dratshev?"

"Yes. However, you must find a believable cover. You cannot pass for Russian. Your accent is terrible. I do not want your presence to compromise the operation."

"Feliks, you wound my professional pride. I am not a virgin at this. After all, my network penetrated the most sensitive sector of Russian nuclear arms. Now, since I believe we have an understanding, there's just one other thing."

"And what is that?"

"A small matter of my payment. You see I negotiated approval for a total sum of one billion Euros. That is your fee of 900 million plus 100 million for me. Since I am in the employ of the Iranian government, I am only entitled to my salary. That does not seem fair. With your widespread international financial transactions, I am sure you can assist in the necessary maneuvers to disguise my commission in view of negotiating a better deal for you."

"Not very patriotic of you, Farzard."

"Patriotism is a very complex thing. I do not think that my properly earned remuneration for delivering such a great service to my country conflicts with my patriotism. It is entirely right that we should both prosper handsomely from this, my friend."

General Oleg Ryndenko arrived at the elegant Grillage Restaurant near Red Square at 8:00 pm. Garnitsky called him the previous day saying there was something of importance to discuss. Savi suggested after concluding business they would enjoy an excellent meal.

Ryndenko arrived on time. He wore a well-tailored civilian gray suit. He understood that Garnitsky would frown on him wearing his military uniform. "Feliks Alekseev, so good to see you."

"Good of you to join me, General. I am enjoying a very good Scotch. Single malt, twenty years old. You should try it."

Their table at the back of the restaurant afforded complete privacy from being overheard. Garnitsky had chosen the Grillage because it would impress Ryndenko. Garnitsky's flamboyant boss Nikolai Krasin introduced him to the restaurant but he was not a regular himself. It was more Krasin's style with its rare books and excellent wine cellar. Garnitsky suspected that it was the kind of place that made Krasin feel less like a criminal.

As they enjoyed their Scotch, Garnitsky said, "How long has it been since we have been doing business, General?"

"I believe it has been four years now."

"And a good four years. For both Rusatomic and for you."

Ryndenko tensed slightly. Where was Garnitsky going with this? "Yes, it has been a most successful working arrangement."

"Let me be frank, General. I believe that your personal work has delivered to Rusatomic even more than the Government's contractual commitment. That is why I have seen to properly rewarding you. The pay of a major general does not begin to compensate you for the level of responsibility you carry. Such is the lot of those in government service I fear."

"That is true, Feliks Alekseev. The pay does not allow for even the basics required of one's position."

"Tell me this, General, where do you see your career in a few years?"

Ryndenko took a large gulp of Scotch. He asked that question of himself repeatedly. But he had no good answer beyond the dreary prospect of eventual retirement on an inadequate military pension. "I still have many years of military service. Like any good officer, I expect promotions. I have reason to expect my second star by perhaps as early as next year."

"And well deserved too. Much overdue. Your skills exceed your office. And meaning no offense, your appetites exceed the pay of even more senior general officers."

Ryndenko knew he was hired help, but he was still a general in the Russian Army. "All of what you say is true. Therefore, I hope there is no problem. What is it you wished to discuss?"

"Certainly this is not about a problem, General. To the contrary, it is an opportunity. One of those opportunities that occurs once in a lifetime. A bold undertaking, but one offering sufficient wealth to indulge all your appetites."

Garnitsky leaned over. Ryndenko leaned closer as well. In barely an audible whisper, Garnitsky said, "We need your assistance to steal three nuclear warheads."

Ryndenko physically recoiled backwards. His face drained of color. "What? That is madness! Why do such a thing? Are there not enough profits in the special arrangements Krasin has made with the Ministry of Defense? I am a general. Do you expect me to be a traitor? You go too far, Feliks Alekseev. I will hear no more on this."

"Calm down, General. I can well understand your reaction. I am prepared to convince you that this is a practical endeavor. But you have not asked the most important question."

"Which is what?"

"How much you would be paid for your part."

"It doesn't matter. There is no amount of money worth the risk of a firing squad."

"What about 10 million Euros?"

Ryndenko's eyes widened. He drained his Scotch. "Euros? That would be my fee?"

"Yes. Placed in a foreign numbered bank account. More than that, you could retire from the military and become an employee of Rusatomic. I am offering three times your general's salary and you would still get all the special bonus entitlements you currently receive. Your job would be to work with your replacement at the 12th Chief Directorate on behalf of Rusatomic. When you eventually retire, you can live anywhere in the world in style. Live off the interest discreetly and no one will ever know the source of your wealth."

Ryndenko signaled the waiter for another drink. Garnitsky could see he had sunk the hook.

"Is this for some terrorist group?"

"No. There is no terrorist group with that kind of money. Terrorists also do not have the capability to make use of such sophisticated weapons."

"Therefore a foreign state? What state?"

"Does it matter?"

Ryndenko speculated. It must be North Korea or Iran. Probably Iran.

"It matters because of the aftermath."

"Your involvement will be entirely concealed. That is integral to the success of the operation. There will be no evidence pointing to you. Once I explain the plan, you will understand."

"How many others will know of my involvement?"

"Only Yuri Dratshev who you know. Not even the foreigners paying for the weapons. We have several army officers working within the facilities that we have enlisted. They will know nothing of your involvement. They believe they are working on secret orders from President Putin to conceal supposedly decommissioned weapons from the American inspectors. Once the operation is completed, altered records will make it impossible to uncover the theft. False orders over your signature will be destroyed. Once that is completed, the officers involved will be eliminated. All will meet naturally explained accidents."

"And why should I not also be killed?"

Garnitsky smiled. "No need, General. There is no reason you would tell anyone. And given your rank and sensitive responsibilities, your death would undoubtedly raise threatening suspicions if linked to the others. We also have future needs for your unique skills."

"What exactly will you require me to do?"

"The details are being worked out, but essentially you will be issuing orders. Those orders are to relocate three specifically designated warheads from the weapons disassembly plant in Trekhgornyy to the fuel reprocessing plant in Ozersk 180 kilometers away. That of course is a normal event. The fissionable material from the decommissioned weapons is reprocessed for use in reactors at the Ozersk plant.

"However, these warheads will not undergo disassembly. I know little about the technology other than these weapons are complex assemblies surrounding a nuclear core of uranium or plutonium.

"Very complex," Ryndenko said. "Actually there are two nuclear fuel cores that detonate in stages. The primary core consists of plutonium-239, tritium, and deuterium. This is surrounded by a conventional explosives detonator called a lens. The secondary core consists of uranium-235 surrounded by a casing of uranium-238. Advanced designs incorporate shielding to reflect back the neutrons to increase the energy yield. Every aspect consists of precision machined components."

"Are you familiar with the technology of how the bomb works?" Garnitsky asked.

"Yes. I have a basic engineering understanding. The detonation of an outer shell of conventional explosives causes an imploding force to uniformly compress the fissionable material in this primary stage achieving critical mass. The compressed plutonium core therefore reaches a state of uncontrolled chain reaction.

"Achieving critical mass, the plutonium atoms give up their binding energy in a nuclear fission explosion. Energy released in this primary stage then triggers a secondary stage event. In a fraction of a second, high enough temperatures are generated to induce nuclear fusion in the secondary uranium core configured around another fissionable sparkplug core. The massive release of energy in the atomic fusion process is what makes these compact weapons so powerful.

"An over simplification to a complex process in a precision engineered device that yields the staggering energy release possible. The evolution to current weapon design makes possible the small size necessary for missile delivery."

Ryndenko's explanation made clear to Garnitsky the incalculable benefit to the Iranians in leaping forward in weapons technology by acquiring these Russian warheads.

"I'm impressed, General. You know more about the technology than I do. At any rate, these three warheads will not undergo the normal disassembly to extract the nuclear fuels. Instead, they will be placed intact in special crates for shipment to the reprocessing facility. All of this requiring orders from you, General."

"But warheads are fully disassembled before the fissionable material is shipped to the reprocessing facility. It is only the nuclear core that goes to the reprocessing facility. What is the purpose of transporting the entire warhead assembly there?"

"Because the tightest security is at the disassembly facility. After all, that is where the intact operational warheads are stored. That is where the international inspectors account for the decommissioning of each warhead to satisfy the nuclear disarmament treaties between Russia and the United States. Little chance of falsifying records there to cover a theft. But security is much less rigorous at the reprocessing facility."

"But the transfer of complete warheads to the reprocessing facility will violate procedure. It will be too obvious."

"I do not believe so. First, only one officer at the disassembly facility will understand these warheads are destined for the reprocessing facility. He is under our control. He is the one that will destroy your orders. Then he will falsify the records to account for the transfer of the appropriate amount of fissionable material.

"The transport personnel are simply following orders to move material. The crates will just be larger than typical. For all they know, they are just from larger bombs.

"Now once the warheads are at the reprocessing facility, another shell game is played. Again on your orders, the warheads are immediately transported to another secret military installation. That location a decommissioned former installation operated by Rusatomic's predecessor, Mayak Chemical. At one time this location stored nuclear material. Rusatomic closed the facility many years ago because of contamination but it remains secured behind high-security fencing but no guards. My people will be in army uniforms providing the appearance that this is a functioning facility under military security. They simply take delivery of the warheads."

"How is that part of the audit trail concealed?"

"Another officer, also under our control will destroy any records related to the shipment to this phantom military site. That includes your written orders. Like the other officer, he also thinks this is part of a high-level ordered military maneuver to hide weapons from the Americans."

Ryndenko shook his head slowly. "You still have the problem of unaccounted weapons grade fissionable material. A lot of material. Physical inventories are conducted every six months."

"We have a third asset that resolves that problem. A colonel. He is in charge of auditing the inventories at the reprocessing facility. He will substitute an earlier receiving record with one that shows lower quantities. The difference is equal to the fissionable content of these three warheads. Therefore, when the physical inventory comes up short, an audit of the records will identify the discrepancy as being from a prior transactional error. The substituted documentation will be meticulously crafted."

Ryndenko stared at Garnitsky dumbfounded. "My God. You have bribed the whole fucking Russian Army. I feel like I am swimming in shit. We once stared down the mighty Americans. Now we scavenge for scraps by taking money from criminals."

"Criminals? Is that what you think I am, General?"

"I did not intend offense, Feliks Alekseev."

Garnitsky smiled to dismiss any sense of hostility. "I understand your anxiety, General. But you must look to the huge personal reward for your services."

Ryndenko let out a long sigh. "And what is the next step?"

"Yuri Dratshev will be in contact with you. He will manage all the details. Now let us enjoy a superb dinner."

Throughout dinner, Ryndenko was uncharacteristically quiet. Trapped with no options. Always had been since his first association with Feliks Alekseev Garnitsky.

Garnitsky ordered cognacs and coffees after the waiter cleared the dishes away.

"General, you must relax. Cheer up. All will go well. Perhaps the two women walking this way will divert your thoughts."

Two women in short, tight dresses made their way among the other tables of diners. Heads turned. One was fair and blonde, the other darker with black hair.

"The dark one is named Elena. Looks Middle Eastern, but actually Georgian. A belly dancer. Wonderfully strong body. She will be your companion tonight."

Ryndenko's gloom receded slightly.

Ten weeks later a tractor-trailer rig pulled onto the docks of the northern Caspian Sea Russian port of Astrakhan. The flatbed trailer carried a large piece of equipment encased in wooden crate. The outside markings in Cyrillic letters identified the equipment as a compressor.

Yuri Dratshev closely supervised the transfer of the load by crane to a waiting Russian freighter. The manifest described the equipment as oil drilling equipment. The freighter bound for the Iranian port of Bandar-e Anzali.

Dratshev remained seaside until the freighter pulled away from the dock. He sent a couple of photographs from his phone to Garnitsky with the message: *The ship has sailed. Will arrive on the seventeenth.*

For Dratshev there should be relief after the unrelenting stress of the past weeks. The theft went according to plan with no glitches. The warheads now concealed and secured within the large compressor tank. He was to be wealthy beyond his imagination. Professionally situated as the right-hand man to a powerful person. Yet a sense of unease overrode other thoughts.

Feliks Garnitsky was himself a key subordinate to the powerful oligarch Nikolai Krasin, close to Putin. Krasin would have no reason to involve his subsidiaries in this unless on orders from Putin.

Conceivable Putin might have a reason for sanctioning the theft. But Dratshev could not fathom any logic for Putin wanting to arm Iran with advanced Russian thermonuclear warheads. It did not feel right. He suspected this scheme might be a Garnitsky rogue operation. Regardless who was behind this, he too was a liability like the involved army officers. Regardless who was behind this, why should he consider himself safe?

CHAPTER 5

CHELYABINSK OBLAST, RUSSIA – 2014

At a popular restaurant in Chelyabinsk, the location of the regional headquarters of the Russian Army's 12th Chief Directorate, a colonel dined with a junior officer. The colonel was Savi's asset in charge of auditing nuclear weapons decommissioning and fuels reprocessing. The restaurant clientele consisted mostly of military personnel in uniform working at the various nuclear facilities in this once closed city. Midway through their dinner a car parked in front of the restaurant and the driver hurried away. Minutes later, the car exploded destroying the restaurant.

The colonel was among twelve victims killed in the blast. The official position declared it the act of Chechen separatists. The convenient scapegoat for any act of terrorism in Russia.

In the nearby town of Trekhgornyy, a young army major and a woman were found shot to death in a hotel room. Police arrested another army officer for the murder of his wife and a fellow army officer. Newspaper accounts attributed the murders to jealousy over an adulterous affair. The accused officer maintained his innocence.

In Ozersk, a lieutenant colonel died behind the wheel of his car in a head-on crash with a tractor-trailer truck. The truck driver claimed losing control trying to avoid a large dog crossing the highway.

MOSCOW, RUSSIA

General Oleg Ryndenko and his mistress had just made love in the afternoon. She had been particularly responsive sexually after he presented her a gift of an expensive watch. Afterwards she cooked his favorite dinner.

Ryndenko was in a relaxed mood. His mistress kept refilling his glass with vodka. It was a celebration, but he declined to explain his exuberant mood. The theft worked out the way Garnitsky planned. Ryndenko was suddenly wealthy beyond his imagination. He would soon resign his commission and take up a high paying civilian job with Garnitsky. Life turned very good.

After finishing nearly a fifth of vodka, Ryndenko fell into a drunken stupor on the sofa. Once he started snoring loudly, his mistress went into the bathroom. Minutes later, she returned with a hypodermic needle.

When injecting medications, it is necessary to expel some fluid from the syringe to prevent injecting air into the patient's circulatory system. An air bubble could cause an embolism, an obstruction to a blood vessel, resulting in a heart attack or stroke.

The woman injected Ryndenko with an entire syringe full of air.

Within minutes, Ryndenko was in visible distress. The sharp pains in his heart revived him into confused consciousness. Struggled for breath, his eyes widening in terror as the pain increased. Unable to form words, not only by the physical distress but the odd reaction of his mistress left him perplexed. Across the room she stood calmly with her arms folded across her chest. Smiling.

No matter the generous money paid to be with him, Ryndenko disgusted her. The pig would never humiliate her again.

Three months later, an American freelance journalist released a serialized story to the New York Times. His well-documented stunning revelations toppled the New York headquartered corporation Martinelli Global. Martinelli Global stood accused of engaging in wholesale criminal enterprises around the world. The scandal far more reaching than the demise of Enron. Martinelli Global's illicit activities went well beyond the white-collar largely fraud and tax-related crimes of Enron. MGI's business model sought opportunities in countries where they could collaborate with the ruling economic interests through corrupt governments. Lucrative monopolies, price fixing, money laundering, currency manipulations, public no-bid contracts enhanced with kickbacks also involved them as accomplices in the violence of their criminal partners.

However, the most spectacular revelation was the journalist's harrowing survival by escaping Russia. Whereas Martinelli Global found welcoming partners mostly in Third World countries, Russia became its most important sphere of investment over the last ten years.

Exposure of vast amounts of documentation incriminating to Martinelli Global came about from a dissident Russia employee. The computer systems administrator and accomplished hacker employed by the Russian holding company, sixty percent owned by Martinelli Global, also provided direct electronic access into the parent corporation databases. Moscow Capital Partners was itself at the top of a pyramid of Russian, Ukrainian, Belarusian, Georgian, Kazakhstani subsidiaries with further entanglements like Enron obscured through offshore tax haven subsidiary corporations.

Moscow Capital Partners was the creation of a successful oligarch by the name of Nikolai Krasin. Krasin navigated the purges of the earliest oligarchs by Vladimir Putin. Krasin was a bootlegger at heart that saw the shift away from democratization when Putin came to power in 2000. Krasin held no lofty aspirations to make Russia into a Western market economy republic. Far more financial opportunity in an autocratic environment siding with the center of power. He was apolitical therefore never posing any threat to Putin. His entire ambition was to make himself wealthy. Use Western market mechanisms while leveraging advantages by partnering with the evolving Russian Federation state riddled with corruption through lack of regulatory controls. He quickly saw the new Russian president as a kindred buccaneer. The archetypical strongman arriving on scene during the unstable transition from the dark Soviet decades to lead the motherland.

Where Krasin saw illicit opportunities in Russia, Martinelli Global recognized Russia with its vast natural resources could be more lucrative than provincial opportunities with unstable Third World despots. A natural partnership formed.

Now the entire rotten structure fell apart. With the origin of the stolen documents originating in Russia, events moved swiftly against the oligarch Nikolai Krasin. Unlike grand jury indictments for Martinelli Global executives in New York, Krasin was immediately arrested by the FSB. Unfortunately for him, he could never be brought to trial to incriminate Vladimir Putin's regime through public testimony. Even in a country where the opposition press was threatened, Russia was not yet a completely repressed society.

A week after his arrest, the press released a statement saying that Krasin had committed suicide by hanging himself with a bedsheet in his cell.

As bad as the unraveling financial scandal damaged the Putin government, the journalist Mark Reynolds revealed something more threatening at the end of his bestselling book, *Shell Game.* Released only months after the New York Times series, a postscript in the book made a startling allegation. Citing transcripts and photos from hacked cellphone conversations, Reynolds alleged this represented evidence of the theft of Russian nuclear warheads. The cellphone intercepts involved conversations of a senior executive with Moscow Capital Partners named Feliks Garnitsky.

According to Reynolds this information cost the life of the insider hacker and the death of a Russian journalist colleague in a bombing intended to silence him while escaping Kiev in Ukraine.

For President Vladimir Putin, it exposed something more damaging than financial wrongdoing allegations he could obscure internally in Russia. However, the alleged loss of nuclear weapons meant military incompetence. If proven true, it also damaged Russia's stature in the international markets for its nuclear energy industry.

Worse yet, Reynolds suggested the obvious beneficiaries of these Russian nukes to be Iran. Already struggling with sanctions imposed for his annexation of Crimea from Ukraine, the international community might now accuse Putin of nuclear weapons proliferation.

That was not the case. Putin had no knowledge of the theft. Putin knew of Garnitsky. Both being ex-KGB, Putin was aware Garnitsky remained close to senior FSB officers. Garnitsky also had business associations with the largest Russian Mafia syndicate, Solntsevskaya Bratva. Garnitsky facilitated the Mafia move into Russian banking during the last years of Yeltsin's presidency. In fact, Putin had found Garnitsky useful in bringing the Solntsevskaya Bratva within the sphere of his broader control by exploiting symbiotic opportunities.

Putin's instincts suggested this theft was most likely to be a Garnitsky rogue operation. Krasin had no reason to do something so foolish. As an executive of the Moscow Capital Partners, Garnitsky had access to the Rusatomic operating subsidiary involved in the weapons management processes. He had access to operational procedures. He would know the military officers. Regardless, the investigation must be exceptionally secret, involving as few people as possible.

The head of the Federal Security Service of the Russian Federation, the FSB, General Valerik Mikhalitsyn reported an intense nationwide search had yet to locate Feliks Garnitsky.

Putin said to Mikhalitsyn, "Whatever is uncovered about this supposed theft, Garnitsky is too much a liability to national security. If he left Russia, it probably was with the assistance of the Solntsevskaya Bratva. Make it their problem to find him. Let it be clear that it is in their direct interest. Garnitsky is to vanish without a trace. I expect this to happen within a matter of days. Are we clear on that, General?"

ROME, ITALY

The Solntsevskaya was Putin's kind of criminal organization. Moscow based with its name derived from the Solntsevo District of Moscow, it evolved from low-level crime into a sophisticated modern-day criminal organization. In their three decades of existence, their tentacles now reached throughout Europe.

They also had a history of rivalry with the Chechen Mafia. The Northern Caucus Chechen Republic of Russia being Putin's recurring scapegoat for any form of organized criminal or terrorist activity, the Solntsevskaya made a good partner.

Boris Stepanovich Lebedyenko, the Solntsevskaya boss operating in Italy, met Feliks Garnitsky at the Hotel Locarno near the Piazza del Popolo.

"What brings you to Rome my old friend?" Lebedyenko said as he joined Garnitsky in the garden patio next to the hotel. It was a gloriously sunny afternoon. Garnitsky had the bartender make them drinks.

"Some difficulties back home, Boris. I decided to leave for health reasons."

"Serious health matters?"

"Very. That is why I came to you. I need to disappear. Willing to pay for protection, I thought of my old friend, Boris."

"Does this have to do with the work we did for you in Odessa?"

The reference to Odessa involved cleaning up after the failed attempt to kill the American journalist. It gave Garnitsky an out rather than fabricating something else to account for his predicament.

"Unfortunately, yes."

The vodka martinis arrived. Garnitsky leaned forward. "I can pay well for this help, Boris."

"And who is it that you have offended? I don't want to inherit your enemies, Feliks Alekseev."

"Certain people in the Government. After the arrest of my former boss Nikolai Krasin, they reported he committed suicide in his cell. Obviously killed so he could not implicate others in the Government. I intend to avoid that same fate."

"And how much would you pay for my help?"

"Two million Euros, Boris. Plus expenses of course."

"You must have really pissed off some important people."

"Can you help me, Boris?"

Lebedyenko looked at Garnitsky for a moment before answering. "Yes. We have a deal. Where do you wish to go?"

"Here in Italy somewhere. A city of some size. Yet someplace obscure enough not to be noticed."

"What documents are you traveling under?"

"A false Polish passport. I speak a little Polish. I will need a new identity. Better to continue to obscure the trail. Ukrainian perhaps. Explains speaking Russian without being Russian. Can that be arranged, Boris?"

"Yes. I have an excellent source. Expensive, but he uses stolen official blank passports. I will have to see about Ukrainian. But it can be done."

"Now about location. Do you know of Catania?"

"Only that it is in Sicily."

"Large enough city so you will not stand out. Good restaurants. An airport. More importantly, I have a business associate there. Young guy. Italian Mafia. Took over from his old man. Understands modern methods, but still respects the old ways. Controls things in Eastern Sicily. Has the local police on his payroll. Smart guy. I will discuss your situation with him. You'll need to pay him too."

"I would expect to. When can you set this up?"

"I'll need at least a day. I will send two of my people to pick you up here at noon the day after tomorrow. Italian guys. Angelo and Tommaso. They will take you to the airport. Only a short flight to Catania. They will deliver your new passport and the hotel reservation in Catania. If my friend agrees to help, they'll have information on how he will contact you there."

"I appreciate this, Boris. You're a dependable friend."

"Thank you, Feliks Alekseev."

Lebedyenko took the napkin from the table and a pen from his pocket. He wrote out a long series of numbers on the napkin and handed it to Garnitsky. "Swiss numbered account. I trust you can arrange the deposit by tomorrow?"

As promised, Lebedyenko's two Italians showed up at the Hotel Locarno at the appointed time. They were polite but said little on the drive to Rome's Aeroporto Leonardo da Vinci.

As they left the city, the driver Angelo did not take the sign marked to the airport via the autostrada. Garnitsky started to look around with some anxiety. They spoke only Italian and English. Garnitsky only spoke Russian and bits of Polish and English. The man in the backseat next to him tried to explain in poor English and hand gestures there was an accident on the autostrada. They were taking the route toward Ostia south of the airport.

Garnitsky relaxed after getting the general idea of what the Italian meant. That was until they passed another sign indicating the exit to Route 296 north to the airport. When he turned his head, Garnitsky faced a silenced 9mm automatic pistol.

Arriving at a marina, the gunmen escorted Garnitsky aboard a thirty-five foot sport fishing boat with its engine idling. After leaving the protection of the harbor breakwater, the boat accelerated at high speed into the Mediterranean.

Once out into the Mediterranean, Boris Lebedyenko emerged from below deck. "Hello, Feliks Alekseev. I must say I am not glad to see you. This is most unpleasant what I must do. You did indeed piss off very powerful people in Russia. Unfortunately, they are far more powerful than you. You also lied to me, Feliks. It was not about killing those Ukrainians."

"Then you're going to kill me, Boris?"

"Yes. However, sadly I have more unpleasantness, old comrade. My orders are that it should be a bad death."

Lebedyenko nodded to one of the Italians holding his gun on Garnitsky. The man shot Garnitsky in each thigh. Garnitsky writhed in agony but said nothing. He was to die and there would be no reprieve.

The Italians then brought out a chain and secured it to Garnitsky's ankles. Attached to the chain was a hundred-pound anchor hung over the side of the boat. The two men lifted and pushed Garnitsky over the railing, as Garnitsky remained silent but with a wild terror in his eyes.

CHAPTER 6

Moscow, Russia - 2015

The publication of Mark Reynolds *Shell Game* sent reverberations throughout the financial world. The exposé of Martinelli Global and Moscow Capital Partners reached into the West through banking and investments. In Moscow, Putin's technocrats began damage control. The possibility of a serious breach in Russian nuclear weapons security held different ramifications.

Yet that assertion seemed unbelievable as staff immediately briefed Putin on the elaborate security protocols. Protocols further verified by international inspection.

Guards at each base belong to independent organizations. Some are federal security service, the FSB, others report to the 12th Chief Directorate of the ministry of Defense. This makes collusion more difficult. Even those guards in the 12th Directorate report to a different battalion command than those working inside the facility.

Electrified fencing, guard dogs, motion detection, separation of an outer and inner technical zone comprising the nuclear depot added another layer of physical security. Several restricted zones of differing levels of security access further divided the technical zone.

Putin took immediate charge of the investigation. At his core, Putin was a thug, even describing his early years in those terms.

A career as a KGB officer reinforced his personal ambitions for power. Now he more resembled a mafia don than a political figure. His inherent brutality surfaced through calmly delivered orders using blunt language that left no ambiguity.

He kept his first meeting intentionally to a small group. Any intelligence leaks to the West of an investigation would exacerbate the international furor. Therefore, it included only the Minister of Defense, the Chief of the General Staff, the head of the Main Intelligence Directorate of the General Staff of the Russian Armed Forces, the GRU, the commander of the Ministry of Defense 12th Chief Directorate, the head of the federal security service, the FSB, and the foreign security service, the SVR.

Putin addressed the Minister of Defense, General Basilevsky, "Are nuclear warheads missing?"

"That has not been confirmed, Mr. President. Our preliminary assessment reveals no anomalies. A thorough investigation is underway to audit every level of management of our nuclear arsenal."

"No *anomalies*? *Audits*?" Putin exploded, slamming his fist down on the conference table.

He turned to address the head of the 12th Chief Directorate, "General Sobolev, are any nuclear weapons missing?"

Sobolov said, "Immediate physical inventories were conducted within twenty-fours of the allegations appearing in the Western media. No discrepancies were found."

"Then your answer is this did not happen? What about the evidence appearing in the media? Just a marketing tactic for this reporter to sell books?"

Putin doubted that to be the case. This reporter had penetrated too deeply into his regime's collusion with the oligarch Krasin's financial empire. The assertion that Russian nuclear weapons were missing was unnecessary to his core story. In fact, it brought on a flood of criticism. Unlike the incriminating documentation produced to make the case for the financial wrongdoings of private corporations, the evidence supporting the reporter's assertion of the theft of Russian nuclear weapons was inconclusive.

Sobolev's expression displayed extreme discomfort. Other than the theft seeming inconceivable, he simply did not know.

"We can find no evidence of missing nuclear weapons. But ..."

"But what?" Putin shouted. "These are big fucking objects under the strictest security. Can your people count?"

"Let me explain better, Mr. President," Sobolev said regaining his composure. "Our nuclear arsenal is spread out at various different levels. These range from deployed weapons, readied reserve weapons, all the way to ordinance in various stages of disassembly. Maintenance of viable warheads requires periodic refurbishing or upgrading, typically to new generations of guidance, triggering, and detonation technology. At the final stage of a weapon's life there is decommissioning and the reprocessing of the fissionable material."

"Get to your point, General."

"What I mean, Mr. President, is a good deal of our arsenal exists in the form of components. A mixture of components from different generations of weapon designs. Components are not necessarily interchangeable. Other than deployed or depot-ready weapons, how many equivalent functioning warheads this represents is a difficult evaluation."

Putin grasped the implications. Could components have been stolen? Would that be easier to accomplish?

"So the answer is components representing operational weapons could be missing and you have not determined that?"

"Not yet, Sir. However, I believe it only to be a theoretically possibility. We of course are working to determine if any components appear missing. It is the highest priority of the security audit section."

"I have been briefed on security measures at our nuclear facilities. My question remains, could such a thing have happened?" Putin said.

General Sobolev knew this would fall on his head if proven true but did his best to lay a defense, however weak.

"Extremely unlikely, Mr. President. To accomplish such a feat would require defeating multiple levels of security redundancies in different forms. However, no security apparatus or set of systems can ever be absolutely secure. As long as people are integral to the security there always remains some risk."

"I'm not interested in a fucking lecture, General. Do you have something material to add or just more blather like General Basilevsky?"

Sobolev said, "Acting on General Basilevsky's orders, we began an immediate investigation. Even a foreign intelligence penetration would require complicity from within. It is too premature to draw conclusions, however we have discovered something that appears unusual."

"And what might that be?"

"To my point, Sir, if a breach in security occurred, someone within the Army must have been complicit. Therefore I ordered an immediate review of all active personnel within the 12th."

"A review? Is that double-speak for bureaucratic masturbation?" Putin interrupted.

"A poor choice of words, Sir. I meant a rigorous database search to establish a starting point for investigating personnel. I ordered the personnel department to search our personnel database of directorate personnel with officer rank going back twelve months. My staff created a search criterion. We searched for officers with disciplinary actions, known financial irregularities such as unusual expenditures, foreign travel of family members, deviant sexual activities, domestic violence, divorce, drunkenness, gambling, anything that could suggest some emotional instability, stress, or compromising behavior. Several thousand officers of course in the 12th.

"The results revealed an expected list as with any such group. It also revealed something else. Although not a sort criteria, the program sorted the entire personnel rooster as active, retired, transferred, or deceased.

"I thought it odd that during this period ten officers died. That seems statistically unusual."

"Died how?" Putin asked.

"A range of causes. Several died naturally, four in that terrorist bombing east of the Jurals, one in an automobile crash, and another murdered by a jealous husband, the perpetrator another army officer appearing on the list. We are looking into each situation in greater detail."

Putin raised an eyebrow conveying the impression he did not see a smoking gun there.

"Turn the information over to General Mikhalitsyn. He will head this investigation. There shall be no turf warfare in this. Every aspect of your respective investigations is to carry the highest secrecy. This is the now top national security matter. I expect confirmation within the week if in fact any warheads or fucking pieces of warheads are missing."

General Valerik Mikhalitsyn headed the federal security service, the FSB. He was Putin's enforcer, a throwback to Soviet era KGB chiefs. Mikhalitsyn personally arranged Krasin's murder in prison then strong-armed the Russian Mafia syndicate to locate and dispose of Garnitsky.

As a trusted functionary within the Yeltsin inner circle, the obscure but ambitious former KGB lieutenant colonel, Vladimir Putin, became head of the KGB successor agency the FSB in 1998. Mikhalitsyn was an FSB colonel at the time. Recognizing Mikhalitsyn's inclinations as similar to his own, Putin relied on him for dark undocumented operations.

His first test was to conduct an operation against Russia's prosecutor general Yuri Skuratov. The prosecutor was mounting a concerted corruption investigation touching on Yeltsin's inner circle. Among those targeted was Yeltsin's own daughter.

A staged black and white, purposely blurry videotape aired on Russian television. The claim on the news broadcast was that the man in the video with blacked out censor strips of his genitals, was the state prosecutor, naked with two prostitutes in a hotel. Mikhalitsyn personally cast the man posing as the state prosecutor and arranged for its airing with a bribe backed by a physical threat to the television station owner. FSB chief Vladimir Putin officially validated the video.

Following the firing of the state prosecutor, the ailing President Boris Yeltsin showed his gratitude to his young protégé Vladimir Putin by promoting him to prime minister. Soon after, Yeltsin designated him as his successor as Russian president. Mikhalitsyn then replaced Putin as head of the FSB.

Putin adjourned the meeting with the admonishment, "This investigation must be conducted in absolute secrecy. No leaks. Use limited staff and only trusted subordinates. You will turn over any and all information to General Mikhalitsyn's office *as it develops*. I am to be briefed daily."

Investigations into the ten deceased officers yielded nothing toward confirming any plot to steal nuclear warheads. The deaths of the four army officers involved in the car bombing in Chelyabinsk raising the number of deaths during the preceding year was the only reason that made the statistic stand out. As part of Garnitsky's post-theft obscuring of the plot, two other bombing incidents occurred the same week as the Chelyabinsk bombing. Unnamed sources attributed this sequence of bombings to Chechen separatists.

Nothing cast doubt on the initially reported details for any of the deaths. Five of the deceased functioned in positions sufficiently remote to each other to seemingly preclude involvement with stealing warheads given the layers of security.

If any warheads are confirmed as missing, the consensus among the investigators pointed to an administrative operation. A paper trail manipulation while the physical warheads or components moved according to normal routines. Investigating these avenues would take time.

In the process of the investigation, the FSB arrested a range of people associated with Krasin and Garnitsky. The entire senior staff of Moscow Capital Partners endured days of unrelenting interrogations while incarcerated in the notorious Lubyanka prison. Some suffered physical abuse in the dreaded lower levels of the iconic symbol of Soviet secret police repression since the 1917 revolution.

Garnitsky's associates suffered harsher treatment. Unlike the white-collar business types working for the oligarch Krasin, Garnitsky's subordinates' backgrounds were more sordid. If there was any substance to this nuclear warhead theft allegation, Garnitsky must be involved. His subordinates suffered arrest on an array of contrived charges as a means of coercing information. Even under brutal interrogations employing harsh physical maltreatment, none of those questioned revealed any knowledge of a scheme to steal nuclear weapons.

Confounding the FSB investigators was the inability to locate Garnitsky's right-hand man Yuri Dratshev. Dratshev's father and mother pleaded knowing nothing of their son's whereabouts, nor did his married sister. Nothing surfaced under physical surveillance and their telephone monitoring of the family. If Garnitsky was involved then it certainly meant so was Dratshev.

No leads existed to explain Dratshev's disappearance. No personal effects other than clothing remained in his rather austere furnished apartment. Nothing found at his apartment suggested any foul play in his disappearance.

All indications pointed to Dratshev going to ground. His modest bank account recorded a sizeable withdrawal leaving only a small balance months earlier, about the time of the exposé by the American journalist. No further activity since then. No credit card activity. Weeks of accumulated mail.

Only one uninvestigated lead remained. Dratshev's older brother, Fyodor. Estranged from the family for twenty years, the elder sibling sought a secluded existence as an Orthodox Christian monk. Brother Fyodor lived a contemplative existence in a monastery on Mount Athos Greece.

❖ ❖ ❖

Major General Anton Grigoryev held the position of Senior Deputy Director, effectively the second highest-ranking officer in the Foreign Intelligence Service, the SVR. He previously headed the political intelligence directorate of the SVR. At the time he first met Victoria Prescott, he was a young colonel newly appointed to that post by the first post-Soviet president, Boris Yeltsin.

His career in the predecessor KGB started in the final years of the Soviet Union. The Gorbachev era saw fundamental changes in a desperate attempt to salvage the Soviet state from a multitude of worsening problems. Characterized by *Perestroika*, the restructuring of the political and economic system, and *Glasnost*, the openness of new social and political reforms, presented opportunities even within the repressive KGB. His appointment came about partly because of his age as well as his achievements viewed in the context of these profound changes.

Joining the former KGB First Chief Directorate, responsible for foreign operations and intelligence, immediately involved Grigoryev in foreign cultures and politics. In his case, the West.

Born to an academic mathematician mother and senior foreign ministry official father, he came from what amounted to privilege in the Soviet system. Those connections, a keen intellect, and acquired proficiency in English from his parents gained him entry into Moscow State University. His background laid the groundwork for an intellectual interest in the avowed enemy world of capitalism. Taking degrees in western economics and political science fed an interest in the West.

Why a career path in intelligence? Difficult to answer with the passage of decades. At the time, the Soviet Union entered what would be its final decade of existence. A sixty-year radical experiment that by any measurement had devolved into dismal failure. An experiment in Communist-styled socialism where the average Soviet citizen suffered substantially greater economic disadvantage than those in Western democratic-capitalist countries. All this while denied even basic personal liberties and held under constant threat by a corrupt and repressive autocracy.

What choices for a bright well-educated young man? Private enterprise did not exist in any semblance of what he studied of the West. His academic background was not in the sciences. Conventional government service seemed a pathetic career path in a dysfunctional system feeding on its bloated bureaucracy. Yet he felt himself Russian.

Not all was perfection in the West under capitalism and market economies. Classes of people still suffered. The other great superpower, the United States remained locked in a contest for international influence. Modern day imperialism. If you were not American then you might suffer any fate under the weight of U.S. military and economic power.

Perhaps his joining the First Chief Directorate was a place on a team that could still challenge at a level equal to that of the United States. Here he could play in what the Americans called the big leagues. His father's career in the Soviet Foreign Service gave him a sense of the contest during his formative years.

The First Chief Directorate conducted foreign espionage. It was not the dark, internally repressive directorates of the KGB feared throughout Russia. Although less malevolent by the 1980s, the KGB was the latest incarnation to Soviet secret police brutality. Originating from the Cheka as it solidified the revolution with the blood of dissenters in the 1920s, the next incarnation as the NKVD became the instrument of Stalin's purges of the late 1930's. The KGB First Chief Directorate was the foreign intelligence. These were spies confronting the West rather than brutalizing the Russian citizenry as police thugs.

Therefore, the KGB became a career choice made against other dismal options. Embracing the intellectual challenges if not Communist ideology, Grigoryev's display of a range of skills rapidly advanced him within the First Directorate.

Grigoryev's role in the investigation of the alleged nuclear weapons theft ran to accessing any intelligence indicators among likely recipients of these devices. In this endeavor, the SVR was not the only Russian foreign intelligence organ within the government. The much larger foreign military intelligence organization, the Main Intelligence Directorate, the GRU employed many more foreign agents. Both foreign intelligence services maintained a rivalry since well before WWII. Grigoryev enjoyed particularly good relations with the GRU. Putin however sidelined the GRU in this investigation, holding the military indirectly responsible for lax security if a theft occurred. The inability to confirm even if nuclear weapons or fissile components were missing further suggested flawed security protocols.

Neither Russian foreign intelligence branches had highly placed intelligence sources within foreign countries that might represent possible recipients of the warhead. Consensus suggested that probably meant Iran, possibly North Korea, and more remotely, unstable Pakistan concerned with their archenemy India's warming ties with the United States. Of course, the terrorist organizations of Al-Qaeda, Islamic State, and the Taliban remained unlikely outside possibilities.

Like the chief of the FSB, General Mikhalitsyn, the head of the SVR, General Dubrovsky was also an ex-KGB contemporary of President Putin. Putin appointed both to their current posts. Putin's bias toward those with KGB or its successor agencies backgrounds stemmed from his greater patronage leverage compared to the larger military GRU intelligence organ. For this reason, Grigoryev was assigned the task of making contact with Brother Fyodor to explore any knowledge as to his younger brother's whereabouts. Given the circumstances of the estrangement between the brothers, it appeared unlikely to yield anything useful.

Grigoryev delegated the task to the SVR head of station in the Russian embassy in Athens. The Russian agent occupied the post of third secretary for cultural affairs as his cover. The cover story to Brother Fyodor concerned a major financial scandal in Russia involving his brother Yuri's boss. His brother is missing and possibly in danger because of what he knows. His brother's best chance is to become a witness under the protection the government.

Once back in Athens, the excited SVR agent called Grigoryev personally on a secure scrabbled embassy telephone.

"General, I spoke with Brother Fyodor yesterday. I gave him my cover story. Registering little surprise, he removed an envelope from a bureau drawer then handed it to me.

"His only comment, *my brother Yuri chose a wicked path to follow years ago. I pray for him every day. He visited me months ago. Confessed to committing some great evil. Believed his life to be in danger. Gave me this sealed envelope and a message before departing."*

"What was the message?" Grigoryev said.

"Should anyone come inquiring about me, give them this envelope. Better not to open it for your own sake. It shall mean that I am no more, brother. Signed Yuri."

"You opened it?"

"Yes, Sir. It opens with a declaration. *The following is a detailed account of the successful theft of three operational Russian thermonuclear warheads and deliver them to agents of the Islamic Republic of Iran. The fact that I am being pursued means I like others involved in the theft have also been eliminated by Feliks Garnitsky. This was his operation along with an Iranian agent I knew only by his operational code name as Achaemenes."*

"And what else does it say?"

"There are five pages of handwritten details, General."

"Read it to me."

The agent read the entire document, interrupted frequently by Grigoryev to repeat certain details. Dratshev also explained how he and Garnitsky arranged for the murders of complicit Russian army officers using hitmen from the criminal syndicate Solntsevskaya Bratva.

After the agent concluded the reading, Grigoryev said, "Listen carefully. You are to fly immediately to Moscow bringing the document you just read. Do not make any copies. Do not discuss this with anyone under any circumstances whatsoever. To your immediate superior you are acting under my direct orders, which come directly from the President. Is that understood?"

Grigoryev and his boss General Dubrovsky gave the news directly to Putin in the presidential office.

With the details of the weapons theft by Dratshev's first-hand account, there was little question that the weapons were in Iranian hands. Putin tasked Grigoryev to determine the identity of this Iranian code-named *Achaemenes*. Who in the Iranian leadership backed such an audacious operation? How might Iran leverage possession of these weapons? What are the ramifications for Russia? How can Russia mitigate the international blowback? What revised security measures are necessary given the culpability of army officers of the 12th Main Directorate?

While Russian foreign intelligence had limited human assets in Iran, they had no one highly placed within the government, much less anyone in the Iranian Ministry of Intelligence. However, identifying the probable identity of *Achaemenes* with Dratshev's physical description proved relatively straightforward. Given this must have been a very senior intelligence officer with a working familiarity of Russia, the list of possible candidates proved short. Every intelligence service maintains dossiers on senior officials of foreign intelligence services both friendly and hostile.

Achaemenes, mythical founder of the Persian royal house, was probably Colonel Farzard Heydar Savi. Savi spoke Russian and even received training at the SVR academy in Moscow twenty years ago. As a minor figure of interest to Russian intelligence in a difficult place to acquire human intelligence, personal details on Savi were scarce. Grigoryev issued priority orders to expand the Savi dossier. Iranian objectives might become clearer by probing Savi more deeply.

The larger unanswered question remained, who within the Iranian leadership backed this plot? A plot undoubtedly authorized by the Supreme Leader, but understanding the advocates in the leadership might suggest Iranian intentions.

All such efforts came to an abrupt halt within days after Grigoryev presented Putin with Dratshev's account of the theft operation. Grigoryev's superior General Dubrovsky delivered the order to him in his office.

"The President informed me just an hour ago that all further investigative efforts into this nuclear theft affair are to cease immediately."

"Cease?"

Grigoryev bolted out of his chair across from Dubrovsky sitting behind his desk."

"Easy, Anton Vladimirovich. Sit back down. I am as shocked as you."

"And what reason did the President give?"

"National security. Leakage of the security breach itself will itself cause irreparable damage the President said. More important to mitigate the damage."

"Damage? Islamic fanatics now possess thermonuclear warheads. Damage will likely be far worse than exposing the gross incompetence of Russia to manage its nuclear arsenal. This final insult also confirms we are no longer a superpower. That is what Putin is afraid of."

"The President also ordered all files and electronic records purged. Turn everything over to
General Mikhalitsyn. Retain no copies," Dubrovsky said.

Unlike Dubrovsky, Grigoryev knew other reasons for Putin wanting to lock away everything surrounding the international scandal growing out of the published exposé by the American author. Missing thermonuclear warheads just one aspect. The other was exposure of the Putin regime's direct involvement with the oligarch Krasin, now the subject of international scandal. Further probes could proliferate further damaging exposures by directly connecting the warheads theft to the government's involvement with Krasin, Garnitsky, Moscow Capital Partners, and Rusatomic. A financial corruption scandal could represent domestic problems for Putin. So Putin intended to continue to deny any loss of nuclear weapons indefinitely. It could be sometime before Iran could find the means to exercise any advantage based on possessing the weapons.

Grigoryev knew those details of financial corruption from his brother-in-law, Stepka Lytkin, a financial expert within the sister internal security services the FSB. For years, Lytkin secretly worked with high-ranking officials close to Putin to participate in moneymaking schemes engineered by Krasin.

From that moment, Anton Grigoryev consciously committed to a course of action. No longer could he be part of this criminal regime. Putin's autocratic rule denied the kind of future he hoped for Russia. He must become a dissident in more than just private thought. His whole life nothing more than a lie if he continued serving this despotic regime.

Grigoryev's brother-in-law shared his views. Yet did he have any right to suggest that his brother-in-law risk his family in the kind of conspiracy he now planned?

CHAPTER 7

MOSCOW, RUSSIA

To Grigoryev's amazement, four years later Iran still did nothing that might suggest they possessed operational thermonuclear warheads. Iran even signed an agreement in 2015 with the world's major powers, including Russia, to curtail nuclear programs that could support weapons development in exchange for relaxing associated sanctions. He speculated they might be waiting to increase their ballistic missile capability. Iran already possessed missiles with a range of 2000 kilometers, capable of delivering the Russian warheads within range of any regional enemy. However, successfully delivering a nuclear warhead involved more than missile range. From technical briefings, Grigoryev understood the technical challenges associated with guidance, detonation, and overcoming defensive jamming countermeasures.

During this time, Grigoryev and his brother-in-law Stepka Lytkin began assembling a package of incriminating material on the Putin regime. How they might use this evidence of corruption remained uncertain. Yet both felt a compelling moral obligation to resist in some manner.

Grigoryev's contribution to their project was the nuclear theft investigation results from the FSB, the SVR, and the Ministry of Defense. Dratshev's confession detailing the theft led to uncovering the trail of falsified paperwork. A secret physical inventory and records audit confirmed the identified warheads missing, and identified the falsified documentation trail revealed by Dratshev. One of the few officials with total access, Grigoryev easily downloaded electronic files. If ever questioned, the digital record of his download explained as following orders to purge all databases and archive the files under highly restricted access.

The active clandestine work and therefore the constant risk fell on Lytkin.

After the scandal of the American exposé involving Moscow Capital Partners, Putin not only sidestepped any political fallout, but also avoided personal financial loss. At worst, only a few cronies suffered with frozen foreign assets and a few Russian banks and corporations fell under Western sanctions. Emboldened, Putin set out to replicate Krasin's methods of feeding off Russian resources and using private enterprises with the state's collusion. All for the personal benefit of his closest subordinates and the functionaries necessary to execute the necessary international maneuverings. What better way to maintain power of a criminal kleptocracy?

Lytkin again became a key player partnered with a team of well-compensated technocrats. In the course of his covert work, he electronically stole documents and communications that he gave to Grigoryev for safekeeping given his brother-in-law's high rank in the foreign security service.

"Look at this," Lytkin said handing Grigoryev a piece of paper. They sat in the back of a bar. One of several they frequented ostensibly to share a drink each week but actually to exchange information. Given their positions, they assumed the likely bugging of their apartments. As for Lytkin, he never shared with his wife what he and her brother were planning.

Lytkin said, "This is how much I have amassed from all the illegal money we are paid. Safe in foreign bank accounts. I am sick of this, Anton. Is this enough to start a new life in the West for my family?"

Grigoryev looked at the figure. More than he managed to hide abroad. Of course, his brother-in-law was helping to steal tens of millions, his bribes commensurate with his greater value.

"The money is sufficient, Stepka. The trick is in escaping Russia. What you are doing places you under constant scrutiny. Even getting Helga and the girls across the border requires careful planning. But the greater danger lies with making contact with Western intelligence."

"Does that mean the Americans?" Lytkin said.

Grigoryev nodded. "Most likely, possibly the French. Not the British. Too much of a history of being compromised by Russian infiltration." He smiled trying to lighten the fearful prospect. If caught, Lytkin would suffer the same fate as Nikolai Krasin. Putin could not afford a public trial with the details Lytkin possessed. Perhaps worse for Grigoryev. If not executed for espionage then buried in a Russian maximum-security prison under concentration camp-like conditions. Both men knew that discovery meant an unpleasant death.

"I shall begin preparations, Stepka. As of now, stop downloading any more information. We have more than enough material to buy asylum in the West. No need to increase the risk. Just do your job quietly. By summer at latest we will make our move."

It was now February in Moscow.

"I shall miss our homeland but not Russian winters," Lytkin said forcing a weak smile.

With the decision made, Grigoryev and Lytkin began serious preparations. Part of that planning meant a means of alerting each other should something go wrong. The greater risk was discovery of Lytkin's clandestine data mining activities of the classified databases involved with his secret work. If discovered, arrest would come without warning. As the practice of secret police, typically the knock on the door in the early morning hours. While Lytkin served in the economic security sector of the FSB, other divisions within the service engaged in secret police tactics reminiscent of the former Soviet KGB.

Unlike his brother-in-law, Grigoryev could prepare for an immediate escape. Lytkin's wife and two daughters however knew nothing of the dangerous game played by their father. Even the planned orderly escape from Russia would be exponentially more difficult for Lytkin's family compared to Grigoryev.

To alert the other in the event of emergency, Grigoryev purchased prepaid cellphones. Three times every day at predesignated intervals, one would send a text message and await a response. A chess move as if from an ongoing match. Actually, a historic match with the moves memorized. Lytkin played white, Grigoryev black. No response from the other within an hour suggested something was wrong. The sender was to leave immediately to a predetermined safe location. The sender would resend the same text for the next three hours. No reply then triggered an emergency escape for the other. A reply with an incorrect move confirmed arrest.

They fixed on a date in July. Lytkin arranged for his family's annual holiday to the seaside Russian resort of Sochi on the Black Sea. It would serve to conceal from his family what this was about until the last moment.

"This is the plan, Stepka," Grigoryev said. "You will train from Moscow to Sochi on an overnight train. Twenty-six hours. You book rooms in Sochi for a week. On the second day you tell Helga and the girls what's happening."

"What if Helga refuses, Anton?"

"You must convince her. Tell her I am involved. We have planned this together for a long time. Tell her we cannot turn back. Things are already set in motion."

Lytkin nodded. "What then?"

"Buy tickets on the high-speed ferry leaving Monday, Wednesday, and Friday afternoons for Trabzon, Turkey to give us flexibility. A four and a half hour trip. Trabzon is a popular seaside destination. Buy the tickets at different local travel offices, not online."

"Why Turkey? In fact why not just fly out of Russia?"

"Fly to where? It would raise suspicions and might provoke surveillance given the sensitivity of what you do. The train trip is within Russia. Security checks on boat trips are not checked against databases. And Turkey is one of the few countries requiring no advance visa for Russian citizens. You will use your actual passports.

"Once in Trabzon you rent a car. You will drive south four hours where you will pick up a train to Ankara then on to Istanbul. I shall meet you in Istanbul.

"And how will you get to Istanbul?"

"I will fly. Also a holiday but in my case I frequently travel outside Russia."

"Then what?"

"That is to be determined, Stepka. Istanbul is a crossroads for every intelligence service in the world. Easy access by air or sea. A big enough city in which to conceal ourselves until exfiltrated by our future host country."

"America?"

"Possibly but I'm uncomfortable with the state of affairs under their unstable new president. Our experts conclude he suffers from various mental disorders. Difficult to anticipate how he might react when appraised of two high-level Russian defections. He is at odds with his own intelligence services and publicly too friendly with Putin for my liking.

"I'm thinking perhaps the French. But we shall see. Any Western intelligence service will welcome what we bring in exchange. However, for our safety, the United States is more secure. Putin's has a long reach and has mounted assassination attempts in Europe."

Grigoryev knew the best deal was with the Americans but he was uneasy. He was actually considering the Canadians. Close to the Americans but not tainted by this strange President Trump. Whatever country he chose, it still remained a delicate task making that first contact. Taking that step immediately elevated the risk while relinquishing control to others he did not know or trust.

Grigoryev spent considerable effort setting up an alternative Canadian identity as his means of squirreling away money outside of Russia. It represented his sole lifeline. Better to conceal even the mention of Canada from his brother-in-law should circumstances go badly.

Lytkin did not heed Grigoryev's admonishment to stop gathering information. In a heated exchange just two weeks earlier, Lytkin argued, "But. Anton, this is huge. Not only billions are involved but the strategic implications for Putin are enormous. It could solidify his hold on power beyond what should be his last term in office."

Although Lytkin agreed after that last confrontation to cease his activities, Grigoryev still assumed that was the reason everything fell apart six weeks before their scheduled date to leave Russia.

Lytkin's text message came at four in the morning. Two hours early. And instead of simply the expected next move all-okay signal of *K-B7*, the message read, *I believe you have mate in the next move. Well played.* Not the result of Lytkin's *K-B7* move in the memorized match. Grigoryev starred at the message understanding its dire meaning. He retrieved his prepared go-bag and left the apartment immediately.

The next hour would determine if he was next. He must get away from the apartment immediately without signaling his next move. He therefore parked his car at a large public lot a short distance away then hailed a taxi to the train station. Escape by air clearly out of the question.

He planned his escape route over months with the scheduled train departure times for each day of the week memorized. The step involved getting out of Moscow as quickly as possible before the police cordon could close off all escape routes. Purchasing a second-class ticket, he boarded the 7:10am high-speed express train to Smolensk, Russia. No security screening for train travel. The final travel segment would involve crossing the Russian border into Lithuania.

Conventional Russian passport holders require obtaining an advance visa to enter Lithuania. Holding a Russian diplomatic passport exempted him. Nevertheless, it also meant he was leaving a potential trail of his location.

The risk seemed acceptable. Lithuania was an EU country. He carried his Canadian passport as Byron Laurent with a French commercial visa, entry stamped in France five months ago. Once entering the EU, you could travel without individual visa within the entire EU. As Laurent, he could then easily make his way to Paris.

The nine-hour train journey took him out of Russia into Vilnius, Lithuania. Arriving at one in the morning, the night shift Lithuanian border guards checking passports on the train took no particular note to the rarely encountered diplomatic passport.

In a couple of hours his train would depart Vilnius. Russian Anton Grigoryev now became Canadian Byron Laurent.

Two days later Grigoryev arrived by train in Paris. By avoiding air travel, his movements were not recorded in any database. Even the arrival by train in Lithuania under diplomatic passport may have gone unrecorded. The Russians were now searching for him. Assuming he fled to Europe, arriving in Vilnius gave away nothing since he now slipped into his well-constructed alternative identity.

The attempted early morning arrest of Stepka Lytkin went badly. Hoping to save his family, Lytkin shot himself before security agents could enter the apartment. The cryptic text message to an untraceable cellphone number obviously a code meant an accomplice or possibly a foreign intelligence control officer. When Lytkin's high-ranking foreign intelligence service brother-in-law could not be located, Russian intelligence went into panic. Was this a broader foreign intelligence penetration? What was the nature and extent of the compromised sensitive information?

FSB chief General Mikhalitsyn reported to President Putin, "The immediate superior of this man Lytkin working in the Economic Security Division made a report raising suspicions about Lytkin's activities."

"What kind of suspicions?" Putin asked.

"Mostly access requests for information outside his clearance. His superior granted the access but remained uneasy. Further interaction with Lytkin caused him to make a report leading to an investigation tracing Lytkin's computer activities. That investigation yielded results indicating an alarming range of files accessed by Lytkin. Highly sensitive communications. These involved highly sensitive communications with the chairman of the board of directors of the central bank, the deputy minister of economic development, the businessman Sergei Terekov, and … " he paused for a moment, "even … certain materials from you, Mr. President."

Putin scowled. "Go on."

"The security division chief handed me the report late Tuesday night. I ordered the immediate arrest of Lytkin. Agents raided his apartment in the early hours of the following morning. Lytkin refused to open the door. As agents forcibly broke in, Lytkin shot himself.

"Next to his body was a cellphone. Just moments before killing himself he sent a text message to an untraceable cellphone number. The message obviously a coded warning to a confederate. We found a USB storage device with stolen files recently accessed. No additional classified materials were found other than those files on the single USB."

"But you believe Lytkin may have stolen other files?"

"Undoubtedly. This was not a singular act. We are trying to determine the extent of the breach. Using forensic methods, experts are looking at his history of database access. With added difficulty because of his level of authorized access as part of his work. Slow work since I have limited the number of security people working on this due to its sensitivity. But we must proceed on the premise that Lytkin stole much more than what we discovered after falling under suspicion."

"His wife? Has she been questioned?"

"She's still undergoing intense interrogation. Claims she has no idea why her husband was arrested. Charged with espionage, she understands the gravity of her position. Concerned about the welfare of her daughters which she has not been allowed to see since her arrest. They are also being interrogated separately. According to her, Lytkin had no particularly close friends other than her brother, General Grigoryev. Says they were very close."

"And Grigoryev is now missing. So who was Lytkin working for, General?"

"We believe that Grigoryev must be behind this. Lytkin's wife says her husband looked up to Grigoryev."

"Then who is Grigoryev working for?"

"That we don't know, Sir. We are using every means to gather any intelligence on his whereabouts. Looking at everyone he has interacted with these last few years. Unfortunately, he traveled to Europe frequently as part of his position. He could have easily made contact with a foreign service. No reports however of any security breaches during any of his foreign trips. But then again he was the number-two man in the SVR. Might have been able to cover up something.

"He and Lytkin were in different security services. Seems like an unusual enemy intelligence penetration going off in entirely different directions," Putin said reflecting his background in KGB counterintelligence.

"Maybe Lytkin was just a target of opportunity Grigoryev discovered by his family association and decided to vacuum up more intelligence."

"Possibly. However, if you were Western intelligence having turned the First Deputy Director of the Russian Foreign Security

Service you would think the interest would be foreign policy, military information. Information Grigoryev controlled without risking theft of documents related to financial dealings."

"Do you have a theory then, General?"

"I believe that Lytkin and Grigoryev might have engaged in their own conspiracy, rather than part of a foreign intelligence penetration. Perhaps both planned to use these stolen materials to bargain for asylum terms in defecting to the West. However, we must assume Grigoryev now has no alternative now but defection, Mr. President."

Putin raised an eyebrow.

Mikhalitsyn continued, "Grigoryev has reportedly been a changed person since his wife died five years ago. Almost reclusive according those questioned. He is sixty-two. Nearing the end of his career. General Dubrovsky confides he has never liked Grigoryev."

"That's because Grigoryev is smarter than Dubrovsky and worried about Grigoryev taking over his job. This fiasco demonstrates Dubrovsky's incompetence. But for the moment, assuming you are correct, what do you think Grigoryev is up to?"

"Regardless if Grigoryev is working for Americans or someone else, he is now on the run. His disappearance appears sudden. Yet Grigoryev would have certainly prepared contingency arrangements. He might still be in Russia but most likely has left the country by now. However, there still might be time to locate him and remove him."

"Why's that?"

"Even if his original intent was to defect, he may have never signaled his intent. If I were in his predicament, I would not contact a foreign intelligence service until I was in some secure place and ready to make the move with a well-planned extraction. Once he makes contact, he is at great risk. His security in the hands of people he does not know. Since Lytkin was still actively stealing material when discovered, this forced Grigoryev to disappear immediately. Undoubtedly, the text message was a prearranged warning by deviating from the rehearsed chess moves.

"But it takes time to contact the right opposition official. Longer still to make it up the chain of the foreign intelligence bureaucracy for approval. Then of course, Grigoryev will want to negotiate terms for defecting. At best, this offers a small window of opportunity. There is still a chance that he has not made it over to the other side. That is particularly likely if Grigoryev planned the defection without prior collusion with any foreign intelligence.

"I've already ordered an intense search focus throughout Western Europe. That is where Grigoryev spent the most time outside Russia. Fluent in French and English affords him a range of options. Best possibilities are France, Belgium, Switzerland, and England.

"And why not the United States?" Putin asked.

"Possible, but if I were Grigoryev I'd prefer to negotiate from outside the U.S. We do not know what false identity he may be using but entering the U.S. falsely would compromise his position.

"Dubrovsky already dispatched two Zaslon strike teams to Europe. One to London the other to Paris. So we have mobile strike assets already on the ground should we locate Grigoryev in Europe."

Within the Operations Department of the SVR's Directorate S is the shadowy Zaslon. A small group of elite secret special forces recruited from other *spetsnaz* units of the Russian military. As experienced operatives fluent in multiple languages, their principal mission was to conduct black operations in foreign countries. With their very existence never officially acknowledged, they represented the equivalent of U.S. Navy Seals or the French Service Action.

"Does Dubrovsky understand what is to be done when Grigoryev is located?"

"Yes, Mr. President. I conveyed your orders. Because of the sensitivity of Grigoryev's defection, an attempt at capture risks losing him. He is no fool and probably armed. He must be prevented from contact with foreign intelligence at all cost. Dubrovsky assured me his clandestine personnel are under orders to eliminate Grigoryev at the first opportunity."

Following Victoria Prescott's departure from the Relais Christine, Grigoryev decided to make a visit to his art gallery. Undoubtedly his last visit. How he longed to disappear permanently into Byron Laurent, the Canadian art broker and owner of the Paris Ile St. Louis art gallery. Unrealistic now. Eventually Russian intelligence would uncover his identity. Montreal did not represent an indefinite safe haven. His course in life set long ago. What lay before him was perhaps the best alternative he could envision. What else for an aging spy profoundly disillusioned with his government?

A great guilt hung over him. He should never have encouraged his brother-in-law in his virulent resentment of the Putin regime. Never should have allowed that resentment to take on active form. To what end? His fault for endangering his only remaining family. Stepka was like the younger brother he never had. The fate of his sister and nieces uncertain. Their lives undoubtedly destroyed.

With Prescott returning to New York and the process of his defection to the United States in motion, Grigoryev booked a flight to Montreal for the next day. Paris was too likely a place for Russian intelligence to search for him given his many documented trips and fluency in French. He will visit the gallery a last time and make arrangements with his manager for his extended absence.

Walking north, Grigoryev crossed over then the River Seine at Pont Saint-Michel arriving on the Île de la Cité after crossing the Quai des Grands Augustin running parallel to the Seine. With the westbound traffic one-way stopped at the signal, a black sedan with two men waited for the light to turn green. The man in the passenger seat suddenly leaned forward staring at Grigoryev crossing on foot in front. Saying something to the driver, the man immediately exited the vehicle and stepped to the sidewalk on the river side of the wide boulevard.

Unknown to Grigoryev, the nondescript license plate of the car bore the code and diplomatic status for the Russian Federation.

Against all the odds of chance, the resident Russian SVR station chief in Paris was on his way to the Russian Embassy west of the Eiffel Tower that morning.

The previous day he received an unusual priority alert communication from Moscow to report any information regarding the whereabouts of General Anton Grigoryev. He had twice met Grigoryev. Not often the SVR hunted one of its own.

Remembering his early days of field training tradecraft, the agent followed Grigoryev keeping at a maximum distance. Grabbing his briefcase as he left the car gave him the appearance of someone headed to an office.

Walking east alongside Notre Dame Cathedral, Grigoryev crossed over the Pont Saint-Louis connecting the larger Île de la Cité island with Île Saint-Louis. He then headed down the rue Saint-Louis, the center street bisecting the small island of affluent apartments and small shops in the River Seine.

After Grigoryev entered the art gallery, the SVR agent called the embassy.

Thirty minutes later, still in the same spot watching the art gallery, the agent took a call. After confirming Grigoryev was still inside the gallery, Moscow ordered the agent to return to the embassy. Other resources were in place to manage the situation.

Victoria Prescott arrived at New York's JFK Airport early in the afternoon. After disembarking the aircraft, she called her father.

"Dad, it's Victoria. How are you?"

"I'm fine. So good to hear from you, dear."

"I just arrived at JFK. Unexpected last minute trip or I would have called will some warning. Are you at home?"

"Oh my, Victoria. I'm at Frank's right now. A boring conference in Chicago but a good excuse for a quick visit with Frank and Judy. Not back in New York until Friday."

"Damn. Just my luck." She certainly was not about to discuss this matter over the phone.

"Are you in New York long, Victoria? Can you spend the weekend?"

"Sure, Dad. That sounds good."

"Excellent. I'll call Isabella and tell her to expect you today."

Isabella was her father's long time live-in Puerto Rican maid and cook. At least she would have time to dive into Grigoryev's files before confronting her father. He would want to see more than just what a Russian spymaster related to her before getting involved. Her father knew nothing of her former intimate relations with Grigoryev, just his assisting in her research while in Moscow twenty-years ago. That of course formed the basis for his wanting her to act as backdoor intermediary knowing her father to be a former State Department official.

Ensconced in her father's study at his Upper Westside apartment overlooking the great expanse of Central Park, she dialed the special number for Grigoryev. Had to tell him about the delay in getting things moving forward. Actually wanted to hear his voice, reassure him.

No answer after several rings. Odd. She disconnected the call. Thirty minutes later, a second try yielded no answer. Worried now, she anxiously placed another call thirty minutes later. She remembered his admonishment, leave no voice messages and speak only in Russian.

On the third try, the call picked up but without any verbal response.

After waiting a couple of seconds, she said in Russian, "Hello?"

In Russian came the reply, "Who is calling?"

It was not Grigoryev.

Waiting a moment the male voice asked again, "Who is calling? Who are you trying to reach?"

She disconnected.

CHAPTER 8

MANHATTAN, NEW YORK

After the failure to reach Grigoryev and the troubling answering by an unknown Russian speaker, Victoria Prescott spent a sleepless night. Did this mean the Russians had found him? If so, what did that mean? Morning did not relieve the anxiety. Her only outlet was to explore Grigoryev's material. By that evening, she completed a first review gaining a solid familiarity of its breathtaking scope. So engrossed, she hardly broke for meals prepared by Isabella or the stunning view of Central Park.

The details of the nuclear theft by this Dratshev character left her shaken. Unlike uncovering a previously unknown Soviet spy from fifty years earlier, this presented something of frightening immediate implications. To think that the Russians and the Iranians both concealed this for years added another sinister aspect.

A more disturbing thought struck her. Did the U.S. know or at least suspect? They undoubtedly embarked on a crash program to determine if what the journalist Reynolds suggested was true. Perhaps they had signals intercepts beyond those few cellphone conversations between Garnitsky and Dratshev and the two incriminating photographs published by Reynolds. Yet all the major powers including the U.S., Russia, China, the UK, and

France still signed an agreement with Iran. Did only Russia know the truth, or did the U.S.? If so, did the U.S. keep other allied nations in the dark?

Weighty stuff. Prescott's field of expertise as a Russian expert specializing on the modern Soviet era left her with a cynical view of the venality of all governments. Given confidential information, those in power most often used it to further their own agendas. Agendas invariably tainted by bias or politics often resulted in concealing information from other agencies within their own government.

That included the United States. Her research revealed the sordid details and rationalizations of countless officials bent on using or distorting confidential information. Her own breakthrough project resulting in her book *Critical Mass* a perfect example. President Roosevelt concealing the Manhattan Project from Congress and his own vice president. The personal experience of FBI directed harassment toward her for revealing evidence of a previously undiscovered Soviet spy making the agency look bad. Once the evidence became uncontestable, they mounted a concerted effort to shift blame to military security inadequacies. A public relations campaign waged by senior FBI officials and FBI historians specifically to shift blame of the treasonous army officer to the Manhattan Project commander General Leslie Groves. All about an event fifty years earlier.

If something bad happened to Grigoryev, this information still must get to the U.S. government. Something bad like what? She hesitated to contemplate his possible death. Had he suffered the same horrible fate as the Russian defector Litvinenko years ago in London? Or like his brother-in-law, taken his own life? Best not to dwell on such distressing thoughts. Could be reasons for his failure to make contact but the Russian voice answering his cellphone dispelled any real hope. Not practiced in this sort of thing left her nothing to do but wait and hope Grigoryev might call with an explanation. Not clear what her next move should be, especially if Grigoryev never called.

One thing for certain, she would not share this whole affair with her father until she could reconnect with Grigoryev and let him plead his own case. If his fate were otherwise then it would not matter. Right now her explanations would only trigger fatherly advice to stay clear of the matter. Certainly, he would counsel that duty demanded turning over the information on the nuclear weapons theft to the proper U.S. authorities.

As much as Hamilton Prescott despised Donald Trump and his entire administration, he remained a traditionalist. A believer in the nation's fundamental elasticity to survive the virulent infection presented by the Trump presidency. He may be right, however she was not sure she wanted to become a witness, involved again with the FBI. While not a lawyer, she knew enough of the legal jeopardy minefield by even speaking to the FBI. Their threats of intimidation experienced twenty years ago made personal what she saw in today's headlines.

She resolved to spend the weekend with her father catching up on family matters. Their last visit was at Christmas. A tough time for the family. Mother died of cancer the previous year. At seventy-seven, Hamilton Prescott was in reasonably good health but the loss of his wife of fifty years left an emotional void. Her cover story then of the unplanned trip was to consult with her current research project collaborator, her father's former state department colleague, Josef Novak. She had unexpectedly come into possession of some astounding new material that she must review with Novak right away. *Decided to spend the weekend in New York with you then train down to Washington to confer with Josef on Monday.*

Share the voluminous trove of financial double-dealing buried in the files she assumed came from Grigoryev's brother-in-law with Novak. As Professor of International Business at the School of Foreign Service, Georgetown University outside Washington, Novak possessed the financial expertise to make sense of the Russian material. But she had no intention of sharing any part of the material with the U.S. government. That was her material with the potential of another groundbreaking work like the

Critical Mass project. Her first amendment right best exercised before the government could clamp some odious restriction to seize the materials under some FISA court order claiming national security. Especially given the uncertainty of this bizarre administration. A White House at odds with its own intelligence agencies, the FBI, and even the State Department left doubts about how new information involving Russia might be received.

Prescott did not intend becoming either a pawn or victim in that destructive internecine conflict within the Executive branch. Nor would she disclose to Novak the conclusive evidence of missing nuclear warheads now in the hands of Iran. He would advise the same course of action as her father. That remained Grigoryev's bargaining chip to play. If he was still in the game.

Realizing that obligation to reveal the confirmation of the missing Russian nukes would fall to her if something happened to Grigoryev, prompted setting a decision deadline. She would give it no more than two weeks. The theft occurred four years ago so a few more weeks should not matter. If she heard nothing from Grigoryev by then she must assume the Russians got to him. Dead or buried incognito in some Siberian prison.

A plan came into focus. Why not release the material regarding the stolen Russian nukes to the media? Anonymously, but along with the source documents? Perhaps approach the journalist-author Mark Reynolds for assistance? Give him the material regarding the theft. He would fall all over himself given incontrovertible evidence of his earlier assertion. He would know how and where to make such an extraordinary story internationally public. That would satisfy her ethical obligation while deflecting attention away from her as a mere peripheral player of convenience. If nothing changed in two weeks that became her plan.

Still implicated but with the material made public, the U.S. government could not exercise legal intimidation. As to the other incriminating material on the elaborate financial corruption of the Putin regime, she would keep that to herself sharing only with Novak. That did not carry the same national security implications as missing nuclear warheads in Iranian hands.

"So what precipitated the sudden trip to consult with Josef?" Hamilton Prescott said to his daughter over coffee in his study.

The elder Prescott returned to New York Saturday morning. Brightened by seeing his daughter, she nonetheless could see advancing age intruding on his vitality.

"Some interesting material related to my current project of post-Soviet Russia. A trove of insider information. New financial stuff on what I'm calling the 21st century rise of a new autocratic kleptocracy shaping the Russian state under two decades of Putin rule. The technical economic stuff is Josef's expertise."

"Like everything else, follow the money," her father said.

She smiled. "Exactly. I'm trying to integrate these financial underpinnings to characterize the evolving political structure."

"And like everywhere, the internal political environment determines a state's international conduct. So how did you come by this new information? An insider source you said?"

"Yup."

With no further comment from his daughter, he raised an eyebrow. "Care to be more specific, Victoria?"

She would not lie to her father, however she was not ready to be entirely candid. Associating with a Russian spymaster in today's charged environment would itself alarm him. Certainly no mention of his defection apparently gone wrong. For that matter, avoiding mention of stolen Russian nuclear warheads. Parental concern would invoke his admonition to turn everything over to the government. That in turn would lead to unwelcomed questioning by government types. Why her? What was her association with this Russian intelligence officer? An endless ordeal perhaps jeopardizing her academic career.

"My own *Deep Throat*. Highly placed."

"And the motivation for this whistle-blower?"

"Hates Putin. Same sort of hostilities surrounding Trump by a lot of U.S. career bureaucrats."

The most effective untruth steered as close as possible to the truth. The unsaid details however left her feeling guilty for creating the false narrative to her father.

"And why would this person know of your interest and then favor you over some media outlet?"

"Because father, this whistle-blower is my old benefactor Colonel Grigoryev of the Russian SVR. Actually, he's a general now. Had high hopes for a brighter Russian future twenty-years ago when he helped me by opening up old NKVD and GRU archives.

"Christ, Victoria, you've been communicating with a Russian intelligence officer? A bit dicey with all this Russian related flap going on don't you think?"

"He contacted me. Couldn't very well turn away such an offer."

"I meant dicey for him. Risking career and probably a lot more because he's disenchanted with Putin? Is there something more to this, Victoria?"

She should have known to prepare a better half-truth. Her father came from the big leagues of political intrigue during his tenure at the State Department.

"I asked him what he expected me to do with this information. Grigoryev said the information released first from an academic source would give greater weight when made public in the media. Said he alone knows the actual source. Thought of me as the prime instrument to make this public. His hope is to damage those close to Putin and inflict a scandal large enough to erode Putin's popular domestic support."

"And this material has the potential for that?"

"Maybe, but I'll need Josef's expertise to understand the scope of what I have."

Hamilton Prescott finished his coffee setting the cup back on the saucer with deliberation.

"That all sounds pretty thin, my dear. As your father, just be careful. You're an academic not an investigative journalist. Don't trust intelligence types. They are self-righteously duplicitous, whether ours, or especially the Russians. But I won't press you further. I intend to enjoy your company this weekend."

Although distracted with no further contact from Grigoryev and the dire implications of someone else answering his burn phone, she enjoyed the weekend with her father as best she could. Something to sustain her as she navigated the expected minefield ahead.

Before her father returned to New York, she reread Mark Reynolds' book *Shell Game*. This time to immerse herself in the mechanics of the criminal financial empire created by the defunct corporation Martinelli Global. Particularly the material on their Russian partner Moscow Capital Partners. After disposing of the oligarch Nikolai Krasin, Grigoryev said Putin embarked on his own venture. This time maintaining absolute control over the process. Her cursory sampling through the voluminous files confirmed the need for expert assistance.

The picturesque campus of Georgetown University dominated by its iconic Healy Hall, occupies a hill on the north side of the Potomac River a mile west of downtown Washington D.C. Professor Josef Novak occupied a typically cramped faculty office. In his case, compensated by a grand view of the Potomac from his window.

Victoria Prescott phoned Novak early Monday morning. "I'll be at your office by noon, Josef. I'm in New York at the train station right now."

"New York? Noon? I have a faculty working lunch today, Victoria. Busy afternoon schedule as well for that matter. Can't this wait till tomorrow?"

"Not to be indelicate, Josef, but you'll wet your pants when you see what I have."

Years younger than his friend Hamilton Prescott, Josef Novak looked older. Short and slightly stooped, he looked the archetypical disheveled academic. Prescott loved him as an uncle. A brilliant analytical mind tempered with a warm collegial demeanor. Willing to share his vast knowledge, collaboration with

Josef Novak balanced the more impetuous aggressive style of Victoria Prescott.

Novak did not read Russian fluently. Relying on translation software to do the bulk of the work, this often resulted in a stilted syntax that could confuse the meaning. Therefore, it fell to Prescott to translate summaries of some of the more revealing documents to produce a truer reading. Knowing this, she came to Washington armed with selected translated material.

After giving Novak the same cover story about the acquisition of the material she gave her father, she presented her first exhibit. Sitting next to him in his cramped office, she pulled up a document on her notebook screen.

"This is my translation of a summary report by another whistle-blower close to Grigoryev, His brother-in-law actually. The original is below.

"This guy is employed by the federal security service, the FSB. A financial expert. Part of team tasked with creating a shadowy Kremlin directed financial network."

To avoid explaining Lytkin's death, she referred to him in the present tense.

"A secret financial network? For the Russian state?" Novak said.

"Not exactly. Although it involved state funds and state controlled banks, it did not benefit Russian economic interests. Intended for the personal financial benefit of the ruling elite of the United Russia Party and key government appointees. The project is under Putin's direct control."

The United Russia Party created by Putin in 2001 currently controls 75% of the seats in the Russian parliament. A center-right party advocating no coherent ideology other than fervent Russian nationalism. Cynically, it embraces a range of political views provided only in support of Vladimir Putin. So dominant is United Russia, Russia functionally is a single party state. With a strongman at the helm, Putin has systematically consolidated power and crushed political opponents while largely silencing media opposition through coercion and even violence.

"And the purpose?"

"Josef, don't be naïve. For the purpose of amassing wealth for ranking members of the current regime. Putin's funding scheme compensates his power base to insure their support. Just like any Third World despot. This entire data dump I've been given reveals a level of corruption beyond imagination."

Prescott chose Stepka Lytkin's own long summary concerning schemes running through the Russian nuclear energy industry as her starting point. This particular avenue struck her particularly relevant in light of Putin maintaining secrecy over the nuclear warhead theft. The nuclear energy sector represented Russia's showcase technological enterprise. The state corporation Rusatom runs all military and civilian nuclear operations. A trillion ruble per year industry.

Created in 2007 under Putin's direction, the agency controls 360 businesses and research facilities. Two of its board of trustees actually held titles as assistant to the President of Russia. Prescott made the connection that its creation coincided with the Putin regime's entanglement with the oligarch Nikolai Krasin as exposed by the journalist Reynolds.

According to Reynolds' stolen electronic files from Krasin's Moscow Capital Partners, the scheme was to privatize certain unprofitable state-run enterprises to obscure the costs. In particular, looming environmental problems stemmed from decades of Soviet era indiscriminate practices for dealing with nuclear waste. The problems with the Hanford nuclear site in the State of Washington paled compared to the worsening scope of Russia's problem east of the Urals.

The Putin regime's stopgap was to coerce Krasin into taking over operation of poorly performing nuclear enterprises. Get the losses off the state's books. In compensation, Krasin's other enterprises received highly profitable government no-bid contracts as offsets.

Within the publicly traded holding company RusEnergy, Krasin created a new subsidiary called Rusatomic to be the loss leader in a larger profit scheme. Even the name played on its common misassociation as just another state-owned Rusatom operating unit.

Of course, everything fell apart with the downfall of Krasin and Moscow Capital in the scandal of the New York based international corporation MGI. While Putin understood the enormous potential for illicit economic gain derived from the Russian nuclear industry, it also represented international prestige. With consolidation of vastly increased power to the office of President, Putin concerned himself less with such details as masking losses in state enterprises. The Russian flagship nuclear energy sector when coupled with the Russian nuclear weapons arsenal, greatly inflated Russian international stature beyond its more modest GDP ranking of only eleventh in the world.

Reading through the summary, Novak commented, "Ah, Sergei Terekov, appears in this cast of crooks."

"Yup. Putin needs skilled business and banking types to manage his criminal empire. Especially if he wants to run with the big dogs on the international stage."

"Eloquently phrased, my dear. Putin destroyed the old oligarchs of the 1990s like Berezovsky and Khodorkovsky, guys he couldn't control. Products of the waning years of the Soviet Union and the subsequent Yeltsin era. Terekov is a new breed. Just as ruthless as the original oligarchs and clever enough to adapt to the changing political environment. Recognizes that Putin now represents the power in Russia."

"Precisely. I've scanned this whole data dump, Josef. Among the complex financial dealings, which are more up your alley, it paints a picture of Putin's team engaged in all sorts of corruption. Unprecedented in scale. We have names and documented evidence of their conspiracy."

"Is this principally Russian internal corruption or something broader?" Novak said.

"Can't tell, but some of the material suggests sophisticated financial dealings internationally. That's what I need you to explore. Ultimately we'll need to run down a lot of rabbit holes to corroborate all this stuff."

"Think this material changes the premise for our project, Victoria?"

The working title for their project was *Post-Soviet Russia – Dictatorship by Another Name.* The premise being to define where the increasingly authoritative rule of a single political party might take Russia while controlling a heavily state-influenced market economy. How did these domestic factors impact Russian international relations? While all authoritarian regimes suffer corruption, Grigoryev's material suggested Russia was moving closer to a Putin dictatorship.

"I don't know. Grigoryev paints this as a state-run criminal enterprise. Maybe this is the framework of 21st century Russian state corruption. But the scary implications come when Putin serves out his final fourth presidential term. Then what?"

After Novak read Lytkin's lengthy summary, he commented with an uncharacteristic expletive, "Sonofabitch. What's really scary about this, we're talking about an enormous nuclear industry with a troubling history. Think Chernobyl technology and operating protocols. Marketing Russian technology internationally for illicit gain brings into question all sorts of environmental and safety concerns for the world."

If Novak only knew the extent of Russian nuclear insecurity, Prescott thought.

"Lot of work ahead, Josef. However, let's start with Terekov and his Eurasian Energy Industries. Look at these documents I've translated," Prescott said as she brought up preselected documents on her computer.

"To your point, you can see by this that Terekov moved in to replace the defunct Rusatomic private contracting management of significant parts the Russian nuclear industry. Particularly waste management and fissile fuel reprocessing."

"Yes of course," Novak said. "That oligarch Krasin caught up in the downfall of Martinelli Global."

Prescott said, "Cost Krasin his life. Officially, hung himself in a jail cell. Not likely a suicide. Putin could not afford Krasin going to trial. What do you know about Terekov?"

Novak was an expert on Russian economics. "Well he's the big player in Russian natural resources development. Came on the scene soon after Putin came to power. An interesting footnote, Sergei Terekov holds an actual graduate degree in mining engineering from St. Petersburg Mining University. Unlike Putin's questionable PhD. from the same institution.

"Terekov may have first met Putin in St. Petersburg during Putin's earliest political involvement in his home city's municipal government. After the abortive 1991 coup against Gorbachev, Putin left the KGB becoming head of a committee promoting international relations and foreign investments for St. Petersburg.

"With the demise of Krasin's financial empire, Terekov's Eurasian Energy picked up not only the Krasin assets but quietly moved in to fulfill all the government contractual connections held by Krasin owned enterprises. Terekov at the time dominated the Russian minerals and metals sectors. According to estimates, he acquired the assets of the defunct RusEnergy for ten percent of their true value. Apparently, Putin manipulated this secret underreported transition asserting national security interests. It also helped obscure the Krasin public relations debacle."

Prescott said, "Putin's way of also avoiding the fallout of his regime's association with Krasin?"

"Probably. From your summary, it suggests Putin's functionaries have since taken direct control. They won't have a repeat of the Krasin affair."

"Well this material suggests some new twists from what Reynolds uncovered with the stolen material from Krasin's Moscow Capital Partners." Prescott said.

"If I remember correctly from his book *Shell Game*, that insider that breached the Russian affiliates' databases was murdered. What about this new whistle-blower?"

Prescott said, "Also dead. Shot himself rather than face arrest I'm told."

Novak looked at her with a grim expression, "And do I guess your benefactor once again is this spy chief Grigoryev?"

"Yes."

"And he's still with the SVR?"

Prescott nodded. "A general now. The number-two guy at the foreign intelligence service."

"Victoria, I know you too well. Something more is going on. You're saying he gave you this stuff so he can embarrass the Putin regime to which he is a ranking intelligence official? Come on. Why you? Not for old times' sake, so what gives?"

Since Novak was a partner in this, only fair he should know the gravity.

"Okay, Josef. But only you're to know. I did not tell Dad quite everything. The actual source for this is Grigoryev's brother-in-law. For security reasons, Grigoryev kept the stolen electronic files."

"And the brother-n-law is dead? What about Grigoryev?"

"The brother-in-law and Grigoryev knew they were playing a dangerous game. They intended to defect using these damaging files as bargaining chips to the U.S. for asylum. Unfortunately, the brother-in-law slipped up. Cost him his life and triggered Grigoryev's immediate escape from Russia."

"Jesus Christ! And?"

"I met Grigoryev last week in Paris. He handed over the stolen files. Wanted me to enlist Dad's help in arranging his defection. Didn't trust approaching Western intelligence operatives for fear of Russian infiltration, or simple bureaucracy wrangling."

"So your father is working on that?"

She shook her head no. "Afraid not. I tried to establish contact with Grigoryev when I returned to New York. Something there has gone wrong as well. I fear the Russians may have gotten to him."

"My god, Victoria, what have you gotten into?"

"Since I can't establish contact with Grigoryev I didn't go into all the troubling details with Dad."

"And if Grigoryev does not surface then what?"

"Then we make public this damaging information on the Putin regime. Drive a sharp stick in the eye of that malevolent little shit. Sure as hell not going to turn it over to the U.S. government."

She still manipulated the entire truth to keep her options open. No mention of the nuclear warhead theft evidence, nor mention of an unknown Russian voice answering Grigoryev's burn phone.

Prescott and Novak spent the remainder of the afternoon digging into the detailed supporting materials to Lytkin's summary of the illegal manipulations of Rusatom.

"Now this is interesting," Prescott said. "This bank, SLT Bank. According to our *Deep Throat* source, it's 65% owned by Terekov. Through alternate shell entities apparently. Here's the kicker. The remaining 35% is owned by the trustees of state-run Rusatom, and by Vladimir Putin personally. Ownership is obscured through various offshore legal shell entities then funneled through shares in a Russian hedge fund run solely for the benefit of the Putin regime.

"You'll have to try to untangle all these artificial business connections, Josef. Is that possible given these are offshore tax haven companies and Russian legal entities?"

"The offshore companies are a roadblock of course," Novak said. "However, everything leads from and then back to Russia. Russia may be corrupt but records exist. Confirming shareholders by name may not be as easy as in the West, but there exists a paper trail even if difficult to read."

"*Deep Throat* claims the illicit flow of money to these officials comes in the form of unusually high dividends."

"A form of money laundering. Excessive profits through what I assume are all sorts of illegal manipulations in collusion with the government become legitimate dividends to the bank's shareholders. Pays the graft to these senior government functionaries, but the real black money is concealed in larger scams I would think."

"You're right. Like this. In a special piece of legislation passed by the Duma, majority controlled by Putin's United Russia Party, Terekov's SLT Bank enjoys specific authorization to borrow from the Russian Central Bank at half the prevailing interest. Ostensibly intended to compensate Terekov Holdings in their contractual arrangement to manage problematic state nuclear waste recycling. However, according to *Deep Throat,* the borrowed money goes well beyond just those earmarked operations. Terekov therefore borrows at half the interest rate to fund operating capital for his entire financial empire.

Prescott took a break to sit in on a late-afternoon scheduled lecture by Novak. A break from this emotional roller coaster ride of the last week. Nothing resolved, only worsened. No clear path to pursue without uncertain pitfalls. Stubbornly she resisted telling the whole story to her father or Josef Novak hoping to find a clear path.

The outlook for Grigoryev seemed bleaker with the passing of every hour. His plight a sickening gnawing. Their once again brief intimacy awakened long buried feelings only to end in despair.

Returning to Novak's office, Novak said, "How long will you be staying in Washington, Victoria?"

"A few days at least. Enough to familiarize you with the scope of this data."

"Well in that case, Martha will insist you stay at the house. In fact, I'll call her. She'll be delighted. Then let's leave early to beat the beltway traffic. Don't know about you but I could use a drink."

"Okay. But let me show you one more exhibit. You asked earlier if this was principally internal Russian corruption. I want to show you something that appears to add a different dimension beyond simply colluding with Terekov.

"Are you familiar with the hedge fund of Gordon Investments?"

"Of course. A major hedge fund. You're saying they're involved with the Russians?"

"According to *Deep Throat* more than involved. I prepared a summary of sorts but it only identifies a bunch of names I culled from various documents. Complex stuff. Again, there are these stubborn offshore tax haven corporations and banks. You'll need to connect the dots.

"Sounds a whole lot bigger than the Trump and Kushner mere financial coziness with the Russians."

"Gordon Investments? That is interesting. Real estate hedge fund. Rapid growth, even competing successfully with this long-running bull stock market. Consistently profitable. Multi-billions in assets."

"*Deep Throat* claims it's a repository for laundering Russian money on a vast scale. The starting point is creating various Russian legal entities, corporations, partnerships, trusts, whatever. Any method to obscure individual ownership involving enterprises generating illicit profits. With government collusion, I might add. These Russian entities then invest in various offshore investment funds, for example in the Cayman Islands. Those Cayman Island shell corporations then invest in a United States Fund of Funds. An FOF. I've never even heard the term."

"Gordon Investments is an FOF. I'll explain the meaning later. Go on," Novak said.

"Well Gordon Investments then invests money in what are termed underlying real estate hedge funds."

"So you're saying the origin of this dirty money is the by-product of Russian corruption. Laundered first through the opaque Cayman Islands corporations then further washed through Gordon Investments as it invests in these underlying hedge funds."

Prescott said, "Seems like a lot of trouble when you control most everything like Putin does."

"How much does this *Deep Throat* say is invested through this scheme?"

"Not sure about this particular scheme, but he estimates the total amount laundered abroad by the current regime to be at least $100 billion maybe as much as $200 billion over the last several years."

Novak looked at her with a look of surprise.

"It's quite simple, my dear. To launder that kind of money you need a much bigger environment than Russia offers. You've certainly have captured my interest. Now let's get out of here and have that drink."

After another day huddled with Josef Novak, it was now a week since leaving Paris. The further she explored the stolen FSB data the richer the material. Complicated legal and financial maneuvering while beyond her expertise in deciphering, still painted a damning mosaic of unprecedented corruption. With Novak's partnership, this could be not only another academic coup but also a headline-dominating exposé.

This complex web of the Putin regime's financial corruption would take months to unravel then organize into understandable form. She and Novak must also explore the backgrounds of the large cast of characters. More a journalistic endeavor. The larger academic project however involved relating this to what had become of post-Soviet Russia. How did you characterize the current regime? What happens when Putin departs office? Will he depart? How might the West respond to a criminal state with a massive nuclear arsenal?

Of more immediate concern was turning over the information confirming Iran now possessing advanced thermonuclear warheads. Maybe missile-capable? Did Iran's current missiles possess sufficient range to present a viable immediate threat? A truly scary thought.

She must give over that information to the U.S. government. Doing that would drop her into not only an awkward situation, but could threaten her ability to control and use the corruption information on the Putin regime. Even Grigoryev warned her about that. Her experience with the FBI in 1999 left a lasting resentment. When she went public with her book *Critical Mass* about the discovery of previously undiscovered Soviet spy the FBI acted as if it were under criticism for something that occurred fifty years earlier.

Do not trust the FBI to act fairly. This was more complicated than just turning over the material. Yet ethically she must share this information on the nuclear warheads. Obviously, she needed help. With her father as the obvious choice, she preferred not to drag him into this unknown snake pit. Not fair to burden Josef Novak with that problem either. Keep his involvement to deciphering the technical maze of Russian financial corruption.

Her best option seemed obvious. Seek out Mark Reynolds. This was his story. He would jump at the chance to validate his assertion about the theft of the Russian warheads. Let Reynolds make the facts public. Put Putin in a terrible position while perhaps taking the scrutiny off her. What could the U.S. government do once the information was public?

Recounting Reynolds' book *Shell Game,* he would know what to do after all he went through dealing with the FBI and the Justice Department according to his account. Reynolds grasp of international financial crimes might also prove useful.

CHAPTER 9

MANHATTAN, NEW YORK

The story in the Washington Post the following morning hit Victoria Prescott in the gut. Even though anticipating potentially bad news about the fate of Anton Grigoryev, when it materializes it is no less devastating. On the front page, the secondary headline read, *Russian Intelligence Chief Murdered in Paris.*

> PARIS – Paris police along with the French internal security agency the DGSI have issued a statement revealing the name of a homicide victim. The shooting death of a Canadian national in the affluent 7th Arrondissement was particularly unusual. According to French police, the victim a Byron Laurent with residences in Montreal and Paris suffered three gunshot wounds, in what they characterized as an execution-style murder. The body was discovered a week ago in the courtyard of an apartment building on Rue Barbet de Jouy by a neighbor in the same building. The murder took place at dusk yet no witnesses claim to have heard any gunshots.
>
> The investigation took a turn a few days later after the Canadian RCMP uncovered inconsistencies as they investigated the background of Laurent. While possessing valid Canadian documents including passport, driver's license, and health card, Laurent's identity seemed unusual for its lack of depth. Few people could

recall seeing him. His Montreal apartment apparently rarely used. A property management firm oversaw long absences by Laurent. According to the manager of the firm, Laurent explained that he spent most of his time in Paris.

Laurent possessed a Canadian business license as an art broker and a French commercial visa. According to the RCMP, banking records showed a normal history of commercial transactions related to his art brokerage business. Canadian income taxes filed for only the last three years immediately raised questions.

Laurent also owned a small boutique art gallery on Ile Saint-Louis in Paris. He paid French income taxes on what is reported as a modestly successful business, but again only for the last three years.

While the identity of Byron Laurent appeared solidly constructed with valid rather than forged documents, it nonetheless proved shallow. Suspecting possible criminal or even espionage associations, the French Direction Générale de la Sécurité Intérieure, the DGSI charged with counterespionage and counterterrorism protection entered the investigation.

Facial recognition quickly identified the victim as Lt. General Anton Vladimirovich Grigoryev, First Deputy Director of the Russian foreign intelligence service, Sluzhba Vneshney Razvedki, the SVR.

In a news conference yesterday, Inspector Maurice Delacroix of the French Police Nationale stated they are investigating the murder as a possibly politically motivated attack rather than a common murder. The victim suffered two 9mm gunshot wounds to the chest and single shot to the head suggesting an execution killing. Delacroix pointed to no indication of robbery, nor any indication this was a crime of passion. Delacroix declined to speculate further as to motive or possible perpetrators.

Repeated inquiries to the Russian Foreign Ministry have met with either no response or a terse 'no comment'. Unconfirmed sources have suggested that Grigoryev may have fallen out of favor with the ruling Putin regime fueling further speculation that this could be a

> failed defection attempt. At this time, there is no evidence to support such a theory. Several U.S. intelligence sources however indicate that assassinations of opposing intelligence operatives, especially ranking officials, are extremely rare. All suggest this is either a Russian operation or something totally unrelated to Grigoryev's professional work.
>
> Comparisons are already being made to the grisly murder of Alexander Litvinenko by radioactive poisoning in London in 2006. Litvinenko was a dissident internal security officer with the FSB. After discovering high-ranking FSB officials had ties to Russian organized crime, Litvinenko fled Moscow in 2000, finding asylum in the United Kingdom. Overwhelming evidence points to Litvinenko's murder as ordered by Moscow. Before his agonizing death, Litvinenko named Vladimir Putin personally responsible.
>
> Earlier this year a former Russian military officer and British double agent and his daughter suffered serious injury in a nerve agent attack in Salisbury, England. Overwhelming evidence attributes the attack to Russian intelligence operatives.

Sitting in Novak's kitchen over coffee, Prescott finished the article and dropped the newspaper on the table. Tears came as she cupped her face in both hands.

MOSCOW, RUSSIAN FEDERATION

Following the death of Stepka Lytkin, General Anton Grigoryev went missing. Considering his relationship with Lytkin, that meant he was in hiding, likely seeking asylum in some Western country. That meant Grigoryev represented a looming disaster for Vladimir Putin.

Grigoryev possessed the details of the nuclear warhead theft four years earlier. In all likelihood, his close association with his brother-in-law also provided him with all that Lytkin knew about the clandestine financial empire created under Putin's control. Lytkin was a central player in the creation of the Byzantine interconnection of corporations, holding companies, offshore foreign subsidiary shell companies, and the many channels for funneling money to benefit those in Putin's orbit. Lytkin knew all the names and secrets. Caught accessing confidential data outside his sphere of clearance, resulted in his arrest for interrogation. At the time, there was no specific suspicion of a broader breach of security. His self-inflicted bullet to the head to avoid arrest suggested something much larger.

Grigoryev's sudden disappearance seemed to confirm a conspiracy. Yet no incriminating evidence was uncovered at Lytkin's apartment. However, the government must operate on the assumption that Grigoryev knew everything from Lytkin's activities at the FSB. With Lytkin dead, it was impossible to determine the scope of Lytkin's breach, much less identifying specific information accessed. How long had Lytkin been at this? A disaster of potentially even greater proportions to the Putin regime than the missing nuclear warheads.

All that and the associated disaster of the defection of a senior intelligence official. Someone with specific knowledge of Russian cyber warfare activities, strategic planning, and a range of insider information of incalculable value to an enemy, caused Putin to take direct control in managing the fallout.

With the break of the sighting of Grigoryev by a Paris embassy staffer, Putin moved immediately to contain the damage. Under his legal prerogatives as president, he could directly issue secret orders to the SVR without consulting any other branch of the government.

Within Directorate S of the SVR is an ultra-secret elite special forces unit known as Zaslon. Unlike other Russian military *spetsnaz*, special forces, who openly display the prestige of their status, there is no official acknowledgment even of the existence of Zaslon.

Putin issued an order to Major General Volkov, deputy director of Directorate S, for a Zaslon team to assassinate Grigoryev and retrieve any incriminating materials they can discover.

The assignment fell to Major Ivan Kozlovsky and his team already deployed to Paris as a likely destination for Grigoryev having traveled there frequently over the years and fluent in French.

Major Kozlovsky personally shot Grigoryev.

"And you searched the apartment?" Putin asked Kozlovsky.

With Kozlovsky's return to Moscow, Putin convened a crisis meeting with General Volkov of the SVR and General Mikhalitsyn of the FSB.

"Yes, sir. Given the brief amount of time allowed following liquidation of the target."

Kozlovsky's orders were to eliminate Grigoryev without delay. Any attempt at an abduction risked complications. Grigoryev must not escape to the West. Therefore, Kozlovsky shot Grigoryev as he was opening the common entrance door to the apartment building courtyard using a silenced 9mm. Since his team only responded to the visual sighting of Grigoryev, they did not know his destination once he left the art gallery.

"We found nothing related to Grigoryev's intelligence work. In fact, the apartment appeared impersonal. More like a hotel room. No personal effects. No photographs, no papers. Just a lot of paintings."

"Computer or electronic storage devices?" Mikhalitsyn asked.

"No computer or storage devices we could find. However, time did not allow the kind of thorough search necessary to be sure. The only items we took were his official cellphone and another cellphone."

Volkov said, "And tell the President what happened regarding that other cellphone."

"The cellphone was a prepaid device. What is known as a *burn phone*. A throwaway device where the number is not associated with any account therefore untraceable. The following day, Saturday, three calls were placed to this phone."

"All three calls came from the same calling number, Mr. President. From another unrecognized prepaid number we learned later. We have to believe it was someone working with Grigoryev," Volkov said. "Continue, Major."

"I picked up on the third call answering in Russia. The caller was a woman saying only hello in Russian. I replied, who is calling? She remained silent so I asked who she was trying to reach. After making no response she disconnected after a few seconds."

"And?" Putin said.

"Unknown who this might be," FSB Director General Mikhalitsyn said. "Not his sister-in-law since she is in custody. Grigoryev had no known women acquaintances. Those women in his office are under investigation as well as close surveillance. We have widened the search to include any recurring personal interactions in his daily routines such as shop clerks or housekeeping staff"

"Rumor at headquarters painted Grigoryev as reclusive since the death of his wife," General Volkov said. "Some even say bitter but without speculating as to the reason."

"And the possibility of his working with Western intelligence?" Putin asked.

"Certainly possible. He frequently traveled outside Russia as part of his official duties," Mikhalitsyn said. "And this well established alternative identity as a Canadian suggests possible assistance."

Volkov offered, "Yet possibly not. Grigoryev and Director Dubrovsky were not on the best of terms. Perhaps Grigoryev felt his career in jeopardy. As to the false Canadian identity, Grigoryev was a clever intelligence operative. Engaged in a conspiracy with his brother-in-law he would insure that a contingency plan be in place should things go wrong. If he were working presumably for the Americans, they would safeguard him then immediately extract him out of Europe. Yet he remained in Paris for a week.

"I am inclined to believe he was negotiating this sudden defection while remaining incognito in his self-created alternative identity. Perhaps attempting to negotiate a better asylum deal which would take longer, Mr. President."

Although the warhead theft evidence would be internationally damaging, Putin's greater concern was the Lytkin material. That could have domestic ramifications and prove disastrous to the financial underpinnings of his power base.

As a senior official, the FSB assumed Grigoryev would hide his *supplemental* income in a foreign secret account. Other officials typically did. All those in the regime participating in illicit sources of income, however came under constant scrutiny by the FSB. Direct orders from Putin elevated security on the flow of corrupt funds to a strict need to know and tightly compartmentalized. Bank accounts, investments, and personal habits filled highly detailed dossiers on everyone. Just like the bad old days under the oppressive KGB intrusion into all facets of life. Even the oligarchs in partnership with Putin were not immune. Although not at the highest-ranking level within the government, Grigoryev was sufficiently senior to share in the institutionalized graft. Most senior officials receiving unofficial payments did not know the origins of the funds unless part of the active group of conspirators managing the complex financial enterprise. Grigoryev of course knew the most intimate of those dealings from his brother-in-law, an insider with the highest security access.

Grigoryev understood that with such vast sums of illicit money moving secretly, the FSB must be tracking every ruble or foreign currency account hidden by anyone in the regime. Planning for an eventual departure from Russia and disappearing into a different identity, including perhaps defection, he wanted easy access to his money once outside Russia. Secret foreign accounts would raise red flags and presented other difficulties for concealment. Conventional foreign accounts might be subject to hacking. He knew intimately the cyber capability of the FSB and its contracted hackers. Therefore, he carefully crafted a dual purpose subterfuge, serving to hide his wealth in seemingly plain sight while establishing a background for his secret alternative identity.

The FSB assumed Grigoryev's periodic but significant expenditures for art were Grigoryev's way of investing while enjoying his supplemental income. Better yet the art remaining in Russia so as not to raise suspicion. A regular pattern of purchases, typically the equivalent of 5,000-10,000 Euros. The art shipped from a Paris gallery to Moscow. With Grigoryev's government connections, he obtained a commercial importation license to avoid sales and value-added Russian taxes.

The immediate search of Grigoryev's Moscow apartment revealed a large number of paintings and several sculptures. Many other paintings were stacked in a spare bedroom closet. According to records of periodic wire transfers from his Moscow bank account, the art purchases came from the same Paris art gallery. The Russian importation declarations identified the consignee as Moskva Art. The fictitious company operated under a state license allowing Grigoryev to avoid import taxes. A satisfactory arrangement for the regime for a senior intelligence official to keep his share of institutional corruption inside Russia.

PARIS, FRANCE

The joint investigation of the French Police Nationale and the French DGSI, working closely with the Canadian RCMP, were in a better position than the Russians to uncover Grigoryev's elaborate scheme for secreting money out of Russia. Not only did Grigoryev hide the funds from Russian scrutiny but also laundered the origin of the money in the process.

After several weeks, the French investigation explained Grigoryev's scheme for concealing sufficient money to disappear into his fabricated new identity. The creation of his new cover legend over years meant eventual defection. French police released only general facts to the press, sufficient to support the claim that Grigoryev's murder in Paris came from Kremlin orders to thwart his defection.

Unraveling the whole scheme revealed his meticulously crafted plan to attempt the seemingly impossible objective of hiding from the long reach of the Kremlin.

Investing in the purchase of the small boutique art gallery on Île Saint-Louis laid the foundation to both move his money out of Russia while giving financial substance to his Canadian identity. It further supported a plausible cover story for only limited residence in Canada.

Employing a manager and one other employee, the gallery also returned a reasonable profit. Therefore, it remained a sellable investment at some future time without loss. It further provided the basis to secure a French commercial visa, which did not limit his stays in France and allowed him to maintain a Paris residence.

The flow of money started with the wire transfer of funds from his Moscow bank account to the Paris gallery explained as the purchase price for a piece of art. By way of example, assume he wires €10,000 from Moscow to his Paris gallery for the purchase of a painting. €9,000 is then electronically transferred from the gallery bank account to his Montreal brokerage account representing payment for the art less a 10% brokerage fee for the gallery. The €9,000 is booked as a payables expense for the gallery. €8,000 of this represents *payment* to the fictitious painting seller and €1,000 as the Montreal brokerage commission. €1,000 is booked by the Paris gallery as commission and French taxes paid accordingly. His Montreal brokerage firm claims income of €1,000 for Canadian tax purposes.

Grigoryev still has the problem of laundering the bulk of the funds wired from Moscow. He cannot just bank these kinds of transactions in either France or Canada without eventually raising questions from tax authorities. In Canada, he books €8,000 as a payables expense representing payment to the fictitious painting seller. To account for those funds and come full circle back to him, he invests the €8,000 in art from other dealers in the United States, Canada, and Europe. The Paris gallery receives the art as *consigned inventory*, listed from fictitious Montreal brokerage clients. Eighty percent of his corruption-sharing income therefore resides in the form of full-valued art under his control but obscured as owned by others. Twenty percent is recognized as income and appropriate French and Canadian taxes paid.

The gallery of course sells some of that high-value art. With astute buying from select dealers that valued Laurent as a discerning repeat client, his gallery sells the art for a legitimate profit. When this occurs, it however repeats the task of concealing that previously laundered money. The Paris gallery pays Laurent's brokerage account in Canada for the consigned art, less commission. He books as prepaid revenue in Canada and simply buys more art with those funds in a bookkeeping Ponzi scheme requiring creative accounting.

As his Paris gallery ships an inexpensive painting to Moscow, the charade concludes full circle. With this seemingly unduly complex sequence of maneuvers, Grigoryev exported his money out of Russia while hiding the actual assets from Russian security oversight. It further served to construct a documented foundation for an alternative identity established in both Paris and Montreal.

"This is explosive stuff, Victoria. Grigoryev's murder proves that," Josef Novak said. "The Kremlin didn't attempt to disguise his killing. Every intelligence agency in the world knows it was the Russians. The parallels to Litvinenko and that recent fiasco in the UK are obvious."

Prescott just nodded.

'We could be in danger, Victoria. Tell me about what went on in Paris when you met Grigoryev."

She related the course of events in detail, excluding the nuclear warhead theft and her renewed night of intimacy.

"There's no way to know if the Russians identified you with Grigoryev, so we need to take some precautions. Most importantly, we need to secure these electronic files in a safe place.

Multiple places, each of us. I have an attorney who will keep a USB drive. How 'bout you?"

"No attorney but I have good friend, a colleague at Stanford."

"Okay. I'm no computer expert but I suggest we each get a separate computer to compile our work product. No connection to the Internet. No one is better than the Russians at hacking.

"Which also means no emails. So let's exchange files, notes, whatever by next-day FedEx. Clunky but safer.

"What about phones?" she asked. "We'll need to talk occasionally."

"Since I'm being paranoid let's do what Grigoryev setup. Get those prepaid cellphones. And don't use any incriminating or suggestive words. Never mention Russia. Remember the NSA might not be our friend either."

Prescott looked deflated and distant.

"You alright, Victoria?"

"Not really. I can't believe Grigoryev is dead. Gunned down in Paris. So close to his objective. He was a good man, Josef. Sounds silly to say about a Russian spy chief. I couldn't have identified Voronin as a Manhattan Project Soviet spy without his help. Things were so different twenty years ago. In Paris he was bitter, bent on bringing down Putin."

"Well with what I've seen, this might do it. Sure as hell will cause the miserable little bastard a world of grief. Let's just be careful. We'll be at this a while. Only really safe once this stuff becomes public.

Prescott told Novak she was returning home to San Francisco. Another lie. She was taking the train to New York to meet Mark Reynolds. Enlist Reynolds as the point person in dealing with how to handle the missing Russian nuclear warheads material.

She sent him a message through his literary agent since he praised his agent by name in the acknowledgments of his book *Shell Game*. Her message to the agent said *I have some new information that corroborates certain claims Mr. Reynolds made in his book. He can verify my background on the Stanford University faculty website.*

Reynolds called within a few hours. He would meet her at New York City's Grand Central Terminal at noon the following day.

Central to the French investigation into the murder of Grigoryev was retracing his movements and contacts after leaving Russia. Once Grigoryev was discovered to be hiding under the name Byron Laurent, his contacts proved limited. Only his art gallery manager, the leasing agent for his apartment, and a couple of other tenants in the same building that never exchanged in more than greetings could be identified. Interviews with these people produced no leads. The Canadian RCMP discovered nothing of value in Montreal. Victoria Prescott remained unknown to the French authorities.

In Moscow, the Russians were more successful.

Two FSB agents broke into Grigoryev's apartment. Both fluent in English, they turned the place upside down for any information that might expand on any aspect of Grigoryev's life. Their initial search turned up no trace of any written or electronic files other than normal personal paperwork. A computer held nothing incriminating. Nothing in his personal email account. In fact, there is little evidence of communication with anyone on a personal basis other than his sister and two nieces. The only photographs found were of his deceased wife and his sister's family. No emails exchanged with his brother-in-law. Yet the investigators recorded every scrap of information, every contact no matter how seemingly innocuous.

Paintings decorated all the walls in the modest apartment, including the two bedrooms. A closet contained additional paintings stacked on the floor. One of the more astute investigators thought such careless treatment odd considering the rumored value of the Grigoryev's art collection. They found purchase receipts and customs declarations with the consignee as his bogus *Moskva Fine Art*. An art expert called in to appraise the collection quickly confirmed that all the pieces were only of modest quality and relatively inexpensive. No known artists among the pieces. Most probably worth less than 10,000 rubles, nothing certainly more than 80,000 Russian rubles. Equivalent to 150-500 Euros each, a fraction of their declared value.

On a large bookshelf stood several small sculptures and bronzes, all inexpensive. Beyond a respectable collection of classics, in both Russian and English, the majority of volumes consisted of western politically oriented publications. An extensive selection of the First and Second World War histories in English. A particularly large collection of Soviet era works in both Russian and English occupied an entire shelf.

Not unusual for a foreign intelligence officer, Grigoryev possessed an extensive range of intelligence related books. Subjects including the CIA, British MI6, the Kennedy assassination, the Cuban Missile Crisis, the British Profumo Affair, the Cambridge Five Soviet spies, and the Soviet penetration of the Manhattan Project. Among the later was a 1999 book titled *Critical Mass*, the author an American academic and expert in twentieth century Soviet history. The book exposed a previously unknown spy within the military command structure of the Manhattan Project.

This book however included something unique. The author's signature scrawled boldly inside on the title page. Among the author's acknowledgments, are special thanks to Colonel Anton Grigoryev, Deputy Director for Political Intelligence of the Sluzhba Vneshney Razvedki of the Russian Federation. Below that page another signature. This time, *affectionately, Victoria.*

A foreign personal relationship? The investigator immediately called his superior. Even practiced spies fall victim to the smallest errors in trying to preserve every possible secret.

CHAPTER 10

MANHATTAN, NEW YORK

As Victoria Prescott disembarked the train at Grand Central Terminal on 42nd Street, she looked for the main concourse information booth clock, the typical connecting location. She and Mark Reynolds could both recognize each other from their respective website photos.

"Professor Prescott," came a voice from behind her.

Turning she recognized Reynolds. A good-looking guy about her same age stylishly dressed in a blazer and button-down shirt.

"Mr. Reynolds," she extended her hand. "Thank you for meeting me."

"After our conversation how could I not?"

"How about we have lunch and you can tell me what you've come by relating to missing Russian nuclear warheads. Certainly tantalizing but you were vague on the phone."

"Didn't mean to be. Just didn't want to say anything specific over the phone. Maybe just paranoia but when you hear my story you will understand. And lunch sounds good."

"Excellent. There's an Irish pub on the Upper Eastside, a favorite watering hole of mine. A short taxi drive. Stout Irish fare. Great Irish stew."

"Are you familiar with New York, Professor?"

"Very much so. Grew up here. Took my undergraduate then masters at Columbia. My father is a retired professor from Columbia and still lives in Manhattan over on the Upper Westside, so I visit occasionally."

Finnegans Wake on 1st Avenue at 73rd Street was a charming place on the inside. The sort of place an American expected of an Irish pub. A social place of gathering. A slightly older clientele came for simple basic fare Irish food and a well-stocked bar.

After they took a table in the front by the window, a cherub of a character with bushy unkempt gray hair and muscular arms came around from behind the bar.

Offered a hand to Reynolds. "Good to see you as always, Mr. Reynolds. And this pretty lady?"

"Professor Prescott, meet Murphy Callahan, proprietor of this fine public house."

"Pleased to meet you. You folks taking lunch or something liquid?"

"A hot day so why not a pint of Guinness?" Prescott said.

"Make that two, Murph, but we'll be having some lunch too," Reynolds said.

It takes a couple of minutes to pull a proper pint of Guinness letting it settle before serving.

"Ever read Joyce's' *Finnegans Wake,* Professor?" Reynolds asked to make small talk as they waited for their drinks.

"No. Is it any good?"

"Only to stuffy literary critics. Unreadable as far as I'm concerned, but then again I didn't like *Ulysses* either."

Anxious to get to the reason for their meeting, Prescott said, "Let me get right to it, Mr. Reynolds. First of all, are you familiar with my book *Critical Mass?*"

"Only vaguely as I remembered from long ago news stories. Your unmasking of a previously unknown Soviet spy from WWII. After you called, I got hold of a copy and read it yesterday. A fascinating read. Well written. Speaking as a journalist, an astounding piece of investigative journalism."

"Thank you. Do you then recall the chapter where I discuss assistance I received from a Russian intelligence officer?"

"Yes. Seemed unusual a Russian helping an American navigate old KGB and GRU archives."

"Unheard of in today's Russian under Putin," Prescott said, "However that was 1997. Still the heady times of openness and the prospect for a democratic Russia. The Yeltsin era when Russia ceased to be the intractable adversarial superpower. That changed when Putin came to power just a couple of years later. That history lies at the center of my personal story."

Callahan brought their beers. Prescott resumed after he left.

"Did you recognize his name?"

Reynolds looked puzzled.

"I don't think so. Should I?"

"The New York Times piece two days ago. The murder in Paris. The victim identified as one Lieutenant General Anton Grigoryev, First Deputy of the Russian foreign intelligence agency."

Reynolds came bolt upright and leaned across the table closer to Prescott.

"Jesus Christ! You're saying he's the source of this new information you have?"

"Yes."

"What's the nature of this information, Professor?"

"Electronic files from the Russian FSB and SVR investigations into the allegations you raised three years ago. Those files confirm the theft of Russian nuclear warheads four years ago."

Reynolds remained silent for a moment, stunned by the implications.

"More than merely a confirmation, the material provides the names of the perpetrators and the details of the theft. Details revealed by one of the central characters in a confession to his brother before murdered along with the other Russian army officers involved. "

"But how is this ..." Reynolds began but Prescott interrupted.

"The man's confession specifically identified Iran as the recipient of three fully operational thermonuclear warheads."

As the first time communicating this terrible secret, Prescott appeared as shaken as Reynolds by the implications of which she possessed.

Reynolds took a breath. "Okay. And you say Grigoryev passed this information to you? How?"

"Electronic files on USB drives. In person. He contacted me and convinced me to come to Paris. Something of life and death importance but he would not discuss specifics on the phone. I could hardly refuse after what he did for me twenty years ago. It made my academic career.

"Once in Paris, he said he was seeking to defect to the United States. Said the Russian government was already searching for him. Wanted me to act as a back channel conduit with the U.S. government. He knew my father was a former State department official and would know the right people and the protocols involved in arranging a high-level defection. Gave me the material in electronic form. It was his bargaining currency to get the best possible asylum deal."

"When was this?"

"A week ago. The French newspapers reported his murder occurred the day after I returned to New York. The story didn't break until days later since Grigoryev carried false identification. They shot him outside his apartment."

She reached for the napkin to dab her eyes now welling with tears.

Quickly composing herself, "Although we did not remain in contact all those years, I feel like I lost an old friend. I want to exact revenge on those that murdered him.

"Grigoryev explained that he joined the KGB in 1980, the First Directorate responsible for foreign intelligence. A rival to the military GRU even today. With the collapse of the Soviet Union, he remained in the successor agency the SVR of the new Russian Federation.

"He saw hope for a democratic Russia. That's when I met him during the Yeltsin era when the new Russian Federation opened and shared old Soviet espionage archives with the world. His help was crucial to my project.

"In the intervening years, Russia changed since Putin came to power in 2000. Grigoryev became sufficiently disillusioned to eventually take action."

"What caused him to do something as extreme as defecting?"

She decided on the train ride up from Washington to confide in Reynolds. Do the right thing by getting this information out about the missing Russian nukes. At the same time, try to insulate herself from the repercussions of going directly to the government. Do what Mark Felt the real *Deep Throat* did in the Watergate scandal or Daniel Ellsberg did by publicly releasing the Pentagon Papers. Go public rather rely on the government. Avoid the government hording the information under the guise of national security. With a vested attachment to the subject, Mark Reynolds was the perfect vehicle.

"His brother-in-law was a senior official in the internal security service the FSB. A guy named Stepka Lytkin. Equally disenchanted with Putin. Seems Lytkin was part of a secret group of experts constructing a shadow financial empire dedicated to enriching senior members of the Putin regime. Grigoryev even admitted to me his own participation in taking what he called regular supplemental payments derived from illicit sources. Profit sharing in the massive graft.

"Grigoryev and Lytkin were planning an orderly defection when something went wrong. Lytkin sent a prearranged warning message to Grigoryev. Grigoryev immediately activated his prearranged escape plan from Russia."

"What happen to his brother-in-law?"

"Grigoryev didn't know. Nor the fate of his sister and two nieces. Considering what his brother-in-law knew, Grigoryev suspected arrest or possibly death."

"I appreciate your sharing this, but why me, Professor?"

"I had a difficult experience twenty years ago with the FBI after I came out with my story about the Soviet spy they never caught."

"Yes, the army officer on Groves' staff. Continued to spy well into the Cold War as I recall from your book," Reynolds said.

"Even though the information became public the FBI threatened all sorts of punitive actions. Working with a foreign intelligence agency, making false statements to the FBI when I explaining the background and sources for my research, and making a knowingly unauthorized release of classified information. All posturing bullshit that died away since there was clearly no legal basis to pursue any serious prosecution against me. But it left a bitter impression, one I care not to repeat.

"These missing Russian nukes started as your story, Mr. Reynolds. You're a newspaper journalist ..."

"Freelance now. My current work now directed more to writing books."

"But you know the media. Where and how to leak this. How to keep me as the source out of it. Like the Nixon era *Deep Throat*, I'll have done my moral obligation to rid myself of this secret while giving Vladimir Putin a world of grief."

"We have a deal then, Professor. Provided what you have is as solid as you say."

"Oh it is. I'll give you the original electronic files in Russian and my English translations so far. It unequivocally corroborates your earlier discovery. Got someplace where we can work this afternoon?"

"My apartment. Not far from here on 67th between Park and Lexington. Now to that lunch I promised. I recommend the bangers and mash or the shepherd's pie. They have good salads too if you're looking for something lighter.

They ate their lunch making small talk to become better acquainted.

"That was good. Didn't realize I was so hungry," Prescott said finishing her Caesar salad and freshly baked soda bread.

"Another Guinness?"

"I think not. Got a lot to show you. We should get down to work. Anxious to get your take on what this all means."

"I agree. I also understand your reticence in going to the FBI and handing over what you got from the Russian spy chief. I've had my own battles with the government too. In my case more with Department of Justice attorneys.

"Thought I was giving them evidence to pursue the corrupt multinational corporation Martinelli Global and their Russian partner Moscow Capital Partners. They not only did not welcome that pile of shit dropped in their lap, but they applied political pressure trying to suppress me. In the end, I obviously got even with Martinelli Global and their partners throughout the world. Through no support from U.S. law enforcement until they couldn't avoid my evidence. So I too am wary."

"Thank you. To be candid, Mr. Reynolds, I have another motive for not wanting to talk to the FBI. Grigoryev gave me something entirely separate from the investigation report on the warheads theft. Equally explosive material, no pun intended."

"There's more?"

"Plenty. A mountain of documents I need to sort through. Complicated financial dealings. Similar to what you encountered with MGI. I read *Shell Game*. Seems you have a good understanding of high-level financial double-dealing."

"Actually I'm no expert. A lot of that international corporate stuff with offshore tax haven shell companies and such came from two colleagues at the newspaper working on stolen files from my own Russian whistle-blower source."

"Well I also have an expert in financial matters. An academic colleague working jointly on a Russian project we started before Grigoryev gave me this material. Anyway, I do not intend to turn this stuff over to the U.S. government, Mr. Reynolds. It is my find. A First Amendment issue as far as I'm concerned. No different from my discovery published in *Critical Mass*."

"And the nature of this material?"

"All sorts of dirt on Putin and his regime. How they are raping Russia and amassing personal fortunes. My colleague and I think it is integral to Putin's unchecked expansion of authoritative power. Keeps everyone well compensated and beholding to him. Banana republic despotism.

"I intend to publish this material before those in this administration so friendly with Putin start obscuring the trail of this mass corruption. Moreover, I relish poking Putin in the eye with something very sharp. The least I can do to revenge Anton."

Reynolds nodded. Another blockbuster story. Prescott struck the mother lode.

"Then let's get to it, Professor."

It was a nice day and Prescott suggested they walk to Reynolds' apartment.

"I left the newspaper three years ago," he said

"Why did you leave?"

"The project that eventually became the book *Shell Game*. The managing editor wouldn't publish what I deemed thoroughly documented evidence of Martinelli Global's illegal dealings in corrupt foreign countries. I suspected outside pressure on the publisher just like the DOJ. People died helping me get that information. I was more than pissed. Quit the newspaper and finished the project without their support.

"Never returned. Besides, investigative print journalism unfortunately is an endangered species. Relegated now to only a few major market papers. Probably could have found a home with one of them. But I can make a living freelancing without the corporate bullshit."

A several block walk brought them to Reynolds apartment building in an upscale neighborhood close to Central Park. Pricy apartments typically populated with successful middle level Manhattan professionals.

She found the apartment's décor tastefully decorated. A large window with good light streaming into a small living area decorated with the look of a professional interior designer. A separate larger office space had a matching window with two walls of bookshelves. Neater than her office at Stanford. Well equipped with two computers and four large monitors. The other wall included photographs hung over lateral file cabinets matching the desk and bookshelves.

"Who's the attractive lady?" Prescott said.

"Her name was Katerina Nikolaevna Avramenko. Nicky died in an explosion in Kiev."

"Oh my god. The Russian journalist in your book. And you were badly injured in that attack as I recall."

Reynolds nodded. "My project cost many lives" Pointing to another photograph, "This is Abejide Ojukwu, a Nigerian journalist. And this is Juan Cortina a Columbian journalist. Both killed by either criminal organizations or complicit police. "

"And this young man standing with Ms. Avramenko?"

"That was my Russian source. A computer geek, an IT systems administrator for MGI's Russian partner, Moscow Capital Partners. Ilya Sergeyevich Varvarinski. Unfortunately he also died. Clever young fellow. Somehow he designed a way to send incriminating files to me postmortem. Brought down the whole rotten house of cards. Had his revenge."

"What was his motive?"

"Claimed it started with the death of his sister. Blamed a guy by the name of Feliks Garnitsky."

"The same Garnitsky that played a prominent role in the theft of the Russian warheads according to the files Grigoryev gave me?"

"Same guy. A real piece of work."

Prescott said, "You'll be gratified to know that in the files Grigoryev gave me there is a reference in the FSB investigation reporting Garnitsky as dead. Liquidated is the term used.

"But I'm getting ahead of myself. Let me show you the major pieces of what I have then we can dig into the detail. I'm sure you'll have all sorts of questions."

Sitting next Reynolds, Prescott booted up her notebook computer on his large glass desk.

"Let me start with this file first. A confession from a guy named Yuri Dratshev. Identified as Garnitsky's key subordinate, the document unravels the whole operation in detail. Here is the original Russian document. That's the letterhead of the Sluzhba Vneshney Razvedki, the foreign intelligence service, the SVR. Now here is my translation."

"You read Russian?"

"Speak it as well. Essential for my academic sphere of interest."

Reynolds read Prescott's translation of Dratshev's confession given to his brother the monk. The lengthy text stretched to a dozen pages describing the theft in detail.

"And this Iranian Savi he names? Is there more about him?"

"Of course. Here is his Russian intelligence dossier."

She pulled up another file first in Russian than switched to her translation.

"Holy shit! Then the Iranians do have these weapons?"

"Looks like it."

"Does anything in these files tell us more about this Dratshev?"

"No. Only the revelations of the deaths of the Russian Army officers by Dratshev's own admission. Russian intelligence assumed Garnitsky arranged for Dratshev's death to leave no direct witnesses, but a body never turned up."

"What about Garnitsky? Does anything in your material reveal what happened to him?"

"Nothing specific except an brief reference appearing in the FSB report. Let me see if I can find it?"

Pulling up the appropriate file in her translation folder, she did a search on Garnitsky.

"Here," Pointing to the passage. *A reliable source confirmed that Feliks Alekseev Garnitsky was killed in Rome by persons unknown and his body disposed of at sea following the Moscow Capital Partners scandal.*

"Reliable source? Why be vague in this top secret report?" Prescott said.

"Because the Kremlin, probably Putin himself, obviously ordered the hit. Better not to put such things in writing. The oligarch Krasin was obviously murdered in a jail cell, not a suicide. That was certainly on Putin's orders. Garnitsky was Krasin's chief henchman. My guess a few other people at Moscow Capital also disappeared, but for different reasons than Garnitsky.

"You didn't overstate this treasure trove. The Russian equivalent to the *Pentagon Papers*. Makes them look grossly incompetent or complicit in nuclear arming Iran."

"If the Russian government was complicit then why conduct a sham investigation?"

"They were not in on this, but the world might not see it that way. Seems clear to me it was Garnitsky's rogue operation. Must have been for a hell of lot of money for the risk. Anything in there about that?"

"Afraid not."

"Well that leaves this Iranian MOIS officer. He's the link to these weapons. Let's see what the Russians know about this guy."

Prescott called up a previously translated file for Reynolds. "Here you go."

After reading through the many pages, Reynolds let out a whistle.

"Impressive background. Started his career a few years after the revolution by joining the successor to the Shah's notorious SAVAK. Not the internal security side of the security agency, but rather their nascent foreign intelligence section. Made himself a name by building his small directorate into an effective operational intelligence organization. The key Iranian intelligence liaison to Hezbollah. Trained in Moscow at the SVR academy. Then he pulls off that clever deception against the CIA using that German code named *Curveball.* That's certainly new information. Educated, multi-lingual. An audaciously clever bastard."

"So what's the next step, Mr. Reynolds?"

"Not sure. Need to go through everything you have. Then devise a strategy to unburden ourselves of this knowledge but in such a way we're not sucked up in the backdraft."

"Can you stay on in New York for a couple of days?" Reynolds asked.

"Sure."

"Where you staying?"

Prescott shook her head. "Haven't thought that far ahead. Not with Dad across town since I want to keep him out of this. Any hotel suggestions close by?"

"There are a couple of acceptable boutique hotels."

"Good. Then we'll pick up on this tomorrow, Mr. Reynolds."

"Professor. Please don't think I'm being forward but I'd be less than gracious without offering you to stay here. There's a spare bedroom with its own full bathroom."

"Oh I don't think so, Mr. Reynolds. Kind of you to offer but better I get a hotel room."

"I understand. You hardly know me. However, I assure you it would not be an imposition and it might optimize our time to work on how best to handle this explosive material. We both have a stake in doing this quickly. And getting it right.

"And by the way, your presence will not create any awkward personal circumstances for me. I am not in a relationship. My lifestyle is not conducive to stable domestic relations."

Prescott bit her lip while mulling over the offer. Probably not a good idea but Reynolds seemed a decent guy. Did not want to put him off since he offered to help get her out of this ethical predicament. It made logistical sense provided things did not become *complicated.*

"Very well, Mr. Reynolds. Makes sense, so I'll take you up on your offer."

"This has been quite a day. What say I make us a drink? Then we can go out to get something to eat. Not much in the refrigerator. I can't cook other than breakfast stuff."

"Okay. Let me freshen up and I'll take you up on that drink."

"Martini, gin or vodka, single malt Scotch, or wine?"

"How 'bout a dry gin martini? With olives?"

"Coming up. By the way, why not call me Mark?"

"Sure. And I'm Victoria."

"Not Vicky?"

"No. In a family of intellectual professionals, with a father named Hamilton and a mother named Lydia, they discouraged common nicknames. But I'm not really an intellectual snob," she said smiling. "I do appreciate you helping with this."

Returning to the living room, Prescott sat and took a sip of her martini.

"Needed that. Are we doing the right thing by releasing this material publicly instead of going to the government?"

Reynolds sipped his Scotch. "No way to know. I tried that years ago and got a lot of grief for my efforts. Government types don't like problems handed to them from outsiders. Then of course, there's this bizarre president with no foreign policy. Since this is about Russia, no telling the attitude this White House might take. If they were indifferent to the Russian interference in the 2016 elections, why not ignore this as well? What is certain is that we will not know what is being done if we just turn over your material. Possible the government could seal the information under a court order closing off all our options using a national security argument. Probably a host of legal maneuvers they could use to control the information."

"Yet might the Israelis simply take unilateral military action if we go public? Even the Saudis might react in some manner."

"Maybe. However, there are no target coordinates for air strikes to take out the threat. Iran will immediately relocate the warheads fearing their location might be compromised. And the U.S. may have always suspected Russian warheads went missing which therefore means they may have already shared that intelligence with the Israelis."

Prescott said, "But if the U.S. suspected the warheads missing does that suggest they do not suspect the Iranians? Otherwise why do the Iran Nuclear Agreement in 2015 to limit Iran's nuclear weapons capabilities in exchange for reduced sanctions?"

"Good point. However, if they found out well into the negotiations, or just recently, then who knows the twisted political rationalizations that made it preferable to conceal. The Russians were also part of the Iran agreement. Why did they go forward obviously knowing the truth? Avoiding international embarrassment for nuclear security incompetence? Fear of the accusation this represented a provocative act indirectly targeting the U.S.? Who knows?

"Whether revealed publicly or not, the real problem is what options does the West have? If not made public they can continue to deny without committing to any strategic recourse. Once it is out there all hell will break loose. At the least, it puts Putin in a deep hole. The whole world will turn against him no matter how he tries to spin this."

"I like the sound of that," Prescott said.

"Resolution of the crisis will only come from pinning this firmly on Iran. That requires more than a confession from a Russian criminal and a Russian intelligence report. What matters is understanding where the nukes are hidden, are they deliverable, and Iranian intentions."

Prescott said, "Grigoryev speculated that the Iranians have given no signals suggesting they are leveraging possession of these weapons. Maybe because a viable delivery system is not yet ready? What's your guess?"

"That could make sense. They might not be technologically ready. Look at what the North Koreans have been doing. Now it is more about delivery capability than nuclear detonation testing. Iran's missile technology ironically comes from Russia, and more recently from North Korean. Iran's missile development falls under the auspices of their space program. The world knows that's a bullshit cover ploy. It is about increasing range, warhead payload capacity, and advanced guidance systems.

"The wild card here is the Israelis. Once there is confirmation that Iran not only has a nuclear weapon capability but several 400-kiloton thermonuclear operational weapons, they'll go ape shit. Current Iranian missile capability puts Israel within range. Who knows how that will play out? But that's a reality whether we go public or turn the material over to U.S. intelligence."

"So regardless, this might result in a new Middle East War?"

"That is a real possibly. Neither Israel nor the United States will tolerate a nuclear-armed Iran. All manner of possible scenarios once someone makes a move. Think about the change in regional dynamics. You now have four nuclear-armed states in the broader region. India, Pakistan, Israel, and Iran. Two sets of avowed enemies and the major nuclear world powers of the United States, Russia, and China all competing for regional influence. With that mix of competing interests, things are bound to turn confrontational."

CHAPTER 11

MANHATTAN, NEW YORK

Prescott walked into the kitchen and poured herself a cup of coffee. Reynolds was already in front of his computer in the study.

Looking up, he said, "Sleep well?"

"Not bad considering what's ahead of us." Sitting down in a chair at the end of the desk she said, "Last night I thought back on my graduate days. My PhD thesis, titled *The Political Dynamics of the Manhattan Project & the Legacy Effects for Military & Foreign Policy*. Got the nuclear bug because my maternal grandfather worked on the Manhattan Project."

"Really? Doing what?"

"A chemical engineer. Worked on the conventional explosives implosion detonator for what became the *Trinity* test weapon and the *Fat Boy* bomb dropped on Nagasaki."

"So you know something about nuclear weapons."

"A working understanding of the technology and construction but my bent was more on how it would shape international events. I wrote it during the time of *mutually assured destruction* by the two superpowers as the conventional approach to deterrence. The work addressed the continuing unsustainable arms race and the possible outcomes. Remember this was the Reagan era of the Strategic Defense Initiative, so-called Star Wars. Everything focused on the U.S. and Soviet Union. Unfortunately, I was not prescient enough to foretell the impending collapse of the USSR just a few years later. That served to redirect my academic focus to Soviet era history.

"Where I was going with this relates to how much has changed. It's now about all the nuclear states other than the U.S. and Russia. Once the genie was out of the bottle, the technology became easily assessable. Now it's these lesser nuclear states that threaten world peace. A complex interplay of multidimensional chess with no rules."

Reynolds quipped, "Possessing nuclear weapons, even just a few gives that country a sense of security even if it's like holding a grenade with the pin pulled."

"I just want this burden put on someone else's back. Someone whose job is to deal with this stuff. I'm an academic not a policy maker. Which brings me to the question, what are you suggesting we do with material?"

The previous evening over dinner, Reynolds furthered his impression of Prescott. Tough minded and smart. Her brilliant exposé *Critical Mass* was a work of first-rate investigative journalism.

He certainly wanted to know more about this financially incriminating stuff on the Putin regime, but did not want to press her. That was her find. Sharing this nuclear theft material and asking his help made him feel protective. As smart and accomplished as she was, in this quicksand she felt vulnerable. For good reason. U.S. federal law enforcement can be pricks when they didn't get what they wanted. Intelligence types were something far worse.

Going public with this would piss off the entire government establishment as they confront recriminations for not uncovering this earlier. Especially this bizarre administration populated with unqualified stooges following erratic and incoherent policies. A White House that reacted in the moment, or followed the whim of an unstable president. Add to that, again involving Russia.

Was Prescott up to the shit storm if they released Grigoryev's material to the media? He could refuse to reveal his source but that might not hold up for long.

The idea he was toying with would be far worse. He must tread cautiously before suggesting such an extreme scheme that would undoubtedly scare the hell out of her.

He said, "I'm a journalist first. Same instincts I think you share. Neither of us feels comfortable in turning the material over to the government. If we release it, we achieve the same end. The government has confirmation that Iran possesses three advanced 400-kiloton yield thermonuclear warheads. The difference is now everyone else in the world knows. Every country must play their cards face up."

"And do you think that's better, Mark?"

"Have you read Daniel Ellsberg's latest book, *The Doomsday Machine*?"

"Yes. A chilling read."

"I think it further reinforces going public. It explains why he released the *Pentagon Papers,* the Rand Corporation report, in 1971. Look at the Snowden NSA breach. Christ. If we cannot trust the United States government we sure as shit cannot trust any other country. All that stuff revealed could only happen if kept secret. Why give them this intelligence football to further the game playing?"

Prescott looked him in the eye, "So you're saying go public?"

"For sure. If you agree of course. We are not making matters worse by disclosing the secret. People have a right to know. Of course, the government will not see it that way. Once it is out there they can't come down us. The material is not classified. If we give it over to them first then it will immediately become classified as top secret."

"You're sure we won't be in legal hot water?"

"Reasonably sure. But that does not mean they won't try. So before we take the plunge, I think we should consult with an attorney."

She let out a deep sigh. "Christ."

"Then there is the issue of this other stuff you have on Putin and his cronies. The FBI and DOJ will immediately launch investigations. Since it involves Russian actions possibly intended to damage the United States, the Special Prosecutor will have an interest. I assume the material directly incriminates high-level insiders?"

Prescott nodded, "Paints a condemning picture of Putin's financial corruption. Points to his means of consolidating and controlling power."

"Does this material also incriminate Americans or Europeans?" Reynolds said.

"My colleague and I are still going through the mountain of material. I suspect it might. At least it involves extensive investment in the West. Western banks are involved."

"Unfortunately, once we go public the FBI will go after us to reveal the source. I still think that it is a first amendment issue, but the FBI and DOJ have all sorts of coercive ways to apply pressure. You do not want to give up the corruption material on Putin before you publish, or they will stop you.

"So an attorney is a must, Victoria. Not just any attorney though. The guy I'm thinking about ironically is named Ellsberg, Phillip Ellsberg. No relationship to the Pentagon Papers' Daniel Ellsberg. Phillip is a former DOJ attorney. Guy turned out to be on my side when I brought them evidence of MGI's financial wrongdoing.

"He was ordered to cease his investigation. Suspicioning outside political pressure he became disillusioned leaving the DOJ a year after my book came out. Kept in touch. We talked about the U.S. government maybe believing my assertion about missing Russian nukes but then sticking their heads in the sand. At the time, the U.S. was in the middle of negotiating the Iranian nuclear agreement. Ellsberg has a decidedly cynical opinion of how Washington functions.

"So he's more than just an attorney. By the way, he is also an expert at complex financial crimes. He was working on stuff I discovered in Columbia involving money laundering traceable to MGI when ordered to cease the investigation by his superiors. Might be someone you and your colleague want to consult for legal issues when you dive into the other information Grigoryev gave you.

"Even though we might be within our first amendment rights, the FBI is sure to want to talk to us. That is a minefield. Any false statement even issued by mistake could result in a federal felony charge. You never talk to the FBI without a lawyer."

"Okay. That makes sense. Where's this attorney's office?"

"Here in New York."

"Convenient at least."

She sat silent for several moments. "Then I guess you need to start working on the media release. Who gets first crack, the *New York Times* or the *Washington Post*?"

"Not quite that simple, Victoria. The original documents Grigoryev gave you will need scrutiny to verify their authenticity. They undoubtedly will secure their own translator to corroborate your work. First thing is to learn as much as they can about everyone named in the documents from other sources. Once that background vetting is complete and the decision made to publish, the managing editor will approach top intelligence officials for comment. I can imagine how that will go. Evidence of another major U.S. intelligence failure.

"But the real issue that will bother the newspaper is how and when did I come by this information? Who did the translation? How can the documents be corroborated? Is this some kind of elaborate setup? The FBI will most certainly want to question me as to the source. Obviously, I'll refuse. I have a plausible cover since Ellsberg can make the argument that I was the obvious conduit for this unnamed whistle-blower because of my earlier allegations about the warhead theft. A recognized journalist that first broke the story, publicly denied by the international community.

"That of course will only buy you some time, Victoria. The FBI can be arrogant but they are very good at what they do.

Eventually your former connection with Grigoryev will be cause for questioning you. His death is the subject of a high-profile French homicide investigation. By treaty, that will obligate the FBI to interview you. If it comes to that, you need Ellsberg with you. At that point there's no point in refusing to discuss what happened."

"Shit. That will still prove awkward," she said. "The FBI will obviously ask all sorts of questions about what I know of Grigoryev. His motivation for defecting. They are sure to ask if there is anything else Grigoryev told me or gave me. I'm not about to lie to the FBI, but neither am I willing to turn over this other stuff. What if a FISA court subpoenas the documents then seals them on national defense grounds?"

"What about going public with all this other dirt you have on Putin at the same time?"

Prescott shook her head no. "Great headlines for a short period. The documents just point to illegal financial dealings. A smoking gun. It needs a lot of investigative work to burrow down into the details. Especially schemes involving the U.S. and Western Europe. Proving violations of foreign laws for money laundering and bank fraud will take time to develop. That is where Putin is more vulnerable if that leads to sanctions isolating Russia from the international capital markets.

"Going public with just the overarching story allows Putin to obscure the tracks. He will suffer damage but the fallout will be more domestic which he can manage.

"Anyway, I'm an academic. I don't need the byline and the unwanted notoriety. Possessing this nuclear warhead theft information obtained from a defecting Russian intelligence officer who is then murdered, is awkward enough for a Stanford professor of history. Not how you advance your career in academia."

Reynolds got up from the desk and went into the kitchen. "How 'bout some scrambled eggs and toast? Best I can do."

"Sure," Prescott said, her tone downcast after this morning's discussion of all the uncertainties. "And some more coffee, please."

They ate breakfast in silence.

"Easier I suppose if we just dumped everything into the lap of the FBI," she eventually commented dejectedly.

"Not necessarily for you, Victoria. There is still the matter of direct contact with the murdered Grigoryev immediately following your departure from Paris. It will prove impossible to retain the financial corruption information you want to keep secret until ready for release. You either lie to the FBI, not recommended, or refuse to answer which breeds other problems."

"Wonderful. I just want to rid myself of this political contamination. Go back to my comfortable life at Stanford."

The thought passed through her mind reminding her that her personal circumstances were not ideal before Grigoryev called her. Truth was she was professionally bored. The Grigoryev material breathed new life into her boring academic research of post-Soviet Russia. She had yet to fix on a core thesis to explain Russia's arch of history following the abrupt repudiation of seventy years of Soviet-style rule to descend into yet another variant of Russian totalitarianism. Grigoryev's material provides a rare window into the new totalitarianism of the Putin regime.

Although emotionally traumatic, the last ten days breathed renewed enthusiasm into her life. A hell of a thing to think with Grigoryev's murder. Selfishly, he was a lover from a distant past. Their one night of intimacy in Paris did not reprise a relationship, but did restart her sexual awareness. It had been a long time since having sex much less any kind of relationship. An unsatisfying status quo now energized with this extraordinary excitement but tinged with uncertainties

She said, "Right now I'm going to take a shower and hopefully get a positive take on where this is headed."

When she returned, Reynolds was working on his computer.

"Writing your press release? Need some help?" Prescott said after pouring another cup of coffee and walking into the study.

She did feel better. At least resolved to go public as Reynolds suggested. The consequences preferred over the government confiscating this treasure trove on Putin.

He turned toward her and smiled. At age fifty-two, she could still turn heads. With his distinct weakness for smart women, she looked even more attractive. Last night over dinner Prescott confided being unattached. Nevertheless, he told himself to remain professionally focused.

"Actually something else. Started with an idea late last night after you went to bed. Back at it this morning before you got up. Had to reexamine it with a fresh perspective."

"Okay. So what's this idea?"

"Now hear me out before you reject the idea. I've already played my own devil's advocate. It still holds up."

A little apprehensive with that preamble, she said, "Then let me hear it."

"The singular lead to pursuing what was behind the nuclear warhead theft is this Iranian Savi. Whether we make the Russian reports public or hand them over to U.S. intelligence, Savi remains the focal point."

"Obviously. But so what? How's knowing that advantage anything?"

"It doesn't. Unless Savi were to share what went down and what happened to the warheads. And most importantly, what are Iranian intentions?"

She gave him a puzzled expression."

"Let me explain. No reason of course Savi or anyone in the Iranian leadership would acknowledge the incident. But once we make it public and implicate Savi, he's potentially in a world of shit."

"How so?"

"First of all, as far as we know, Iran has kept this secret. The Russians of course have known but for their own reasons have kept it secret. Doubtful the U.S. knows given they concluded the nuclear agreement with Iran in 2015. Unless the Iranian leadership thinks Savi is a national hero, sacrificing him might further their denials. Then again, it is possible some militant Iranian faction within the leadership authorized the theft. A rogue operation perhaps like Garnitsky's.

"The Russians will want Savi's head. They will threaten Iran forcing the leadership to scapegoat Savi. Maybe ending in a contrived suicide?

"With the world knowing his name, he can never travel outside Iran. You have translated the Russian dossier on Savi. He spends a fair amount of time outside the country. Certainly Syria and Lebanon with their ties to Iran, but also Western Europe. Russian intelligence comments on his Western tastes in clothes, expensive watches, fine wine and liquor. Not known to express Islamic religious sentiments. Might this mean a professional with less than nationalistic allegiances?

"The Russians note in some detail his long-standing relationship to a Lebanese woman, a professor at Beirut University. He frequent travels there to interact with Hezbollah and assess their military guerrilla capability largely funded by Iran.

"As to the U.S., Savi would be a prime target for black ops. Another Bin Laden. Procuring nuclear weapons for Iran not to mention what the Russians claim is his scam to cause the United States to invade Iraq in 2003 on the pretext of possessing weapons of mass destruction."

The Russian dossier revealed Farzard Savi as a middle-level intelligence officer with the Iranian MOIS engineered a brazen scheme to inflame tensions between the United States and Iraq. Masquerading as a fellow Iraq defector, Savi recruited Rāfid Ahmad Alwān living in Germany since 1999. Claiming asylum because of accusations of embezzlement in Iraq landed him in a refugee camp. Savi, working undercover as a member of the Iraqi Red Crescent humanitarian organization, discovered him there.

Alwān was exactly what Savi sought. Savi identified him as a practiced liar, undoubtedly a petty criminal, willing to pursue any opportunity for personal gain. Claiming a background in chemical engineering, Savi determined Alwān had a working familiarity in the field. A week later, Savi suggested Alwān claim his real reason for defecting was his forced work on a biological weapons project for Saddam Hussein. Schooling Alwān in some basic process designs and procedures, along with providing a photograph of what he told Alwān was a mobile weapons laboratory, Savi instructed him this was a sure way to assure asylum in Germany.

The simplistic ploy worked beyond Savi's wildest expectations. German intelligence passed on intelligence extracted from Alwān, code named *Curveball*, to the United States but refused to allow U.S. intelligence access Alwān directly.

Even though U.S. intelligence found numerous flaws in the German information, *Curveball's* assertions found their way into a hundred U.S. government reports from 2000 to 2001. Famously it even made its way into Secretary of State Colin Powell's address to the United States Security Council in February 2003 as a justification for the invasion of Iraq a month later.

Although years later the U.S. determined *Curveball* as a fraud, the Russians alone seemed to possess knowledge that the Iranian MOIS instigated the hoax.

"So what does Farzard Savi do once he is exposed?"

Prescott shrugged her shoulders.

"If he's already a national hero then he becomes a footnote in history. Doubt that is the case. More likely he becomes a liability.

"While this changes the Middle East political dynamic, the premature revelation places Iran in deep shit. This voids the nuclear agreement between Iran and the five permanent member states of the UN Security Council, Germany, and the EU. They may have three nukes but may not be ready to leverage that threat. Israel may not wait for the rest of the world to debate. At the least the Iranian leadership faces difficult domestic circumstances with the immediate economic impact of renewed punishing sanctions."

"Likely that Savi will be viewed as an embarrassment along with whoever in the leadership championed this audacious move. So Savi is then in an untenable position. No place to turn for sanctuary. The Iranians make him the scapegoat, perhaps publicly accusing him of being a double agent for the CIA or the Mossad. A dead man walking."

"Fine, I get that. Now what's this idea you have, Mark?"

"What if we can coerce Savi to defect before releasing this information?"

Prescott nearly choked on her coffee.

"Are you out of your mind?"

"Like I said, hear me out. The quid pro quo to Savi is to defect before we out you in the press. He will understand the alternatives are life threatening. The price for asylum in the United States is identifying who was behind the theft, the strategic purpose, and of course the current location of the warheads.

"If he rejects our proposal then we go public without having lost anything. For that matter, neither has the United States. This happened nearly four years ago. A few more weeks doesn't change anything."

"Mark, stop right there. How could you possibly make contact with someone in Iranian intelligence? And make direct personal contact without anyone else knowing? Christ this is Iran. You can't go poking around over there without ending up in some hellhole prison."

"There's a crack in his armor. A woman of course."

"Yes I know. Remember I translated the Russian dossier. So he has a girlfriend in Beirut?"

"Don't you see? I can get to her in relative security. Beirut's no longer the active war zone it used to be."

"Really? I recall bombings at various times over the last few years."

"Probably no more dangerous than what goes on in Israel as a regular occurrence. My point is we can get a message to ... let me see ... her name is ..."

"Her name is Leila Hajjar," Prescott said. "Associate professor of art history at the American University in Beirut. Jesus, Mark, this is Beirut. Savi's extended turf. Hezbollah is a terrorist organization based in Lebanon. The reason Savi goes there so frequently. It also borders Syria. Damascus itself is not that far from Beirut. Refugees from the Syrian civil war crossover daily into Lebanon.

"The whole region is a war zone. You can't play amateur cloak and dagger games in this kind of place. I'd guess Beirut is crawling with all sorts of foreign intelligence agents."

"I'm not staying there. In and out of Beirut quickly. I deliver a message to Ms. Hajjar to pass onto Savi but I am gone before he even gets it. Retreated to the safety of Rome. If I hear from him, we take it from there. If not, I'm back in New York and we make the material public."

"So he comes to Rome along with his assassins then kills you. No different than what happened to Grigoryev."

"If we meet, Savi will know others have the information to be released should anything happen to me. I'll create a failsafe mechanism just in case."

Prescott caught herself thinking that Reynolds' screwball plan did sound plausible. Simple enough in theory. Nothing to lose unless of course it got Reynolds killed. By reputation, he thrived on going after the deeper story, the story that revealed more than just the headline exposé. Spectacularly successful given his past journalistic record.

"Extorting an Iranian spy master is just too crazy, Mark. I can't get my head around doing something so utterly foolhardy. Why do you need to do this? "

"I don't of course. But if I'm successful in luring him to defect, it changes the impact of your revelation about the Russian warheads. It also provides immediate corroboration of the leaked Russian material. We still release the material to the media once we have connected Savi with U.S. intelligence. Perhaps enlisting your father as Grigoryev intended. So the government can't bury the information in secrecy."

"Isn't it really more about getting an even bigger story, Mark?"

"The bigger story is always the more important story. That's what investigative journalism is all about. Think about what Savi can offer. He will not defect after we expose him publicly."

Prescott said, "Okay. I still think you are crazy, but I'll do my part. Just want to get this off my hands. From a shellfish perspective, how much time do I have once the shit hits the fan before I'm identified as your source?"

"Truthfully, very little time. Even without my cooperation the FBI will make a full-court press to discover my source."

"What happens then with this mountain of material documenting Putin's financial corruption?"

"That is the real problem. I don't have a solution but I agree we must find a way to retain control without turning over to the government. Right now, let's draft the media release about the nuclear warheads. Also the message I'll deliver to Leila Hajjar to convey to Savi. Then of course we need to schedule a meeting with Phillip Ellsberg. Make sure we are not in violation of any U.S. laws. Maybe he can suggest how we keep corruption stuff without revealing it to the government."

The book *Critical Mass* sat on General Mikhalitsyn's desk. Found in Anton Grigoryev's apartment and signed by the American author. A paperweight held open to the acknowledgment page. Among many other sources, the author cited Grigoryev effusively for his contribution. Then she scrawled by hand, *affectionately Victoria.*

Could this be Grigoryev's connection to the West? Lying next to the open book was a hastily prepared dossier on Professor Victoria Prescott. Nothing in the intelligence files, the information came from public domain sources available on line.

Stanford University professor of history. Russian expert. PhD thesis on the international implications of nuclear proliferation. Speaks and reads Russian fluently. Her father a former U.S, State Department official. Perhaps the caller to Grigoryev's untraceable cellphone reported by Major Kozlovsky after dispatching Grigoryev?

Mikhalitsyn placed a secure scrambled call to the Russian Federation Embassy in Washington.

The call routed to the resident legal attaché, in reality a colonel in Russian foreign intelligence, the SVR. His counterpart's, General Dubrovsky's service but Putin made this clear that Mikhalitsyn and therefore the Federal Security Service was in charge of this investigation. Furthermore, Mikhalitsyn anticipated Dubrovsky might become a casualty as a result of the Grigoryev debacle. As for himself, he was lucky that Putin did not assign a measure of blame for Lytkin's complicity. Mikhalitsyn wasted no time before lopping off heads within his FSB.

Dubrovsky's fate further sealed by Mikhalitsyn's ambitious intrigues. Not only was Mikhalitsyn a trusted confidant of Vladimir Putin but he represented Putin's muscle. Former KGB like Putin and a hardline nationalist, Mikhalitsyn was a staunch advocate of annexing the Crimea and fostering the continued conflict in eastern Ukraine. During the Soviet era, the KGB engaged in foreign intelligence, competing with the military GRU. Mikhalitsyn envisioned a return to reconstituting the post-Soviet separation of the former KGB federal security service, his FSB, and the foreign intelligence service, the SVR into a single ministry with him at the head.

What Lytkin may have stolen over a long period concerned Putin and Mikhalitsyn more than the documentation confirming Russian knowledge of the nuclear warheads theft. As damaging as the theft was, the international repercussions were manageable. Renounce Iran by calling the theft a state-sponsored terrorist attack, claiming the Russian Federation as a victim.

The regime's secret financial dealings were another matter entirely. Nothing found in Lytkin's apartment meant *copies must be hidden elsewhere*. Was his coconspirator brother-in-law General Grigoryev in possession of some unknown Lytkin cache of confidential information? Yet nothing was found in Grigoryev's possession. Hidden elsewhere or had Grigoryev handed it over to someone?

"Colonel, I am personally heading a most sensitive investigation on direct orders from the President. This is to take priority over anything else. What I am seeking is to be reported to my office directly and no one else. That includes anyone within the SVR including General Dubrovsky. This order comes directly from the President. Is that understood, Colonel?"

"Yes, sir."

An unusual order most likely tainted with Kremlin intrigue at the highest level. Although the colonel was an SVR foreign service officer, the FSB represented Russian internal security and Russia's counterintelligence arm, equivalent to the U.S. FBI. Known to be particularly close to the President, General Mikhalitsyn, former KGB like so many around Putin, carried a feared reputation.

Mikhalitsyn said, "I need someone in the United States placed under surveillance, around the clock. More than that, I need to know her movements and any contacts she has made within the last three months. And her current whereabouts."

"Yes, General. And the name of this person?"

"Victoria Prescott. An academic. I will send her particulars by coded transmission. Moreover, Colonel, this needs to be done discreetly. You cannot use Russian personnel. Can that be managed and implemented immediately?"

"I believe that can be arranged, General. There is an American law firm we have used on many occasions. I shall fabricate a reason about needing to obtain information on this woman related to a civil litigation. They in turn will hire a licensed private investigative firm to do the fieldwork under a legitimate cover. Provides a cutout since U.S. law protects attorney-client privilege."

"Excellent. This requires results quickly, Colonel. You will transmit a report to my office daily detailing your progress."

CHAPTER 12

TEHRAN, IRAN

Colonel Farzard Savi of the Iranian Ministry of Intelligence and Security sat outside the office of the Minister. Savi headed the Foreign Intelligence Directorate of the MOIS. He requested this meeting with Minister Mahmoud Alavi, an Islamic cleric, as were the heads of most other ministries.

Even though those like Alavi held religious credentials, relationships and political factions dictated an individual's authority. Politically Alavi was a *Principlist,* literally followers of principles or fundamentalists. Interchangeably the label connotes them as conservatives, right wing, or in western terms, hardliners. Alavi was also personally close to President Hassan Rouhani and Supreme Leader Ali Khamenei.

Given Savi's secular views, he was keenly conscious to be deferential to the religious ideology of the ruling Iranian clerical hierarchy. Fortunately, his role within the Ministry allowed him to avoid engaging in areas of repressive activities within the conservative theocracy. Domestic policing of dissidents and counterintelligence of foreign ex-patriot organizations came under the purview of other directorates. Not unlike the feared SAVAK of the former Shah of Iran's regime. Funding for these policing functions received better funding than his sphere of operations, but his portfolio allowed him to operate more independently. It also allowed frequent professional travel from cloistered Iran to foreign countries.

Still in high school at the time of the 1979 revolution, Farzard Savi grew up in a middle-class household. A time of rapid modernization patterned on Western cultures, driven by the Iranian ruler Mohammad Reza Pahlavi, the Shah. With the 1979 revolution, the Shah became the last Iranian monarch ending 2,500 years of continuous Persian monarchy.

Savi's family painfully adapted to the post-revolution theocracy. All sectors of government now came under control of fanatical Islamic clerics. Replacing the absolute authority of the beleaguered Shah, that same absolute authority now transferred to an exiled Shiite cleric Ayatollah Sayyid Ruhollah Mūsavi Khomeini, the new Supreme Leader of the Islamic Republic of Iran.

Savi's father was a physician, his mother a teacher. As the youngest of three siblings, Savi was still in high school in 1979. A sister was married to a banker and an older brother served as an analyst in the Shah's feared secret police, SAVAK. A potentially dangerous occupation in the retributive chaos of the populist revolution. However, as with all new regimes, pragmatic demands of governing often meant retaining existing expertise. While the new Islamic regime purged the senior ranks of SAVAK of those that did not flee the country, many midlevel functionaries like Savi's brother remained employed. In his case, being an analyst rather than directly involved with torture and murder of the former regime saved his job, and probably his life.

Yet the family still struggled to adapt to the new overtly religious social order. None of the family observed daily prayers. Relishing Western fashion, Savi's mother was now forced to wear unstylish dresses then cover herself with a long coat or tunic, while always covering her head with a scarf. Violations might invite a physical attack by even a bystander.

Easier for the teenaged Farzard Savi to adapt. He was young enough to avoid the influence from the rebellious disaffected university students. The student revolt, a combination of factions fueled by left-wing politics, nationalist identity, Islamic religious fervor, saw a common enemy in the Shah's embrace of Western-styled secular-based modernization. Not imbued with any ideological position, Savi turned his attention to personal advancement under this radically different environment.

Unlike females suddenly relegated to inferior class status with life-altering restrictions, for Savi the only change required superficial adherence to the imposed religiosity. Male facial hair became required as a reflection of appropriate religious observance. Wanting to look older, Savi welcomed adopting a well-groomed close-cropped beard. The imposition of daily prayers was a burdensome ritual with mumbled only half-memorized words, but so were many other demands for a teen.

Savi was a brilliant student. His father wanted him to pursue an education leading to a profession in the sciences. In his second year at Tehran University, he opted instead to change from his engineering curriculum. Three years later, he graduated with dual undergraduate degrees in history and economics. Two years later, he obtained a graduate degree in international finance.

His higher education experience provided a wider view of opportunities. Iran was a backwater. Now a pariah state to the United States and their European allies after holding their Tehran Embassy staff for over a year. Iran was a theocratic oligarchy. A career in Iranian banking or academia held no interest. He was old enough to remember the pre-revolution times. The return of ancient culture norms now clashed with the modern Western world. Everything regressed to an older conservative Persian era reminiscent of the early twentieth century.

Yet emigrating from Iran would now be fraught with increased difficulty. To where? With no experience, how could he expect to secure a position? Abandon his family? Before reaching a decision point, his brother suggested a possibility never considered.

Close to his older brother, he often shared his uncertainty about his future. However never going as far as suggesting that he considered going abroad even though his brother talked fondly of life before the revolution under the Shah's westernization. Although corrupt and repressive against certain elements of Iranian society, life for a non-political professional family under the Shah's regime was better than under this Islamic theocracy.

"Farzard, what about a position within my government ministry?" his brother said as they sipped tea at his brother's home.

"You're joking. Doing what? Beating up guys holding hands or girls in short skirts? Your MOIS is a secret police force just like SAVAK."

"That's not the sort of work I am involved in. You know that. I am in the foreign intelligence directorate."

"So what is it you do, Masoud? "Does that involve spying on these Iranian ex-patriot groups we read about in the newspapers?"

"No, that's the counterintelligence directorate. Because of security I cannot give you details but we do work outside Iran. My function is to try to make sense out of the information we receive from ... well let's just call them sources from around the world."

"What do I have to offer for your group of spies, Masoud?" Farzard said with a smile.

"Can't say specifically. The chief of my directorate, Colonel Yeganeh is looking to build our capabilities. The work I did when we were SAVAK concerned domestic security. Assessing threat intelligence on left-wing political groups. What I do now is different. This is what the American CIA does. Yeganeh is building from scratch. You speak English. Understand computers. Educated in history and international finance. You therefore have knowledge of how things work internationally. If you're interested I can speak to Yeganeh?"

A month later after hours of interviews with MOIS staff, Farzard Savi landed a position in the MOIS Directorate of Foreign Intelligence. Entry level work with computer programs and databases but a chance to demonstrate his talents.

The MOIS formed only a year before Savi hired on. Now thirty years later he occupied the post of chief of the foreign intelligence directorate. During his career, he transformed the directorate into a professional intelligence service. From the ashes of the Shah's secret police to the successor Islamic Republic MOIS, Savi set out to create a functioning foreign intelligence organization. Patterned on major spy agencies of the world, the U.S. CIA, British MI6, Soviet KGB, and the Israeli Mossad, he set out to narrow the mission to maximize results with his limited resources. Even though a small and underfunded agency, the Iranian Foreign Intelligence Directorate of the MOIS claimed a remarkable set of achievements. From his earliest days, Savi began making his mark, seemingly born to intelligence work.

His brilliant mind reveled in the creative challenge of the intelligence game. A talent for languages, he spoke English from an early age then learned German at the university. Following the 1979 revolution and the violent split from the United States, Russia quickly moved to fill the vacuum. With close military and intelligence ties, he acquired proficiency in Russian. This led to advanced training at the Russian foreign intelligence training center of the SVR in Moscow in 1995.

By that time, Savi was already accomplished in basic tradecraft. An uncanny skill for assessing opportunities augmented a natural inclination toward deception. Advanced Russian tradecraft burnished his skills. Since the Russians had been at this longer than anyone else, the Moscow training introduced him to uniquely KGB-origin methods.

His successes came not only from his abilities but also from his innovative and bold operations. He reveled in the high stakes game of wits. What he was about to propose to the Minister of Intelligence and Security far exceeded anything previous in its audacity. The stakes could not be higher. If successful, he would achieve national hero status. If it unraveled, the damage to Iran would be considerable. The responsibility his alone. Those in the leadership approving of the operation would disavow any responsibility for his actions. The most powerful would purge the others. For Savi, not even a secret trial. Summary execution or contrived suicide.

Summoned into the Minister's office, Savi greeted Alavi, "*As-Salam-u-Alaykum*, Minister Alavi."

An austere office with an overt Islamic feel. In his sixties with a graying neatly groomed beard and wire rim glasses, Alavi dressed in typical Shiite cleric fashion including a black turban.

"*Wa Alaikum Assalam*, Colonel Savi. This is your meeting, please proceed."

"As you well know, Minister, our Azerbaijan network's penetration of Russian nuclear weapons facilities has produced a wealth of technological intelligence."

"I agree. Although an unseemly business from your reports of methods employed, the results are proving to be of great value in furthering our weapons technology."

The flow of nuclear weapons intelligence extracted by Savi's penetration of Russian facilities in the Chelyabinsk Oblast a year earlier not only benefited the Iranian knowledge base but also proved a valuable bartering commodity with North Korea.

Both men knew of the ongoing pursuit of the secret weapons program in spite of the Nuclear Agreement that restricted Iranian uranium enrichment. Enriching uranium represented the foundation for developing weapons. Natural occurring uranium consisted of less than one percent of the fissionable isotope U-235. The remainder was the stable isotope U-238.

Enrichment was the process to increase the percentage of U-235 to 3.5-5.0% for powering reactors and over 80% for weapons. A laborious process impossible to keep secret from international monitoring. The current accepted method was gas centrifugal separation of gaseous uranium in the form of uranium hexafluoride. The slightly different masses of the chemically identical two isotopes separate in centrifuges spinning at 90,000 rpm. U-235 concentration increased as the output of one centrifuge is successively fed into a cascade of additional centrifuges.

Moderately enriched uranium is essential for powering specifically designed reactors to produce the manmade isotope plutonium Pu-239. Plutonium is a more efficient fissionable weapons fuel than uranium-235, and more cost effective to produce. Yet U-235 was still necessary to power a nuclear breeder reactor. Everything led back to uranium enrichment producing sufficient quantities of suitable U-235.

With the agreement not to enrich uranium to weapons-grade levels, the Iranian weapons program effectively stalled. However, nuclear agreements can be difficult to monitor. Iran therefore never stopped the technology side of nuclear weapons development. The current United States administration's retreat from the agreement and the unilateral reimposition of U.S. sanctions confirmed Iran's foresight. Savi was keenly aware of the prevailing attitude of the Iranian leadership never to abandon the objective of developing a nuclear weapons threat.

"If you mean enlisting the services of the Russian criminal syndicate Solntsevskaya Bratva, I agree. Unfortunately, the world of international espionage operates in the darkest of places. Pursuing Iranian interests and security often necessitates employing unpleasant methods."

As an Islamic cleric, Alavi found the more unsavory aspects of Savi's operations repugnant. The Solntsevskaya Bratva assisted in infiltrating Savi's agents into the Russian Chelyabinsk region east of the Ural Mountains. Heavily urbanized industrial Chelyabinsk contained much of Russia's nuclear weapons related facilities. The Russian criminal syndicate controlled drugs, gambling, smuggling, black market commerce, extortion, and prostitution. To infiltrate Russian nuclear facilities, Savi's agents worked under the protection of the crime syndicate. High-class prostitutes provided the principle means to entrap sources working within the secret facilities.

The Solntsevskaya Bratva knew this was an Iranian intelligence operation. Their cooperation stemmed from another Savi arrangement that returned tens of millions of rubles annually to the syndicate. A deal brokered by Savi with certain Afghanistan warlords allowed the Russians a regional access monopoly on raw opium production. Savi arranged for transport through bordering Iran then by ship from a Caspian Sea port directly into Russia. Everyone gained. The Afghans received a higher price for the opium, with the Russian syndicate justifying the added cost by elimination of intermediaries establishing a secure smuggling route. Savi's directorate received not only a substantial *service fee*, but also cooperation for his intelligence activities in Chelyabinsk, Russia.

With his Azerbaijani network, Savi also facilitated two-way smuggling through the unstable Caucasus region between Russia and Iran to avoid Western sanctions. In these endeavors, the Russian Solntsevskaya Bratva played a key role and connected Savi into the economic underbelly of Russia. With these revenue-producing enterprises, Savi's Foreign Intelligence Directorate became almost self-funding.

Under the new Islamic regime, the Minister of Intelligence and Security must be a *doctor of Islam*. Hardliner Mahmoud Alavi justified the use of harsh measures for enforcing conservative Sharia laws on the Iranian domestic population. Savi's collaboration with criminals, trafficking in drugs, and using sex to achieve results was morally abhorrent to Alavi. Although Savi was as vague as possible and avoided details in his reporting, certain facts were still necessary.

Always a delicate issue for Savi. Yet he knew the Minister relished taking credit for his Ministry's foreign intelligence successes. Savi decided to approach Minister Alavi this day because of Alavi's expressed support of the Iranian the nuclear weapons program. Equally important, Alavi enjoyed a close relationship with President Rouhani.

While considered a political moderate, Rouhani spent many years negotiating with the Western powers as they sought to curtail Iranian uranium enrichment. The Iran Nuclear Agreement of 2015 negotiated under his presidency achieved a measure of economic sanctions relief but did not eliminate Iranian nationalistic aspirations. Rouhani strongly supported the sovereign right for Iran to possess nuclear weapons. With a belligerent nuclear-armed Israel threatening Iran, the agreement driven by the Americans was nothing more than continued efforts by the United States to impose hegemony in the region with their surrogate Israel.

The Supreme Leader also held Rouhani in high regard. What Savi was to propose required Rouhani's support to gain the ultimate approval from the Supreme Leader Ayatollah Ali Hosseini Khamenei.

"Because of our success in penetrating Russian nuclear weapon sites, we have uncovered an array of security weaknesses. The central weakness with any security system is always the people involved. Russian technical personnel and military staff are no exception. Their security protocols are inadequate. I suspect essentially little has changed since the collapse of the Soviet Union. Pay is low, advancement opportunities limited. An environment proven susceptible to bribery and other inducements."

Minister Alavi just nodded waiting for Savi get to the point of this meeting.

"I merely cite this background because I believe an opportunity exists to enhance our nuclear weapons aspirations in a great leap?"

"Colonel, while your intelligence acquisition of Russian technology has been of great benefit, our program is now more theoretical than practical. This agreement to curtail uranium enrichment effectively stalls any practical progress."

"Exactly. What I am proposing cuts short the problematic hurdle of enriching sufficient quantities of uranium."

Alavi leaned forward, "Very well, Colonel, you have my attention."

"Minister, I am suggesting it may be possible to acquire several fully operational Russian advanced thermonuclear warheads."

Alavi's expression changed from initial shock to incredulity.

"Really? Acquire you say? You mean steal?"

"In a manner of speaking. However, not by our people or anyone connected to Iran. The theft will be carried out by those undesirable Russian elements co-opted for this purpose. We will fund the enterprise. Iran can maintain deniability whether the theft is successful or not."

"And will the Russians not immediately suspect us and react militarily?"

"Because the theft will not be discovered. This is not a military-style operation. Russian nationals will perpetrate the theft, but the participants will not know the true nature of what they are doing. The operation involves a routine transfer between facilities engaged in the maintenance of nuclear warheads and repurposing the nuclear cores. The key is a sequence of falsified paperwork by well-paid insiders."

"That sounds like many people with knowledge of the operation. Traitors. People that accept bribes cannot be trusted to remain silent should it become in their interest to divulge what happened."

"Of course. Each participant will only know a piece of the operation and never the actual intent. The people most directly involved believe they are following orders from President Putin. A secret program to conceal operational warheads to circumvent armament agreements with the United States. Once the operation concludes, all parties will be eliminated in *accidents*."

Alavi remained silent for several moments digesting Savi's argument.

"But do you not expect the Russians to discover the missing warheads at some future time?" Alavi said.

"Unlikely since the records will show the warheads as dismantled and their nuclear cores recovered. That audit trail is part of the paperwork alteration. Even if the discrepancy might be suspected during some future physical audit, the Russians already have significant quantities of unaccounted for fissionable material. The unaccounted quantity of the missing warheads will be lost in the larger record keeping inaccuracies."

"Should the theft ever be discovered by the Russians, it is highly unlikely they will acknowledge the loss of nuclear warheads fearing damage to their nuclear energy export sector through loss of prestige. Or the accusation of complicity in nuclear weapons proliferation. Of course we can easily deny everything."

"How is that? What use are these weapons unless we can leverage them?"

Alavi would harshly reject anyone else making such a wild proposal. Too many of his fellow hardliners were fanatics with unrealistic aspirations for Iran. However, Savi was no fanatic. Rumored to shun Islamic customs, he was a brilliant pragmatist. As bizarre as this sounded, it was undoubtedly the product of a great deal of thought.

"Many strategic options might be considered. Possession of these warheads will provide an exponential leap in our weapons technology. Reverse engineering will transcend years of engineering and shortcut the typical testing cycle to acquire empirical data. I believe it will become a significant tool from which to bargain with our friends of the DPRK to share in that technology. Perhaps sufficient for them to clandestinely become a source for providing Iran with weapons-grade fissionable material, uranium or even plutonium. In short, from these advanced warheads we might leverage the ability to circumvent foreign scrutiny and create a viable nuclear weapons arsenal."

Alavi took a deep breath absorbing this audacious idea.

"I'm still concerned with the number of people involved. Impossible to insure secrecy. These Russians you speak of, who exactly are you dealing with?"

"Apart from several Russian army officers already compromised, essentially one man. His name is Feliks Garnitsky. Former KGB with strong ties to Russian organized crime. A large-scale smuggler turned businessman. Works now for an oligarch named Krasin who is close to President Putin."

"And what does he get for doing this?"

"A great deal of money. I have not yet approached him, but he holds the key to the plan with his high-level connections within Krasin's empire. One of those companies operates many nuclear facilities under government contract. Garnitsky is essential. If he turns me down then we do not proceed."

"For how much money, Colonel?"

"At least 600 million Euros. The total project cost perhaps as much as one billion Euros?"

Alavi's mouth dropped, "That is an impossible sum, Colonel."

"Unfortunately that will be what it takes for Garnitsky to risk his life. He is doing this all on his own initiative. No connection to Krasin."

Alavi displayed a negative expression shaking his head.

Savi countered with his last best sell, "Think of the possibilities, Minister. This money buys Iran three operational thermonuclear warheads each with a yield of 400 kilotons explosive power. Twenty times more powerful than the bombs dropped on Japan in 1945.

"These weapons become the foundation from which to develop a nuclear arsenal to rival the Israelis. It will provide Iran the leverage to dominate the region. And it will provide Iran security against military attack by its enemies."

One week later, Alavi summoned Savi to his office. This time ushered into a small conference room. Seated with Alavi were three others, two in uniform. Savi knew all of them and greeted each with the traditional embrace.

As Savi took a seat, one of the two men in military uniform bluntly said, "Do you actually believe you can pull this off, Colonel Savi?"

The question came from Major General Qasem Soleimani. His heavily muscled physique not the only reason for reference behind his back as the *bull,* Soleimani was outspoken and quick on the attack.

Briefed by Alavi on Savi's proposal, these senior military commanders were here to find fault with the plan or tacitly concur with its feasibility. Alavi needed the weight of these officials to present a united front in proposing the plan to President Rouhani.

Savi replied, "Yes it is possible, General. Remember, it will not be our people or anyone directly connected to Iran involved in the operation. We become involved only when the warheads successfully reach Iran. Any failure during the operation provides Iran with complete deniability. Execution of the plan carries risk, but little risk to our exposure."

General Soleimani commanded the Quds Force. In the complex reorganization of the Iranian military following the revolution, the new regime did not trust the remaining officers of the former Shah's armed forces. The solution became the creation of a parallel military force, the Islamic Revolutionary Guards Corps, commanded by known loyalists to the new theocracy leadership. During the Iraq-Iran War, the Quds Force became a special forces command within the Revolutionary Guards. By the 1990s, the Quds Force evolved into carrying out extraterritorial military operations in the Middle East. The United States designates them a supporter of terrorism.

Soleimani was however more than just the Quds commander. Supreme Leader Ali Khamenei who promoted him and called him a living martyr, also held him in high regard. Western intelligence referred to him as the *Shadow Commander*, describing him as *the single most powerful operative in the Middle East today*. He greatly influenced the Iraq government following the Second Golf War, and become the architect of the military wing of the Lebanese Shia party Hezbollah. Soleimani remains the principal military strategist and tactician to combat Western influence while expanding Iranian influence throughout the Middle East.

Savi and Soleimani professionally respected each other. Fortunate since their respective spheres of operation often found them working together in Syria and Lebanon. Yet both could not be of more differing motivations. Soleimani was a soldier as well as a fanatical Iranian nationalist. To possess nuclear weapons, Savi suspected Soleimani to be willing to accept almost any risk.

Alavi said, "Gentlemen, before we start questioning Colonel Savi on specifics of his audacious plan, allow him to explain in fuller detail what he outlined more generally to me. Colonel, please proceed."

Savi launched into explaining the plan this time in much greater tactical detail. He must convince this audience not only of the practicality of the plan but the ramifications for all conceivable contingencies. Collectively they were necessary to sell this President Rouhani and then to the Supreme Leader. That meant all of them would share in the success or failure.

The other two participants were Major General Mohammad Ali Jafari, commander of the Iranian Republican Guards Corps and Hossein Taeb, deputy commander for intelligence of the IRGC, an Islamic cleric the same as Alavi.

Jafari in contrast to the assertive hard-charging style of Soleimani exuded a studied demeanor. A technical military officer educated as a civil engineer, he however possessed an extensive military background including combat commands throughout the Iraq-Iran War. A hardline conservative, he was an expert in asymmetric warfare strategies. If the theft proved successful, it would fall to Jafari to secure the weapons in absolute secrecy.

Taeb like Alavi was an Islamic cleric and dressed accordingly. Yet he formerly commanded the *Basif*, a paramilitary volunteer militia formed in 1979 by order of Ayatollah Khomeini, leader of the Iranian Revolution. Under his command, the *Basif* was active in suppressing protest over the controversial 2009 election with Western allegations his forces were guilty of mass beatings, murders, detentions and torturing of peaceful protesters. In public statements Taeb expressed a hardline accusing the United States of subversively trying to overthrow the Islamic Republic.

The common thread among the group was virulent anti-Americanism. Soleimani, Jafari, and Taeb were all under personal sanctions by the U.S. Alavi escaped inclusion, perhaps a reflection of how Western intelligence undervalued the Iranian MOIS. More importantly, all saw that an Iranian nuclear weapons program was the only way to defend against American-Israeli military threat. North Korea clearly affirmed that strategy.

For three hours, Savi explained every detail, every contingency, parrying questions from all the participants. Although preaching to the choir, this was all about risk management. Indicative of the seduction of the possibility of Iran possessing high-yield nuclear warheads, no one questioned the enormous financial cost, where the funds might come from, and how to conceal the expenditure. A lively debate occupied the final hour as to how to leverage the acquisition of the warheads. Savi shared his idea of bartering access to the warheads in exchange for weapons grade fissile fuel from North Korea. He argued for using the Russian warheads as a precursor to secretly establishing a larger nuclear arsenal with missile delivery capability to be the more successful long term strategy.

Pleased with how things went, there was nothing more he could do. At the conclusion of the meeting, the group announced no collective decision. Individual positions were difficult to gauge. However, he felt it perhaps even odds they would recommend the plan. None of the participants expressed a negative position. Beyond that, there was no way to foretell the prospects of Rouhani supporting the plan, or the prospects of obtaining the required final approval by the Supreme Leader.

Savi sensed Alavi's personal support of his plan by the convening of this group. All were conservative hardliners previously expressing views in support of an Iranian nuclear weapons program. Notably absent were any members of the leadership known to oppose nuclear weapons development. This was to be a clearly partisan operation, thereby also tightening its surrounding secrecy.

Even if Savi had convinced this group, the unknown remained convincing President Rouhani. While not a reformer, he was more politically moderate. Although closely associated with Iranian nuclear aspirations in negotiations with the West, he was a clever intellectual, noted for his diplomatic skills. Would he view this bold plan to circumvent the spirit of the 2015 agreement he engineered as a personal affront? Rouhani was important to the process even though the decision ultimately rested with Supreme Leader Ayatollah Khamenei. If Rouhani vigorously opposed the idea, it might be sufficient for Khamenei to scuttle the venture.

CHAPTER 13

TEHRAN, IRAN

Two weeks later Savi received a summons from Minister Alavi. Seated in Alavi's office was General Soleimani as Savi took a seat around a conference table.

"Some tea, Colonel?" Alavi said.

"Thank you, Minister."

As Alavi served Savi tea, "Your proposal was well received by President Rouhani. Naturally he asked many questions. Surprisingly, he centered more on the risk factors than on the core concept. Paraphrasing, the President said, *with the antagonism of this new American President toward Iran, and their abandonment of the nuclear agreement, we have little choice but to move forward to protect ourselves. With the aggressive tone from Netanyahu and now Trump, along with Saudi military adventurism, Iran increasingly faces military threat. The North Koreans have demonstrated the change in posture of the United States by possession of a viable nuclear weapons arsenal.*

"President Rouhani is uncertain about American intentions. The Americans wish to inflict harm on Iran by renewing crippling sanctions. The nuclear agreement signed in 2105 without the United States is no longer valid. Imperialists now in power in the United States have reverted to economic warfare to restrict Iranian influence in the Middle East by denying Iran's right to nuclear weapons. Treaties with the United States are proven to be meaningless. It ignores the reality that India, Pakistan, and most importantly Israel, all allies of the United States, possess such weapons.

"Therefore, the President persuaded Khamenei that we must develop a nuclear weapons program to insure Iranian security. If your mission proves successful, we can improve our economic situation while secretly pursuing a different path to achieve the necessary weapons to defend ourselves. It is written that Iran shall stand against America's war on Islam.

"He told me your efforts to penetrate the Russian nuclear weapons facilities yielded valuable technical intelligence. Not only for our own scientists but it has served as valuable barter with the North Koreans."

Savi was well aware of the benefits of sharing his stolen Russian nuclear technology. He was the principal conduit passing intelligence to a highly paid agent in the DPRK Tehran Embassy.

"The President did have one immediate question. Why such an excessive amount of money to this Russian criminal, Garnitsky?

"Then the President will present the proposal to the Supreme leader?" Savi said.

Soleimani answered, "No, all of us that know of the plan will convene together. The President expects all of us to share collectively in the responsibility. That is why you are here today. You will explain again to Minister Alavi and me every facet of the operation. Convince us down to the smallest detail. All of us have a personal stake in this, Colonel. If we agree the plan is workable with contingencies appropriately considered with alternatives, and if the risks deemed manageable, you are to prepare a comprehensive written plan. Remember you must do this personally, no subordinates or secretary. Produce no hard copies. Secure your electronic files as assessable only by you.

"The President even selected the operational code name. Your mission will be called *Sword of Allah*, Colonel," Soleimani said. "Code level only authorized security."

Alavi said, "At our last meeting you provided the essentials of how the operation will be conducted on the ground. The General and I need to examine the operational details further. We also need to understand the mechanism for financing this operation, Colonel. All of us see the money trail presenting the most serious risk to disclosure of Iran's role in this act."

"I should add, this enormous payment for this Russian's assistance has us all questioning why so much?" Soleimani said. "You said the operation could be as high as one billion Euros. That is many times even our annual funding for support of Hezbollah."

Savi answered, "Felix Garnitsky is essential because of his unique access to the nuclear weapons facility as an executive of the managing private firm Rusatomic. While I have conceived the plan, Garnitsky must carry it out. First because it involves high security installations in Russia, and second because it must involve only Russian operatives to shield our involvement.

"Only Garnitsky can coerce a key army general under his control to redirect the intact warheads by issuing false orders to junior security officers at two key facilities. Furthermore, the cover to the junior officers is explained as a secret operation personally authorized by the President. Explained as a deception to conceal warhead disassembly from scrutiny under the prevailing arms control agreement with the U.S. The general involved is essential to that deception. Garnitsky is the only person in a position to initiate the operation. Garnitsky is already a successful criminal but he will be concealing this from his boss Krasin as well as committing treason against Russia.

"Let me explain Garnitsky's background. Former KGB still connected to high level FSB officials. Well paid by Krasin, but not wealthy in the class of an oligarch like Krasin. Krasin brought him into his business empire because of Garnitsky's extensive involvement in smuggling with close connections into the leadership of Russia's largest criminal syndicate. Those same people we are using for cover in our penetration into the Russian nuclear environment in Chelyabinsk Oblast. Through the Russian crime syndicate Solntsevskaya Bratva I connected with Garnitsky years ago to facilitate smuggling to mutually circumvent Western sanctions on both our countries.

"I am asking Garnitsky to risk his already lucrative position to use his insider connections to Krasin operations under contract from the Russian government to operate certain nuclear facilities. I am also asking him to betray his country. The cost is commensurate with his degree of risk considering Putin's record of killing traitors.

"And remember, Garnitsky might turn me down. If so, there is no way to implement the plan. However, we will have lost nothing by the effort. Garnitsky must convince a this Russian general to initiate the critical orders necessary to launch a sequence of various record falsifications. Therefore, I must entice Garnitsky by an offer he cannot refuse. I will first offer a lower amount but Garnitsky will surely demand more."

Alavi said, "Very well, Colonel. Now explain if you will how the operation is funded so as to shield Iran and your Russian traitor."

"We purchase a controlling interest in a small Austrian consulting firm. A failing enterprise with only ten employees. A modest expense. The inducement to the owner is a large project management contract for a new Iranian petroleum refinery. The purchaser is the National Iranian Oil Refining and Distribution Company. I negotiate the deal and retain powers of attorney as the owner representative for the Iranian government. In my alternative identity, I am recognized in Vienna as a trade specialist for the Ministry of Economic Affairs and Finance. To legitimize the venture, we will use construction plans for the Shahid Tondgooyan refinery here in Tehran with the documentation altered to the fictitious location.

"We execute a contract with this firm to negotiate purchase contracts of equipment and services from predetermined Russian companies. The lack of competitive bids is explained as a means to satisfy a financial offset agreement with Russia. For this, the consulting firm receives lucrative management fees, and the ability to buy back their sold shares at the original sale price at the end of the construct project. To the owner of the consulting firm, our reasoning for this seemingly added complexity is to transact the three-year project in Euros to avoid currency fluctuations of the ruble and Iranian rial. We also chose to insert an intermediary gatekeeping function for oversight given the corrupt business environment of Russia.

"For saving his business and providing immediate profitability with a long-term revenue stream, the owner will not raise questions. I of course will authorize all payments and construct the false purchase agreements with nonexistent Russian companies for the eventual larger payout after successful delivery of the warheads.

"To finance concealment of the illicit funds flowing to Garnitsky, I negotiate a line of credit with the Austrian bank Wiener Handelsbank for 150M Euros backed by a guarantee from the Iranian Central Bank. We already have relations with Wiener Handelsbank for legitimate trade transactions with the EU. Austria has proven more cooperative on financial matters than other EU countries therefore I expect no undue scrutiny to this deal.

"This represents the down payment to Garnitsky of 100 million Euros. Disbursement flows to a small Russian engineering firm purchased by Garnitsky to act as a shell company for just this transaction.

"And the other 50 million?" Alavi asked.

"I will use that for various expenses to facilitate the concealment and shipment of the warheads to Iran."

The same arrangement for funneling the down payment to Garnitsky provides Savi with the perfect cover to skim millions into personal accounts using the same fictitious payees. Payments to those nonexistent entities route through foreign bank accounts in Switzerland and Lichtenstein controlled by Savi.

"And how is the balance of whatever fee is demanded by Garnitsky transacted?" Soleimani said.

"The remainder of his fee is released once the shipment is loaded onboard the ship at the Russian port of Astrakhan, ready to embark to the Iran port of Anzali on the Caspian Sea. A ship under our control. Garnitsky holds a letter of credit for the shipment of machinery associated with the petroleum refinery. The credit arrangement is funded by the Iranian Central Bank and transacted by the Austrian bank for a handsome commission."

Alavi said, "And how is a payment this large concealed by Garnitsky? He cannot use a Russian bank I trust?"

"Garnitsky knows better," Savi said. "Remember he is an accomplished major smuggler. Sophisticated operations done with government collusion in most cases. He understands how to hide large transactions and launder the money. His early criminal background evolved into sophisticated white-collar crime working for the corrupt oligarch Krasin.

"Should Garnitsky accept, I shall impress on him the need to satisfy our security concerns."

"And how would you redirect this money if you were Garnitsky, Colonel?" Soleimani said.

"I will provide a list of invented financial transactions. Garnitsky will fill in the names. He will create shell companies to act as brokers, consultants, investment banks, or any entity acting as intermediaries in what shall appear a large-scale construction project. Money is recorded as payment for fees, commissions, engineering services, advance down payments for equipment flowing through these intermediaries. Remember, Garnitsky can always justify this new cash-stream flow as part of his many illegal business dealings. I suspect he will then quickly launder the money onto tangible foreign assets through offshore tax haven accounts."

Alavi said, "Very well, Colonel. Garnitsky then has to bank the money we have paid by interbank transaction to these intermediary shell companies. Where? In Russia initially, or someplace else? A paper trail therefore exists. Easily discovered as false with little probing."

"We have to trust that Garnitsky realizes that and finds satisfactory methods of laundering the funds to obscure transparency," Savi answered. "Keep in mind, Garnitsky is practiced in illegal financial transactions."

Alavi said, "We cannot leave the risk of exposing Iranian complicity to reliance on the financial skills of a criminal."

"Gentlemen. Consider this. Once the warheads are in our possession, if Garnitsky is found to be involved, he is dead. A bullet to the head, probably a much worse death. He is highly accomplished at this sort of thing. He understands discovery of the theft means forfeiting his life no matter where he might flee.

"Even if the Russians eventually suspicion warheads are missing, what can they possibly do? Remember there is no physical inventory of the warhead cores that will reflect a discrepancy. The only trail becomes a disparity of fissionable fuel inventories, further obscured by falsified records accountable as errors. Russian inventories of fissile material already reflect significant missing quantities. These three warheads add only slightly to the total discrepancy.

"Admission by the Russians exposes them to charges of gross incompetence or maybe even suggestions they engineered the theft. Russian trade in nuclear technology becomes sanctioned universally. Iran disclaims the theft as Russian disinformation. No proof will exist. If the Russian of losing nuclear weapons is true, might this be the act of Sunni terrorists like ISIL or Al-Qaeda? Why single out Iran?

"But I suggest it would never come to that. Russia can do nothing even if suspicions are raised, therefore they will remain silent."

Soleimani said, "Let's discuss the more obvious risk concerning those participating in the theft. How do you mitigate that?"

"After completion of the mission, the active participants are immediately eliminated. I shall use the Solntsevskaya Bratva organization for that task. They are already aware of our intelligence penetration operation. I claim something went wrong. The discovery of a double agent. All involved must be silenced to cover our penetration. For money, they will suffer various accidents. The same for anyone actually seeing the warheads during transport and concealment. Other peripheral participants are ignorant of what is happening. To those higher up in the Solntsevskaya Bratva, we are smuggling out enriched uranium. Talking to authorities is a death sentence within the Bratva.

"Those in my Azerbaijani network know nothing more than our continued intelligence penetration. They are not involved in this separate theft operation. That leaves only Garnitsky and I suspect his right-hand man, Yuri Dratshev. Dratshev is Garnitsky's fixer. Garnitsky will either pay him well or more likely arrange for his death."

"Then Garnitsky and his subordinate Dratshev remain the risky loose ends," Soleimani said.

"Very well, I will then insure that Dratshev becomes a casualty. But I see no way to eliminate Garnitsky. He stays mostly in Moscow. Well-connected with personal bodyguards. Attempting anything would be unacceptably risky and raise questions. Furthermore, it could unnecessarily expose our involvement. We must accept some level of risk for the potential benefit of this venture. Again, once the warheads are in our possession the risk becomes remote regardless of Garnitsky. We have plausible deniability. Who would believe Iran to be behind such an elaborate intelligence penetration involving Russian nuclear weapons security?

On September 14, 2014, a small cargo freighter with rust lines streaking down the hull loaded a large open crated piece of machinery to its deck at the Russian port of Astrakhan on the Caspian Sea. The cargo manifest read *petroleum drilling equipment compressor*. The consignee listed as a state-owned Iranian corporation. The export documents were in order with money changing hands to insure no delays. Supervising the loading of the *Caspian Princess* flying the flag of Azerbaijan was Yuri Dratshev and Farzard Savi. Savi wore the disguise and carried credentials as the first officer of the *Caspian Princess*, his Azerbaijani network having bribed the captain and his two subordinate officers. Just routine graft in the lucrative smuggling trade of the Caucasus region.

Savi was here to take custody of the warheads and deliver the necessary paperwork to Dratshev for Garnitsky to redeem his funds through the letter of credit with the Austrian bank. The vessel would steam south stopping first in Baku to take on more cargo before proceeding to the Iranian port of Bandar-e Anzali.

Arriving two days later, the equipment offloaded the vessel while Savi presented the manifest and bills of lading in the Iranian customs office. Several military vehicles and a company of soldiers spread across the dock next to the *Caspian Princess*. This day the small office included only officers of the Republican Guard, including the commander Major General Mohammad Ali Jafari.

Jafari embraced Savi.

The weapons now became General Jafari's responsibility. For added security against foreign intelligence, they would not be concealed within known Iranian nuclear facilities. Arrangements called for their dispersal to three different locations and held under tight layered security. The concealment from the exterior suggesting something innocuous. It would take time for the leadership faction that knew of the acquisition of the weapons to adopt a consensus strategy before widening the knowledge to select scientists and weapons engineers.

Savi now turned his attention to monitoring the elimination of those intimately involved in the theft. He was aware Garnitsky would contract this dirty work probably to the Solntsevskaya Bratva. Therefore, he apprised Garnitsky of his earlier network penetration of the Russian facilities in Chelyabinsk. He suggested Garnitsky use this knowledge as the justification to Solntsevskaya Bratva for eliminating Russian army officers. The cover ploy being that Garnitsky's sources in the FSB alerted him to suspicions of a possible foreign intelligence penetration of certain nuclear facilities. As the private operating contractor, this could place Rusatomic in an awkward position. As an executive with Rusatomic, Garnitsky could not afford an investigation that could jeopardize the profitable contractual arrangement Rusatomic enjoyed with the government. The Russian army officers were all corrupt. Taking bribes from both Rusatomic and Savi's agents, they presented a risk if arrested and subjected to harsh interrogation. Aware of Savi's penetration, Garnitsky was therefore sacrificing Savi's intelligence network for his own reasons and compensating the Solntsevskaya Bratva for eliminating the corrupt officers.

In their final exchange as the false compressor concealing the nuclear warheads hoisted onto the deck of the *Caspian Princess*, Dratshev assured Savi of the immediate elimination of all the complicit army officers. To the extent possible, all would appear as unconnected events.

Dratshev said to Savi, "General Ryndenko, the key to issuing the false orders, has already met with a natural death in Moscow."

"And those other officers at the Trekhgornyy disassembly plant and the Ozyorsk reprocessing plant?"

"I have assurances that will happen within the week."

Savi said, "In such a way without raising suspicions? Might not the deaths of several army officers in a short span of time draw attention? Why will they not be linked?"

"Their deaths have been carefully planned. With Ryndenko's fatal heart attack, only four army officers between the two plants participated in falsifying the records. Trekhgornyy is also 200 kilometers from Ozyorsk. Thousands of military stationed throughout the area. The deaths will appear in substantially different and unrelated form. Certain other non-military individuals involved will simply disappear. Their deaths not as sensitive. Happens all the time in the criminal underworld."

Without knowing the details, Savi could not be totally convinced. However, that part of the operation remained beyond his control.

"Even among those knowledgeable in the theft, it was conveyed as a secret operation authorized by Putin," Dratshev added.

"And those involved from the Solntsevskaya Bratva?" Savi said.

"Garnitsky is handling that. But he told me to maintain the cover story. *His sources within the FSB are investigating a possible foreign intelligence penetration into these nuclear facilities. That dictates the sacrifice of all those involved trading in classified information.*"

"And those on the ground masquerading as soldiers in that phony facility?"

Dratshev said, "They are under the impression they participated in the theft of nuclear material, not functional warheads. None understood the entire plan through careful compartmentalized. The few that actually saw the warheads did not know what they were looking at, yet they also will be killed as a precaution. The Bratva bosses know nothing about warheads, only the theft of fissile material."

After handing over the documentation for Garnitsky to redeem the letter of credit, it was a tense forty-hour trip to Bandar-e Anzali. Now exposed with possession of the warheads, Russian warships could detain the Caspian *Princess* landing in Iran should anything go wrong.

Once the ship pulled into the Iranian port, Savi relaxed and absorbed his victory. The achievement of an intelligence coup to rival anything the KGB carried out during the Cold War. Even if some loose thread unraveled to expose the operation, Iran now possessed thermonuclear warheads. Short of a full military invasion, the U.S. and Israel would have no idea how to remove the threat with targeted air strikes alone.

This was not about just three warheads. If played cleverly, they represented the ability for Iran to leverage the acquisition into multiplying their arsenal. Kept secret from the West advancement of the Iranian weapons program could proceed. The key was getting North Korea to provide weapons grade nuclear fuel and share in their advanced missile technology.

The successful undertaking meant something more important for Savi. He was now a wealthy man. Of the fifty million Euros allocated for *operational expenses,* he managed to siphon off over forty million. The funds secure in numbered accounts in various countries. However, to enjoy that wealth meant leaving Iran. No way to account for a sudden lavish lifestyle should he retire from the MOIS. Furthermore, Iran was no place to enjoy the kind of life he envisioned. As the ex-chief of foreign intelligence, openly leaving Iran was not an option. He must disappear. That required establishing a new foreign identity. Moreover, to fix on a country suitable to his lifestyle tastes while safely out of reach of his many domestic and foreign enemies.

Best to give it a couple of years. See what transpired now that Iran possessed these weapons. Enjoy the personal accolades and let some time pass before secretly leaving Iran. When that time comes, he shall just disappear into his new identity once outside the country.

Only a few months after the success of the mission, catastrophe struck. The headline story broke in the United States, European, and Russian media announcing the spectacular demise of the large international corporation Martinelli Global. Savi's interest focused however on an associated story a few days later. As the scandal widened, it enveloped the powerful Russian holding company Moscow Capital Partners, and its head, the prominent oligarch close to Putin, Nikolai Krasin.

In the United States, news video footage showed the arrest of executives of MGI, and the announced search for the Chairman and CEO Steven Martinelli now wanted as a fugitive. In Russia, the only media announcement was a terse short article appeared in *Izvestia* and short sixty-second segments on evening news broadcasts based on a released statement by the Russian state-owned *RIA Novosti* wire service. The report concluded with the statement that Russian businessman Nikolai Krasin was under arrest.

A week later, Russian news reported the suicide death of Krasin in the Lubyanka Prison.

A month later, more disturbing news appeared in the Western media. The scandal broke with evidence secured by an investigative reporter, Mark Reynolds. Promotions for his forthcoming book on the financial scandal, *Shell Game*, made an unrelated but astonishing assertion. Through hacked cellphone conversations, the author connected a close associate of the Russian oligarch Nikolai Krasin with the theft of Russian thermonuclear warheads. Reynolds suggested the recipient of the weapons most likely as Iran.

In an untraceable and coded online message in social media two weeks after the warheads arrived in Iran, Garnitsky informed Savi that Dratshev was no longer a threat. That welcomed prior news now overturned by news of the arrest of Krasin and the scandal enveloping Moscow Capital Partners. What did that mean for the fate of Garnitsky?

The continued fallout of the expanding corruption scandal of the American corporation MGI implicated Moscow Capital Partners' questionable business practices. More alarming was the revelation their subsidiary Rusatomic held government contracts to operate various state-owned nuclear facilities. The reporting in the foreign press clearly made the connection of those implicated in the international corruption scandal to the alleged nuclear warhead theft. Vladimir Putin's close association with Krasin indirectly implicated him in the widening scandal. Garnitsky was therefore already dead or gone into hiding.

If Garnitsky was still alive, it was only for limited time. The FSB had a long reach. Putin had a long memory and despised traitors. If captured, Garnitsky would give up Savi as the mastermind behind the theft in exchange for a merciful death.

Savi braced himself for the Russian response whether public or covert. Even though it would take the Russians some time before determining if functional warheads were missing by the false paper trail, they would eventually confirm the theft. With the hacked cellphone conversations published by Reynolds the Russians possessed the knowledge of the deaths of several army officers involved with Russian nuclear weapons unknown to the West. It would unravel quickly.

Over the next several weeks, Russian officials repeatedly denied any nuclear weapons were missing. A ridiculous fantasy according to Russian Foreign Minister Lavrov. The cellphone conversations related illicit activities involving Moscow Capital Partners. Nothing substantiates the wild claims of missing nuclear weapons. A brief statement from the Ministry of Justice announced the businessman Nikolai Krasin's immediate arrest, however choosing to commit suicide while in prison instead of facing trial. Others within his organization are also under arrest. As for one of his Krasin's subordinates, Feliks Garnitsky, mentioned in the cellphone conversations, he is charged with several illegal offenses related to smuggling and other financial wrongdoing. He remains a fugitive.

An investigation is underway to examine government contracts held by Moscow Capital's subsidiary Rusatomic. After a comprehensive security audit of all inventories, the Russian Federation emphatically declares no nuclear weapons are missing.

As for the Americans, the preoccupation of the Obama administration centered on concluding a nuclear agreement with Iran. The U.S. Secretary of State claimed the assertion of a theft of Russian nuclear warheads as journalistic speculation exploiting unsubstantiated evidence. Unhelpful in view of current negotiations with Iran by the United States and other major world powers including Russia, seeking an agreement to curtail Iranian nuclear weapons technology.

Secretary Kerry seemingly ignored the creditability of this journalist in bringing down a major international corporation with hard evidence of criminal wrongdoing obtained through great personal risk. A scandal involving Russia with one of the principal characters even identified in the alleged nuclear theft.

Publicly, Israel flatly stated such an event did not happen. What else could they say to avoid domestic panic?

Iran of course claimed this was journalistic sensationalism playing on anti-Iranian sentiment in the West.

Savi determined that if the Russians did confirm that warheads were missing, most likely they would never acknowledge the finding to the West. Far too much risk of accusing Putin of another audacious offensive move targeted at the United States by further destabilizing the Middle East.

Savi's own high-level contact within the Russian crime syndicate Solntsevskaya Bratva informed him that they liquidated Garnitsky on orders from Putin. They knew only that they assisted Savi's network in stealing nuclear material. They also knew Savi and Garnitsky cooperated in smuggling for years. Savi claimed the sanction on Garnitsky was about the financial scandal involving Moscow Capital and Rusatomic. Even the Solntsevskaya Bratva discounted the idea of stolen warheads as an exaggerated claim.

Savi conveyed to his superiors that Garnitsky was dead. No witnesses remained. He assured them the money funneled to Garnitsky would not implicate Iran in the warheads thefts. The money untraceable after funneling through cutout channels eventually comingling with Garnitsky's vast illicit financial transactions.

One year later President Rouhani signed the Iran nuclear agreement framework with the major world powers including the United States, the United Kingdom, France, Germany, the European Union, China, and even Russia. Iran agreed to limit uranium enrichment to less than weapons-grade level and the other signatories would eliminate associated sanctions.

The leadership faction knowing of the existence of the warheads continued to preserve secrecy. In light of the agreement and easing of sanctions, the weapons remained buried for some time. No scientists permitted to examine them. The Russians kept silent and so did Iran.

Two years after the theft of the warheads, the geopolitical landscape changed following the election of a new American president in 2016. A strident unpredictable aberration that caught the world off balance. To Iran, Trump was an avowed nationalist with virtually no knowledge of international affairs. Worse yet, his presidency swept into the U.S. Executive a number of senior officials harboring aggressive views toward Iran. Although probably an unilateral move, it was increasingly likely the United States would withdraw from the Iran Nuclear Agreement and reimpose sanctions. With the Trump administration's closer ties to the hawkish Israeli President Netanyahu, Iran could expect a new era of political pressure.

American-Iranian relations deteriorated immediately following the election of Donald Trump. Following his election, a select group of Iranian scientists and engineers gained access to the Russian warheads. Summoned to meet General Soleimani at his office at the Quds Force headquarters, Savi assumed a strategy was possibly forming for using Iran's newly gained nuclear capability.

Soleimani embraced Savi and offered tea. It was only the two of them.

"The time has finally come, Colonel. The Supreme Leader has agreed with a modified plan to move forward with our nuclear weapons program.

"President Rouhani is extremely upset with the United States withdrawal from the nuclear agreement. I sense he feels a personal betrayal by the Americans. They have lurched from a negotiated treaty to this new hardline stance. Iran has lost these last three years to advancing our stockpile of enriched uranium based on American lies.

"American Middle East imperialism increases with new threats with this new president while encouraging their surrogate partner Israel. Both speak of the potential for preemptive military strikes on Iran. Rouhani said it forces Iran to seek alternatives. Your successful theft of the warheads now presents us with new possibilities. Once the North Koreans learn of these weapons, Rouhani believes we can negotiate an arrangement with the DPRK. Our bartering position with the DPRK greatly elevates. With their assistance we may very well achieve an arsenal of nuclear weapons sufficient to blunt any American or Israeli military threat."

Savi nodded. No surprise since it was his idea to leverage acquisition of the weapons with the DPRK when originally selling the scheme for the theft. The 2015 agreement forestalled the leadership from acting on their possession of the Russian warheads at that time. Savi believed the delay was to allow the removal of sanctions to take effect while simultaneously forming a strategy to secretly move forward with a weapons program. Similar to the DPRK's years of delaying tactics while pursuing nuclear weapons development.

Soleimani continued, "Do you still have a close personal relationship with the woman intelligence official at the North Korean embassy, Colonel?"

Ye-jin Sung was a high-ranking intelligence agent in the North Korean embassy using the cover of third secretary for trade affairs. Ms. Sung was the daughter to a senior general and close to Kim Yo-jong, the younger sister of Dictator Kim Jong-un. Sung therefore had a direct pipeline to Kim Jong-un. Savi had used her as the secure conduit to funnel stolen Russian nuclear weapons intelligence gathered by his Azerbaijan network prior to the warhead theft.

The relationship turned intimate. Sung was ambitious as well as pretty. Even when his flow of intelligence stopped following the purge of the Russian Army officers, she maintain the sexual liaison. Savi told her only his intelligence penetration fell apart when the Russian FSB reassigned certain army officers under suspicion. Savi's relationship with Sung continued to serve as a back channel for Iranian leadership directly to Kim Jong-un.

So this was probably the reason Savi's superior, Minister Alavi was not present. As a cleric, Alavi was uncomfortable in discussing the use of sex in Savi's trade. The prostitutes that compromised Russian Army officers, or his rumored sexual intimacy with a North Korean spy.

"Yes. I see Miss Sung socially on occasion."

Soleimani already know that by his own intelligence.

"Then I have a new mission for you, Colonel. President Rouhani with the concurrence of Supreme Leader Khamenei wishes to explore opening negotiations with the DPRK. In broadest terms, we propose offering full access for their scientists and engineers to study the Russian warheads. In exchange, we expect to purchase North Korean produced enriched weapons-grade uranium and plutonium.

"Because of the sensitivity of exposing our possession of these weapons, you are to be entrusted with this mission. You are the best person to explain how these weapons came into our possession. Your established communications pipeline to the highest level of the DPRK shall now prove invaluable."

That opening up of direct access to the advanced design of the Russian warheads to North Korean technical experts appeared a windfall for North Korea. In 2017, they conducted six nuclear test detonations. The West estimated the sixth test at a yield of 120 kilotons. Eight times the yield of the Hiroshima bomb of 1945. The Russian warheads were more advanced and therefore physically smaller while more powerful.

A naked Ye-jin Sung walked from Savi's bed to a table holding an ice bucket with a bottle of Champagne. Not Savi's type, petite with small breasts, she nonetheless was an energetic sex partner. Of course, she was a practiced intelligence operative so he did not accept their relationship as anything more than fucking in the line of duty.

They enjoyed intimacy only sporadically. With Ye-jin, it was not romance but she seemed to enjoy sex. He wondered if she might have a lover in her embassy to fill her needs on a more regular basis. All he knew of her personal life was her age, forty, never married, and fanatically devoted to her parents and Kim Jung-un. A committed intelligence professional of the Reconnaissance General Bureau, the agency responsible for the DPRK's clandestine operations, she possibly reported directing to Kim Jung-un. Before the posting to Tehran, she served at DPRK embassies in China and Russia. Given her sexual proclivities, he assumed she used sex to entrap sources. Perhaps their sexual couplings were nothing more than the habit of an accomplished intelligence operative.

Returning to the bed with two refilled glasses after sex, she handed a glass to Savi.

Running her hand over Savi's hairy chest, she said in heavily accented English, their only language in common, "I like your hair, Farzard. Very arousing. Korean men are hairless."

Her hand moved from caressing his chest down to his genitals under the sheet.

"Not as well-endowed either."

No wonder Savi thought. Stunted growth through inadequate nutrition. As a result, small in stature possibly including penile development. He could not imagine living in North Korea even among the ruling elite. A shithole by any assessment. Kim Jong-un ran a Stalin-like paranoid police state where even the top people were never safe, even his own family members.

Back to business, she said, "I have some good news for you to pass along to your leadership, Farzard. Our Great Leader expresses his personal gratitude to Iran for sharing the Russian weapons design. And to you personally for achieving such a spectacular intelligence feat by stealing these from the Russians. He personally believes the access to the Russian technology already advances our weapons development efforts by years.

"To fulfill his part of the bargain, the Great Leader feels the DPRK is now in a position to share an initial quantity of enriched uranium with Iran. A quantity I understand sufficient to assemble two fission warheads of modest yield. He will also provide technicians to work alongside your technical people to develop an efficient weapons design, capable of missile delivery."

Savi's immediate reaction came from a personal perspective. With this new move, it would be difficult to maintain secrecy from the international community if the Iranian nuclear weapons program rebooted. Even without the need to enrich uranium, other technical processes difficult to conceal from Western surveillance remained. The number of people involved increased exponentially. Iran might quickly become untenable for Savi. He meant to enjoy his millions somewhere other than Iran's climate of oppressive theocracy. That meant a quiet escape from Iran not a rat leaving a ship under attack.

Up to now, Iran had kept secret the acquisition of the warheads. The Russians may well have discovered the falsified record trail, or the physical fuel inventory discrepancies. They certainly would have vigorously investigated given Garnitsky's exposure in the Moscow Capital scandal and the American journalist's book. Yet there was no outward change in Russian relations with Iran. If they did discover that warheads were missing, they logistically would attribute the operation to Garnitsky given his criminal background. Even so, they still must conclude the buyer to be Iran. Or might they suspect North Korea?

With Garnitsky and Dratshev dead, there was a chance Savi's name might not be connected with the operation. He hoped that to be the case. Putin had a long reach and a penchant for revenge.

CHAPTER 14

MANHATTAN, NEW YORK

The cascade of unsettling events since Prescott's fateful trip to Paris continued. The decision to enlist the help of the journalist and author Mark Reynolds to expose the details of the Russian warhead theft seemed the best way to fulfill her moral obligation. Now Reynolds' audacious plan to attempt to coerce the Iranian intelligence mastermind behind the theft presented a new level of anxiety.

Regardless of Reynolds' pursuit for a more dramatic story, her basic problem remained. Once the story released publicly, she could not insulate her from U.S. government scrutiny indefinitely. No way to escape giving over the information once confronted by the FBI. As yet another scandal involving Russia, the material on the illicit financial dealings of the Putin regime likely becoming compromised by this president's self-interest. The material classified under a cloak of national security. Academic access denied.

"Once you go public with the details of the Russian warhead theft, the U.S. government will come down on you to reveal the source of this information," Prescott said to Reynolds. "You won't be able to stonewall them for long. If Savi agrees to defect then you will have to offer that up immediately. That means me as well. And that means my other stuff will likely be blocked from publication by the government."

"Maybe not. That's what we need to discuss with Ellsberg."

They were having their morning coffee at Reynolds' apartment before launching into the day's work of compiling the press release exposing the theft of the warheads.

Reynolds said, "This other material? It's that powerful?"

"I read your book, *Shell Game*. The dirt you dug up brought down MGI and their Russian oligarch partner Krasin. This material is just as damaging. Incriminates Putin himself along with the entire Russian power structure, not to mention individuals, banks, and corporations outside Russia. A scandal of pandemic proportions."

"Damaging enough to cripple Putin?"

Prescott shrugged, "Hard to say. The damage internationally will undoubtedly be severe, especially coupled with the missing Russian nukes. Russia will become even more a pariah state. Domestically, who knows?"

"What about this idea, Victoria. Go public with the financial material immediately following the release of the missing Russian warheads evidence."

Prescott slammed her coffee cup down on the dining table. "Jesus, Mark. That's not even remotely possible. Novak and I need months to just assemble a coherent mapping of the Putin regime's financial dealings much less research each thread. It's a mass of complicated transactions using foreign shell companies just like MGI used according to your book. Then god knows how much more research time is needed to flesh out the details. Are you suggesting we wait before doing something about the nukes?"

"No. I am suggesting we release all the Russian material with its broader elements to the international media. Collectively, this is the story of the decade. Pare it down for public consumption. However, populate it with names, organizations, legal entities, and the flow of major money sufficient for government investigators to latch onto. You must have enough to assemble a fact-based story that will rivet the public and instigate official investigations."

"How's that help? Won't the U.S. government still try to suppress the scope of my work? Confiscate all my files? Threaten me in some way?"

"I don't think they'll be able to. They'll demand you turn over all materials you have, but that's irrelevant since you have dumped everything into the public domain therefore it cannot be classified. How can they suppress what is already out in the public domain? But that's why we need to talk to Ellsberg.

"Here's the other argument. You're not in this for the journalistic bang yet you already achieve that by delivering this massive scoop. You are however interested in the larger implications for your academic project. Nothing is lost there. In fact, you now have investigative journalists around the world in a feeding frenzy to further connecting the dots. Hundreds of collaborators with you as their clearing house if you play it right. Your initial story will breed a sustaining attack on Putin's criminal enterprise. All their findings only adding to your source material for your academic project.

Prescott understood Reynolds' strategy. Made sense but it still felt as if she would be giving up her story prematurely. Yet going public with everything probably was the only way out of her dilemma. They must get this information about the Russian warheads out there soon as a moral imperative. Counterintuitively, the only way to retain control of the financial corruption material was to release it publicly, even if prematurely. Reynolds reminded her that her interest was academic. So what if the material first made front-page headlines? That was Reynolds' expertise. Let him take the lead on that as well. He had the right background. The deeper implications for post-Soviet Russia remained for her and Novak to explore as part of their academic study. The preceding news release painting the current Russian government an undeniable criminal enterprise would only support their scholarly work exploring the larger implications.

This corrupt U.S. president with an inexplicable affinity for Vladimir Putin would find a way to impede any investigation into Russian international financial wrongdoing. Not only was this her story, but the only sure way of inflicting assured damage on Putin was a public dump of all the incriminating information. Reynolds idea made sense.

She said, "How long do we have to put together something? And should we even wait? What about the nukes?"

"Perhaps a few weeks if we work together. It's been four years since Iran acquired the warheads. A couple of more weeks doesn't change anything."

Prescott shook her head. "I don't know, Mark. Give me a couple of days to see if I can shape this into something collectively incriminating rather than just unconnected pieces."

As crazy as Reynolds' scheme to coerce Savi to defect seemed, she understood his motivation. If he pulled it off, the public release of the warhead theft gained greater impact by cooperation of a key participant. Following with the financial corruption material could prove overpowering for Putin.

Reynolds continued to sell the idea. "Listen, Victoria. You and your colleague are working toward a scholarly academic publication. That is what historians do. However, think of the advance promotional benefit for your finished book following the blockbuster media exposé of Russian corruption and nuclear irresponsibility. Another bestseller like your *Critical Mass.*

"This is your find, Victoria. I'm simply the journalist reporting the story of the tenacious academic and a defecting Russian spymaster teaming to bring down a corrupt autocrat threatening the world."

That approach appeared be the only way to do the right thing while preserving her use of the material. She was not a journalist looking for a scoop. She had original material from which to build on her current project of explaining the evolution of the Russian state since the collapse of the Soviet Union.

Reynolds also appeared to be the perfect collaborator for more than just the journalistic elements of making the material public. He was the author of two books. Both dealt with Russian subjects. Both dealt with the current circumstances revealed by Grigoryev's materials. *Nuclear Threats for Our Time* dealt largely with the uncertainty of the vast Soviet arsenal following the collapse of the USSR. *Shell Game* followed years later with the criminal financial empire of an American corporation partnered with a Russian oligarch. The shocking assertion that Russian nuclear weapons were missing now coming full circle.

Prescott's swirling confusions then came into focus. *This was not her story*. Not a product of her tenacious research and ingenuity like *Critical Mass*. It just fell into her lap from Anton Grigoryev. This was a real-life political thriller of global nuclear threat, spiced with intrigue and murder.

"I see what you mean, Mark. It does seem to solve my dilemma. I'm neither a journalist nor a writer of thrillers whether real or fiction. But you are. How about we collaborate? Once we make public everything we have, we each write our separate books?"

"Separate books? What do you mean," Reynolds asked.

"Come now, Mark. You want to go after Savi for the chance of a bigger story. Even if he does not defect, you have confirmed the lingering question you raised in *Shell Game*. You also have a hell of a non-fiction adventure thriller. Use the Dratshev's account to reconstruct the theft. God only knows what the aftermath of our revelations will cause. A perfect sequel.

"That's your arena. For me it is the broader implications of a new type Russian autocracy not seen since Stalin. What circumstances brought that about? What does this political trajectory portend? Does Russia become another Third World despotic, economically failed-state with an insecure arsenal of nuclear weapons? The deeper questions considered from broader academic research and conjecture. That's my arena."

Reynolds smiled broadly. "This is your find, Victoria. Aren't you being overly magnanimous by sharing this treasure?"

"Had I discovered something like the Rosetta Stone then I would not probably share. However, this is different. A straightforward news story. A startling discovery with potentially dire consequences for the world. Material that needs to become public as soon as possible. It needs the treatment of an investigative journalist."

"Okay. Since this is now a broader project than either of us envisioned, are you saying you want to move forward with simultaneously releasing the financial dirt on the Putin regime?"

"Yes. I can see no other way to retain control over the material Grigoryev dropped into my lap. I can't in good conscious withhold revealing for months that Iran now has Russian thermonuclear warheads. And even Putin laundering money in the United States needs immediate exposure."

"In that case, what about adding another resource to our band of conspirators?"

"What do you mean?"

"All that complicated financial maneuvering by MGI explained in my book *Shell Game* became understandable through the expertise of a colleague named Bernie Poole. He was the financial editor when I worked for the Daily Press. Indispensable contributions explaining the criminal connections of MGI and their Russian partner Moscow Capital. Knows a good deal about the current Russian oligarchs financial empires."

"Can he be trusted to keep this quiet?"

"I believe so. He retired when I left the paper but I've stayed in touch. He delighted in the challenge of untangling the financial legal maze we unearthed working on my project at the time. Took him out of the mind-numbing daily grind of covering boring Wall Street. Lives by himself in Brooklyn. He'll jump at the chance to get back in the game."

"Okay. Let me discuss that with my colleague, Josef Novak, an economics professor at Georgetown. How long can we postpone your ploy to approach Savi?"

Reynolds hesitated for a moment. Material like this had an uncertain shelf life. The sooner the better. Yet still a very long shot that Savi would defect. Therefore, the likely scenario had them going public solely with the evidence they had concerning the stolen warheads. Following immediately with a second blow would make the story earthshaking even without the Savi angle. He contemplated the longevity of the story by sustaining the attack on Putin with the serialization of continuing revelations of Russian financial wrongdoing.

"We don't have the luxury of much time. No telling what the Russians are up to after murdering Grigoryev. Let's say two weeks, no more than three. We must put together what to release about the financial wrongdoings during that time. We'll draft the press release about the stolen nukes first. That is easier since it's essentially Dratshev's detailing of the operation while we just explain the background and key players.

"Two weeks?" Prescott said thinking how to adequately translate and cover all the material in such a short time. "Guess I'll have to let Josef in on the stolen nukes to explain the urgency. And the reason to enlist additional help."

Having established a plan after the unrelenting uncertainty since going to Paris, a weight felt lifted from her shoulders.

"Thank you, Mark?"

He smiled. "It's me who should be thanking you for inviting me to participate in such a journalistic triumph, Victoria. Got a lot of work ahead of us, shall we get to it?"

Prescott first needed to tell Josef Novak of the change in plans. Not enough time for her to train down to Washington and explain in person.

"Josef, it's Victoria," she said as he answered his office telephone. "Something's come up. It has to do with that material we acquired. After I left you, I returned to New York. I looked up the author of that book that led to the collapse of MGI."

"I don't understand, Victoria? He's a journalist. Don't tell me you shared this Russian material with him?"

"There's something else that I needed his advice about. Something that changes our timetable, Josef. I can't explain on the phone. Can you come up to New York tomorrow?"

"Tomorrow? That's somewhat difficult. Can't you come down here?"

"Please, Josef. I'm here with Mark Reynolds. Best if we meet in New York considering this new urgency. I know it's an imposition but you'll understand when I explain."

Novak reluctantly agreed. He would show up at Reynolds apartment the following afternoon.

She and Reynolds spent the rest of the morning preparing the press release exposing the evidence for Russian nuclear warheads in the hands of Iran. A straightforward piece of work framed around the Dratshev confession.

Prescott began with her connection to Anton Grigoryev. His intended defection before his murder. Reynolds followed with the background of Feliks Garnitsky from his work on *Critical Mass*. The closing concluded with the range of speculations of Russian complicity, Iranian motives with the theft occurring during the period of negotiations for the Iran Nuclear Agreement, and the range of consequences. How would Russia respond? Would they claim the entire story as a CIA contrived fiction? Would the United States respond with calls for severe sanctions on Iran, or with military threat? Would Israel threaten military action or unilaterally launch air strikes?

Prescott suggested they publish the original Russian documents accompanied by her translations to bolster the authenticity of the source material.

Reynolds contacted Bernie Poole. Told him he was working a new story. Bigger even than the *Shell Game* project. Was Poole interested in lending his expertise to untangling another financial criminal conspiracy? Poole agreed to meet for lunch.

Prescott and Reynolds returned to the Finnegan's Wake tavern. Poole was already there.

A small slender man in his late middle age. Wire rim glasses and thinning gray hair. Always a smart dresser, Reynolds was happy to see Poole had not retreated into a disheveled retirement as he sported a stylish blazer and slacks. He knew Poole left the newspaper under a cloud. Involvement in some impropriety but he never confided specifics to Reynolds.

"Bernie, so good to see you?" Reynolds said.

Poole stood and extended his hand to Reynolds but quickly changed his attention to Prescott.

"This is Victoria Prescott, Bernie. Professor Prescott. We're working together on a project."

"Pleasure to meet you, Professor," Poole said shaking her hand. "And with what university are you associated?"

"Stanford. History is my field."

After they all sat down, a waiter arrived taking drink orders. Poole ordered a Guinness while Reynolds and Prescott stuck with coffee. They had a full afternoon of intense work ahead, better not dulled by alcohol.

"Let me get right to the point, Bernie. Professor Prescott has come into possession of some extraordinary material. Russian in origin. Some of it reminiscent of the MGI and Moscow Capital web of interlocking legal entities spanning the globe. I'll let her explain."

"In the course of doing research on a current academic project, some material fell into my lap," she said. "Highly incriminating material of Russian corrupt financial dealings in the West. I came to Mr. Reynolds because of his work several years ago in the MGI scandal. While my academic project has a broader scope, I feel this material must be publicly exposed immediately."

Poole said, "And the urgency?"

Prescott looked at Reynolds and nodded.

"Something else came into the Professor's possession that has a shorter shelf-life. Before we get into specifics, Bernie, are you available to work with us? Maybe a two-week stint. Actually working with Victoria's colleague, a Georgetown economics professor by the name of Josef Novak."

"Novak? I know the name from years ago. Read some of his articles. Smarter than a lot of economists and financial experts like me. He identified the vulnerabilities of the U.S. financial market's house of cards. Unlike the rest of us, he got it right by anticipating the 2008 Wall Street-driven recession debacle.

"And to your question, I'm available. Haven't done anything interesting these last few years. Retirement is not all it's cracked up to be."

"Can't promise you much compensation, only some share of what we get for selling the story. Journalistic credit of course."

"Money's not my problem, Mark, just boredom. When do we start?"

"Right after lunch," Reynolds said.

They returned to Reynolds's apartment. Prescott explained the material related to the financial issues so far translated. She wanted to get a sense of Poole's grasp of the international financial maneuvering of Putin's functionaries. How much could he contribute given the short time frame?

For Reynolds it would be his first glimpse of what Prescott claimed to be earthshaking. Something far more pervasively sinister than Russian business deals or Russian bank loans to Trump or his son-n-law Kushner.

Prescott took charge. Although feeling as if she was giving up her personal trove of information, she was anxious to move forward and offload this troubling burden. She wanted nothing more than to return to San Francisco and quiet academic life.

With Reynolds and Poole seated in the living room, she plugged her notebook computer into the large screen television.

"Professor Novak and I have been working with a large cache of electronic files for the last two weeks. A great deal more work remains. However, you will agree that what we have is explosive from different perspectives. It's slow going because the source material is all in Russian. I'm the translator. There's no summary because we have not gotten that far. I was not expecting to do a crash project in order to go public. We'll explain the reason for the urgency later. This should give you a sense of what we have."

"How did you come by this material, Professor?" Poole asked.

"A disaffected Russian, Bernie," Reynolds answered for her. "Victoria will also explain those circumstances later. Right now we need to get a sense of the scope of her material."

Prescott brought up the first file on the screen.

"I will broadly summarize this material as a blueprint for the current Russian regime to steal Russian assets then launder billions of dollars abroad. All controlled by a group of Russian officials and private sector power brokers. Undoubtedly under the direction of Vladimir Putin. A massive conspiracy like some African dictatorial regime. These are original files naming people and institutions. Bad enough if these criminal profits remained internal to Russia, but the documents reveal the launder assets transforming into predominately Western investments.

"This is similar to the *Panama Papers* leaked a couple of years ago implicating all sorts of politicians and others from around the world hiding vast sums of money in secretive places. Another Panamanian law firm like the one that set up the tax haven secret accounts for the world's despots as revealed in the *Panama Papers* is also instrumental in this Russian enterprise. This firm however exclusively handles Russian legal work. And it's not just about concealing money out of sight.

"The data suggests the stolen Russian assets become laundered into investments outside Russia. Legitimate investments intended to generate a return. This is evidence of Vladimir Putin heading what might be the largest criminal enterprise in the world. Outright theft of state assets and corrupt profits laundered into Western investments. Only possible in Putin's police state."

"And this list of names, corporations, and such?" Poole said.

Prescott said, "Like I said, there's no prepared summary so I thought I'd just lead off with this list. What you are looking at is a list of people and entities complicit in these secret financial transactions. Both Russian and Western conspirators. I'm sure some of these names are familiar to both of you."

Poole leaned forward in his chair while Reynolds stood up.

Reynolds exclaimed, "Holy shit! Your material names all these?"

Before Prescott could answer, Poole exclaimed, "And you're saying your material explains what these guys are up to?"

Prescott said, "Yes. More than explains. Implicates with specifics. This is original source material. Highly sensitive material stolen directly from FSB databases."

Poole looked at Prescott with an expression of amazement. "And the source?"

"An FSB operative intimately involved with constructing this ...whatever this is called. Might have broader implications than just Putin and his cronies lining their pockets."

"Is your source known? Is he still in place?" Poole said.

"The source is dead."

"Jesus. Then the Russians know this material is missing?"

Reynolds answered, "No way for us to know. But that's why I persuaded Victoria that we need to go public as soon as possible."

Prescott added, "To do develop a full picture of this Russian investment infiltration into the West will take months of work for team of researchers."

"But we don't have that kind of time," Reynolds said. "So we've decided we must go public in three weeks before the Russians start covering their tracks. That's where we need your help."

Poole shook his head in dismay and mumbled, "Three weeks?"

Reynolds continued, "Once it becomes public, the U.S. administration cannot downplay this as they have done with other outrageous moves by Vladimir Putin. If the public outcry is loud enough, the collective resources of Western intelligence and law enforcement will mount operations to penetrate the veil of secrecy of foreign business-friendly tax haven countries.

"Once the genie is out of the bottle with a host of pissed off countries feeling political pressure to act, the Russian scheme becomes exposed in detail. Even if government agencies try to maintain secrecy, leaks to the media will sustain unrelenting public pressure."

Prescott continued with her overview, "The material essentially provides the framework of the Russian operation. It identifies the players. However, the opaqueness of using interconnected shell companies in tax haven countries lacking banking transparency obscures the money trail. The task will be to connect the two sides of this wall of secrecy, the Russian side and the international investment side."

"Here is a rough flow chart Josef Novak and I plotted from our initial work on the material. Having to translate makes for slower going. From the documents we know more about the Russians than their conspirators outside Russia. That requires much further investigative work."

Poole said, "The principals seem to be the oligarchs Alexei Balakin and Sergei Terekov?"

"Certainly they're the key players in the Russian private sector, if there really is such thing. On the government side is the Chairman of the Board of Governors of the Central Bank of Russia, Dimitri Marakrov, Putin's own banker the Minister of Economic Development, Ilya Rabrenovich, and the head of the sanctioned bank Rossiya, Oleg Sochinsky. The name of General Valerik Mikhalitsyn, Director of the FSB appears often in these files.

"Note the names of Eurasian Energy, RusEnergy, and SLT Bank. These are Terekov enterprises with management contracts in the Russian nuclear industry, including the nuclear weapons sector. Contracts formerly held by the oligarch Krasin who met a bad end after implication in the Martinelli Global international scandal uncovered by Mark."

Reynolds said, "The name Boris Lebedyenko adds another sinister aspect. Russian Mafia. He's an important figure in Russia's largest organized crime syndicate, Solntsevskaya Bratva.

"How's he implicated?" Poole asked.

"We haven't gotten that far," Prescott said looking at Reynolds. "Where his name appears suggests perhaps smuggling to circumvent sanctions. Needs more work to see how the Russian Mafia profits."

Both Prescott and Reynolds knew the connection went beyond smuggling. Solntsevskaya Bratva worked all opportunities within the corrupt Russian state. Having helped the Iranian Savi penetrate Russian nuclear installations, they then murdered those Army officers involved in the warhead theft. A Savi and Dratshev deception portrayed as smuggling Russian enriched nuclear fuels to a Middle East client. Years of profitable collaboration with Feliks Garnitsky made Solntsevskaya Bratva a willing conspirator.

Josef Novak arrived at Reynolds apartment by taxi midafternoon.

Prescott answered the door after Novak buzzed the entrance intercom.

"Josef, thank you for coming," she said wrapping him in an embrace.

"You're difficult to resist, Victoria."

"Come in and I'll introduce you to Mark Reynolds and his associate, Bernie Poole."

After introductions, Prescott got to the point.

"I wasn't entirely candid with you Josef. The material I acquired from General Grigoryev included something else beyond the financial wrongdoings of his regime. That's the reason I came to see Mark.

"I felt a moral obligation to do something immediately but I didn't want to involve you or father. I also didn't want to risk the government confiscating and burying this treasure trove of dirt on Putin."

Bernie Poole said, "Excuse me Professor, you say your source was this Russian Grigoryev? The Russian intelligence officer reported murdered in Paris a week ago?"

"Yes. Lieutenant General Anton Vladimirovich Grigoryev, first deputy director of the Russian foreign intelligence service, the SVR. A benefactor that assisted in my research twenty years ago.

"Disgusted by Putin's corruption, he and his brother-in-law conspired to amass this highly confidential body of material. Russian security discovered the brother-in-law's unauthorized access forcing Grigoryev to flee Russia. He approached me as a back channel to arrange his defection while he hid in France. The information he gave me was his admission for asylum and a new identity in the United States.

"But even with Grigoryev's murder, obviously on orders from the Kremlin, they may not know the extent of what we have. He likely secured copies of the material carefully. However, this financial corruption is not the urgent reason I've asked you here. I'll let Mark explain."

"Bernie of course is familiar with my project of several years ago that lead to the demise of MGI. At the end of my book, *Shell Game,* I made a seemingly wild assertion that Russian thermonuclear warheads were missing. Hacked cellphone conversations suggested a theft operation with the nukes smuggled into Iran. But I had no corroborating evidence. The story dismissed for lack of indisputable evidence.

"That is the reason for urgency. We now that undeniable evidence. Victoria did not reveal to you that Grigoryev also passed to her Russian classified intelligence documentation confirming Russian thermonuclear warheads were in fact stolen in 2014."

Novak exclaimed, "Oh god. You're absolutely sure?"

Prescott said, "I'll show you my translation of a confession of the person on the ground overseeing the theft. A confession made to his brother fearing for his life because of what he knew. He explains the ingenious operation in detail.

"Now you see the urgency," Reynolds said.

"I don't understand, Victoria. Just turn over the material about the theft to the government," Novak said.

"I'm not going to do that. Mark agrees. The government might just bury it. They will certainly confiscate everything we have on the Putin regime. Classify everything and get a court order to suppress everything based on overriding national security interests. I remember the hard time I got from the FBI twenty years ago. So to protect our find we'll go public with everything."

Reynolds added, "Once public, there's no basis for the government to suppress."

"We can then proceed with our broader academic work, Josef," Prescott said.

Novak looked at her. "Don't be so sure about that, Victoria. This is kicking a hornets' nest. Lots of powerful bad characters involved. Russian and American."

She thought if her colleague only knew that they were planning to approach Savi to coerce his defection, he would bolt immediately from being part of such a screwball scheme.

Parked on the opposite side of the street from Reynolds' apartment building was a white delivery van with commercial markings advertising a security systems company. At the wheel sat a driver. Within the van interior sat a young woman at a console viewing three computer monitors. One monitor displayed a closed circuit video camera focused on the front entrance of the building. The other display was a street map with two different colored blinking lights. A third displayed the view for from a remote controlled digital camera with zoom lens and motor-driven shutter. Centered now on the building entrance, the camera could take high resolution images in rapid sequence.

The woman spoke into a microphone attached to her headset.

"Seventeen thirty-hours surveillance report. Female subject A and male subject B remain in apartment as indicated by cellphones GPS."

The blinking lights signified cellphone locations obtained from hacked access into the service provider system. The client of the private investigation firm running the surveillance was the law firm of Mallory, Smith & Reinhart. The investigation firm often engaged in illegal activities for their most lucrative client. As usual, the ubiquitous cover story being pending litigation, gathering compromising political material, or other suitable inventions.

This and another van similarly equipped rotated surveillance after tracking Victoria Prescott to Reynolds' address. Video footage and close-up stills of everyone entering or leaving the apartment building since her arrival the day before captured the images of Bernie Poole and Josef Novak. Identifying all the faces of the other tenants and their visitors required considerable investigative resources.

Mallory, Smith & Reinhart's best client was a Cayman Island law firm whose sole client was the *Federal'naya Sluzhba Bezopasnosti Rossiyskoy Federatsii*, the Russian Federal Security Service, successor to the former Soviet era KGB. Reynolds immediately became a person of special interest from a list of all the building tenants once his online background revealed him as an investigative journalist and author of a book unflattering toward Russia.

Should either Prescott or Reynolds leave the apartment, the surveillance van personnel would radio a mobile team parked in a car two hundred yards away to take up the surveillance by car or foot.

"Nineteen-thirty-two hours, surveillance alert," the woman at the console said into the microphone. Female subject A and male subject B exiting the building. Accompanied by two middle-aged men walking east on 67th Street. See video feed timestamped 19:30 to 19:32 hours. Mobile team alerted to take up foot-surveillance."

CHAPTER 15

MANHATTAN, NEW YORK

Over drinks and dinner, Prescott, Reynolds, Novak, and Poole strategized the tasks necessary to compile a coherent media story within the short span of two weeks. Reynolds and Poole understood seemingly impossible deadlines from their newspaper days. Prescott and Novak wrestled with having to rush the product. It ran counter to the methodical and careful pursuit of academic protocols.

Novak remained uneasy about the entire plan to make public such earth shattering information. Without saying so, he harbored professional concerns about possible adverse publicity. How was he to explain why they did not take the obvious route and turn this over to the proper U.S. authorities? Would they be labeled a group of antigovernment conspirators or opportunistic headline seekers? Tenure would not protect against damage to his professional reputation.

After Reynolds suggested to everyone not to communicate anything related to the *project* via cellphone, Novak commented, "Now this sounds even more nefarious. Who are we afraid of?"

Reynolds said, "Just a precaution. We want to control this information, not leave it to this administration as yet another Russian threat for President Trump to obsess over. No telling his reaction. Cellphones are just not secure."

Prescott added, "And frankly I'm paranoid about the Russians since they murdered Grigoryev. What if they somehow link me as having been in Paris before they killed him? That's reason enough for me wanting to get this out there to remove any possibility of a target on my back."

Novak nodded. As a longtime close friend and colleague of her father, he was genuinely fond of Victoria Prescott as he watched her career develop. She was the sole reason for his participation in this dubious venture.

"What about emails, Mark? They're not exactly secure either," Bernie Poole said.

"Good point. However, we have little choice. Have to communicate by some means," Reynolds said. "But let's make that more difficult for hacking. All of us should set up new Google email accounts with some obscure address. Continue to use your personal or professional email addresses for everything except communications about our project."

Prescott said, "Here's my idea for the division of tasks given the tight time frame. I will continue to review and translate what I think to be the most pertinent or damning documents then distribute to all of you.

"Mark will research the publicly available information on all the people mentioned. He will construct bios and cite any known or rumored associations. Mark will also finish editing the release related to the nuclear warhead theft based around the translation of the detailed confession of the guy supervising the operation.

"Josef, we'll rely on you to explain the macro elements of the financial schemes perpetrated by the Putin regime. Where and how they have concealed billions in looted Russian money. Perhaps you can also use your former State Department contacts to add to the available backgrounds of all these Russians referenced in the documents. What are their affiliations? What do they actually do? How are they connected within the regime?

"Bernie, according to Mark you are particularly skilled at connecting the dots to make sense of this maze of entangled legal entities. Show how the money moves out of Russia using shell companies in tax haven countries then ends up laundered into U.S. or European investments. Explain in such a way as any reasonably intelligent reader can understand. Mark says that's what you did to unravel Martinelli Global's financial empire.

"Mark and Bernie will then draft the final press release. They're the journalists. There is enough material to allow dividing into segments for a serialized series of releases over weeks to give the story sustaining inertia. Did I cover everything, Mark?"

"Most thoroughly, Victoria. I'll add this comment. This is internationally explosive material with wide ranging implications. At the top of the list is a nuclear armed Iran. Not an arsenal, only three powerful weapons, and perhaps with no viable method of delivery. Nonetheless, the world will react. Perhaps with another regional war. The Israelis might immediately contemplate a preemptive military attack. The Saudis will elevate their state of readiness. Once exposed, no telling the Iranian reaction. No way to predict the U.S. response but given this administration's posture toward Iran, military action of some nature is likely, probably in coordination with the Israelis. Hard to predict how the world reacts toward Russia.

"The other corruption stuff should prove an unprecedented scandal for Putin. Domestically he has such a dictatorial grip on Russia he can probably weather the storm. However, the rest of the world will further relegate Russia to a pariah state, especially with the missing nuclear warheads. Increased sanctions, severely curtailed trade, and exclusion from Western capital markets could well tank the Russian economy. Impossible to predict the reaction in the United States with another major scandal involving a new form of Russian intrusion."

Following dinner, Novak and Poole left the restaurant by taxi with Novak getting a late train at Grand Central Station to return to Washington. Prescott and Reynolds walked back to his apartment enjoying the warm evening.

All four harbored decidedly different perspectives on what lie ahead. Josef Novak clearly was uneasy about releasing the information publicly. At the least, all of them faced intense scrutiny by the FBI when the story broke. Novak understood the logic of the ploy to go public rather than turn the material over, but still dreaded the aftermath.

However the prospect of working on this material delighted Bernie Poole. A welcome diversion from his dull routine as an investment adviser since leaving the Daily Press. It brought back the thrill of financial detective work with Reynolds on the MGI story.

Mark Reynolds was right in his element. For an investigative journalist, this could not be bigger. Stolen nukes, the prospect of an unexpected Middle East military confrontation, Russian financial corruption spilling over into the United States. What could be better? Chance also favored him again by teaming with a like-minded attractive colleague. His weakness for smart women.

A constant barrage of the thrill of discovery, tempered with endless misgivings, and the specter of real danger considering the adversary, proved unsettling for Victoria Prescott. Everything clouded in uncertainty brought only a sense of dread.

During her pursuit of the undiscovered WWII Soviet spy, the task may have been daunting, but always straightforward, mostly academic research. Only when confronting the elderly spy did things become personal. Everything about this was intensely personal. Not even sure how it would play into her current academic project. Grigoryev murdered only a day after she left Paris. Could easily have been her as well. Reynolds not only convincing her to go public but also wanting to double down by coercing this Iranian spy to defect. His explanation logical but still wildly crazy.

Then there was Mark Reynolds. A real buccaneering investigative journalist and interesting raconteur recounting his career. She could not deny her physical attraction to Reynolds after these few days. A longtime since being seriously involved with a man. Relationships never seemed to develop deeply enough. Self-examination concluded the failures to be largely her fault.

Bad pairing? Too particular or self-absorbed for a relationship? Yet in spite of her intellectualizing, she still had emotional and physical needs. Being over fifty only intensified her doubts.

All these conflicted emotions occupied her thoughts as they walked. If only this could be just a summer night's stroll in New York with a handsome, interesting man.

As the taxi with Novak and Poole pulled away from the restaurant, a car followed. Engrossed in conversation, neither Prescott nor Reynolds noticed the unobtrusive foot surveillance by a changing team following them as they returned to the apartment.

The following day Prescott began a preliminary draft summary of the work she and Novak accomplished before bringing Reynolds into the picture. While still incomplete with a long list of documents still requiring translation, it would help Reynolds and particularly Bernie Poole to understand the scope of the Russian regime's secret financial activity.

After hours of work, she handed Reynolds several pages off the printer.

"Take a look at this draft opening summary, Mark. More than these damning revelations we will make public, Josef and I need to explore the macro implications of what this means for the future of Russia. Putin is into his fourth term as President. Can he circumvent the constitutional presidential term limit again? After serving two terms, Putin installed his man Dmitry Medvedev as President while he took on the role of Prime Minister to wait out one presidential cycle. Would he dare try that again or has his power grown sufficiently to arrange for a constitutional change? Difficult to see Putin leaving his unchallenged position of power. Neither will his gang of thieves willingly relinquish their lucrative criminal enterprises. But that's an academic challenge that will take much longer."

Reynolds took the hardcopy pages from her.

'As a result of two disaffected Russian intelligence operatives, the world now understands that Russia is governed by an autocratic kleptocracy with a despot in control. A state-run criminal enterprise on an unprecedented scale, surpassing anything previously seen in Third World dictatorships. At the head of this Russian criminal enterprise is President Vladimir Putin. As will be shown in the documented evidence, Putin is clearly directing the systematic looting of state funds, theft of state-owned assets, avoidance of taxes, and circumvention of Western economic sanctions. Yet only the West offers profit-making investment mechanisms to conceal the vast sums of money involved. Therefore elaborate means of laundering the illicit funds by concealing the true origin, becomes essential to funnel these funds through the international banking system. Russian government officials and their private sector oligarch conspirators hold title to these laundered assets. They exercise control through an obscure trail of ownership involving foreign subsidiaries based in tax haven countries. These are countries with tax and banking laws preventing any reporting of transactions, scrutiny of the sources of funds, or ownership to any foreign government.

The whistle-blower source of these secret documents was a ranking officer in the Russian Security Service, the FSB. He worked directly on designing the financial schemes, subsequently stealing electronic copies of incriminating documents. Discovered, he took his own life before arrest. His accomplice was his brother-in-law, the number-two man in the Russian Foreign Intelligence Service, the SVR. He also is dead, murdered in Paris a month ago. France now considers the murder of General Anton Grigoryev to be a Russian state-sponsored assassination.

Fortunately for the world while in hiding before his murder, Grigoryev prepared for defection to the United States by preserving evidence of the Putin regime's crimes.'

Reynolds looked up from his reading and said to Prescott, "A powerful intro. Sets the stage and the expectations of what will follow."

Prescott said, "The rest of this cites the various origins of the money and the means for moving the money out of Russia. We have a sense where some of the money winds up in the United

States and Europe, however the details of how it is laundered remains unclear. As you encountered in the Martinelli Global and Moscow Capital affair in your book *Shell Game*, layers of tax haven shell companies and straw men fronts make it difficult to connect the source of the funds to the laundered destination.

"Josef will expand with much more detail of course. And Poole probably can add some insights."

'The span and scale of these illicit funds amounting to billions of dollars is breathtaking in its audacity. The origins of the money covers every conceivable opportunity when the thief controls the enterprises and all regulatory and law enforcement, plus repressing a free press.

At the heart of this criminal enterprise is the conspiracy of tightly organized high-ranking government officials with selected private sector oligarchs. The origin of the money comes from government non-bid contracts, cost-plus contracts with falsified accounting, discriminatory licensing, inflated pricing, falsified records of product deliveries and services, grants for nonexistent research, defaults on government-underwritten loans, tax avoidance, controlled market sector monopolies, and outright smuggling of state-owned assets.

Yet the architecture of this sophisticated criminal financial enterprise does not end with the theft from the Russian economy. Nor is the money just hidden away in bank accounts in secretive foreign countries. These schemes intend for the unlawful funds to appreciate through investment in secure domains outside Russia. To accomplish that requires elaborate laundering schemes since funds of this size must move through international banking systems and withstand scrutiny. Once these funds comingle with assets involving legitimate investors, the funds are not only hidden, but also protected against confiscation by foreign governments.

Maintaining disciplined secrecy among the conspirators is the same as for any criminal enterprise. Beyond the lure of greed, the regime invokes coercion, the threat of ruin and imprisonment, and the implicit threat of physical harm including murder.

There is no rule of law in today's Russia. Opponents of the regime of all types are routinely imprisoned on contrived criminal charges or die under questionable circumstances. Gone is the brief period of hope for a democratized Russia Federation following the collapse of the Sovi-

et Union. Vladimir Putin's rise to power in 2000 changed any such allusions within only a few years. Russia has since increasingly moved closer to now resembling something closer to the Stalinist era repression of the fifties rather than even the later Soviet decades. Vladimir Putin possesses a penchant for personal gain perhaps as another expression of power to compliment his outsized international ambitions. The power of this modern-day Russian strongman surpasses any Soviet era leader other than Stalin.

Documented evidence describes the mechanism for moving of these vast sums of money out of Russia. The first obstacle for the conspirators in moving substantial sums of money out of Russia involves concealing its origin as it enters the international banking system. Therefore, the money initially passes into shell Russian companies or straw men front enterprises. Easily accomplished with no government regulatory oversight. In turn, these sham enterprises move funds disguised as revenue streams and operational expenses through Russian banks cooperating in the conspiracy.

The majority of funds flow through two colluding banks, Rossiya and Chelyabinsk Commercial, both sanctioned by the United States after Russian annexation of Crimea in 2014. This of course inhibits their ability to move money internationally. Various government officials closely associated with Putin represent the principal shareholders of both banks. Many documents specifically implicate these individuals in a broad conspiracy of illegal transactions.

The funds then move from these closely controlled banks through the Russian Central Bank. Evidence points to direct control by Putin personally working through Dimitri Markarov, Chairman of the Board of Governors of the Central Bank of Russia, and Oleg Sochinsky, Minister of Finance.

The Bank of Russia then secretly moves money for Rossiya and CCB through international banks ultimately into the dark hole of offshore tax haven companies. A practice legitimately used by all major corporations in the world as well as criminal enterprises and corrupt governments. While legitimate corporations use such foreign subsidiaries for legal tax advantage, illegal enterprises use the secrecy and the inability to access these foreign shell companies by foreign regulatory authorities to conceal their activities. These tax haven host countries tout the advantage of almost absolute secrecy. No financial accounting is required, nor any registering of officers, partners, shareholders, etcetera. The perfect repository for illegal money. Obscuring the audit trail further, business is often transacted through a secondary layer of foreign subsidiaries.

These foreign shell corporations then invest the money outside Russia or maintain deposit accounts in secretive banking countries, specifically, Switzerland, Liechtenstein, and Panama. By this time the illicit origins of the money have been laundered away often through multiple washings.

Documented evidence points to Alexei Balakin, the prominent banking and financial services Russian oligarch as orchestrating this elaborate blueprint to launder and conceal money derived from a range of illegal sources.'

"I love it. Sounds like the opening statement at trial by a U.S. district attorney," Reynolds said. "A reasonably intelligent reader could follow without being familiar with the legal structure of business or international banking."

Handing him several more pages, Prescott said, "The rest of the draft cites some of the specifics we've already culled from the material," Prescott said. "Here's a partial list of names and entities with their relevant connections Josef and I assembled, cross-referenced to the source document. Maybe Poole can unearth additional information fitting them into a larger picture."

Reynolds scanned the pages listing individuals and business names.

"You're saying there is evidence that Russian dirty money wound up invested in U.S. real estate?

"Yes. Apparently in a very big way it seems. Probably well into the billions."

"Jesus. And the large hedge fund, RK Investments, is involved? Holy shit! RK's CEO, Russell Koning, is tight with Trump."

"So far we haven't discovered anything that incriminates them as conspirators, but documents identify investments from hundreds of tax haven LLCs. Not only these offshore shell companies but also several European investment funds are mentioned adding another layer of complexity to the money trail. Josef has not yet determined how Russian money flows to them without causing Western banking scrutiny. So there's a lot of work needed to map the money flow through these secret shell companies."

"Well that's where Bernie can help. Other than RK Investments and the two sanctioned Russian banks, none of these names means anything to me. However, the connections you have cited will give him a starting point to work backwards and forwards.

"I already forwarded the information to him. And what have you been working on all day?" she asked.

"Planning the specifics for making contact with Farzard Savi. Listen to this. A draft of the message I'll deliver to his Lebanese girlfriend in Beirut. If he doesn't defect, he'll at least know he is generally fucked."

'My name is Mark Reynolds. I am an investigative journalist. Perhaps you know my name? Recall my book Shell Game*? About your Russian friend Felix Garnitsky's involvement in an international financial scandal. Of course, he was involved in something far more sinister as you well know. Recall the intercepted hacked cellphone conversations between him and Yuri Dratshev included in my book? Those exchanges and photos led me to make the allegation of the theft of Russian nuclear warheads.*

Russia of course denied the theft. The U.S. and even Israel discounted my allegation. Iran has done a remarkable job in keeping this a secret for four years. Time has now run out. The consequences for Iran and you personally will soon prove dire.

Wondering how I got your name? Another whistle-blower. Are you familiar with the term? In this, case a dissident Russian intelligence officer seeking to embarrass the Putin regime. Russian intelligence assembled an extensive dossier on Farzard Savi, head of the foreign intelligence directorate of the Ministry of Intelligence and Security. Or your alternate working cover name Farhad Sattari, a trade bureaucrat within the Iranian Ministry of Economic Affairs and Finance. Classi-

fied documents reveal that Russia knows of the theft of the nuclear warheads, and the part you played.

From that dossier I learned of your romantic relationship with Professor Leila Hajjar of the American University Beirut. She presented the perfect means of secretly delivering you this message.

Both Garnitsky and Dratshev are now dead. However before Dratshev met his fate he set down in writing every detail of the theft. Read for yourself the original document attached. All the way from every step of the warhead theft in Chelyabinsk Oblast to shipment of the warheads to Iran from the Caspian Sea Port of Astrakhan on the vessel, Caspian Princess *concealed within the tank of a large industrial compressor. I assume your Russian is still adequate. You may ask why would Yuri Dratshev commit this confession to writing? Because he feared also ending up dead just like those he ordered killed. A post-death revenge entrusted to his estranged Orthodox monk brother secluded in a Greek monastery.*

The Russians therefore know what happened and for obvious reasons have kept the incident secret. Not very well as it turned out since I am now in possession of their secret intelligence files. My compliments since that evidence names you as the mastermind behind the theft. A national hero in Iran I assume. I suspect that will dramatically change once this material becomes public. Obviously disclosure will alter the Iranian strategic plan held in secret. Might your Supreme Leader now see you as a liability as the weight of the United States and their surrogate Israel conceivably take military action against Iran?

Your choice is this. Defect to the United States before this becomes public. I will make the right contacts within the U.S. government to facilitate your asylum in return for your assistance in understanding the location and Iran's intent for these weapons. You get to live and I get a larger story. Decline the offer and everything I have still becomes known to the world.

I am no longer in Beirut. Not foolish enough to attempt direct contact in a location you can control. I will be in the Piazza Navona in Rome near the great fountain between 13:00 and 15:00 hours on Saturday and again on Sunday. I will be alone although someone will watch me from a distance. Should you attempt to harm or abduct me, it will not prevent everything from becoming immediately public. If I per-

sonally do not present myself in person at a particular place in New York City on Tuesday morning, a prepared story along with the source documentation will be released to the international news media. You therefore have little time to make your decision.

Since this will be me personally making contact, and given my past unpleasant experiences involving Russians, this is not likely a Russian intelligence ploy. I have also not yet contacted U.S. authorities. I am working for my own interests as a freelance journalist.

Whether you choose this option to save your life or prefer your chances in Iran, I still have my story and Iran suffers its fate. I will see you in Rome, or your picture displayed on television and newspaper front pages of the world.'

"What do you think?" Reynolds said.

Prescott shook her head. "I still think it's a terrible risk. He'll understand the threat. Like a cornered animal, he might retaliate rather than embrace the logic of your alternative. Might he not just kill you in Rome and take his chances on the run?"

"Possible of course. But reading Savi's dossier, I doubt he will react emotionally. Nor as a martyr. He is not a practicing Muslim. Self-serving, ambitious. A risk-taker but not reckless. Going into hiding with every intelligence service in the world searching for him is not consistent with his past."

"Are you misjudging his standing in Iran when this goes public? Just because it was his scheme doesn't mean the leadership will scapegoat him?"

"No, I agree that remains a possibility. Regardless, even if he considers that, my bet is he will choose a life outside Iran. Once we go public, Iran is in deep shit. For Savi that means a sort of prison as an international pariah. Shut off from his Lebanese mistress and the ability to travel to Europe. You've read the dossier comments, *secular, enjoys western luxuries of clothing, fine dining, wine and liquor, western sexual norms,* and so on."

"Risky bet, Mark. Could cost you your life. Savi is a trained intelligence operative. By definition that implies ruthlessness."

"I appreciate what you're saying, Victoria. Though I think it's an acceptable risk given the potential. Think of not only the added impact of the story but also the practical consequences of learning of Iran's planned use of these weapons. Learning how they have hidden them so successfully for years may also reveal details of their clandestine weapons development.

"And there's another possibility. Think of the theft. Garnitsky was already in a highly profitable position as a close subordinate to the oligarch Nikolai Krasin. Krasin had no reason to be involved in this brazen scheme to steal Russian nukes for the Iranians. But Garnitsky was a career criminal. I always thought that this was some rogue gamble. If so, it had to involve an enormous amount of money given Garnitsky's already lucrative circumstances.

"Therefore, suppose our friend Savi invents this scheme and sells the idea to Garnitsky. Given Savi's background and proclivities, did he personally profit monetarily? If so, that means he probably has money in some Swiss bank account. He can only access the money if outside Iran and living under a new identity granted by the United States in exchange for his information."

"That's a stretch, Mark. Possible I guess, but nothing supports that theory. He could still be motivated as an Iranian nationalist hostile toward the United States."

"Just the same, as a journalist pursuing Savi is too good an opportunity to pass up. Given we've decided the best course is to release this stuff publicly anyway, it's worth making the wager for a bigger return."

"Okay. I am still uncomfortable but I've agreed to go along with this. What is my role?"

"Should things go sideways in Rome, you'll coordinate the launch of the media release."

"Which is how?"

"I'm a member of the International Consortium of Investigative Journalists, the ICIJ. Two hundred investigative journalists and one hundred media organizations in seventy countries. Headquartered in Washington, D.C. The director's name is Howard Benedict. It will set off a feeding frenzy not only about the nukes but targeting the Putin regime's financial conspiracy."

"And this reference to an attorney? I assume that's the ex-U.S. district attorney you mentioned?"

"Of course. Phillip Ellsberg will have the same instructions as you have for releasing the material should anything happen to me. Work with him. He'll also give you legal cover when the FBI comes calling.

"So you admit there's danger involved?"

"Listen, Victoria, there is always that possibility. Look who we are dealing with. I believe I have gauged the circumstances accurately. This is my line of work. Yet every situation carries different risks. I'm just being cautious."

With an expression revealing her doubts but resolved to the plan, she said, "Then when do we meet with him?"

"I'm thinking the day after tomorrow. Gives us time to finish the broad outline of what it is we have. And to make sure we're on firm legal ground should our government try to interfere."

"And when do you leave for Beirut?" she said.

"I'm thinking two days after we meet with Ellsberg.

She exhaled in the form of a sigh. "If you must to do this, Mark, I'm going with you."

"No way, Victoria. There's no need. I don't want you exposed. Besides, you need to release the material should anything go wrong. The press will want background interviews."

Silent for a moment contemplating what she was agreeing to, she responded, "Ellsberg can do that. I'm going with you, Mark."

"How about a compromise? Go with me to Rome but let me go to Beirut alone. I don't want Savi to know of your involvement."

"I appreciate your concern. I'll think on it. We're in this together, Mark. I'm scared enough as it is without worrying about what's happening to you in Beirut."

He picked up on her tone as more than just professional concern and responded with a warm smile and nod of agreement.

"Then I'll set a meeting with Phillip Ellsberg. Day after tomorrow if possible. Gives us time to complete the press release and edit the pitch to Savi. We'll run all this by Ellsberg to make sure we are not violating any U.S. laws. He also becomes our insurance policy. We leave him copies of the files with specific instructions. If I do not contact him by a specified deadline, he is to release the material to a predefined group of journalists.

"The following day we fly to Rome.

Reynolds liked the idea of collaborating with Prescott. Tempering that thought, he also harbored difficult memories of all those that died working on his past dangerous undertakings. Did those deaths result from his reckless pursuit of the story? This was not her line of work. Had he oversold how straightforward this was to get her agreement? Obviously unknown dangers existed given the adversaries they intended to expose.

"Are we satisfied with what we've put together for release?" she said smiling also.

"Best we can do given the time constraint. But I think we've done an excellent job. Let's discuss it over drinks and dinner."

CHAPTER 16

MOSCOW, RUSSIA

Major General Dimitri Volkov, Deputy Director of Russian SVR Directorate S chaired a small meeting with his chief of staff and two others. Responsible for clandestine foreign intelligence, Directorate S conducted covert operations in foreign countries. The SVR typically focused on political matters leaving the sphere of military intelligence to the larger rival foreign military intelligence agency the GRU.

Vladimir Putin's career in the Soviet era commenced with the predecessor KGB's First Chief Directorate responsible for running foreign intelligence operations. With the collapse of the Soviet Union in 1991, the foreign intelligence functions of the former KGB reorganized into the SVR. In the matter of the Grigoryev and Lytkin stolen files, Putin therefore turned to Volkov to deploy covert resources abroad if needed to contain the damage. For this mission, Putin directed Volkov to report directly to the internal security FSB chief General Mikhalitsyn heading the entire government investigation. Putin recently removed Volkov's previous boss the head the SVR for his command failure after the attempted defection of his chief deputy General Grigoryev.

With Volkov and his chief of staff, Uri Neumenko, sat two others at the large conference table. Although dressed in civilian attire, both men conveyed military bearing.

"Colonel Lukashevich, Major Kozlovsky, the matter of the traitorous actions of General Grigoryev have taken an ominous turn, "Volkov said addressing the officers. "The damaging effects were unfortunately not contained by your elimination of Grigoryev in Paris, Major."

Kozlovsky headed a unit of the SVR's ultra-secret special forces known as Zaslon. A small shadowy force comprised of selected soldiers from other Russian *spetsnaz* units. Zaslon personnel never reveal their affiliation. The government does not even acknowledge their existence. They operate in foreign countries typically in civilian clothing or in the uniform of other Russian military units. They comprise a Russian elite special forces command comparable to U.S. Navy Seals or British SAS. Zaslon missions usually involve hostage rescue, security in war zones, or clandestine assassinations.

Kozlovsky and a team of four Zaslon operatives made the hit on Grigoryev. Kozlovsky himself fired the kill shots from a silenced weapon at close range.

"The FSB has determined this was not a Western intelligence penetration. Grigoryev and his brother-in-law Lytkin did this on their own. No other identified conspirators. We assume they planned to defect but Lytkin got careless. The extent of the stolen classified material is unknown. Although Grigoryev was unsuccessful in his attempt to go over to the West, he likely possessed electronic files for bargaining with the enemy.

"There are serious concerns that Grigoryev may have handed over copies of the material to someone before being killed."

Kozlovsky and his superior Lukashevich the Zaslon commander remained impassive waiting for Volkov to get to the point of the meeting.

"Uri, please explain," Volkov said to his chief of staff.

"Certainly a significant intelligence breach for the number-two man of the foreign intelligence service to attempt defection,

Not only politically damaging, Grigoryev could possibly have stolen operational information that could compromise our strategic interests. Yet as serious as that seems, the extent of the security breach may be even worse.

"What hasn't been generally known is that Grigoryev was in a conspiracy with his brother-in-law, a midlevel officer in the FSB. Routine security auditing discovered Colonel Stepka Lytkin accessing sensitive computer databases without authorization for over a year. While attempting to arrest him at his apartment, Lytkin chose instead to put a bullet in his head. Some signal from Lytkin likely alerted Grigoryev who obviously had a prearranged contingency plan to escape Russia.

"The nature of the stolen material must remain confidential. Sensitive enough to warrant any risk to insure it is not used against Russia."

Neumenko then distributed copies of red-jacketed dossiers to Kozlovsky and Lukashevich.

"These are dossiers on two Americans. The woman is a history professor. Authored a book in 1999 titled *Critical Mass*. Exposed a previously undiscovered Soviet GRU agent that penetrated the American's Manhattan Project that developed the first atomic bomb.

Volkov interrupted his chief of staff, "She is perhaps key to this. Possibly the last person in contact with Grigoryev in Paris before you killed him, Major."

"Why her?" Colonel Lukashevich asked.

"Grigoryev aided her during the Yeltsin era in researching Soviet intelligence archives," Neumenko said.

"An unbelievably naïve time thinking that we could coexist on equal terms with American imperialistic ambitions," Volkov interjected.

Neumenko continued, "And for Grigoryev, perhaps influenced by the more commonplace lure of sex with an attractive woman. Note her current likeness in the dossier at the age of fifty. Investigations of witnesses from that time twenty years ago reveal the certainty that she and Grigoryev enjoyed a sexual affair during her brief stay in Moscow.

"A revealing hand-written personal note found in a copy of her book in Grigoryev's apartment launched an intense probe of Victoria Prescott, Professor of History at Stanford University. Her area of interest, the Soviet Union and now the Russian Federation. You will note she is fluent in Russian.

"Since Grigoryev had few close relationships female or male other than his brother-in-law, Prescott became a likely suspect. We subsequently determined she was in Paris for two days, departing for New York the day before Major Kozlovsky killed the traitor.

"There is no evidence of prior contact between Prescott and Grigoryev until his disappearance and Prescott showing up in Paris. Furthermore, Prescott's father is a former American foreign service officer. At the least, she was likely Grigoryev's conduit to seek asylum in the United States. At the worst, Grigoryev turned over copies of the stolen confidential files to her.

"There is also no indication that she has been in contact with anyone in the U.S. government. Either she possesses nothing to hand over to U.S. intelligence, or she is playing some other gambit. Although believed unlikely, Grigoryev conceivably gave her nothing of value other than his offer to defect. However, that now brings us to the other dossier.

"An American journalist, unfriendly to Russia. His name is Mark Reynolds. He exposed questionable activities of a large multi-national corporation. The scandal brought down the affiliated business empire of Russian businessman Nikolai Krasin several years ago. Reynolds also made an unfounded wild accusation in his book *Shell Game* about missing Russian nuclear warheads.

Volkov added, "An opportunistic journalist who teamed with Russian antigovernment elements using other stolen electronic files. Professor Prescott recently contacted Reynolds in New York. There can be no reason for her approaching Reynolds other than something related to Grigoryev. Whether Grigoryev shared information or handed over electronic files to Prescott is unknown. However, Prescott's collaboration with Reynolds measurably increases the potential threat.

"Prescott joined Reynolds in New York two days ago. She is staying in his apartment. We are maintaining continuous surveillance," Neumenko said.

Colonel Lukashevich said, "Who is conducting the surveillance?"

"An American private investigation firm. Working for a law firm used before with various cutouts of dummy clients. The firm believes the law firm's clients are private corporations or organizations. The reasons given are suitably vague under the claim of confidentiality. They undoubtedly believe much of the work probably to be legally questionable. However they are paid well enough to avoid probing beyond the fabricated cover explanation."

Volkov added, "But they are not special operations, just watchers doing a job for money. Should an opportunity arise, or the situation change, we need our own resources in place. Resources capable of improvising with little notice while remaining undetected. That is why I need the skills of Major Kozlovsky."

Both Lukashevich and Kozlovsky exhibited slight expressions of surprise on their otherwise impassive expressions. The implication that they might be ordered to conduct an assassination or kidnapping mission within the United States represented a staggering political gamble.

"Yes, gentlemen. I understand the risks of such a mission. So does the President. You can therefore understand the importance of our mission.

"The situation remains fluid, gentlemen. The objective is to recover the stolen files if possible. That might be too late, however the fact that this woman appears to have joined with the journalist Reynolds suggests she is up to something. Assuming Grigoryev gave her the material, it could mean she and the journalist intend to release it through the media instead of turning it over to U.S. authorities."

"What specifically are our orders, General?" Major Kozlovsky said.

Kozlovsky did not look the part of a Special Forces operative. A handsome face with stylish hair, of average height and build, he could pass for any ordinary man in his early thirties. The ability to disappear into any identity suitable to the mission was an essential element for most Zaslon missions. Along with his lethal skills, Kozlovsky was a master of disguise.

All Zaslon operatives were multilingual in English as well as at least one other foreign language. Within Kozlovsky's team at least one member held fluency in one of the major European languages, their principal sphere of operation. In addition to Russian and English, Major Kozlovsky was fluent in French and Italian.

"Only preparatory until we know more, Major. You are to position your team in New York. Even that requires the utmost caution. I can assure you the false identities for your team will pass any United States scrutiny at the port of entry. All will carry European passports consistent with their language skills. Each identity originates from actual backgrounds that will pass any entry screening, including the database of the issuing passport country.

"Beyond that, you must devise a method to stay close to the targets Prescott and Reynolds. Moscow will relay instructions to a continuously manned dedicated senior Directorate S unit working out of our New York consulate. Communication will be by a new generation encrypted cellphone to avoid American NSA communications harvesting. It introduces a brief time delay then sends an advanced high-speed unintelligible burst in encrypted text form to your phone. You can send text from your phone using the same method."

"And what alternatives shall we prepare to execute, Sir?" Kozlovsky said.

"Ideally to seize material in the suspects' possession or determine their existence by intensive interrogation. We must determine if they have hidden copies or distributed to others. Regardless what is determined, it will then be necessary to eliminate both Prescott and Reynolds. However, this must be done in such a way to conceal any hint of Russian involvement. This cannot be the same as eliminating Grigoryev in Paris. That served the purpose of sending a message to anyone contemplating treason. Prescott and Reynolds are a different matter.

"The SVR has the task of repairing the damage of this intelligence breach. A great opportunity that also carries great risk. If the Americans even sense this is a Russian intelligence operation, the consequences will be disastrous. It must look either accidental or the bodies prevented from discovery. I suggest you plan possible alternatives since you must improvise with little opportunity for reconnaissance . You will command two teams, Major. The operation is code named *Motherland.*"

"When do we leave?" Kozlovsky asked.

"In three days.'

CHAPTER 17

MANHATTAN, NEW YORK

The following day added more pieces of the puzzle falling into place. First was a communication from Josef Novak with information about the hedge fund RK Investments.

Prescott shared the email with Reynolds.

After reading the attached file, Reynolds commented, "Jesus. RK manages forty billion dollars in assets. According to Novak that makes them the fifth largest hedge fund in the U.S. Actually says they are a fund of hedge funds. Defined as a fund comprised of a number of underlying individual hedge funds.

"Prescott said, "If laundered Russian money arrives from secretive offshore shell companies or an offshore hedge fund, it then transforms into all manner of investments. Not only real estate but other assets such as securities, commodities, derivatives, or whatever."

Reynolds displayed a questioning look.

She said, "You see, in an FOF, the investor purchases shares in the FOF which allows for diversification among all the funds managed by the FOF. Another layer of laundering.

"And look at the growth of RK. It all starts around six years ago. That was when their assets grew dramatically by adding several new real estate funds. Growth in two existing RK funds and newly created foreign funds based in tax haven locations ballooned their holdings. Twenty billion dollars in real estate assets added to RK spread among these half a dozen funds. Guess where the investment came from?

"Josef also points out that this asset growth of RK was fueled by leveraging their buying power through taking on debt. Easy to rationalize if the real estate purchases come from Russian graft. Why not accept a higher risk for increased returns?"

Reynolds smiled. "You're pretty good at this, Victoria. I'm impressed."

"There's more. Josef provided some background on the two Russian banks, Rossiya and Chelyabinsk Commercial named in so many of the documents. Both grew exponentially in the last five years. Both sanctioned after the occupation of Crimea, along with the major stockholder of both banks, Alexei Balakin, the financial oligarch. Balakin is a close associate of Putin and probably the principal architect of this international money laundering scheme according to Josef's take on the documents we have examined.

"When Putin came to power he mounted a concerted attack on several oligarchs. Many in the West mistakenly thought this was a campaign to replace the early corrupt oligarch empires evolving out of the chaos of the demise of the Soviet state controlled economic system. We now see it was simply Putin's move to bring the system under his control through sponsoring a new crop of oligarchs beholding to him.

"But back to the immediate. Josef says Rossiya's commercial client base consistently expands at an inexplicable rate. According to their annual report, energy and mineral resources clients accounted for much of the growth. Rossiya was founded in 1990 during the chaotic times following the Soviet Union collapse. Hijacked by the Putin crowd when he came into office in 2000 after Balakin acquired a majority interest.

"Chelyabinsk Commercial came out of nowhere when Balakin and the former oligarch Nikolai Krasin founded it in 2011. With the fall of Krasin caught up in the MGI and Moscow Capital scandal triggered by your exposé, Balakin quietly took over

Chelyabinsk, which in turn gobbled up the distressed assets of other Krasin banks. The business model for Chelyabinsk Commercial is financing for private firms holding government contracts. This includes all those working in the Russian nuclear industry.

"Josef unearthed an obscure fact in his research. Seems Chelyabinsk has a history of an astoundingly high percentage of bad debts. Although written off, bad debt does not damage them since most of that debt is underwritten by guarantees from the Russian Central Bank. According to Josef, clear evidence of Putin's control of the Central Bank and another means of indirectly stealing state funds."

Reynolds said with a wry smile, "So these government contractors borrow money from Chelyabinsk Commercial with probably nonexistent collateral. The client defaults on repayment and the Central Bank covers the loss. Just like some banana republic despot looting his country."

While planning for tomorrow's discussions with Phillip Ellsberg, Bernie Poole showed up at Reynolds' apartment.

Poole was clearly in a good mood as he took a seat at the dining table and a cup of coffee offered by Prescott. While everybody else involved shared differing anxieties about what they were doing, engagement with something this exciting only stimulated Poole's enthusiasm.

"Had to share this with you, Mark. Ever heard of an attorney named Vincent Fletcher?" Poole said.

Reynolds shook his head no.

"Used to be with the law firm used by your old nemesis Conrad Redek at MGI. Seems that Mr. Fletcher left that firm before it collapsed under the weight of their involvement in the MGI scandal.

"Who is Redek?" Prescott asked.

Reynolds said, "The former CFO of Martinelli Global. Serving a long sentence in federal prison. It was Redek who was responsible for creating the elaborately illegal business model adopted by MGI. Creatively developing ventures in some of the world's most corrupt places by colluding with local power brokers."

"Precisely," Poole said. "And it looks like Fletcher has his hand in these nefarious Russian ventures."

Both Prescott and Reynolds leaned forward toward Poole as they sat on the living room sofa.

"In what way, Bernie?" Reynolds said.

"One of your Russian documents made reference to a Panamanian law firm, Servicios Corporativos de Panamá. Seems SCP set up these hundreds of offshore companies used by the Russians. Headquartered in New York, which is convenient for the managing partner, Vincent Fletcher.

"So I did a little digging into Fletcher. Although named in the sweeping MGI criminal investigations, he avoided indictment for lack of evidence. In the end, only the firm's managing partner took a federal fall for bank fraud, money laundering, and SEC violations.

"Anyway, Mr. Fletcher has a checkered background. Clearly an expert in the world of offshore tax haven corporate structuring. With his direct involvement with Redek, the person responsible for creating MGI's financial empire, Fletcher is an expert at sophisticated money laundering. Since Krasin's Russian crowd was part of the MGI structure, easy to understand why the Russians tapped him.

"Five years ago, Fletcher acquired Servicios Corporativos de Panamá. At the time, it was a lesser-known firm in the Panamanian national industry of legal services in the creation of tax haven shell companies throughout the Caribbean. I did some digging and contacted some sources knowledgeable in that arena. Seems to be more information on SCP than you might expect considering the laxity of Panamanian regulatory reporting. Probably necessary for SPC to attract legitimate publicly traded corporate clients.

"Since the collapse of the large Panamanian legal firm Mossack Fonseca after their data breach in 2015 leading to the publication of the *Panama Papers*, SCP saw a boost in growth. That year they opened offices in New York and London, obviously picking off clients now shunning Mossack Fonseca.

"All this serves to mask their apparently more lucrative work with the Putin regime. Even in the secretive world of off-shore tax havens, word travels with insiders about the origin of shadowy clients like drug cartels and Third World dictators. Fletcher has avoided some of the unsavory criminal types that collaborated with the defunct MGI while obscuring the identity of his new Kremlin clients."

"That's some good work, Bernie," Reynolds said. "Haven't lost your touch."

"Something else. Seems Fletcher's SCP occupies a niche market in setting up offshore LLCs and hedge funds for publicly traded large real estate and property investment corporations. May prove to have some connection with the flow of Russian money into RK Investments. Could be the devious Mr. Fletcher has found a way to cross pollinate the illicit funds into another level of legitimate Western investment."

"Wow. Have you communicated this yet with Josef?" Prescott said.

"Not yet but I will. Considering we're under a tight deadline I wanted to discuss with you two first."

Reynolds commented, "Too bad we don't have a whistle-blower inside this SCP outfit. Seems they're the key segment in the money pipeline between Russian and especially RK Investments."

Prescott said, "Is that background stuff Josef forwarded on RK Investments helpful, Bernie?"

Poole shrugged, "Maybe. Certainly a thorough dissecting of their annual report. But then again, hedge funds do not have the same regulatory reporting demands that mutual funds have. The most striking fact is the timing of RK's growth coinciding with Fletcher's purchase of SCP and its meteoric growth. The common denominator in both centers on real estate investment. RK took a big hit in the 2008 financial collapse and following recession. Russell Koning may have done an opportunistic deal with the devil.

"A hedge fund of funds is a lucrative business for the fund management. Each of the underlying funds charges an asset fee, plus an incentive fee of any profits generated. The umbrella FOF layers incremental fees on top of that by arguing that these additional fees are more than justified by the potential higher risk-adjusted returns offered by the FOF.

"An interesting converging of timelines. If Koning and Fletcher partnered up, it offers the mechanism by which Russian laundered money transforms in investment-grade Western real estate."

Poole laughed and shook his head crediting the audacity of the scheme. "For these crooks, the money's not squirrelled away in secret bank accounts but appreciating through investment. And I have one more thing to add on the real estate angle. You'll love this.

"In your list of legal entities is an obscure German bank by the name of Deutsche Werbung. According to your preliminary notes, something apparently gave Professor Novak reason to believe that Russian laundered money now resides on their books. Seemingly untainted money now in a reputable European bank.

"However, I thought I recognized the name. In semi-retirement with extra time on my hands, I've binged on the many intriguing financial entanglements of our President."

"Don't tell me you've discovered something incriminating involving this German bank?" Reynolds said delighted at the prospect of an increase impact when they went public.

"No, nothing so specific. Maybe not even a smoking gun. But like everything with Trump and Russia, another curious connection. Seems that Deutsche Werbung loaned Trump hundreds of millions. The loans go back to 2015. A collection of loans covering New York commercial properties, luxury apartments, and golf courses.

"May be nothing, or at least impossible to connect Trump with dirty money."

"How the hell did you discover that?" Reynolds said.

Poole smiled. "Professional secret just like your sources, Mark. However, the world of high finance is fraught with gossip and jealousies. When large loans are made for questionable and highly leveraged projects, bankers talk. You just have to listen closely."

Reynolds said, "Can't top all that, Bernie, but later I'm sending you and Novak my research on the Russians identified so far in Victoria's translated documents. Incomplete dossiers but maybe some useful threads you financial guys can unravel. The one common theme is a close connection directly with Putin. Collectively these people span all the important government ministries and the named oligarchs control major sectors of the private economy. The ministers of finance and economic development. The chairman of the board of governors of the Russian Central Bank. The oligarchs Terekov and Balakin. A powerful kleptocractic regime. Interestingly, apart from senior officers in the FSB and SVR, Grigoryev's material does not mention any military general officers."

"Unlike other despotic regimes, you're saying Putin is not backed by the military?" Prescott said.

"No, I wouldn't draw that conclusion. They just don't appear to be part of this financial corruption."

"So what's that mean?"

"Nothing necessarily. Just means that unlike banana republic dictators, Putin's muscle comes from his secret police rather than the military. The same as Stalin."

"And here's another piece of information. Did you know that Putin visited Tehran a year ago?" Poole said.

Both Reynolds and Prescott looked at each other before answering, "No."

"Does raise questions since he's known for some time about his missing nukes that Iran has concealed for years."

"Can't believe Putin would admit to the theft in order to negotiate their return. He's not exactly pals with Khamenei and Rouhani," Reynolds said.

"Suppose you're right. Although farfetched, Putin must know the secret will eventually come out. Puts him in a box. Incompetence then followed by a cover up placing the world at elevated nuclear risk. Sure as hell doesn't support Putin's strategic objectives in the Middle East.

"And on that inexplicable tidbit, I shall take my leave. This will be one hell of a story when it breaks. Seeing this stuff in the public domain will piss off all sorts of powerful people in the U.S. government. Good luck to all of us in the ensuing shit storm. Personally, I can't wait."

Once Bernie Poole left, Prescott and Reynolds updated the draft of the media release. Neither Novak nor Poole realized going public might happen sooner than expected.

That deadline now dictated by milestones. First was the meeting with Phillip Ellsberg the day after tomorrow. That provided only the following day to polish the media release and assemble the entire digital package. A mountain of material including all the original documents provided by Grigoryev plus Prescott's translations, and the team's research, summaries, and conclusions.

Reynolds' *insurance* required not only leaving copies of the entire digital file with Ellsberg, but to establish the deadline requiring his physical presence back in Ellsberg's office. That was to be a week from the scheduled deadline for Savi to show up in Rome. If that came off, it allowed sufficient time to assess Savi cooperation while going to the federal government to arrange Savi's extraction from wherever he was in Europe. To protect their material from U.S. interference to suppress not only the nuclear warhead theft but also the disclosure of the Putin regime's financial corruption, meant the media release must occur simultaneously.

Two days following the meeting with Ellsberg, Prescott and Reynolds were to board planes for Rome. Reynolds would connect to a nonstop flight to Beirut, Lebanon, returning to Rome the following day after leaving the message for Savi with his Lebanese girlfriend.

"What do you say we wrap it up for the day? We're in good shape with tomorrow to finalize everything before meeting with Ellsberg," Reynolds suggested. "I could use a drink and a nice dinner. Things are about to become more hectic."

"Hectic? More like nerve-racking. Frankly, I'm scared to death about trying to contact Savi. What we're about to do sounds absurdly crazy, Mark. And you can't deny it's dangerous."

"Victoria, we've been ..."

"I know. I'm not getting cold feet, just telling you how I feel. I agreed, so I'll do my part. And I could use some downtime. How about fixing me a martini?"

"Coming right up."

In the kitchen he fixed her a dry martini with olives and a single malt Scotch in a tumbler for himself.

"What about dinner? Any ideas?" he said as he brought over her drink. They settled in the living room after she turned on a Stan Getz CD.

"Well, as you said, things are going to get hectic for a while. How about we just get some steaks and salad stuff and eat in? Got any special wine in that wine cabinet?"

"Surely you jest? I can offer a selection of excellent Bordeaux, Burgundy, or on the Italian side, there's Barolo or Super Tuscans.

"Better yet, there's a good specialty market close by that can deliver. The owner's teenage son does neighborhood deliveries.

As she sipped her martini, Prescott said, "Like I said, I'm committed. Cannot let you go this alone and meet up with a Middle East spy you just screwed over. I couldn't bear worrying."

"I appreciate that. However, your involvement must remain unknown. You will stay in the background only to observe. If it goes sideways in Rome and I don't walk away then it is up to you to get the hell back to New York. Help coordinate things with Ellsberg to release the material."

"I know all that, Mark. Just one change to the plan. I decided I'm going with you to Beirut."

Reynolds sat up straight and shook his head. "No, Victoria. I thought we settled that. You must stay in the background. Savi often frequents Beirut. He's well connected into Hezbollah. Iran funds their war against Israel. So it's his turf. Just too dangerous."

Setting down her martini, "My point exactly. I'm not going to be worrying about you while waiting in Rome. All I'll be doing is watching from the background when you deliver the message to the girlfriend. You are in and out in minutes. We take a taxi to the airport and return to Rome. No different than what I'm doing in Rome when you wait to see if Savi shows up there."

"It serves no purpose coming with me to Beirut."

Sitting on opposite ends of the sofa, she reached over laying her hand on his knee.

"It serves my purpose, Mark. Regardless of your logical explanations, I still think this is still highly dangerous. Too many unknowns that might create an unexpected reaction by Savi. God knows what sort of assassins he could call on from his associates in Hezbollah. Being in Beirut with you removes the unbearable uncertainty of waiting alone in Rome not knowing what's happening for those twenty-four hours."

She knew very well where the gesture of touching his knee might lead. Even given the unending emotional roller coaster of the last few weeks, she could not deny her physical and emotional attraction to Reynolds. Something not experienced for a long time.

For the same reasons, he was equally attracted to Prescott. A kindred inquisitive spirit with an outsized intellect. Physically, not only attractive but with that indefinable aura men describe as sexy. Something about her angular face and expressive eyes. According to her Stanford faculty online bio, she was three years older than he was. That meant nothing.

Looking at him intently, her inviting expression was unmistakable. Dressed in tailored gray slacks and a white silk blouse revealing enticing cleavage, immediately stirred his arousal.

Setting down his own drink on the coffee table, he moved next to her on the sofa. Reaching to cup her cheek in his hand, he kissed her. A long lingering kiss to which she responded by reaching to her blouse and unbuttoning it down to her waist.

He stood up quickly unbuttoning his own shirt and pulling it off.

After removing her blouse, she touched his crotch pressing her hand against his obvious erection. Still seated she reached behind her back unfastening her bra. Letting it fall to her lap, she looked up with a mischievous smile as he took in the sight of her bare breasts.

"I've wanted to make love with you for the past couple days, Mark. Let's go to the bedroom."

For the next hour they engaged in trying to please the other. They both had well developed sexual appetites over decades of relations with different partners. However, neither had experienced such a strong physical and emotional attraction for some time. As two experienced but starved people, they made the most of this rare connection.

Lying on his back, she situated herself over his chest with her breasts pressing against him. Neither said anything as they indulged in post coital contented affection.

After a few minutes, Prescott began kissing him. As he responded with renewed passion, she moved her hand down to his cock and began stoking it as she rubbed her crotch against his thigh. To the surprise of both, he became erect again.

"That's impressive," she said as she clenched his cock tightly in her hand working him with long strokes soon bringing him close to climax.

As he groaned arching his body upward at each stroke of her hand, she waited until he seemed at the edge of ejaculating before climbing on top, directing his cock into her still wet vagina.

Her timing proved impeccable as she rode him vigorously for only a minute before he released with another orgasm causing her vagina to contract spasmodically in response.

Minutes later while still sat on top of him, she said, "Hope this doesn't change our professional relationship."

He grinned, "Of course it does. For the better I should say. Knowing that we can consummate our desire for each other is a lot better than the anxiety of secretly lusting.

As she extracted herself by throwing a leg up as if dismounting a horse, she wiped herself with the sheet. "What a mess. We'll have to change the sheets."

"For tonight we'll sleep in your bed. Housekeeper comes tomorrow."

"I'll strip the sheets later. Otherwise she'll identify the smell. No need to advertise your intimate habits. Right now I'm hungry. Got anything we can scavenge to go with one of those good bottles of wine?"

Reynolds sat up in bed admiring the sight of her walking naked out of the bedroom.

"Eggs. Not much else," he called out.

"Okay. What about scrambled eggs and toast with a good Barolo?"

He grabbed a robe and walked into the living room to find her seated on the sofa dressed only in his discarded shirt sipping the remainder of her unfinished martini. He liked the fact she recognized how good her body looked without any qualifiers for her age.

An extraordinary night. Both knew it would be difficult to switch mental gears back to what lay ahead with seeing this daring plan through. Yet this shared venture shaped part of their attraction. Without either saying anything, both knew this was more than a circumstantial sexual encounter.

Each reflected on their personal demons getting in the way of romantic relationships. Neither knew the deep-seated uncertainties of the other that found them both without partners at their age. Might this relationship prove different?

CHAPTER 18

MOSCOW, RUSSIAN FEDERATION

Seated in chairs in front of the massive desk of General Mikhalitsyn, head of the Russian Federal Security Service, were two senior officers of the Foreign Intelligence Service, the SVR. Because of the attempted defection of the deputy director of the SVR, President Putin placed Mikhalitsyn in charge of cleaning up the fallout. The debacle cost the director of the SVR his position, now replaced temporarily by Mikhalitsyn's own FSB deputy.

This was Mikhalitsyn's responsibility as Putin's most trusted subordinate. Although the FSB had their own field operatives trained in black operations outside Russia, Mikhalitsyn chose to use the ultra-secret SVR's Zaslon. Better qualified personnel than the FSB's embarrassing failure in the London poisoning assassination attempt. If this mission went badly, he could direct failure toward the SVR.

This assignment called on the special infiltration skills and situational adaptabilities of the Zaslon, specialized in hostage rescue and assassination in hostile territory. Unlike the clumsy UK poisonings, this operation called for subtlety deflecting accountability away for the Russians.

As head of the SVR's Directorate S, General Dimitri Volkov was operational head of *Operation Motherland*. Seated next to him, Colonel Vadim Lukashevich commanding the Zaslon units. Absent from this meeting was Major Ivan Kozlovsky, field commander for this mission.

The experienced Kozlovsky personally killed the traitor Grigoryev and Paris. He commanded two Zaslon teams now in New York City. After identifying a connection between Grigoryev and a U.S. female academic named Prescott, followed by her contacting a journalist, Mikhalitsyn ordered Kozlovsky and two teams to New York. All this based on the possibility Grigoryev handed over a cache of stolen secret FSB and SVR files to the woman.

Russian sources within the U.S. intelligence community detected no signs the woman turned over any incriminating material to the U.S. government. Her contact with the journalist Reynolds who publicly alleged the theft of Russian nuclear warheads years earlier suggested a more troubling scenario of publication of the secret material. With no previous connection to Reynolds, she was either seeking his assistance to approach the U.S. government or planning going public with the information.

That second hypothesis appeared more likely after under surveillance two associates of Reynolds and Prescott turned up at Reynolds apartment in New York.

Moscow ordered Kozlovsky to plan for the abduction and subsequent killing of Prescott and Reynolds immediately following transmission of the execute signal. The orders repeated the imperative of avoiding Russian implication. He was to interrogate Prescott and Reynolds to determine what information they possessed, and who else possessed the information. With Prescott staying at Reynolds apartment, this presented the possibility of seizing both targets at once.

However, simultaneously with the identification of Novak and Poole, Russian cyber intelligence discovered the purchase of airline tickets for Reynolds and Prescott. A brief overnight stay in Beirut, Lebanon then departing to Rome the following day. Four days later they held return tickets to New York.

The intelligence confounded Mikhalitsyn's mission team by the meaning of this unusual last minute trip abroad by Prescott and Reynolds.

"Gentlemen, an opportunity has come our way to resolve this matter," General Mikhalitsyn said. "We have learned Prescott and Reynolds are leaving the United States in three days. I have authorization to execute Operation Motherland. You are to mount an operation to abduct Prescott and Reynolds once they are outside the United States. We can then confirm if U.S. intelligence possesses the stolen information. With any luck we can contain the damage to Russian national security caused by the traitors Grigoryev and Lytkin."

"Where are they going, General?" General Volkov asked.

"Beirut then Rome."

"Do we know the purpose of their trip, Sir?"

Mikhalitsyn grinned. "Not for certain. Puzzling to the investigative team since neither target has any background connection to anyone in either location. One enterprising officer suggested a remote possibility. However, the connection is unlikely and only speculated as a remote association of something possibly connected with this security breach."

Neither Volkov nor Lukashevich knew of the nuclear warhead theft, only Grigoryev's theft of unspecified top-secret documents.

"There is a remote possibility the journalist Reynolds might be working with U.S. intelligence to make contact with a senior Iranian intelligence officer. If so, the purpose is unknown. However, this Iranian has been under suspicion for some time as possibly a double agent for the American CIA."

That was a fabrication only for this audience. Farzard Savi was the last remaining participant in the warhead theft. Since identified in the Dratshev confession, his dossier grew over the years. The connection to Beirut was a sustaining romantic connection with a Lebanese academic. A frequent stop in his official duties when traveling to nearby Damascus in Iran's support of the Bashar regime, and Beirut in support of Hezbollah. A speculative possibility only. Yet if Savi is the reason for Reynolds trip to Beirut, he became a target of opportunity for the Zaslon assassination team.

"The target is still Reynolds and this woman Prescott. However if this Iranian is the reason for their trip to Beirut, he is to be eliminated."

Mikhalitsyn handed Volkov a thick dossier.

"His name is Farzard Savi, head of the foreign intelligence directorate of the Iranian MOIS. Travels outside Iran under the name Farhad Sattari under the cover of a trade specialist for the Iranian Ministry of Economic Affairs and Finance. Fluent in Farsi, English, German, and Russian."

After eliminating Prescott and Reynolds, Savi was to meet the same fate in war torn Damascus where Russian intelligence maintained a presence.

"We are monitoring Savi's movements. If his presence is discovered in Beirut at the same time as Reynolds, he must also be killed."

"And these associates that appear involved with the woman and the journalist?" Volkov asked.

"Once Prescott and Reynolds are abducted, their associates are to meet with fatal accidents. Easier then killing Prescott and Reynolds I should imagine, yet still carrying risk. Can this be done without the chance of any suspicion falling on us, General?"

Volkov said, "Yes, Sir. Two older men offer many possibilities for accidents."

Turning to Lukashevich, he said, "Colonel, order Major Kozlovsky and one of his teams to follow Reynolds and the woman overseas. I want Kozlovsky to personally supervise their abduction and interrogation at the first opportunity. It is imperative we discover the extent of the stolen classified material in their possession, and if distributed to others. Leave the other team to deal with the two old men in the United States.

"With such short preparation time, will Kozlovsky have the logistical capability to hold Reynolds and the woman either in Beirut or Rome?" Mikhalitsyn asked.

Colonel Lukashevich set his jaw. A difficult mission fraught with its own set of risks if it went wrong and discovered to be a Russian operation. "A difficult challenge. However, Major Kozlovsky is the most resourceful commander I have. It will require situational adaptation as circumstances unfold.

"With the targets only one day in Beirut, the opportunity for abduction there is unlikely. Easier to kill the targets there but I assume that is not an option?"

Mikhalitsyn answered, "No. Short of the targets escaping back to the United States. It is essential we know who possesses the stolen files."

"Understood, General," Lukashevich said, "Rome must be connected with their brief stay in Beirut. The longer stay in Rome suggests something keeping them there. This is not a holiday. Therefore we should plan to execute the abduction in Rome. I will dispatch another Zaslon support team to add to Kozlovsky's resources. He needs to find suitable locations for possibly holding the targets for an extended period. I'll need support from the resident SVR agents at both our Beirut and Rome Embassies."

Volkov said, "I'll see to that personally, Colonel. Anything else?"

"Another contingency arrangement, General," Lukashevich said to Volkov. "We should arrange for a charter aircraft to be fueled and ready to depart Rome in a matter of hours. A private executive jet. A large Gulfstream I would think. Capacity for at least a dozen passengers. Private aircraft with conventional charter ownership.

"If the abduction is successful and the opportunity presents itself, the best resolution is to fly them to Russia or some other location under our control."

"Of course! Excellent, Colonel. I will see to the arrangements," Mikhalitsyn said. "Avoiding any discovery of this being a Russian operation is just as sensitive in Italy. But I assume somewhat easier than in the United States to deflect this as an act by someone else. Islamic extremists seem the best cover. Can this be done?"

Lukashevich smiled. "Our thoughts exactly, General. We incorporated that in our selection of the Zaslon team. Had the operation required execution in America, using the cover of Islamic extremism was the logical approach. Major Kozlovsky himself is fluent in not only English but also Arabic. He and many of his team also maintain facial hair to adopt the appearance of Middle East Islamic adherents."

"Understand, gentlemen, the abduction of the targets must not become known to Italian police. Reynolds and the woman must simply disappear," Mikhalitsyn said. "Execute this mission successfully, gentlemen. The President has personally assured me that if you contain this security breach, each of you will be appropriately rewarded."

A month after the abrupt Singapore summit between President Donald Trump and North Korea's Kim Jung-un, Savi received a summons to the office of General Soleimani at the headquarters of the Quds Force. Soleimani had taken on the role of directly interfacing with Savi on his back channel to North Korea through Savi's sexual relationship with the intelligence operative at the DPRK Embassy in Tehran. The other members of the small leadership group knowing of the existence of the Russian thermonuclear warheads, mostly Islamic clerics, preferred to distance themselves from Savi's unsavory means.

"We must understand how this sudden appearance of détente between the United States and North Korea affects the prospects of acquiring nuclear fuels. In principal, Ayatollah Khamenei has ordered resuming a cautious pursuit of our nuclear weapons program. A delicate act to maintain secrecy and preserve the suspension of sanctions by the European Union.

"That of course brings us back to the fundamental problem of maintaining secrecy in producing enriched nuclear fuel. Difficult at best while also presenting the Americans and Israelis specific military targets. Circumventing that with North Korean nuclear fuel therefore becomes the best solution. Because of your ingenious efforts, Colonel, we hope that option remains open.

"The North Koreans have had two years of their scientists and engineers examining the Russian weapons. True to their methods, they have been vague about commencing delivery of any nuclear fuel to Iran. Now this lowering of the aggressive rhetoric with the Americans casts doubts about the DPRK's position."

Savi asked, "Do you believe the Koreans are foolish enough to negotiate away their nuclear weapons?"

"Iran essentially did. At least stopping weapons-level uranium enrichment that effectively put development on hold. I opposed that capitulation to the West. The feeling among our leadership now sees the error in trusting the Americans. I would hope the North Koreans are not as foolish."

"Unlikely, General. In their case, they already have weapons whereas our position is one of development lacking only sufficient weapons-grade fuel to move forward.

"I agree, Colonel. The North Koreans will protract negotiations indefinitely. Then as in the past, they will abruptly break off talks. That does not necessarily help Iran.

"I need you to use your special relationship with the Korean female agent. Probe for their commitment to our deal. Specifically, when can we receive an initial quantity of weapons grade enriched uranium?"

"Yes, Sir. Can I be allowed to convey some negotiating pressure?"

"In what way?"

"As you say, they have had access to the Russian warheads for two years. Perhaps that might be discontinued if there is no reciprocation?"

Soleimani hesitated for a couple of moments considering Savi's question.

"Yes, but qualified as only your speculation. Emphasize you are only acting as a messenger. Tell her the leadership is however expecting something specific regarding our bargain."

"I understand, General."

Savi wanted to tell the General not to trust the North Koreans. Just because he was occasionally sleeping with their highly placed agent did not provide access to any particular insights. Ye-jin Sung never revealed anything without careful consideration. Never any careless pillow talk. She enjoyed sex without any emotional bond, only as a means to manipulate her partner. Lovemaking was a contest. She would provide him with some vague assurances that he would deliver back to his superiors.

Increasingly Savi thought about cashing in his winnings as they say in Las Vegas according to the American movies. Foreign movies and his infrequent sojourns into Europe served to focus his thoughts of a different life in the West. The first move in that direction was establishing an escape identity a year ago on a series of trips to Austria.

Perhaps the time to consider leaving Iran was close at hand. Surprisingly, the theft of the nuclear weapons remained a secret. He assumed the Russians eventually found out but did not share that information for obvious reasons. Certainly not with the Americans, therefore the Israelis and Saudis did not know. However, if the deal to smuggle enriched weapons grade fuel into Iran from North Koreans materialized, secrecy became much more insecure. Particularly if the Iranian leadership became emboldened to take on greater risk.

His alternative identity as Faisal Drescher, an Austrian citizen by reason of birth, rested on a solid background. Fluent in German from his university years and subsequent work as his alternate identity as Farhad Sattari within the Iranian Economic Ministry provided the linguistic foundation. Researching death records during his frequent trips to Vienna and Salzburg, he discovered the perfect match.

A Salzburg University academic and his Lebanese wife died in an automobile crash on an icy road near Innsbruck in 1969. Under Austrian law, a child born of an Austrian citizen father is entitled to Austrian citizenship. With his Lebanese connections, Savi forged a birth certificate in the name of Faisal Drescher, born 1964 in Beirut naming the parents as Erich Drescher and Noura Khoury. With his German fluency, Savi secured the passport on a trip to Vienna. Used only once to return to Beirut with an entry stamp to validate his return to Vienna when he chose to disappear. This provided a span of time basis supporting his cover of living in Lebanon these past few years. All of Europe was then open to him as a holder of an EU passport.

Obstacles remained as to how and where to disappear without fanfare into this carefully constructed new identity. Simply leaving Iran would not be easy. And certainly not easy to slip into a new identity with no plausible background sufficient to access his hidden fortune. Escape made no sense unless he could enjoy Western luxuries. Unfortunately, this probably meant abandoning Leila Hajjar.

Not realistic to believe he could construct an equivalent new identity for Leila Hajjar. Why would she forsake her career and family to disappear into an unknown life with him once he confided to her his real occupation? She knew him as the Iranian financial official Farhad Sattari from Tehran through his frequent business trips to Beirut and occasionally to Europe. Although he possessed genuine affection for her, life together living under new identities seemed impossible. She would never abandon her family. He would miss her emotionally, intellectually, and physically.

Unlike Leila Hajjar, his infrequent sexual assignations with Ye-jin Sung contained no emotional bond. Strictly professional for Savi. Undoubtedly the same for Sung although she genuinely enjoyed the sex, especially with a non-Korean thereby avoiding any dangerous political entanglements.

Even though both Iran and the DPRK knew the connection between Savi and Sung, it was necessary to observe certain protocols. Iran was oppressively Islamic observant. The DPRK oppressively paranoid. No rendezvous at fashionable restaurants for unmarried couples. Sung lived in an apartment building entirely occupied by DPRK embassy staff. Well-guarded and everything under video and audio surveillance. No place for sexual encounters. Therefore, their rendezvous took place at Savi's house in an affluent neighborhood in northern Tehran.

A modest home surrounded by a wall like others in the neighborhood, closer inspection would reveal a sophisticated closed circuit surveillance system monitored by two armed guards at all times. Isolated to a wing of the house equipped with monitors, radios and telephone communications, they did not interact with Savi unless he requested something.

Leaving a message for Sung earlier in the day, Savi waited in his study watching two different camera feeds of either direction of the street in front of his house. A car parked a distance down the street briefly caught his attention as he sipped a Scotch waiting for Sung's arrival. These houses all had ample grounds for parking. Excepting for large gatherings, cars did not park on his street.

They had not been together for many weeks. Unless she had taken up with another lover, she would expect servicing. Lovemaking with her felt to be just that. A contest in which she expected certain things. The diminutive Ye-jin Sung was anything but the fictionalized subservient Asian female. A Scotch necessary to fortify himself. Undoubtedly, she would want exhaustive sex before they engaged with professional issues. Both understood their roles in the mating dance ritual between their two countries. The giving of information to the other carefully choreographed.

As her car pulled into view on the monitor, he set down his drink and descended the stairs to the first floor. Before she knocked, he opened the door.

She was alone. Iran allowed women to drive in Iran. Nevertheless, she observed Iranian cultural norms for women's dress in public, covering her head in a floral patterned rusari, and a long black coat extended below her knees.

"A long time, Farzard," she said in English since she did not speak Farsi.

After entering and closing the door, they embraced as she passionately kissed him. "Too long."

She freed her hair from the rusari and dropped the coat to the floor. Underneath she wore a form-fitting black knit sheath with black Western three-inch heels. Undoing her hair to let it fall to her shoulders framed an attractive face made up with great care to her makeup. The transformation was remarkable. From nondescript to call girl-sexy.

Like him, she favored Western fashion but unlike some of her prior diplomatic postings, Tehran offered little opportunity to indulge. The dress constraints of the DPRK Embassy staff were best described as 1950s Stalin era with all the bland ugliness that implied. Individuality only expressed in her footwear and a taste for black underwear.

"A drink, Ye-jin?"

"I was thinking of something more stimulating," she said enveloping him with her arms.

Ascending the stairs ahead of him, she was already unzipping her dress.

Two hours later, they sat in the study enjoying drinks. Covered in his robe she sat on Savi's sofa with her legs tucked underneath her sipping a Scotch neat.

"I needed that, Farzard. And this Scotch is superb. So difficult to obtain fine liquor in your repressed country."

She intended the use of the term repressed as an insider joke assuming everything might be recorded. As to the sex, she cared little if Savi taped them screwing.

"As much as I believe I please you sexually, I am sure there was a more official reason for wanting to see me," Sung said.

"Of course. Always better though when you can mix business with some pleasure. In this case, my superiors have asked that I convey their desire to see movement on when we could expect delivery of weapons grade fissionable material. I'm to emphasize it has been two years since our countries reached an accord on technology sharing."

She sipped at her drink. "And during that time, circumstances have changed. Our Dear Leader has successfully eased tensions with the new American president. An extraordinary accomplishment given the hawks surrounding the American leader favoring the threat of military action."

"An astounding accomplishment, I agree. However, nothing of substance was achieved. No one believes the DPRK will ever relinquish its nuclear weapons. Therefore the achievements of the DPRK may be transient as the Americans come to terms with the realpolitik."

"Our Dear Leader has said only that he is seeking to denuclearize the Korean peninsula. Conciliatory talks with the South suggest the possibility of reunification one day. All of this is tied together in a long game."

Propaganda bullshit for North Korea's oppressed people while playing to the naïve hope of a fearful world. Of course, it was a long game. One the current dictator and his father and grandfather before him played over decades. Endless protracted negotiation never leading to meaningful compromise.

Savi replied, "Iran's circumstances with this American president have shown American duplicity. With their periodic change in leadership, former treaties mean little. For Iran, it is essential to possess nuclear weapons. Your country has proven that to be the only path for survival in the long-term."

"And what message would you like me to pass on to my superiors, Farzard?"

"Iran is seeking to begin receipt of nuclear fuel before your country enters into any agreement possibly leading to international inspectors in the DPRK. I am instructed to convey the message that to enhance the bargain, Iran might consider an exchange of one of the operational Russian warheads for a continual supply of weapons-grade fuel. Although your scientists have had access, I am told possession of the actual weapon would be invaluable to the DPRK's continuing weapons development."

That elicited a slight rising of Sung's eyebrows in surprise. "Well that is interesting. I shall convey the information immediately."

"Impress on your Dear Leader Iran's intensions to possess a nuclear weapons capability, Ye-jin. With these Russian warheads we have a start but insufficient to challenge Israel. Iran's weapons development is years away from achieving even a modest arsenal of operational warheads. Iran must surmount the obstacle of concealing uranium enrichment from international scrutiny. Israel will never allow nuclear advancements beyond a certain point before delivering military strikes. Enriched fuel from the DPRK circumvents western scrutiny.

Ye-jin responded, "I am certainly not empowered to negotiate on behalf of the DPRK. However, what if Iran considers trading all three Russian warheads? A good bargain in exchange for a continuous supply of weapons grade nuclear fuel and access to North Korean weapons technology. That allows Iran to fast-track creation of its own nuclear arsenal in secrecy."

Sung did not occupy her high position in DPRK intelligence solely because of her close family connection with Kim Jung-un.

Savi said, "Like you, I will convey your proposed idea. However, I am instructed to convey the message that Iran needs immediate movement on the question of receiving weapons-grade fuel. Iran has honored its side of the bargain by providing North Korean scientists access to study the Russian weapons."

The conniving bitch. For that matter, the entire DPRK regime was a duplicitous gang of thugs. Even though the whole idea involving North Korea originated with Savi, it was to sell the scheme for personal gain. He never thought it might come to this. The North Koreans could not be trusted. However, that was soon to be a problem for others.

Sung said, "Hopefully the resulting negotiation exchanges will flow through us as a direct back-channel. We can therefore enjoy more times like tonight."

After midnight, Sung left the house. He watched her drive away on the security monitor. He watched as she drove past the same car still parked on the street from hours earlier.

Immediately picking up the phone, he issued orders for his guards downstairs to zoom in on the vehicle to capture the license plate. Quickly the screen confirmed Savi's suspicions. The car made an awkward U-turn, disappearing quickly as it followed Sung's car.

One of them was under surveillance. By whom? His own MOIS or the North Koreans? Both knew of Savi's and Sung's sanctioned connection. The Americans? Someone else? Clumsy tradecraft whoever it was. That suggested some foreign intelligence probably using local talent.

Two days later Savi arrived in Damascus on a military flight. A frequent field trip with an Iranian military and intelligence team to assess the status of Iran's interests in support of the Assad regime's ongoing civil war to regain control of Syria. Since 2013, Iran provided logistical, technical, and financial support for training of Syrian forces. Although for different self-interests, Russian and Iranian support sustained the Assad government aligned against most of the Western world and the Sunni Middle East.

Syria is crucial to Iran's regional ambitions. Sufficiently important for Iran to extend its support by reportedly deploying over 70,000 combat troops in Syria. An assorted mix of Iranian military, Afghan Shia militia, various groups of Iraqi Shia militia, Pakistani and Palestinian militia, and Lebanese Hezbollah fighters. Iran also pays monthly salaries to 250,000 Syrian militia fighters supporting the Assad government.

Largely to assess military progress and optimize Iran's investment, Savi was there to assess the current political climate of the Syrian government and obtain what he could from direct contact with Russian intelligence operatives operating in Syria. On this trip he traveled without any other MOIS staff. After three days in Damascus, he would make the two-hour drive to Beirut. Brief consultations with senior Hezbollah leaders then spend a leisurely two days with Leila Hajjar.

With the U.S. withdrawal from the nuclear agreement with Iran, Putin sees the U.S. playing into his greater ambition of recasting Russia as a superpower by Russian support of the Assad regime. A duplicitous move since Russia also signed the nuclear agreement with Iran. Iran simply wants to be the dominant regional power. Savi's specific role in these periodic trips to Damascus was to interact with his Russian intelligence counterparts. Report on the views of the state of affairs in Syria from the perspective of Russian intelligence. His Iranian military counterparts would focus on the pragmatic issues of managing Iran's large military commitment in coordination with the Syrians, and to a lesser extent, the Russian military presence.

Savi was naturally skilled at making relationships. The fact he could speak fluent Russia with his long association with Russian intelligence, provided a perfect basis to ingratiate himself informally with Russians in Damascus. Having received intelligence training in Russia in 1995 at the SVR academy in Moscow known as the Institute, made him a comrade. He could relate first hand to the Russians the rigorous training that included weapons and martial arts proficiency. He told of trainees in his time engaging in brutal hand-to-hand combat competitions. To these younger Russian intelligence operatives, he asked, if such intense training was still practiced as a means of impressing them as an experienced intelligence operative.

A hard drinking lot, Savi always brought along a supply of vodka and whiskey as gifts. Unlike other predominately Muslim countries, liquor was legal in Syria. Even so, Damascus was still tough duty for Russian intelligence officers. Not only an alien foreign culture where they did not speak the language, but little access to women. Savi bridged the cultural divide by speaking not only Russian but also Arabic. When in the city, Savi served as unofficial tour guide to the hot spots for what constituted Damascus nightlife, including access to prostitutes and illicit drugs through the Syrian black market.

His first night after arriving in Damascus, he got down to business. After a day of dull briefings by the Syrians, obviously slanted to suit their agenda, he invited several Russians to join him at a bar he discovered on his last trip.

With the Syrian civil war still raging, Damascus itself was an armed camp, experiencing the violence within its own boundaries. Savi and his Russian colleagues arrived in Savi's rental car at an enormous stone gate within the great wall surrounding the Old City. The high walls displayed posters depicting dead soldiers and loyalists. Pro-government paramilitaries manned the gate. Not the sort of place one expected to find nightlife revelry.

They entered through the gate into the Christian neighborhood of Bab Touma, a warren of narrow cobblestone streets. The area held many pubs and shops walling off the signs of the war. A favorite haunt of Syrians escaping the constant specter of civil war violence into some semblance of normality eased by alcohol.

Still early in the evening, the streets were full of people. Savi led the way to a large bar called *La Méchante Femme*, a French name for *The Wicked Woman*. Savi caught the eye of the woman proprietor behind the bar. Slipping her some money, she motioned for two men back in the shadows that quickly pulled together two small empty tables for Savi and his group of three Russians.

La Méchante Femme was a different kind of bar. The two muscular men that arranged the tables obviously bouncers. While alcohol was legal in Syria, prostitution was not. Although not strictly enforced, establishments frequented by working girls were not common. Those that were only operated with official police corruption. For the sex-starved Russians, this was their kind of local color.

Looking about, the majority of the patrons were men. The few women were all young and attractive wearing short dresses that enhanced their figures. No head coverings here. Unquestionably working girls. Western pop music played to the tastes of the decidedly younger well-dressed clientele. An upper class place catering to those with money seeking the pleasures of Western liquor and sexual freedom.

The proprietress came over to the table bending down to kiss Savi on the cheek. A dark statuesque beauty in early middle age still capable of turning heads, revealing deep cleavage as she bent forward.

"So good to see you again, Farzard," she said in Arabic.

"You look beautiful, Amal. For the vision of you is the only reason I risk my life to travel to Damascus," Savi said with a broad smile while wrapping his arm around her waist.

Amal kissed him sensually on the mouth.

Turning toward the Russians, she smiled seductively then motioned for a waiter.

"You know this woman intimately, Savi?" the senior Russian asked.

"Amal? Not *intimately* as you say, Dimitri. Only met her on my last trip. Colonel Khateb brought me here. You know he likes women and whiskey. Amal owns the place. As a good marketer, she uses her sexy looks to advertise her establishment. I'm a foreigner who speaks Arabic so she remembers me," Savi said in Russian.

Dimitri Markov of the Russian SVR was well acquainted with their associate Colonel Khateb of Syrian military intelligence. Savi chose this place because Markov liked liquor and women. As senior in this group, Markov like Savi traveled in an out of Syria while the other two Russian operatives were resident in Syria. A relaxed Markov might offer up some candid information on the current Russian intelligence view of the Syrian conflict.

After more than an hour of drinking, the place filled to crowding. Several unattached females sipping glasses of wine cast glances about for male company.

Markov liked American Jack Daniels on ice but did not hold it well. Savi had the waiter set a bottle at the table. Between Markov and his subordinates, the bottle was empty within an hour.

Savi motioned for the waiter. After peeling off several Syrian pound notes for another bottle, he directed the waiter's attention to two women standing at the bar. Saying something in a whisper, he handed the waiter more money.

Within a minute, the two women arrived at their table. Clearly, working girls dressed in tight short dresses, lots of exposed skin, and high heels. The two bouncers squeezed two chairs into Savi's group. The waiter returned with a bottle of wine for the women.

Savi's instruction to the waiter was to have the darker complexioned woman cozy up to Markov. The other could take her choice. Find a third for the remaining Russian if he could. Savi provided a generous tip and the promise that he would cover everything including the cost of the prostitutes' services.

Markov soon had his arm around the prostitute looking down at her large breasts. Looking over to Savi he said, "Nadira here speaks some English. Better than mine but we can communicate. Tells me she is Lebanese. That is why she has such exquisite skin coloring?"

"I agree she is beautiful, Dimitri."

Markov took another drink of his whiskey.

"I am told, Farzard, you have a Lebanese beauty of your own in Beirut."

Savi just smiled, revealing no expression of his surprise at Markov's comment. Russian intelligence would be well aware of his trips to Beirut given Iranian support to Hezbollah. Of course a dossier existed which not surprisingly might include his association with Leila Hajjar. Yet there was no reason that Dimitri Markov should have access to that information. He was not high enough within the SVR. Unless Markov was briefed and tasked with spying on him knowing their relationship in Damascus. Was Markov just doing the same thing as Savi, namely to gain intelligence on the other's view of the Syrian situation? Or was there something else?

With heightened sensitivity following the clumsy surveillance in Tehran, Savi could not be sure. He did not know Markov's two junior colleagues. One was obviously measuring his intake of alcohol to the extent he still nursed his first drink. Savi was not able to draw the young man out after he declined the advances of a third prostitute sent over to the table. Savi made a career of recruiting agents by assessing their character and motivations. A spy's instincts that served him well. Something did not feel right about Markov.

"There are many beautiful women in Beirut, Dimitri. Unfortunately professional duties allow me little time to pursue personal interests."

Markov continued to drink but turned the conversation to politics. He noticeably ceased paying attention to the prostitute. So did the other Russian as the other prostitute tried to entice him by rubbing his crotch. Clearly, something was out of place.

Savi said, "Seems these young women are not attractive enough for you and Vassily to take them upstairs. And it was to be my treat."

"Ah, Farzard, not enough sleep and too much whiskey. Not sure I could even get it up."

Savi reached into his pocket and took out money handing it to the two women and motioning with his head for them to leave. Markov was a clumsy intelligence operative and a worse liar.

The women stood up thinking the men would accompany them until Savi said in Arabic, "Not tonight, ladies."

The third Russian nursing his drink excused himself to go to the toilet.

An hour later, Markov pleaded exhaustion by calling it a night. His two associates exhibited no disappointment in cutting short a night of drinking and sex on someone else's money. The SVR Institute training clearly not in evidence among these Russians.

In a parting shot to goad Markov, Savi said, "What happened with your number two guy at *Sluzhba Vneshney Razvedki*?"

Markov's expression turned grim. "Heard he died."

Savi grinned. "The old fashion way with a bullet to the head according to the newspapers. First those hits in London now Paris. You Russians are not subtle."

By Markov's expression, Savi's sarcasm did not amuse him.

The following two days in Damascus proved unproductive toward Savi's mission of acquiring intelligence on the Russian position in Syria. Colonel Markov was curiously unavailable. Sociable to Savi during previous encounters, something definitely was out of place. Savi now wondered if it was Russian intelligence taking an interest in him? Two incidents out of the norm. But why now? Even if the Russians somehow knew of his involvement in the warhead theft, Iran continued to maintained tight secrecy. Or had something leaked?

Was there some connection with the murder of the SVR general in Paris weeks ago? Obviously a Russian assassination, therefore an unsuccessful defection attempt.

Even if the Russian's knew of Savi's involvement with the theft, so what? Then again, Vladimir Putin was a thug at heart with a known inclination toward exacting revenge. And Savi had committed an outrage against his regime. He could not ignore the possibility. Or might the Russians want to use him as a back channel to the Iranian leadership to ensure containing exposure of the warhead theft?

The following day Savi drove west on Damascus International Highway 30 for the two-hour drive to Beirut. A drive taken many times. Since he might be under Russian surveillance, he removed the SIM card from his cellphone to prevent GPS tracking. Ever cautious, communication with Leila Hajjar was always with untraceable cellphones. In turn, he replaced the phones each time he journeyed to Beirut. The drive to Beirut was through territory under governmental control therefore representing no threat from Syrian rebels. With carefully planned stops, the nighttime drive also confirmed no one was following.

Several miles behind Savi another sedan followed the lightly traveled highway where most of the traffic consisted of trucks and military vehicles.

"Target crossed border into Lebanon. Another hour to Beirut, Colonel Markov," the Russian named Vassily said into a cellphone.

"Very good. Follow him and report his location once he leaves his car," Markov replied. "Maintain surveillance on Savi until relieved only by my orders."

When excusing himself to go to the toilet, the quiet Russian slipped out of the pub and attached a GPS tracking device under Savi's car.

Before leaving Moscow, Markov received orders to stay close to Savi when he arrived in Damascus, and to mount surveillance until relieved. The order came directly from General Volkov head of Directorate S.

CHAPTER 19

MANHATTAN, NEW YORK

"Good god, missing nuclear warheads?" Phillip Ellsberg said after Reynolds explained what they had.

Listening to Reynolds narrative, Ellsberg leaned forward intently over his desk as he asked questions of Reynolds and Prescott."

"Thermonuclear warheads, Phillip. First North Korea and now Iran have joined the nuclear fraternity."

"And you want to go public with this rather than take it to the government? Why?"

"Obvious isn't it? It's our story. We give it to the government and they take control out of our hands. Don't they have that power?" Reynolds said.

"Yes. Easiest way is to immediately classify the material and confiscate all your material under court order. Prevents any use under criminal penalty. You could file suit but that could take forever. Moreover, if the President issued an executive order claiming national security implications, you'd get nowhere.

"Therefore we go public. Prevent the administration from burying it."

"Might result in military action against Iran," Ellsberg said. "Want that on your hands?"

"Come on, Phillip. Don't give me that tired government argument about the necessity for secrecy. You're arguing as if you are still with the DOJ. No matter what, the Iranians can expect a military response. If not by us then by Israel. Saudis are also going to be scared shitless with their Shiite antagonist possessing nukes. Same possibilities exist either way. Only difference, all the world knows and Russia takes the fall along with Iran."

"And there's more, Mr. Ellsberg," Prescott said. "In addition to these stolen warheads, my source gave over a massive trove of documents revealing extensive financial corruption directed by the ruling Russian regime. With Trump's affinity for Vladimir Putin and his own questionable business dealings involving Russia, that material undoubtedly becomes suppressed. These documents reveal methods of laundering billions of illicit dollars through investment in U.S assets. As insidious as their cyber-attack on our election process."

Reynolds added, "I agree with Victoria. Plagued by its own corruption, this administration might see the material as a personal threat. There are important U.S. interests implicated in the conspiracy. A major scandal even here in the United States. Why wouldn't they suppress it?"

Prescott said, "We need more time to explore this huge data dump from secret Russian intelligence files. But we can't do that while ignoring the compelling urgency of exposing these missing nukes now in the hands of Iran. Going public is a way of satisfying both objectives."

Ellsberg let out a deep exhale. "Okay. Since both of you have already decided to go public, what do you need me for?"

"Your legal opinion, Phillip. Are we violating any U.S. law? Beyond that, can the government do anything to squash this?" Reynolds asked.

Ellsberg took a couple of moments before answering.

"Don't see this violating any U.S. statues. No violation of the Espionage Act. You acquired the documents in a foreign country. You are clearly not acting on behalf of any foreign power, therefore no involvement of the FISA courts. No evidence of bribing foreign nationals, therefore no issue with the Foreign Corrupt Practices Act. As to the second question, the government undoubtedly will go all out to deny, suppress, and otherwise do their utmost to marginalize this as a media-manufactured story. If for no other reason than you upstaged them. Another U.S. intelligence failure.

"You're the journalist. Won't publications like the New York Times and Washington Post seek corroboration before publishing? During that process the government still might be successful in getting the courts to suppress based on a Presidential Executive Order under a national security claim."

Reynolds said, "But every major newspaper, news service, and broadcast media network in the U.S. and the world will have access to the material. In a practical sense, can they effectively prevent it from getting released?"

"Probably not. Depends on beating them to the draw. If you can get into the public domain before they can react, then their position is effectively diminished, probably thwarted.

"The clear landmark Supreme Court precedent in the ruling on publication of the Pentagon Papers in *New York Times v. United States* in 1971 supporting the preeminence of the First Amendment appears applicable for your situation. I know it well as the ruling in the case of the government military contractor analyst Daniel Ellsberg, no relationship. His story of standing up to power always grabbed me.

"In short, the constitution prohibits any law from abridging the freedom of the press. A few landmark cases in the twentieth century established precedents creating exceptions. These rare exceptions require the government proving a case for the *grave and irreparable danger* to the American public by release of the information. The Pentagon Papers ruling however was not one of those exceptions. The government lost and the Pentagon Papers were published."

"Doesn't that all become a moot point if the material is published by foreign media?" Reynolds asked.

"You would think so, but the President's power to protect national security is broad. This President is wildly unpredictable and surrounded by unconventional aides. With the conservative shift in the high court, I cannot rule out some attempt to go after stopping you and Professor Prescott.

"Mark is a freelance journalist but you have an academic career to protect, Ms. Prescott. This could have unpleasant ramifications for you. Sure you're up to this?"

"I'm already on board to go this route, Mr. Ellsberg, unless you can point out some clear legal jeopardy. Like Mark, I had my own bad experience when the government went out of its way to discredit my revelations unmasking a WWII Soviet spy. However, there is yet another matter we need to discuss. Right, Mark?"

"I think we have the possibility of an even bigger story, Phillip," Reynolds said. "The confession document of the Russian supervising the theft named the Iranian mastermind of the operation. Subsequently the Russian intelligence investigation included a dossier on this Iranian, now the chief of their foreign intelligence directorate. I think there is a very good chance to induce him to defect."

"Jesus Christ! That is the stupidest thing I've ever heard. You can't go mucking about with foreign intelligence operatives. Look what happened in Ms. Prescott's situation. The murder of her source only a day after she left him attests to the seriousness of what you possess. If she had been with him, the Russians would have done her in as well. Now you want to challenge this Iranian? These are professionals playing for high stakes, Mark."

Turning to Prescott, Ellsberg said, "And you're going along with this hair-brained scheme, Ms. Prescott?"

Before Prescott could answer, Reynolds butted in.

"Listen, Phillip. This is not as farfetched as you think. The Iranian is in a precarious position once this is exposed. Iran has kept this secret for four years. Revealing his involvement, throws Iran into a hell of a precarious position, probably facing imminent military attack. Does our guy remain a national hero or liability? At the least, his professional career ends. Add to that his propensity for western luxuries, frequent travel outside Iran, including to Europe. A girlfriend in Beirut. And he's a known secularist. Nothing to suggest an inclination toward Islamic or even nationalistic martyrdom. I simply provide him an escape route to asylum in the United States. A new identity in exchange for identifying the location of the warheads, the plans for how Iran intends to leverage them, and a wealth of secret information as a senior Iranian intelligence official."

Ellsberg shook his head with an expression of disbelief. "Is that it? No further bizarre twists in this scheme?"

"That's the sum of it. I'm not being reckless, Phillip. I simply deliver an envelope to his girlfriend in Beirut at the American University. She is a professor there. I'm in and out then immediately return to Rome. The envelope contains what I hope is an offer he can't refuse. A meeting in Rome in a public place. No worse a risk than I've faced in my career to get a story.

"You're to be my insurance. If I do not show up at your office in a week from today, you will overnight these envelopes. One is addressed to the Director of the International Consortium of Investigate Journalists and the other two to the London Times and Le Monde. That insures it goes public outside the reach of the United States government. Every journalist in the world will be poking in all the dark corners this stuff exposes.

"If Savi never shows for the Rome meeting, I return to New York and we still send the envelopes off immediately. If this doesn't work out then all we've lost is another week before getting the information out there."

"Or you're shot or kidnapped in Rome."

"I don't think so. Once the Iranian knows everything will become public, he has only other three options. He stays in Iran and hopes to survive the aftermath. At best, his life is forever altered in a restrictive country now under real siege. At worst, he becomes a liability. I would guess he probably has enemies. Maybe his superiors authorizing the scheme?

"Or he goes on the run. He might have the means to escape Iran. But where can he go? Now every intelligence agency in the world is looking for him.

"And yes, it's possible he could react desperately thinking he might prevent the media release. My message should convince him otherwise. I'm figuring he won't react irrationally. He's a trained professional. There's a good chance he will see defection and a new identity as his best option.

"My guess he either does nothing, maybe suspicioning this is a CIA or even a Russian trap, or he takes my offer to facilitate his defection to the United States. I'm betting he's logical and pragmatic rather than irrational. Victoria will be watching my back from a distance."

"Really?" Ellsberg said looking at Prescott. "Doubt you've ever had any experience in this this sort of stuff, Ms. Prescott. Two amateur dilettantes playing with high explosives. My advice, just go public. Let events unfold. You don't need to cap it off with getting this guy to defect."

Reynolds said, "We've been all over that, Phillip. Will you help us?"

Ellsberg rubbed a hand on the back of neck. "Yes, of course. I understand your distrust of the government, especially when you are about to intrude on their official turf in a very big way. After all, that's how I became involved with you when I was with the DOJ and you were working to expose MGI. Like to think I still wear a white hat. Don't want you and this obviously naïve academic twisting in the wind once things start to happen.

"So I'll play my supporting part in what I hope is not a Shakespearian tragedy. You two will certainly need a good lawyer to navigate the shit storm once this breaks."

"Thanks, Phillip. Both of us appreciate your help. So if my bet pays off and the Iranian agrees to defect, can you arrange contact with the proper people in the government?"

"I believe so. I know counterintelligence people in the DOJ and FBI. They'll be the people to arrange asylum, witness protection, and so forth. Exfiltrating your guy probably falls more to the CIA but we'll let the Justice Department deal with that. I'll do some discrete poking around."

"Good. Because there will not be any advance notice. If the Iranian shows up in Rome, we are back here next Wednesday. Remember that's my insurance if this goes wrong. Yet even if the Iranian accepts the deal to defect, the Government still does not get any notice before we go public. Nothing changes there.

"Understand this, Phillip, next Wednesday we go to press regardless what happens in Rome. If the Iranian makes contact, I will call you with the particulars of how U.S. intelligence can make contact with him. I am sure the Iranian will want to negotiate. At that point Victoria and I return to New York."

"And what if this Iranian spy has a gun to your head when you call?"

"Good question. If I want you to delay the media release I'll say *Victoria agrees with that*. If things have gone sideways and I'm under duress, I'll say *Vicky agrees with that*."

Looking over at Prescott, while explaining to Ellsberg, "She dislikes being called Vicky. So that response means I'm compromised and you are to release the material for publication. There can be no negotiation., just release the material as I instructed without hesitation.

Prescott gave him a look of real distress. *Compromised? You mean a gun to your head*?

Ellsberg said, "Jesus, Mark. Sounds like cloak and dagger nonsense, but okay. Your whole plan sounds overly simplified. Just hope this doesn't all go wrong. So when are you embarking on this absurd adventure?"

"Tomorrow."

As they left Ellsberg's building, Prescott hung to Reynolds arm. As he hailed a taxi, she said, "Let's pack and relax the rest of day. No more work. I need to get some relief from all this.

And I'm scared of what might happen next week. Then god only knows the ordeal we'll face after the story releases."

He wrapped his arm around her shoulder pulling her closer. "We'll get through this just fine. Glad you're with me on this, Victoria."

He was not entirely that confident. They were playing with fire. While feeling a romantic connection with Prescott, was he putting her in harm's way? Did he downplay the risks too much? If this went all wrong, could this become a repeat of the tragedy with Katerina Avramenko?

"But I agree things are going to be hectic for a while. So let's enjoy the rest of the day, and the night. Nothing more to do in preparation anyway."

Descending the elevator from the same floor along with Reynolds and Prescott was a non-descript woman dressed in office attire carrying a stack of folders.

After reaching the ground floor and exiting the elevator, the woman said into her cellphone, "Both targets spent two hours in the law offices of Goldstein Waterman & Ellsberg at 376 Fifth Avenue in Midtown Manhattan. They are now exiting the building onto Fifth Avenue."

Outside, another surveillance team took over the tail. The woman returned to the law firm office. Approaching the receptionist, she said, "I'm here to deliver these files to Mr. Mark Reynolds one of your clients."

"Oh, I'm afraid you missed Mr. Reynolds. He just left. Would you like me to give the files to Mr. Ellsberg?"

"Thank you, but I'll need to give them directly to Mr. Reynolds since I need to explain some changes and get his signature. I'll catch up with Mr. Reynolds later at his office."

Outside the law office, she placed a call. "The targets met with one of the partners by the name of Phillip Ellsberg."

That afternoon back at the apartment relaxation took the form of lovemaking. Once they uncoupled, she laid her head on his chest. He could feel the damp of her tears.

"Why are you crying, Victoria?"

"Just a touch of self-indulgence. Feeling sorry for myself."

He stroked her cheek wiping away the tears. Not a time for him to ask what she was talking about.

Sitting up she said, "Stupid thoughts. Wish we could just go off to Rome for a holiday not this. Can't help feeling scared. Even when we go public I fear it might turn our lives upside down."

That was only part of it. Something clicked when she met Reynolds. Something far more than the sex. A very long time since experiencing her last serious relationship. That ended disappointingly as did the one before that. Honest reflection concluded things ended badly largely because of her. Might this prove different?

"You could reconsider making the trip, Victoria? Understandable how you feel. But this is the kind of thing I do. Going into strange places relying on my senses to adapt to the circumstances."

"Damn it, Mark, don't you understand what I'm saying? I'm worried about something happening to you in this stupid quest involving Savi. As you pointed out, I'll be in the background. Can't you see I've developed serious feelings toward you?"

Her tears restarted as he embraced her. While she sobbed quietly against his neck, he could not help himself from becoming aroused with her bare breasts pressed against him.

Sensing the same feelings, she began stroking his cock attempting to coax a full erection.

"The will's there but maybe not the ability," he said. "You're insatiable."

"We'll see."

She rearranged her position then wiped his cock clean of the lovemaking with the sheet. As she took him full into her mouth, he groaned with pleasure. With residual sensitivity from intercourse and her oral attentions, his semi-erect member sprang fully erect. Within a short time, he convulsed with another orgasm.

Her performance left her feeling euphoric at how comfortable she felt in her intimacy with this interesting man.

"Why are we doing this crazy trip, Mark?"

Spent from the lovemaking, both experienced feelings transcending the sex. Each wrestled silently with their insecurities.

"Think of the story if I get first crack at interviewing Savi. I get insider material that becomes public before the government can do anything to prevent release. Once he disappears into the classified world of U.S. intelligence and witness protection, that story is forever lost. That's really what the government wants along with those in the Iranian leadership responsible.

"The issue of the warheads gets resolved the same way no matter what Savi does. This other financial stuff becomes a stark example of how far Russia has descended into institutionalized state corruption. Grigoryev's material shows the pervasive decline into despotism of the Putin regime."

"So you're risking your life for a better story?

"A harsh way of putting it, Victoria. My whole career has involved risk. My particular brand of investigative journalism puts me in trouble spots throughout the world. Places without the rule of law therefore dangerous bad actors. That's where I find my best stories.

"Lots of professions carry personal risk. I've known a lot of journalists working in trouble spots. For the most part, they're not adrenalin junkies. All have different reasons for doing what they do, yet most cannot adequately express those reasons in words.

"I'm not unique. Many journalists like me. The three photographs on the wall of my murdered associates working the MGI and Moscow Capital Partners story all had their reasons to take real risks. Think of the Russian investigative journalist Anna Politkovskaya murdered in Moscow for reporting on Russian excesses in the Chechen conflict. Or Marie Colvin killed in Syria trying to get a story out to the world by circumventing government censorship.

"No different with me. I understand the risks and try to balance against the possible benefits. But I don't see this venture to lure Savi to defect as the same I experienced going after the MGI story."

"Okay. But you must have asked yourself over the years why you do this. Your book, *Shell Game*, reads like a thriller with lots of violence. So try to explain to me.

"I see the world as overwhelmed by lies, half-truths, and carefully crafted arguments to sell something. Politics, religion, nationalism, economic schemes. Self-serving interests geared to persuading people. I like to think the facts I uncover help to balance the scale against the evils of power.

"I take seriously the need for a free press. Even those in power you might agree with can succumb to lies and subterfuge rationalized as for the greater good. Always their concept of good. I don't take sides. It's about exposing the truth. In my work, I'm cynical and largely apolitical.

"I don't go so far as to call what I do noble but I feel it's worthwhile. Important enough that it's worth some personal risk. How 'bout that for an existential justification?"

"Wish I shared your confidence, Mark. Seems so bizarre what we are about to do. We're not experienced in this sort of thing. I hope you haven't become inured to danger to have miscalculated this given all your past misadventures."

The following day, Wednesday, Victoria Prescott and Mark Reynolds boarded a nonstop Alitalia flight in the late afternoon from New York's JFK to Rome. Arriving early morning Rome time the following day, they had six hours to kill until their flight departed for Beirut, Lebanon. The three-hour flight with the one-hour time difference put them into Beirut late afternoon after clearing customs and immigration. Too late to deliver the fateful message to Professor Leila Hajjar at the American University. The plan called for spending only that night in Beirut then delivering the message the following day.

After delivering the message they would board a return flight to Rome that afternoon. Reynolds knew those few hours in Beirut represented some risk. He expected Hajjar to contact Savi immediately. If she accessed the USB drive, she would undoubtedly attempt to contact Savi by telephone immediately. If successful, therein lay the real danger. The Russian dossier said Savi frequently traveled to Beirut to confer with senior Hezbollah officials. Therefore, Savi undoubtedly had experienced violent resources probably at his disposal in Beirut. A few hours waiting at the airport before they departed Beirut left them exposed should Savi react by mounting an impromptu attack on them at the airport.

Prescott however was already committed. Reynolds chose not to add to her sense of foreboding by sharing this thought, which would only initiate a protracted argument to abort. He could not deny an element of risk existed. Once again, exposing someone emotionally close to possible physical danger of his making. Going after Savi was solely his doing. Was the bigger story worth it? Did he have the right to involve Victoria?

Since it was not possible to discuss what they were about on the plane, they read and made small talk. They could rest that night in Beirut before initiating the adrenalin-fueled uncertainty of the days ahead.

"What time do we deliver the message to Hajjar?" Prescott said.

"I'd prefer early afternoon. Gives us enough time to get back to the airport while not waiting any longer than necessary for our six o'clock flight back to Rome.

"So what do we do all day?"

"Mount surveillance on Ms. Hajjar. First of all, is she in her office? Possible of course she is not even at the university on Friday. If she's there and leaves early, we must prepare to intercept her and give her the message for Savi.

"So the first order of business is reconnaissance," Prescott said. "Maybe I can help?"

"Listen, I want you to stay in the background. I'll deliver the message to Hajjar. Don't want anyone connecting you to this."

"I understand. But I can still help. I obviously know my way around the university environment. I can ask the right questions without ever giving my name. Find out where Professor Hajjar's office is located and if she is in the office today."

"I already know the location of her office. In a building named College Hall. Close to the university campus main gate. I downloaded a map from the Internet. According to the AUB website, her office number is 421."

"Okay. However, to determine if she's in her office takes closer reconnaissance. As a woman I'm less conspicuous."

"Let me think about that. If I let you participate I still must be the one to deliver the USB to her and speak to her about the urgency in getting it to Savi. I don't want you connected."

"Understood."

From the airport south of the city, they took a taxi to the Three O Nine Hotel in the Hamra-Bliss area on Jeanne Darc Street. The American University is located between Paris Avenue known as the corniche along the Mediterranean coast and Bliss Street running parallel to the south. Their hotel was just two blocks from the main gate to the university. Their target building housing the Department of History and Archaeology and Leila Hajjar's office was just a short walk north of the university entrance gate.

The plan called for delivering the USB to Professor Hajjar then quickly returning to the hotel to retrieve their luggage and taxi to the airport for their 5:50pm flight to Rome. Should Hajjar not be in her office, Reynolds would slip the USB under the door, through a mail slot, or to some available secretary. A plan agreed to reluctantly at the insistence of Prescott. If not for her, he would have allocated at least another day to insure prompt delivery of the message to Savi. Therefore, there remained the risk of Hajjar not delivering the message to Savi immediately.

With a deadline set to release the story, any delay could obviate any motivation for Savi to defect. As a final fallback contingency, Reynolds included his burn phone number should Savi want to attempt a deal before everything became publicly exposed.

The hotel proved modestly upscale, decorated in modern chic with a restaurant and bar. Convenient since they did not intend venturing out to see Beirut at night. Get what sleep they could then check out leaving their luggage at the desk to retrieve later. They wanted to get to Hajjar's office by nine o'clock in the morning. If in the office, they would embark on a long surveillance until mid-afternoon before confronting her. This left them exposed for as short a time as possible in potentially hostile Beirut while waiting for their departure flight.

After a sleepless night both Prescott and Reynolds were anxious to conclude delivery of the message and be gone from Beirut. Privately, Prescott hoped the whole trip proved to be in vain, meaning Savi never showing up in Rome. Return to New York to release the material. Then brace for the blowback as events took their course.

Prescott still felt going public with the information seemed their only course of action. President Trump's inexplicable ignoring of Russian international outrages over the last several years and his affection for Vladimir Putin confounded everyone. Trump never denounced Russian cyber-attacks to affect the 2016 U.S. election, the annexation of Crimea, fostering and actively supporting separatist warfare in eastern Ukraine, support of the Syrian government while the West supports the Syrian rebels, and the flagrant murders and attempted murders of dissident Russians outside Russia. He stubbornly refuses to endorse economic sanctions against Russia. The common held belief was some underlying personal reason. Impossible to anticipate Trump's reaction to anything involving Russian wrongdoing.

After settling the hotel bill and securing their luggage for later retrieval at the desk, they fortified themselves with a light breakfast and coffee before setting out for the AUB campus.

"Ready for this?" Reynolds asked as he placed his hand over hers.

"Hell no, but I'll do my part. I'll just be glad to be on that plane out of here this afternoon.

Using an Internet map of the AUB campus, they approached the building housing the Department of History and Archaeology at nine o'clock. A warm sunny day. The campus surrounded by trees with the feel of cooling breeze coming off the nearby Mediterranean.

Reynolds said to Prescott as he pointed to the building, "Nothing to be concerned about. Just locate her office. See if she is in, but don't make yourself obvious. Understood?"

She nodded. With her heart racing, she told herself this was just a reconnaissance. All she had to do was determine if Leila Hajjar was in her office, or at least on campus. Hajjar's university website image imprinted in her mind.

As Prescott walked into the building, Reynolds found a bench and opened a book brought along to appear less conspicuous.

Prescott made her way up the stairs to the faculty office level. Locating Hajjar's office number, she tried the door finding it locked. To be sure, she knocked then waited a few moments but with no reply. Had Hajjar been in, Prescott would simply say she had the wrong office. Returning to the floor level, she approached the reception desk.

"Excuse me, but is Professor Hajjar in today?"

The young receptionist replied in good English, "Oh, yes. I believe she is giving a lecture right now. Let me check her schedule."

After consulting her computer monitor, the receptionist said, "Yes, her lecture starts in an hour and runs to 11:30. Do you wish to leave a message?"

Prescott said, "No thank you. I'll return later."

Returning to Reynolds, she said, "She's in today. Giving a lecture until 11:30."

After a two-hour wait, Prescott said, "Are you ready? Her office is on the top floor. Her name is on the door down the hallway about half way."

He gripped Prescott's hand. "Just a little longer and we're out of here."

After trying Hajjar's office door, he leaned against the opposite wall hoping she would return before leaving for lunch. Being conspicuous not a concern since claiming he was waiting for Professor Hajjar if asked. Within the USB was his picture and biographical data so it was not as if he was hiding his identity.

Unfortunately, Hajjar never showed. After waiting thirty minutes, Reynolds returned to Prescott outside on the bench. Three tense hours of waiting passed. Reynolds was ready to give up and slip the USB under her office door when they spotted her stepping out of an automobile and walking into the building.

Reynolds followed behind as she unlocked her office door.

"Excuse me. Are you Professor Leila Hajjar?

Turning, she replied in slightly accented English, "Yes."

"My name is Reynolds. I am an American journalist. May I have a couple of minutes of your time?"

"A journalist? American?"

"Yes."

"Very well, please come in."

They both entered the small office and Hajjar sat down behind her desk. "Please be seated Mr. Reynolds. Now what can I do for you?"

He continued to stand. "Thank you, but this will only take a couple of minutes, Ms. Hajjar."

She looked up at him with a puzzled expression. An attractive woman in her late forties with long black hair, dressed stylishly.

"I'm here to give you something." Reaching into his pocket, he extracted the thumb drive laying it down on the desk in front of her.

"What is this?" she said sharply, now apprehensive with this stranger.

"I need you to deliver this to your Iranian friend. You know him as Farhad Sattari. His real name is Farzard Savi, chief of the foreign intelligence directorate of Iranian Ministry of Intelligence. The thumb drive contains electronic files that Mr. Savi will find most interesting. This is very time-urgent, Ms. Hajjar. For his sake, you need to get this to him immediately. If he is in Iran, I suggest you contact him immediately and determine how you can securely transmit the information to him. My contact information is included."

"This is ridiculous. Now please get out of my office or I shall call security," she said angrily then stood up while picking up the USB drive.

"I am leaving, Professor. Understand that your lover's life may be in jeopardy with the information contained in those files. Tell him my offer is good for only a few days. It is his only way out."

"You're threatening him? Now I am calling security."

As she picked up her telephone, Reynolds turned and abruptly left.

Confused, Hajjar followed the now hurrying Reynolds as he descended the stairs two at a time. Once outside he headed at a fast walk toward Prescott sitting on the bench.

From behind him, Leila Hajjar hurried trying to catch up, yelling, "Stop! Please stop! I must know what this is about."

Prescott and Reynolds were already some distance away as Hajjar stopped to catch her breath. In heels, there was no way to close the distance to the departing stranger. Still clutching the USB in her hand, she rushed back to her office.

From another bench under a tree a slightly overweight man with a camera dressed in a cheap tropical suit stood up. Equipped with a telephoto lens, he captured a series of close-up photos first of Prescott and Reynolds movements then of the episode outside with Hajjar following Reynolds out of the building shouting. Two other men with Middle Eastern appearance of close-cropped beards and in casual attire soon joined him.

In Russian, one of the bearded men said to the other, "Follow the targets. Stay close to them until they board the aircraft." To the man with the camera in the rumpled suit. "Bring the car around. We shall stay with the Lebanese woman."

The Russian issuing the orders was Lieutenant Ebrahim Zadeh of the SVR's Zaslon unit. He reported to Major Kozlovsky who took half his team from New York to Rome. Knowing Reynolds and Prescott were only in Beirut for one night then returning to Rome dictated making the abduction in Rome. Zadeh and one other Zaslon operative were there to determine the reason for the brief Beirut visit. They requisitioned the local SVR resident at the Russian Beirut Embassy to act as their driver, evoking the code word *Motherland*.

The embassy staffer sensed they may be Zaslon special forces but knew better than inquire. If they were, this was serious business probably involving violence. Everyone in the SVR knew Zaslon engaged in secret black operations. The best of the best selected from other Russian special forces.

Suspicioning that Reynolds trip to Beirut potentially involved Savi, Kozlovsky sent his number-two, Lieutenant Zadeh. As a Persian fluent in both Arabic and Farsi, should Savi be in Beirut visiting his girlfriend, Zadeh's language skill might prove useful. However, should the opportunity present itself, his orders called for killing Savi. No need to disguise the murder easily attributed as an Israeli Mossad hit.

The scene with Hajjar chasing after Reynolds and Prescott confirmed their reason for being in Beirut. The mission now for Hajjar to lead them to Savi if he was in Beirut. Failing that, determine the meaning of Reynolds' contact by any means necessary.

Within only minutes of Hajjar returning inside the building, she reemerged and walked hurriedly to a parked car. Zadeh climbed into the passenger seat beside the cameraman in the bad suit already behind the wheel.

"Follow her."

Driving too fast for the traffic, Hajjar headed southeast from the university. After just a few miles, she pulled in front of the five-star Sofitel Hotel on Avenue de l'Indépendence. Her fifteen-year old small sedan in need of a wash stood out as she exited in a hurry handing the car keys and some money to the door attendant.

Zadeh motioned for his driver to pull to the curb. Exiting the vehicle, he following Hajjar into the hotel.

He came up close enough to her at the front desk to hear her conversation with the desk clerk while appearing preoccupied looking down at his cellphone scrolling through messages.

"Mr. Sattari's room please," Hajjar said excitedly in Arabic.

"I'm afraid I cannot give out a guest's room number. However, I shall be glad to call his room. Your name, Madame?"

"Leila Hajjar. Please hurry."

Savi arrived at the hotel only an hour earlier.

"You're early, Leila. I'll be right down and we'll have a drink in the bar."

"No, Farhad, I need to talk with you. A man came into my office this afternoon. He made all sorts of strange accusations. Said you were not who you claimed to be. He gave me a thumb drive to deliver to you. Said it was urgent you saw what was on it."

"I understand. Give me the desk clerk. He will give you a key then come straight up."

The clerk processed a key card handing it to her.

She went to the bank of elevators and punched in the sixth floor. Zadeh entered behind her and pressed for the seventh floor.

CHAPTER 20

BEIRUT, LEBANON

Leila Hajjar exited the elevator and let herself into the designated room calling out "Farhad". From the partially open bathroom door came the sound of water running in the shower.

Outside in the hallway the elevator door opened and Ebrahim Zadeh exited. Walking down the hallway, he stopped at the room Hajjar just entered, putting his ear to the door.

From the stairwell door near the elevators, Farzard Savi stepped out holding a 9mm pistol with attached silencer. Seeing the man at his room door, he advanced several strides closing the distance to the man listening at the door. Savi held the weapon in his outstretched arm cupping the butt of the weapon with his other palm.

The room door unexpectedly opened startling the man causing him to step back. As he saw Hajjar in the doorway, he abruptly turned around trying to disguise himself as just another guest in the hallway. Shock registered as he saw Savi approaching only twenty feet away pointing a weapon. As he attempted to extract his own weapon from under his jacket, Savi shot him twice in the chest.

The man dropped his weapon, collapsing to the floor. While not without noise, the silencer eliminated the loud crack of the fired rounds. From inside the hotel rooms, the noise should not register as gunshots.

Hajjar uttered a gasp and brought her hand to her mouth. Stepping into the hallway, she looked down at the prone man's shirt turning crimson with spreading blood from the bullet wounds. To her credit, she did not scream, just continued holding her hand to her mouth as she saw Savi with his gun. It took a couple of seconds for her to process what had just happened.

"Get back inside the room, Leila."

Slow to react, he said sharply, "Now, Leila! And close the door."

She did as ordered.

With no one in the hallway, Savi wasted no time in attempting to conceal the shooting. After picking up the man's weapon and putting it in his own waistband, Savi grabbed him by the shirt collar and began dragging him back toward the stairwell access door.

He successfully pulled the wounded man inside the stairway landing before anyone entered the hallway.

Still alive, the man's breathing was shallow. Periodically he coughed spewing forth blood from his mouth. At least one of the rounds obviously damaged a lung.

The man, about thirty, physically fit, wore a close-cropped beard like Savi. Inside his jacket he wore a shoulder holster.

Propping the man against the wall Savi asked first in Arabic, "Who are you working for?"

The man barely conscious made no reply.

Savi repeated the question in English. Again no reply. Then in Farsi. Could this be Iranian intelligence service?

Asking in Russia, Savi detected an almost imperceptible reaction in the eyes.

In Russian, "It is possible you might survive if you receive immediate medical attention. Tell me who you are?"

Barely audible and accompanied by a burst of frothy blood from the man's mouth, came "*Ебать тебя.*" Fuck you in Russian.

Savi dragged the man to the stairs then sent him tumbling down the steps to the landing below. Assuming only infrequent use of the stairwell on the sixth floor, it might be hours before discovery of the body.

Returning to the room, Savi noticed there was no visible trace of blood on the hallway carpet. No evidence directly linking his room to the shooting. Mattered little anyway since he must now discard his alternative identity as Farhad Sattari. For that matter, his real name Farzard Savi posed a threat. Not only the Russians were after him but soon his own country. He must now disappear into his elaborately constructed identity as the Austrian-Lebanese Faisal Drescher.

Inside the room, Leila Hajjar sat on the bed holding her head in her hands.

Looking up, she said, "What is going on? Who are you? You shot that man!"

Savi came to her attempting to take her hand but she pulled it away.

"I had no choice, Leila. He was about to kill both of us. I will explain later. Right now, we must leave here immediately. I mean leave Beirut. Tonight."

"Leave Beirut? Why?"

"Leila, because that man I shot is a Russian assassin. I do not know why I am targeted. But we need to get to a safe place. Please do as I say."

She reached for her purse and took out the USB given to her by Reynolds. "Here, this is what the American gave me."

Savi took it from her and grabbed his suitcase and laptop computer. "Now listen carefully. We will leave by the back of the hotel and take a taxi to your apartment. You'll pack quickly and then we will leave for the airport."

"What about my car?"

"Leila, I'll buy you a new car. We must leave immediately."

"Why must I leave Beirut? I've done nothing wrong. You shot that man. A Russian assassin you say? Who are you, Farhad?"

"I'll explain everything once we get to the airport. Right now we must leave. Because of me, you are also in danger."

"Flying to where?"

"Anywhere taking us away from Beirut."

They walked two blocks away from the hotel before hailing a taxi.

Hajjar's fear turned to anger, further aggravated by the frustration of not understanding what had just happened and now unable to question Savi in the taxi. Arriving at her apartment, he told her to pack a suitcase, enough for a week, and to bring her passport and laptop computer. He would wait in the taxi. The wait providing the opportunity to determine if there was any surveillance at her apartment.

Hajjar returned to the taxi twenty minutes later. As Savi tried to touch her, she pulled away. Arriving at the airport, she exited the taxi slamming the door.

Checking departing flights on the display board at Beirut-Rafic Hariri International Airport, Savi looked for a way to get to Vienna. It was late at night with few flights departing for any destination until the early morning hours. The best option was a non-stop flight departing at 8:00am for Milan on Middle East Airlines. From Milan they could train north into Austria where he could disappear into his Austrian identity. After purchasing first-class tickets, they settled into the airport's Cedar Lounge for the eight-hour wait until departure.

Planning ahead after securing his Austrian identity two years earlier, Savi opened a checking account in Vienna. He funded the account by periodically diverting discretionary operational funds of the Iranian MOIS, disguised as untraceable expenditures. With a substantial balance accumulated through regular deposits, he obtained various credit cards in the name of Faisal Drescher. Using the cards when traveling to Lebanon or Europe, he arranged for automatic payment of the monthly statements from his Vienna bank account. Possessing a credit history provided additional substance to his new identity as Faisal Drescher. The Austrian bank account provided the means to periodically transfer money from his secret Swiss account concealing his millions from the Russian nuclear warhead theft without raising suspicion.

Anxious to see what this alleged American delivered to Hajjar, he first needed to calm and reassure her. Even though genuinely fond of her, she now represented a liability. As taught during training at the Russian SVR academy, in the event of unexpected events during a field operation, survival meant breaking through seeming chaos by calmly assessing options. Pragmatically choosing a course of action to save your life dictated taking ruthless action. He should quietly dispose of Leila. Yet he knew he could not do that.

Suddenly, all his planning to leave Iran on his own terms fell apart. First the surveillance in Tehran. Perhaps something connected to Ye-jin Sung? Was North Korea somehow involved? Perhaps his own intelligence service the Iranian MOIS? Then the suspicious interactions of known Russian intelligence associates in Damascus. Followed immediately with this person claiming to be American giving his girlfriend electronic files. Unlikely a journalist could have discovered their relationship. CIA? Then an assassination attempt by a Russian. The common threat must have something to do with the nuclear warhead theft of several years ago. Vladimir Putin pursuing revenge? Yet why now?

Priorities dictated first getting to safety. Clearly too dangerous to remain in Beirut. Returning to Iran remained possible depending on what he discovered on the electronic files delivered to Leila. With plans already in place for leaving Iran imminently, these recent events added to the uncertainty of such a move. Once back in Iran, future escape could be far more difficult. Yet the option of disappearing into his new identity outside Iran now carried increased risk. Russian intelligence had a long reach.

With several hours before boarding, he opened his laptop computer. Reading Reynolds' introduction and pitch for defecting to the United States added yet another element to this cascade of disasters.

Sitting next to him in the waiting area, Hajjar stared at him intently for some time as he studied the computer before she said, "Now tell me what this is about."

He looked over at her while closing his laptop. He read enough to begin putting together what might have happened. If Reynolds had this information then conceivably the Russians may fear their cover-up of the warheads theft was about to be revealed. Removing him might assist in their denials.

With the lounge sparsely occupied at this late hour, they remained out of earshot of the few other patrons.

"Very well, Leila. First, this American is correct. My real name is Farzard Savi. I am the chief of the foreign intelligence directorate of the Iranian Ministry of Intelligence and Security. You know me by my operational cover as Farhad Sattari, a trade specialist with the Iranian Ministry of Economic Affairs and Finance.

"I regret deceiving you these past few years, Leila. You must understand that I had no choice. Our relationship could never be possible had I traveled under my real identity. Becoming increasingly fond of you left me no way to be honest without potentially endangering you."

"After what happened at the hotel, that did not work out so well did it?"

He sighed, "What I mean was the danger of all the intrigue swirling about in Beirut. You are aware of my country's involvement with Hezbollah. That alone would make me a prime target for Israel's Mossad. However, I now suspicion everything now centers on the Russians."

"The Russians? Why?"

"I believe this attack on me is rooted in an intelligence operation I directed against the Russians four years ago. The assassin at the hotel was Russian special forces."

"How do you know? And what happened to him?" Covering her mouth in an expression of horror, "Please don't tell me you killed him?"

"I left him in the stairwell, Leila. Unlikely he survived with the gunshots to his chest. I shot him in self-defense. You saw that. He was after me but undoubtedly would also have killed you. Unfortunately my profession puts me at risk, therefore I carry a weapon."

"I thought I knew you. The Iranian government financial official. Handsome, educated, refined, westernized. Now you reveal you are a spy. Someone who carries a gun because others could be out to kill you. I suppose your trips to Beirut were to meet with Iran's terrorist partners Hezbollah."

"Listen, Leila. Whatever I was is now behind me. I have been thinking about leaving Iran for some time. Now I have no choice. However, it is not that easy for someone in my profession.

"This American, if he is actually American, has at least explained what is happening. A complicated story, Leila. You'll understand what's at stake when I tell you the details."

"But where will you go, Farhad, or should I call you Farzard?"

"I have not yet determined where to go. I have ample financial resources hidden away, but these unexpected events have altered how I planned to resign official position and quietly leave Iran. Unfortunately, I know too much."

"And you expect me to follow you like some Bedouin woman? I have a career, a life. I am Lebanese. I embrace my Mediterranean origins, but for me that means identifying more with Europe. I resent the plight of Lebanon sucked into the never-ending sectarian and religious strife plaguing the Middle East.

"Now you tell me you are part of Iran's subversive interference in the Middle East. The West calls it exporting terrorism. Just what do you do in Damascus and Beirut? Helping Hezbollah and that butcher Assad."

"That is all behind me now. I hope that we might find a life together, Leila. Right now it is a matter of getting to a safe location. I promise I will do everything possible to restore your life as it was before today. Just give me a little time to sort this out and plan what to do.

"Perhaps you could get us some coffee. We have a long night ahead and I need to study what this American gave you.

After again reading Reynolds' pitch to facilitate his defection to the U.S. before going public, he poured over the details of Yuri Dratshev's *confession.* Painstaking in its detail explaining the paper trail falsifications that both enabled as well as concealed the theft. Dratshev's record even provided the names of the complicit Russian army officers. He then described their deaths under his own orders at the hands of the Russian criminal syndicate Solntsevskaya Bratva. Dratshev clearly outlined Savi's role and that of Felix Garnitsky.

Once Dratshev disposed of the military witnesses, he worried about his own fate. Although Garnitsky's right-hand man for years, after this he was too great a threat. With the likely promise of a great deal of money, Dratshev chose not to go into hiding although surely fearing for his life. And where could he go anyway? Garnitsky had a long association with the Solntsevskaya Bratva. Both had the means to eliminate him as the only remaining witness no matter where he fled. Trapped to whatever fate befell him, Dratshev chose to pen the full account and ask his brother to keep it, opening it only after his death. Garnitsky should planned better.

Of course this still might be a CIA operation. Using Reynolds either willingly or not. The Americans would like specific intelligence on the locations of the warheads in Iran. If they were convinced that the theft took place, a massive airstrike became vastly more effective with specific target locations.

The more pressing question for Savi if he pursued defection was the receptivity of the Americans to do a deal for asylum. Was providing the location of the warheads, the strategic intent for these warheads, the larger question of details on the Iranian nuclear weapons program, and who in Iran was behind this, sufficient? Or would the CIA just dump him into one of their rumored dark rendition sites?

Reading his extensive dossier prepared by Russian intelligence was disconcerting in its level of specifics. However, the recounting of his career and personal habits perhaps lent credibility to this journalist's approach suggesting defection. The journalist could infer from the information the potential for inducing him to go over to the Americans. A clear inclination for Western culture and fluency in English and German. A fondness for fine living. His secularism and implied distain for Islamic dogma. Savi agreed with the conclusions.

Possession of the dossier by the journalist proved nothing. The CIA might still be using him as bait. However, in view of the Russian assassination attempt, the Russians presented the immediate threat. Of course, it could be both.

The Russians complicated the choice to defect to the Americans using Reynolds as a conduit. Were they also after Reynolds? Was it Reynolds' contact with Leila that led the assassin to the hotel? Of course the Russians knew of Leila so was that a coincidence? Tradecraft training schooled him to disbelieve in coincidences. Therefore, he must assume the Russians were targeting Reynolds as well. How could he then connect with Reynolds? Should he instead simply walk into an American embassy somewhere in Europe? If Reynolds then went public with the story as threatened, did that jeopardize his bargaining position with the Americans?

Hajjar returned with coffees. After allowing him to study the material on his laptop for a minute, Hajjar finally asked, "What does the American want?"

Savi looked up from his laptop. After insuring no one was within hearing distance, he said, "I ran a major intelligence operation against the Russians four years ago. A mission I conceived and sold to my leadership. If successful, the results would prove of vital significance to Iran's national security. It was successful. Absolute secrecy was essential to long-term success. Unfortunately, the Russians discovered the penetration."

"Penetration?"

"Penetration of Russian nuclear weapons facilities. The mission of vital importance to Iran's nuclear weapons program."

"I thought Iran has always denied any such program?"

He put a finger to his lips. "I'll explain in detail later, but not here."

He pulled up the photo of Mark Reynolds on his laptop. "Is this the man who came to your office this afternoon?"

She nodded, "Yes. Who is he?"

"An investigative journalist. Might be working for U.S. intelligence or just freelancing as he claims. Impressive background. Published two books. I must take him seriously. What he has is documented details of that mission four years ago. He is threatening to go public with the story. Claims to want an even bigger story by helping me to defect to the Americans."

"Why does that become a larger story?"

"Because I alone have information of vital use to the Americans. Even more so with recent events as the American President has ratcheted up aggressive threats to Iran."

"So he wants you to betray your country?"

"Perhaps not that simple anymore. Once the details of what happened become public, my situation in Iran may become tenuous at best. This is so explosive to both Iran and Russia there is no way to gauge how my superiors might react. You can see how violently the Russians have reacted."

"What choices do you have?"

Already having narrowed his options, he replied, "After today, only two choices. Simply disappear somewhere in Europe or consider this journalist's solution of going over to the Americans."

She looked at him quizzically. "Really? How could you just disappear? You would need a new identity. How would you live financially?"

Not ready to share specifics about his financial means, he avoided the last part of her question. "I have a new identity, Leila. A valid passport that makes me an EU citizen. I'm traveling under that name right now."

"So I'm to know you by yet another name? And after Milan, what is next?"

"I believe we decide on a destination in Europe. Where depends on accepting this journalist's scheme to defect or vanishing on my own. The American wants to meet me in Rome?"

"Then why are we then flying to Milan?"

"Because Rome might be a trap. The Russians possibly know about the American. I believe they must have followed him to you. American intelligence may also be watching him. Either intelligence organization may have watchers at the Rome airport.

"I need to think this through about whether to consider defecting and seeking asylum in the United States, or just disappearing. If it is to be Rome then we train south. If the later, we train north and leave Italy."

However, Savi already made up his mind to explore the defection option. If legitimate, it offered him the best long-term options. Checking train schedules online, they could be in Rome in three hours from Milan. He would miss the Saturday meeting window Reynolds defined at the Piazza Navona but it would provide an opportunity to canvas the terrain to consider approaching Reynolds on Sunday.

Who was watching Reynolds remained the critical question. Could Savi circumvent the surveillance? Leila Hajjar might prove useful as his canary in the mine.

"And what about me, Farhad? Am I part of your new future?"

As Savi's flight became airborne out of Beirut, it was one o'clock in the afternoon in Brooklyn, New York. Bernie Poole ordered a pastrami on rye at his favorite Jewish delicatessen. Not the best of neighborhoods but it held a special place for Poole.

This was the neighborhood of his youth, returning here frequently for sixty years. The third generation current proprietor was an old acquaintance his own age.

Finishing his sandwich at one of only a couple small tables, Poole walked toward the door. "Thanks, Moe. See you next week."

An old-fashioned doorbell sounded as he exited.

From inside the liquor store next door a shot rang out. Seconds later a man with a ski mask covering his face violently pushed the door open.

Startled, Bernie Poole froze starring at the man holding a handgun. The running man collided with Poole sending him reeling backward but regaining his balance and now facing the gunman.

The gunman shot him from only three feet with a single fatal bullet to the forehead.

Only minutes later, a team of two men carefully broke into Poole's Brooklyn apartment using lock picks. A thorough search found no written materials related to Russia. Unfortunately, the computer access was highly encrypted with professional-grade software. Impossible for this team to penetrate. They found no backup hard drives. Under orders not to disturb anything such as removing the computer hard drive left them few options. At best, Poole's murder outside the delicatessen remained an unsolved homicide of a bystander to a failed liquor store holdup.

As Savi and Hajjar became airborne out of Beirut, Victoria Prescott and Mark Reynolds landed at Rome's Fiumicino International Airport.

After clearing customs and reaching a taxi, Prescott put her head on Reynolds' shoulder. "God I'm glad that's over with. I was scared the entire time in Beirut."

Reynolds wanted to say Beirut was the easy part. The dicey circumstance was this weekend should the Iranian show up.

Always possible it could be for revenge for exposing him. He only knew Savi from what his Russian dossier said. Instead, he just said, "It's almost over, Victoria."

"You mean this cloak and dagger stuff? In some ways, I hope Savi doesn't show. Promise me if he does that, we won't be undergoing the FBI's and DOJ's high-handed methods by our meddling in matters of national security."

"That's where Phillip Ellsberg comes in. It's his former turf and he's good."

"Well it would be nice to enjoy Rome before facing the shit storm when we release the story once back in New York.

"You're still okay releasing all that material incriminating Putin as a thief?"

"You left out murderer. And yes, more than ever. I want to drive a stake in Putin's malignant heart. Most experts in their fields find some personal connection with their subject. I'm no different. I have a great affection for the Russian people. Suffering unimaginable exploitation for hundreds of years. Putin is just the last in a long history of brutal oppressors.

"I can follow up later on with my academic work of attempting to explain Russia in the twentieth and twenty-first centuries. My project is explaining the progression from absolute feudalistic monarchy to the first Communist state. Then those socialist ideals corrupted under the decades of Soviet Stalinist dictatorship followed by the ultimate collapse of the failed Soviet system. The nascent aspirations but doomed experiment with capitalistic democracy during the 1990s only to degenerate in today's kleptocracy under Putin's rule. The central premise being to explain with so many natural and human resources, why Russia regressed to a failed corrupt state?

Reynolds said, "Well the shit storm you refer to should be more from the media. Comments, interviews, network news appearances. Ellsberg should keep the government jackals at bay."

"Tell you what. Once back in New York I intend to decompress. You can do the talk show appearances and such. I'll relax at the apartment. You can make love to me every day to make up for this crazy escapade you seduced me into."

Two Russian Zaslons picked up surveillance on Prescott and Reynolds as they exited baggage claim at Rome's Fiumicino Airport. Their colleague in Beirut transmitted a coded message as the targets' flight departed Beirut. He also transmitted confirmation that Reynolds and Prescott made contact with the Iranian's girlfriend after which Lieutenant Zadeh followed the woman. A subsequent transmission stated his inability to contact Zadeh.

Major Ivan Kozlovsky, commanding the mission, assumed his number-two man encountered serious difficulties. Zadeh's orders included killing Savi if the Iranian proved to be the reason for Reynolds and Prescott traveling to Beirut. According to the other operative, that was in fact what happened and Zadeh separated in order to eliminate the Iranian. Not checking in raised concerns. Perhaps his communications just failed, but it could mean he was dead or incapacitated. Hard to believe an accomplished *Spetsnaz* like Zadeh could not prevail against someone like Savi, presumably alone in Beirut and not known for possessing violent skills. Perhaps Savi was under protection by Hezbollah.

If Zadeh was a casualty, he carried no identification or indications of being Russian. Logic would point to an Israeli Mossad assassination attempt.

Kozlovsky's orders were far more delicate. Italy was not Beirut. His team was to abduct Reynolds and Prescott then smuggle them out of Italy into Russian-friendly territory if possible. Barring that, hold them in a secure location in Italy and extract the information using whatever means necessary. What information did they possess and who else has the information? Kozlovsky then expected further orders to kill them, disposing of the bodies probably at sea to prevent discovery.

CHAPTER 21

ROME, ITALY

Prescott and Reynolds arrived at their hotel in Rome at 9:00pm. A small hotel tucked away on the Via del Teatro Pace, a tiny street just a short distance west of the Piazza Navona. Like all of Europe, Italians dined late. The hotel clerk directed them to a couple of cafes a short walk south. They were both hungry and glad to be out of Beirut after delivering the message to Savi's girlfriend. For Prescott it meant nearing the end of this frightful adventure.

Summers in Rome can be oppressive during the daytime, yet at this late hour, it was perfect for dining outside. After ordering pasta dishes, both dove into the fresh bread with olive oil accompanied by a good bottle of wine. The warm evening while sitting outside with the unique ambience of Rome made them feel like lovers on holiday. Regrettably, not much of a holiday with the anxiety of waiting for Savi to take the bait. Prescott almost hoped Savi would not show. Let this just end. Unlike Reynolds, she worried something unexpected happening. After all, they were threatening a senior intelligence officer of Iran. Not a comforting thought. The next two days would be wrenchingly stressful.

"God this is wonderful," she said. "Wish it was a holiday. I've never been to Rome. Guess we can't see the sights this trip."

"Unfortunately not. Even though I'd guess less than a fifty-fifty chance for Savi taking the offer. Hardly enough time for him to think it through thoroughly. Then again, it wouldn't be safe for us to prolong this. Chances are he'll either hunker down in Iran or make a run for it on his own. He knows his name will soon be in the media. Whatever happens, at least we can enjoy tonight."

She hoisted her glass of wine. "Here's to our successful collaboration."

He touched his glass to hers. "I'm glad we came together, Victoria."

She smiled mischievously. "Professionally or sexually?"

He smiled in return. "Both. However as good as both are, I'm thinking beyond that. Once we're done with this, is there a future for us?"

She felt her heart race. Her very own feelings while trying to suppress her latent anxieties. Don't screw this one up, Victoria. He just might be it.

Grabbing his hand in both of hers, "I hope so, Mark. I've got to be honest though. I'm still scared."

He covered her hand with his other hand, "This will be okay, Victoria."

"No, no. I didn't mean about this Savi thing or shitting on Putin in the media, I mean about us. I don't think I'm very good with personal relationships. There have been several men in my life. Intelligent men, by all accounts good for me. Yet somehow things just never worked out. Always attributed it to conflicts of our respective careers. With introspection over the years, I'm not so sure. If I'm being honest with myself, I think it was me that caused the relationships not to work. Takes a lot of effort to make that work."

"Of course it takes effort. Anything worthwhile does. But that doesn't necessarily mean drudgery."

"I know. I didn't mean it like that. I want there to be a future for us together, Mark."

"I would hope so, Victoria." He leaned over and they kissed. "You know my past is also littered with failed relationships. Most never even got off the ground. The ones that might have worked failed because of my profession. Gone too much. Too much uncertainty for my safety for any woman to pursue a lasting connection. Others were never good fits intellectually."

She smiled. "Just convenient sexual partners?"

"A few probably fit that category. Mostly just circumstances eventually got in the way. How do you share a life in my line of work?

"So I got lucky by you coming along. We make a great team professionally and emotionally. No question about your brains. You are a knockout with that indefinable sexy quality. Our lovemaking couldn't be better. So let's not dwell on past failures. I'm telling you that I want *us* to continue together."

She leaned over to kiss him again with tears running down her cheeks.

They did enjoy the night. After the excellent meal, they walked back to the hotel, both with the same immediate thought on their mind.

Even following lovemaking, sleep did not come easy for either of them, thinking about the uncertainty of tomorrow afternoon. Waking early from a fretful night, they decided to get coffee just walk about. Within easy walking distance this sector of Rome offered some of the iconic Roman sights. Early enough in the day to enjoy the Trevi Fountain, the Pantheon, and the Coliseum before the tourist crowds descended. They ended at the Piazza Navona before one o'clock to wait for Savi.

A light lunch at a café in the Piazza Navona took on a more somber note as they mentally prepared to wait for Savi's possible arrival. Making the strain more pronounced, they left the café at the appointed time. Reynolds walked to his position close to the spectacular Bernini fountain in the piazza. Prescott took up a position far enough away to observe surreptitiously.

❖ ❖ ❖

While Prescott and Reynolds lunched at an outdoor restaurant on the Piazza Navona, Zaslon team leader Major Ivan Kozlovsky was sitting with another man on the opposite end of the piazza.

Speaking in Russian, the other man said to Kozlovsky, "What is your plan, Major?"

"For the moment, we will wait and observe. The two Americans appear to be waiting for someone," Kozlovsky replied.

Kozlovsky knew they might be waiting for Colonel Farzard Savi of the Iranian MOIS. Via his secure satellite phone, Moscow relayed what transpired in Beirut.

Following a visit by the American reporter to her university office, Savi's Lebanese mistress left by car in a rush. Kozlovsky's second in command, Lieutenant Ebrahim Zadeh followed her in a car driven by a local Russian Embassy SVR staffer. After hurriedly parking her car in front of a hotel, Zadeh followed the woman inside after ordering the SVR driver to maintain surveillance outside until he returned.

Zadeh never returned.

The SVR driver followed his orders explicitly, waiting the entire night in the car. He could not afford a mistake given his orders. Clearly, this operative was Zaslon. The mission code word left no doubt it came from the highest level.

Wailing sirens interrupted his lonely vigil in the early morning hours as police vehicles converged on the hotel. Waiting another two hours hoping to learn what happened to his shadowy colleague, a completely covered body on a gurney exited the building to a waiting ambulance.

Hanging about he walked up to the door attendant and offered the man a cigarette while asking what was going on. *Cleaning woman found a dead man in the stairwell. Blood all over. Shot according to staff rumors.*

The SVR man returned to the embassy, immediately reporting to Moscow. New instructions ordered him to determine the identity of the victim while discretely trying to find out if Farzard Savi was among those staying at the hotel. For a sizable cash payment, a source provided the guest list for that night. The name Farhad Sattari, confirmed to Moscow that Savi was the target. Within hours, another bribe at the morgue produced an official photograph of the deceased.

Speaking to his associate, Kozlovsky said, "We maintain surveillance through Monday and see what happens. Moscow tells us the man and woman hold tickets on a Wednesday flight to New York. If the person they are waiting for appears then we must be prepared to move immediately. If nothing happens, we take the targets Monday. Are your people ready?

The other man nodded. He did not like this arrogant soldier. Obviously Russian special forces by his confidence and bearing.

Boris Stefanovich Lebedyenko headed operations in Italy for the Russian crime syndicate Solntsevskaya Bratva. Mostly involved with smuggling, principally drugs, his instructions were to provide *any and all assistance* to this asshole. Lebedyenko understood the order originated at the highest level within the Kremlin. Not the first time he received orders to clean up some mess for Vladimir Putin.

Four years ago, orders came down to dispose of a long time fellow criminal associate, Felix Garnitsky. Garnitsky obviously ran afoul of the Putin regime, however, Lebedyenko never learned any details. With Garnitsky fleeing to Rome, it fell to Lebedyenko to execute the contract. Lebedyenko understood the mutually beneficial relationship between the Solntsevskaya Bratva and the current government regime. As in the Garnitsky situation, this was yet another accommodation to the real criminal boss, Vladimir Putin.

Lebedyenko's instructions were to assist Russian intelligence in the abduction of two U.S. nationals. A sensitive undertaking that must not be traceable in any way to Russia. His instructions specified using Italian criminal resources to support the intelligence operatives. The targets were American journalists threatening to expose criminal drug smuggling of Afghanistan opium through Italy.

The order made clear that secrecy was paramount. The Italians must believe this involved the drug trade. After abduction of the subjects, the plan called for extraditing them to a secure location. Get them to Syria by sea. Secretly secure the subjects on the ship, eventually transferring them to a smaller, fast Syrian vessel once just outside Syrian waters.

Lebedyenko said, "As you requested, I have made arrangements on a freighter. Bound for various ports in the Eastern Mediterranean. A rust bucket tramp steamer past its prime but useful. I trust you can arrange for a fast smaller vessel to rendezvous just outside Syrian waters to avoid warships patrolling the area?"

"It shall be arranged. When is this ship scheduled to depart," Kozlovsky said.

"The *Bella Signora* sails on the tide on Wednesday from the Adriatic port of Bari. The captain is reliable. Worked for us many times before."

"And how do we get to Bari?"

"By truck. A large delivery truck. Six hours."

"Why Bari?"

"Because the ship docks in Bari tomorrow with an already workable itinerary suitable for our purpose. For the right price, I simply delayed its sailing due to *engine problems*. My people already lease a dockside warehouse in Bari. They can make a quiet transfer from there onto the freighter without raising suspicion. You also require a secure place in which to interrogate the subjects. What better place than the hold of a rusting tramp steamer?"

Kozlovsky liked the plan. If it proved impossible to make the transfer to offload his subjects to Syria, he could dispose of them without any trace if necessary. The trip across the Adriatic would take four days. More than adequate time to extract information from Prescott and Reynolds. His team could then disembark in the next port of call of Beirut, Lebanon, easily crossing into Syria to link up with Russian military in the country.

"Then Monday we execute the plan," Kozlovsky said.

"My men will be ready. Care to show me the targets?"

Kozlovsky extracted photos of Prescott and Reynolds from inside his jacket then said, "Come with me and I will point them out. They are seated at a café at the opposite end of the piazza. Two of my people are watching them."

"Where will the abduction take place?" Lebedyenko asked.

"At their hotel a short distance from here. When they leave. The hotel fronts on a narrow street with few pedestrians. We walk them quietly to the end of the narrow street where the truck is waiting."

Kozlovsky and Lebedyenko strolled past one of the Zaslon surveillance team without making any sign of recognition. As they approached near to the outside canopied area of a café at a safe distance, Kozlovsky offered Lebedyenko a cigarette while whispering, "The man in the blue shirt sitting with the woman with dark hair and white blouse."

"Sexy looking bitch. A professor you say?"

"Her academic specialty is Russia. Even speaks Russian. Believed to be the source of sensitive stolen documents."

"A spy?"

"The details are not necessary, Lebedyenko."

Lebedyenko's eyes narrowed. He had killed people daring to address him with such disrespect. Fucking arrogant prick. A killing machine with no character. He employed this type of muscle in his own line of work. Yet he said nothing although a troubling thought occurred. With the Kremlin directly involved, might this be a counterintelligence operation directed against the American CIA? Lebedyenko would not rule out Putin doing something so provocative.

Finishing lunch where neither had much appetite, Reynolds said, "It's noon. Showtime."

"But the instructions told Savi between one and three o'clock?"

Reynolds nodded. "I know. But you must remain unconnected to me. He's a trained professional. He might already be here. That's why I picked this place with this table well back under the canopy in the shadows so I can observe the piazza. He doesn't know about you. So just get up and take a circuitous route to find a place from which to observe me. Don't make it obvious. Act like a tourist. Move about but just keep an eye on me. I'll be wandering close to the fountain at the appointed time."

"And if he shows, I'm to observe and wait for your call on the cellphone."

She did not reiterate the rest of Reynolds' instructions should something bad happen like being led away under gunpoint. In that event, she was to call Ellsberg and trigger the media release. Then get to the U.S. Embassy.

The afternoon passed without event. Following instructions, she returned separately to the hotel ahead of Reynolds in case Savi might be watching him. Reynolds would join her after taking a circuitous route to insure no one following.

Unlike the prior night, stress heightened. Today might have been too soon for Savi to react and get to Rome. Tomorrow ended Reynolds' imposed deadline if Savi intended to meet. Reynolds told Prescott, if he were in Savi's position, he would allocate surveillance time to observe him waiting by the fountain. Determine if he was alone or watched by U.S. intelligence. Then again, maybe not enough time. Savi may have been anywhere when Hajjar conveyed the message. Making such a life changing decision immediately then getting to Rome might take more than a day even for a veteran spy.

While making his way to Rome, Savi planned a couple moves ahead. If Reynolds checked out as legitimate, he would lay out his demands to the Americans then separate from Reynolds while going to ground in his own secure location in Austria. A location where he could hide in plain sight. An untraceable legal identity with a plausible past with access to his Austrian bank account as well as easy access to his Swiss bank account. A location from which to easily travel anywhere in the EU for exfiltration by the Americans.

When he and Hajjar arrived at Rome Termini central train station at 5:00pm, they checked into a modest hotel nearby. After the long exhausting hours of the prior night in Beirut, followed by the four-hour flight to Milan then a three-hour train trip to Rome, both needed to rest. For Savi, he not only needed time to rest physically but also to reassure Leila to insure her cooperation the following day.

On the train ride south, he found the Hotel Gioberti just 150 feet from Rome Termini train station on a travel website. A pleasant hotel in a 19th century building in the center of Rome. Easy to find good restaurants close by.

His plan called for a pleasant evening catering to Leila. Drinks, a romantic dinner, possibly followed by lovemaking to reaffirm their emotional bond. She was smart and no pushover, however. Tomorrow would be fraught with uncertainty. Regardless of the outcome, he could provide only vague assurances about their future together.

They must get an early start. After checking out of the hotel, they would store their luggage at the train station. After he concluded his business with Reynolds, he and Leila would immediately leave to make their way north to Austria.

The first task in the morning was to reconnoiter the Piazza Navona. Savi had been to Rome a couple of times but did not know the city well. The overriding issue was surveillance on Reynolds. He must assume that likely after Beirut. Leila would be the one to approach Reynolds while he watched from a distance. He regretted exposing her to further danger but had no choice.

Could he defeat the likely surveillance on Reynolds, or must he abandon using Reynolds to facilitate defection to the United States? More uncertainty if he just turned himself in at a U.S. Embassy. No ability to negotiate. Perhaps imprisoned. Unlikely to enjoy a life envisioned in the West accessing his secret wealth. How to neutralize the surveillance and move to a secure location could not be preplanned. He must improvise as circumstances unfolded. The only given was to leave Rome as soon as possible. He already had a location in mind.

Another sleepless night passed for Prescott and Reynolds. Difficult to focus on anything other than what tomorrow would bring, each rehearsing the envisioned possible scenarios.

Up early, they spent the morning walking about the immediate area of the hotel, a warren of narrow winding cobblestoned streets. With repeated stops at different places for coffee then a brief lunch, they eventually showed up at the Piazza Navona at one o'clock.

Prescott took up her roving surveillance of Reynolds as he wandered close to Bernini's spectacular 17th century Fontana dei Quattro Fiumi dominating the Piazza Navona. A few more hours and she could put this behind her. Hope for the best, whatever form that took.

After an hour, she thought *just one more hour and this will be over.* Savi's time window ended at three o'clock. Then she spotted her. Leila Hajjar was purposefully approaching Reynolds who was facing another direction. Shit!

"Mr. Reynolds," Hajjar said in English causing Reynolds to turn abruptly.

"Ms. Hajjar. Am I to assume Mr. Savi, or as you know him, Mr. Sattari, is here? Does he wish to take me up on my offer?"

"I do not know. I am simply instructed to call him."

Hajjar dialed her cellphone handing it to Reynolds.

Without preamble, Savi said, "Mr. Reynolds. You will follow Ms. Hajjar to another location. I need to insure you are not under surveillance."

Reynolds said, "I assure you I'm not working with anyone. The U.S. government knows nothing of my activities in attempting to contact you. I am in this for my own reasons and the story. You undoubtedly checked my background."

"Perhaps. However it is my life that is at risk and therefore certain precautions are necessary," Savi replied.

"Listen, Savi, the whole purpose of this meeting was to conduct it in a very public place. For my safety. Now let's sit down at one of these cafes and come to terms about how to do this. Having come this far, I assume you are interested."

"Very well, although not here. Walk with Ms. Hajjar to the Campo de' Fiori only a short distance south of here. Lots of people with an open-air market. Very public just like here."

The call disconnected.

Reynolds looked around to pick out Prescott. Spotting her, he simply nodded hoping she would follow instructions not to approach but follow at a distance.

The purpose of moving to another location allowed Savi to determine if Reynolds was under surveillance. This obviously exposed Leila Hajjar further, but circumstances dictated using any available means to manage the situation.

Savi surveyed the piazza with the practiced eye of an experienced intelligence professional. Since the attempt on his life in Beirut was a Russian operation initiated by following Hajjar after Reynolds made contact, then logically the Russians should still be watching Reynolds. As Hajjar and Reynolds walked the length of the piazza south, he recalled his Russian intelligence training in Moscow over twenty years earlier. They practiced countless field exercises in following targets as well as spotting those following you. As much an art as specific techniques.

Quickly Savi picked up three individuals. On the cellphone, he told Hajjar to tell Reynolds to increase the pace of their walking to help him spot anyone following them.

Two men with Middle Eastern looks, moving separately picked up their pace to remain close to the targets. The third person was a woman perhaps in her forties making little attempt to conceal she was following Reynolds and Hajjar.

Reynolds and Hajjar wound through the narrow streets entering into the small Campo de' Fiori. With the open-air market, a good number of people filled the small piazza. Reynolds found a café with an outdoor table well protected by an umbrella from the afternoon sun, ordering beers to validate occupying the table.

Prescott took up a position wandering about the market stalls in the piazza center while watching Reynolds and Hajjar.

Hajjar's cellphone rang. Answering, she handed it to Reynolds.

"You are being followed by several individuals, Reynolds. Could be American intelligence but I have reason to believe it to be the Russians."

Savi's statement unsettled Reynolds. If correct then he and Prescott were in imminent danger. How could the Russians be on to them?

Reynolds said, "If you're correct that it's the Russians then it may be you they're after. If they were watching Ms. Hajjar, they clearly connected me after her loud fuss in Beirut. Now Ms. Hajjar shows up and leads them right to me. So what do you suggest?"

Reynolds could be bluffing if he was working with American intelligence. After Beirut, Savi's instincts however told him this was the Russians.

"One of those watching you is a woman. A pretty woman in her forties. Dark hair. Brown handbag. Clearly not a professional. Know her?"

Reynolds remained silent gathering his thoughts. "Yes, she is with me. Didn't want her to get involved should this attempt to contact you go wrong."

Savi said, "Like shooting you?" An amateur ploy by a journalist bringing along a girlfriend? "Did you get this stupid idea from a movie? Perhaps I should just shoot you, Reynolds."

"You could but it won't help your circumstances. I assure you the world will soon know your name whether you shoot me or not. Not only the Russians, but every intelligence agency in the world will be looking for you. You cannot disappear without the assistance of the Americans. I figured you never to be the martyr type. Am I wrong? My offer to help you defect is your only option, Savi."

"If you are that confident in your journalistic instincts, here's what I want you to do. Where are you staying?"

No turning back now. He wanted to connect with Savi. What did he expect this Iranian spy to do, just walk up to him in the piazza? Now Savi is saying the Russians are watching them? If true, he and Prescott are in some very deep shit. Yet the chance remained for the larger story that Savi represented. Unless this was a ploy by Savi. Should he opt out and simply try to get to the U.S. Embassy? An incalculable risk with too many variables to weigh. No turning back now.

Staying with his instincts, he told Savi the name and location of the hotel.

"Then gather your woman and return with Leila to your hotel room. Settle your hotel bill and pack. Be prepared to leave immediately. We must relocate to a secure location where we can talk. I will call Leila and give her instructions."

"How are we to rid ourselves of the Russian surveillance?"

"That is what I need to work out."

CHAPTER 22

ROME, ITALY

As Reynolds, Prescott, and Hajjar walked the short distance back to their hotel, Savi followed, observing the two watchers. Both were dressed casually with untucked shirts and jeans. One watcher was moving his mouth, obviously reporting in on a cellphone using a Bluetooth device evident in his ear. As they were about to enter the southern end of the narrow Via del Teatro Pace, one of the watchers broke off and turned into an alley.

Instinctively Savi stopped, wondering if spotted by the man, maybe intending an ambush from the alley while the other watcher proceeded to follow Reynolds and the two women down the street.

Savi was carrying a messenger bag over his shoulder. It provided the ability to hold the weapon in his hand at the ready while fully hiding it in what appeared as a typical tourist accessory.

Although dismantled to obscure the image as a weapon, getting the weapon through Beirut baggage security presented a risk if his luggage became subjected to x-ray. He could only hope security procedures included only random x-raying of checked baggage by Middle East Airlines. A false concealed section of his luggage hid the weapon components sufficient to pass a physical customs search when arriving in Milan. This subterfuge proved successful on two previous test trips.

His fallback position if caught was to invoke his Iranian diplomatic status and attempt to bluff as best possible. However, if that happened, everything collapsed leaving him dangerously exposed. His government of course notified of the breach of international diplomatic protocols raising questions. His carefully crafted Austrian alternative identity destroyed. Given current circumstances, a risk that he must accept. He had no intention of venturing about unarmed after the attempt on his life in Beirut.

Savi followed the man that disappeared into the ally. No one else was visible in the alley. Carefully maintaining a distance to remain unobserved, Savi saw the man stop, leaning against a wall while surveying the rear facing windows of the various buildings. Taking a position to what Savi assumed was the rear entrance to Reynolds hotel, the man lit a cigarette appearing to settle into his surveillance.

There would be no way to approach the watcher unobserved to get within striking distance. The man probably an SVR Zaslon *spetsnaz* operative like the assassin in Beirut. After talking to Reynolds, professional instinct convinced Savi the surveillance was not CIA. After Beirut, it clearly suggested a Russian black operation. Unusual given the risk in a European country like Italy, suggesting Reynolds as extremely important to the Kremlin. The only connection between him and Reynolds must be the nuclear warhead theft years ago. Somehow, Reynolds came into possession of the details. The source likely inside Russia. Russian intelligence now identified Reynolds as the recipient and attempting to contain the damage.

This ambitious reporter therefore had not turned over the material to the American government. That also made Reynolds the perfect conduit to negotiate a defection-asylum deal with the Americans. Savi guessed something went wrong with the Russian source as he tried to transfer the information to Reynolds knowing of the journalist's prior allegations at the time of the theft four years earlier.

Savi decided the effort worth saving this fool and his woman friend if he could achieve his objective. Escape from Kremlin retribution with the potential to enjoy his wealth in the West under American protection.

No quiet way to resolve this problem. The watchers at least employed poor surveillance tradecraft. These were not intelligence operatives but rather special forces assassins. Unlikely they suspected Savi's presence in Rome thereby providing him with some advantage. That and the assassins' obvious problem of creating an international incident if things turned ugly. Bad enough using a nerve-agent poison in the UK but they would do everything to avoid gunfire in the heart of Rome then attempting to escape the police.

Savi's only question remained tactical. Amongst his considerable skills, Savi was supremely analytical, quickly breaking down a problem into a weighted hierarchy of elements.

From a military perspective, this Zaslon team appeared too limited for the mission. With only two assigned to surveillance, they split to cover both the front and rear of the hotel. Obviously reinforcements were nearby, but these two were out of line of sight contact. They did not expect armed opposition. To Savi, he must only neutralize the watcher in the front who had taken a seat at an outside café table just a short distance from the hotel entrance. The café had three two-seat outside tables occupying a narrow strip to the already narrow street closed to normal vehicle traffic. No one else occupied the other tables.

Savi could observe the man from a distance as he leaned against a building partially concealed behind a large potted bush pretending to be talking on his cellphone. Executing the plan was a matter of timing. By nature, Savi was not a violent person. The shooting of the Beirut assassin was a singularly rare event in his long intelligence career. However, old training kicked in when someone was trying to kill you.

Provided he could neutralize the watcher near the front entrance of the hotel quietly, Savi could ignore the watcher stuck in the rear ally for perhaps a critical couple of minutes. Everything hinged on timing.

Savi called Hajjar, "Are they ready to leave?"

"Yes. What's going to happen, Farhad?"

"Nothing to worry about. Once I hang up, walk out of the hotel and turn to the right, going south on the street the same way you walked to the hotel. Tell Reynolds and the woman to follow close behind you.

"Now listen carefully, Leila. Once you come out on the main street, turn left and keep walking past the museum. You should be able to wave down a taxi. Go to the Termini train station. Purchase four tickets for the 4:45 direct train to Verona. First class if possible but just be sure to get on the train. I will make sure no one follows you then join you later on the train. I will collect our bags from the locker at the station and find you on the train. Do not wait for me even if the train pulls out. I must wait until the last second before boarding. Can you do this, Leila?"

"Yes. I understand. Please be careful, Farhad."

He disconnected before she could quiz him further.

A minute later Hajjar exited the hotel followed by Prescott and Reynolds each pulling a rollaway bag.

The watcher immediately laid down his newspaper on the café table, and stood up while reaching into his pocket to pay for his drink.

In the same few seconds, Savi advanced toward him from behind closing the distance to within ten yards while extracting his silenced 9mm from the messenger bag. The man instinctively turned sensing Savi's approach.

Too late, Savi placed a silenced round into his chest. The man stumbled, toppling a chair then dropped to his knees on the cobble stones while trying to pull his own weapon from his waistband. Savi shot him a second time in the head from closer range.

With the muffled low pitched noise from the silenced rounds, no one emerged from the café.

Savi continued walking past the downed man, increasing his pace as he followed close behind Hajjar, Reynolds, and the woman. As all three turned at the sound of someone yelling behind them, Savi motioned them to keep moving. Behind Savi they could see a man lying in the street as the cause of the commotion.

A short distance up the street Savi put his weapon back into the messenger shoulder bag and resumed a normal walking pace. No one else came along from either direction of the Via del Teatro Pace. As he emerged out onto the Via del Governo Vecchio the distinctive wail of European sirens sounded in the distance.

Reynolds and Prescott sat across from Leila Hajjar in a first class train carriage. All three understood what took place in front of the hotel. Witnessing Savi shooting that man in the street made their circumstances completely uncertain.

Reynolds realized the Russians somehow connect Prescott with Grigoryev. Now this was a race to escape Russian assassins with the unlikely help of Farzard Savi.

"I am Victoria Prescott, Ms. Hajjar. Sorry to have dragged you into this affair."

Hajjar glared at her but said nothing.

"I am also in academia. Like you, a professor of history. Stanford University in California."

Hajjar made no reply.

Prescott continued, "I detect this whole affair is a terrible shock to you. Perhaps you only knew Mr. Savi by his cover name, Sattari?"

"Who are you people? What is this all about?" Hajjar said looking at Reynolds. "Farhad only told me vaguely that you wanted him to defect to the United States or you would release information that would endanger him. Blackmail of some sort."

"Did he tell you his real profession, Ms. Hajjar?" Reynolds said.

Lowering her head, "Yes."

"It has to do with his past," Prescott said. "Information that came unexpectedly into my possession. Mr. Reynolds and I must get this information out to the world. However, Mr. Savi, your Mr. Sattari, has additional information that is vital. Rather than take our information to the U.S. government we hoped to have him volunteer what he knows. In exchange we believe we can connect him with the right officials to secure his defection and protection."

"Protection from who?"

"The Russians for one. Maybe his own government of Iran. Probably every intelligence agency in the world," Reynolds said.

Hajjar broke down holding her head in her hands. "That explains what happened in Beirut. He says the Russians know."

"What are you talking about?" Reynolds said.

"The Russians tried to kill him in Beirut after you delivered your message to me. They followed me to his hotel."

"What happened?" Prescott said.

Hajjar shook her head as if to dispel the image. "Farhad shot the man just like he shot that man in front of your hotel."

"Shit!" Reynolds exclaimed. "Then the Russians know what we have, Victoria."

"What do you suppose Savi is doing, Mark?"

Prescott's worse fears confirmed. Things had totally gone sideways.

"I don't know," Reynolds said, "But we're safer here than where we were."

"Unless Savi has his own plans. Remove the Russians then maybe us?"

Reynolds shook his head no. "Don't think so. He's also in deep shit. A fugitive now. The Russians will never relent.'

Hajjar stood up. "I must go to the restroom."

Reynolds looked at his watch. The train was to depart in ten minutes. Whatever was going to happen, there was nothing he could change.

"Sorry to have drawn you into this, Victoria."

She squeezed his hand. "I'm the one who insisted on coming along. Be positive. You connected with Savi. He must be interested in pursuing defection otherwise why not just abandon us to the Russians? If he's successful in removing Russian surveillance then your plan is still in play, Mark."

Reynolds leaned over and kissed her.

Major Ivan Kozlovsky questioned the operative that was watching the rear of the hotel. He and the now dead operative reported to Kozlovsky every five minutes. By the time Kozlovsky arrived at the north end of the Via del Teatro Pace, police barriers cordoned off the entire length of the short street.

"When I heard the sirens approaching I attempted to contact Ilysov. Getting no reply, I rushed to join him. There was no means for the targets to escape the rear of the hotel without coming back into Teatro Pace. A waiter and another man stood over Ilysov lying face down in the street. Blood pooling around him. I left as quickly as possible without attracting attention.

"But I never heard any shots, Major. I was close enough to have heard them. There was no traffic noise on this quiet street. Must have been a silenced weapon."

Who was assisting Reynolds? Kozlovsky wondered. A silenced weapon meant a professional. The CIA? The mission now blown. Reynolds and Prescott were gone.

He quickly made a call to Boris Lebedyenko, "Reynolds and Prescott are gone. Someone killed one of my men. Doubt it could be Reynolds. Looks like the work of a professional. I need you to deploy all available resources you can manage to find them."

Lebedyenko smiled as he disconnected the call. Fucking arrogant soldier with his special forces crew screwed up.

Kozlovsky placed another call to his superior Colonel Lukashevich in Moscow.

"We have a problem, Colonel. Someone is helping the American reporter. Killed one of my best men with a silenced weapon allowing Reynolds and Prescott to escape their hotel."

Doing everything to deflect blame by ascribing speculation of a silenced weapon as fact, Kozlovsky knew he would still shoulder the blame. If General Mikhalitsyn did not call for his head then probably President Putin would. He might find himself doing hard labor in Siberia or the victim of a *training accident.*

Colonel Lukashevich offered no words of encouragement only expletives. He had his own problems with explaining his selection of the operational commander in this particularly crucial black operation ordered by the President himself.

Twenty minutes later Lukashevich called Kozlovsky on the secured cellphone. "Perhaps you have been reprieved from a bullet to the back of your head for your failure, Major. A chance to redeem yourself. The cyber people have just hacked a cellphone call from the Iranian Savi's Lebanese girlfriend, Leila Hajjar. A call to her mother and another to her sister in Beirut. To the sister she was more candid in revealing her situation. She is onboard a train leaving Rome Termini station headed for Verona, Italy in the north. We have checked and believe it probably the train arriving in Verona at 7:37pm.

"Hajjar told her family she is on a short Italian holiday with two Americans, one a history professor like herself along with her visiting Iranian boyfriend, Farhad Sattari. A spur of the moment trip with a visiting American professor and her boyfriend. She would return to Beirut in a week.

"So this professional that disrupted your plan for Reynolds and Prescott seems to be Savi. A formidable opponent apparently, since he likely also killed your man in Beirut. And a much worse situation if he has teamed with Reynolds and Prescott. I suggest you resolve this quickly, Kozlovsky."

Verona? Kozlovsky was a professional soldier. His mission now turned uncertain with the lack of specific intelligence on the ground. Why did Moscow not separately target the Iranian? What was Savi's involvement with Reynolds? A double agent working for the CIA? Two subordinates killed and the mission compromised because Moscow did not share essential information. What did they fear from the journalist Reynolds and the woman academic?

Immediately he placed a call on his cellphone. "Lebedyenko, I have new information. The targets are on a train that departed Rome less than an hour ago headed for Verona. Arriving 7:37pm. Do you have people in Verona?"

"Verona? No. Although I have associates I can call on near there in Bologna. I will have to check but the train may stop in Bologna since it should be on the route to Verona. If so, what is it you want done, Major?"

"Get enough people on board the train to determine where they go after arriving in Verona and keep them under surveillance. They cannot be allowed to leave Verona. If necessary, you must abduct them and take them to a secure location. Same plan we had for Rome.

"And something else, Lebedyenko. There are now four people involved. The two Americans plus another woman and an Iranian intelligence operative. He is the one that killed two of my men and appears to be working with the Americans. He should be the only one armed."

"And if things go badly with this Iranian gunman?"

"I'm only interested in the two Americans. Kill the Iranian and his Lebanese girlfriend at the first opportunity. I will join you in Verona with my team. There is a later high-speed train out of Rome tonight that we can make, putting us into Verona at 10:23pm. Keep me updated on your progress. I do not need to remind you how critical this is, Lebedyenko. We fix this and I can assure you President Putin will be particularly grateful."

To himself, Lebedyenko thought, fuck you. You are the one who screwed up, Major. If it does not get fixed then it is your head. Yet if the Solntsevskaya Bratva proved crucial to delivering up these Americans where the Zaslon failed, it greatly advanced Lebedyenko's stature.

The *associates* Lebedyenko referred to were Italians. Italian Mafia. This new task would entail far more than then just assisting the Russian *spetsnaz* with the logistical side of their abduction mission. Cost more money for his Italian associates but a good investment especially since he had little choice. Lebedyenko did not want any personal blowback because of Kozlovsky's failures.

Lebedyenko would not allow another mishap. Unlike Kozlovsky, he would not be as delicate to avoid creating a potential international incident for the Russians. Especially against four people that knew they were in the crosshairs. If this turned violent, best to make the attempt with the targets contained within the train. Take them just before disembarking in Verona. Cover the collateral damage as best possible. Provided they captured the Americans without injury, they could still make the sailing of the *Bella Signora* out of Bari on Wednesday.

He placed a call to an Italian underboss he knew well in Bologna. Somewhat risky discussing such matters in the open but time dictated the necessity. At least he was using an untraceable cellphone but did not know how careful his Italian colleague was.

For years, they worked together smuggling all manner of contraband out of the Balkans through Italy then distributed throughout Europe. The Italian controlled the Bologna criminal underworld. At his disposal was a crew of experienced violent muscle.

The Italian responded to Lebedyenko's request, "Of course, Boris Stefanovich. Not much time but I believe I can put the right people on this train. This might be messy. You okay with that?"

"Keep it contained but do what you have to. I want the Americans taken unharmed. Kill the Iranian agent, the one with the beard, and the Lebanese woman. I will forward photos. The Iranian should be the only one armed."

"Very well, my friend. Now as to the fee for this service?"

"Not a problem, Fabrizio. I trust you will charge a fair price."

Twenty minutes after the train departed Rome Termini station, Farzard Savi entered the train carriage and placed two bags on the luggage rack at the front. The messenger bag remained over his shoulder with the flap unsecured. Quickly surveying the carriage, he saw nothing threatening in the five other passengers. Seated at the far end of the carriage, he saw Leila Hajjar facing toward him with Reynolds and his woman seated opposite, facing away from him. Hajjar stood abruptly then came down the aisle to embrace him.

Reynolds and Prescott turned around and stood up. An awkward moment as they looked at Farzard Savi with no one knowing exactly how to react.

"Please sit down. We have a lot to discuss, Mr. Reynolds," Savi said then looked at Prescott. "And you are?"

"My name is Victoria Prescott, a professor of Russian history at Stanford University," she said in Russian.

Savi registered surprise and responded in Russian. "I see. Mr. Reynolds' translator?"

"No. His collaborator. Actually his source."

Savi smiled, returning to English. "Interesting. So it was you that uncovered this information?"

"Obviously not. The material came from classified Russian intelligence files. But I am not a spy just a conduit. Like most such revelations of state secrets, the source is a disgruntled insider."

"Yes, of course. And your source?"

"I'd prefer not to say. Does it matter?"

"No. Just professional curiosity."

Savi however guessed this sudden sequence of events might have something to do with the senior Russian intelligence official murdered in Paris weeks ago as reported in the Western media.

"What happened back in Rome, Mr. Savi? The man you shot? You're sure he was Russian?" Reynolds said.

"Yes, I am sure. A second man was at the rear of the hotel. A tactical mistake on their part or only limited resources available. But there will be others trying to catch up to us. Russian special forces."

"Jesus Christ!" Reynolds exclaimed in a hushed tone.

Prescott looked as if she had been slapped.

"Don't appear so shocked. What kind of game do you think this is? I am here only because another Russian assassin tried to kill me in Beirut. Understand this, I care nothing about what happens to you two. I am only interested in your assistance in arranging my defection to the United States."

"What happened in Beirut?" Reynolds said.

"I also killed that assassin. Before he died, he confirmed he was Russian. *Spetsnaz*, a special forces group known as Zaslon I suspect. Black operations people of the Russian SVR. These are the Russians after you, Reynolds.

"The Russians were following you. Probably since you left the United States. You led them to me. I was a just target of opportunity. You are amateurs playing in a life and death game.

"The Russians know what you know. They also suspect you have not yet given it over to your government. As a professional, I would guess they are planning to abduct you. Undoubtedly torture you to understand what you have, who gave it to you, and who now has this information. After that, you disappear. Both of you."

Leila Hajjar was even more appalled as she listened to her urbane Dr. Jekyll lover transform into the grotesque Mr. Hyde. Not only a spy but a killer.

"I am helping you only because you represent the best conduit to make contact with the appropriate American officials. You two can credibly present what I have to offer in exchange for asylum."

"And what exactly are you offering, Savi?" Reynolds said.

"The precise locations of all three Russian warheads. How they remained secured in secrecy for several years. More importantly, the current strategy to use them as a means for reactivating Iran's nuclear weapons program and instantly advancing it by years. I will also offer tantalizing information concerning North Korean involvement in the Iranian weapons program. All that plus every detail of Iranian support to the Syrian regime and Hezbollah. A year's debriefing I should think."

Prescott was stunned at the sheer scope of what they were hearing.

"Sounds impressive, assuming you can deliver. Now what do you want?" Reynolds said.

"Simple demands considering what I am offering. Let me be clear however, demands nevertheless, not negotiable. Asylum and a new identity to live in the United States. Not in some prison, but with a passport and the freedom to travel. A fair exchange I should think for telling the Americans and your friends the Israelis where and how they can destroy three thermonuclear warheads in the hands of Iran."

Reynolds said, "I will get things in motion once we arrive in Verona. I have someone that knows how these things work ready to make contact with the right government officials. But why are we going to Verona?"

"Because it generally suits my plans. You will make your call and I will also speak with your go-between person. Then we part company. You and Ms. Prescott must immediately return to the United States. The Russians cannot reach you there if you take basic precautions. Regardless, according to your threat, you intend to make everything public very soon. I suggest you take the next train to Milan and seek protection at the U.S. Consulate."

"And you?"

"I will be somewhere in Europe. Secured underground until I have assurances from your government. You will remain as my contact up to the time I am satisfied with the details of my exfiltration. Your government needs to move quickly. No telling how Tehran will react to my unexplained absence."

Reynolds looked at Prescott who just nodded. Fixed on Savi's chilling pronouncement the Russians probably sought to abduct then torture them for information before killing them, she could not dispel the conjured images that evoked. The situation further intensified by Savi's admission to killing two Russian operatives. She clung to the hope that this might all end soon by refuge in a U.S. consulate.

"Tell me something, Reynolds. What made you think I would bend to your blackmail to defect and give up my country's secrets?"

"I read the Russian dossier on you. You are a non-practicing Muslim. Decidedly secular. Nothing suggests an ideological identification with the current Iranian Shiite theocracy. I suspect you probably even resent the clerics dominating the leadership as Islamic fanatics. You on the other hand are a devout pragmatist. You're not the martyr type for either god or country. Your brother even worked in the former Shah's feared SAVAK. Not even clear that you are particularly nationalistic. Personally ambitious the dossier concludes."

Leila Hajjar listened with rapt attention as Reynolds revealed details of a different person than the man she knew as Farhad Sattari, an Iranian trade specialist.

"Then of course there is your obvious attraction to Western culture. Designer clothing, expensive watches, liquor, fine wine. You speak English, Russian, and German in addition to Arabic and your native Farsi. A degree in international law. Sufficiently knowledgeable in finance to function abroad in your cover identity as a trade specialist within the Iranian economic ministry. You have a lover outside of Iran. A true cosmopolitan. Given the personal repercussions once your complicity in the warhead theft becomes public, remaining in Iran might be risky with nowhere to turn. Perhaps the gallows. At best, your life forever altered. Unable to enjoy those former luxuries while trapped inside a repressive internationally besieged Iran."

Savi listened without comment. Leila Hajjar looked at Savi with an expression of bewilderment as the sound of the train on the tracks filled the silence.

Let this arrogant American think he is clever. The Russian information just fell into Reynolds lap through Prescott who obviously had connections inside the Kremlin. So anxious to get at the even larger story of cornering the mastermind behind the theft, they both risked their lives oversimplifying this foolish amateur venture. Yet Reynolds was right. Savi was a pragmatist. Given the circumstances, Reynolds and the woman represented his best option.

CHAPTER 23

BOLOGNA, ITALY

Prescott booted her laptop using the Wi-Fi connection on the train.

"Mark, I have an idea. Why not call Ellsberg before we get to Verona? I want to get to Milan tonight. I just checked and there are several direct trains. We can then show up at the consulate first thing in the morning. Besides, it further obscures our trail from the Russians."

Reynolds looked at his watch. "Good idea. Does that work for you, Savi?"

Savi nodded affirmatively.

The recorded message on the train announced *next station Bologna Centrale.*

"We shall wait until we see what other passengers join our car to ensure privacy on the call."

Currently no one else occupied the nearby seats but that could change with newly boarding passengers.

As the train began pulling out of the station after the brief stop, several passengers disembarked while no new passengers joined.

"Okay to talk right here?" Reynolds said to Savi as he prepared to dial Ellsberg's cellphone. With the six-hour time difference, it was shortly before 1:00pm in New York.

As Savi nodded to go ahead, two men entered the car from one end. Immediately he was wary. Something did not feel right. This was a first class car with only less than an hour to Verona. They did not appear the type to pay for first class seats for such a short distance. The men looked to be in their late twenties dressed in jeans. Both carried gym bags. They were laughing and bantering in Italian as they walked through the car exiting into the next car.

Savi sat in the aisle seat with Leila Hajjar seated next to him. As the men entered the car, he placed the messenger bag on his lap with his hand inside gripping the 9mm.

Only two other people currently occupied the car, a well-dressed older couple seated at the opposite end of the car.

"Make your call," Savi said to Reynolds.

Two young people, a man and a woman, entered taking a seat opposite to the older couple. Savi eyed them critically but relaxed noting both as better dressed than the two men that walked through the car five minutes earlier. The man wore a sport coat and the woman tailored slacks with a large designer handbag.

Since Ellsberg had the untraceable cellphone Reynolds gave him, he answered, "Reynolds?"

"It's me, Phillip. Listen closely. Things did not exactly go according to plan."

"Not surprising. What happened?"

"I'd rather explain later. The kicker is the Russians are on to us. They know we have something of value."

"Jesus! How do you know that?

"No time to explain right now. The objective of the plan worked out though. I'm sitting here with Colonel Farzard Savi. He saw the personal benefits in seeking asylum in exchange for all he knows. But he wants assurances."

"What kind of assurances?"

"I'll let him tell you himself. He's okay if you want to record it. Play it back for whomever you're going to contact in the government."

Reynolds handed the phone to Savi. "The name is Phillip Ellsberg. He is a former attorney with the U.S Department of Justice. Now in private practice."

Savi and Ellsberg conversed for the next fifteen minutes with Savi repeating what he told Reynolds and answering Ellsberg's questions.

Handing the phone back to Reynolds, "Hard to believe you pulled this off, Mark. Remarkable."

"But it went badly, Phillip. Turned very ugly. To help himself, Savi saved Victoria and I. So do your best. And quickly, Phillip. What Savi has to offer has a shelf life. And we're still in some real danger over here."

"Where are you?"

"In Italy. Moving about staying out of reach of the bad guys. We're trying to get to the U.S. Consulate in Milan by tomorrow morning. So alert the cavalry. Tell them about Savi but nothing about the stolen files in our possession. Tell them it's just an investigative journalist doing his job. They don't get to see the source material until they read it in the news.

"Let's also delay the media release by a few days since I might not make it back by my imposed deadline with these new developments. Once Victoria and I are safely inside the consulate, I'll call again and give you an update."

"Very well, Mark. But aren't you forgetting something?" Ellsberg said.

"What's that?" Then recalling his own coded signal, "Yeah, right. And Victoria agrees."

By the time the call to Ellsberg concluded, the high-speed train began slowing as the audio system announced arrival in Verona.

Savi leaned forward handing Reynolds a cellphone.

"Untraceable. My untraceable number is the only listing under contacts. You are my conduit. Pull this off and you have not only an enormous story but the material for another bestselling book.

"We shall of course talk but it is unlikely we shall see each other again," Savi said extending his hand then turning toward Prescott. "And a pleasure meeting you, Professor Prescott. I suggest you stick to academic pursuits rather than engaging in international espionage."

As the train jerked to a stop, everyone in the car stood to disembark. The older couple left first at the far end of the car. Ever aware, Savi fixed his stare on the younger well-dressed couple from his position standing on the opposite end of the car near the door to the adjoining car.

The door from the next carriage behind opened. Savi turned at the sound to see a pistol extended at a distance of only two feet. It was the last sight Farzard Savi saw. A round entered his face below the left eye followed by a second shot to the chest dropping him immediately.

Blood from the exit wound to Savi's head splattered across Leila Hajjar's face. Releasing a scream, she bent down to touch Savi. The assailant immediately fired a bullet into the back of Hajjar's head.

Prescott and Reynolds recoiled, unable to escape while expecting they might be next.

The assailant was one of the two men walking through the car earlier raising Savi's suspicion. The second man joined him as the young well-dressed couple hurried toward them down the aisle. All four now pointed guns at Reynolds and Prescott.

The train car was empty except for Reynolds, Prescott, and the four assailants. Possibly the gunshots not heard beyond the confines of this carriage alone.

The well-dressed assailant said in heavily Italian-accented English, "Come with us or you will be shot like the others."

The killer pushed Reynolds into the aisle while his associate grabbed Prescott pulling her along. The woman assailant led the way out of the train car while her partner covered the rear should anyone enter the car from the opposite end.

At the luggage storage rack at the front of the car, the woman stopped and said to Reynolds in English, "Which are your bags?"

After making no reply for several moments, the woman conveyed a non-verbal message with her head at the killer holding Reynolds. The man immediately smashed the barrel of his pistol across Reynolds' forehead crumpling him down onto one knee.

Prescott uttered an exclamation of distress then pointed to their bags saying, "Those two."

The well-dressed man grabbed both leaving Savi's and Hajjar's luggage on the rack.

Everyone exited the train onto the station platform. The men holding Reynolds and Prescott concealed their weapons inside the gym bags slung over their shoulders.

The woman assailant said, "Say nothing and do not attempt to escape. We will shoot anyone you call out to for help."

As they moved along the platform toward the terminal, behind them a frantic conductor exited the train blowing his whistle incessantly and waving his arms. Two Italian police officers came running past on the station platform as the assailants pushed Prescott and Reynolds forward.

Several police vehicles with flashing lights pulled to the curb as they exited the Verona Porta Nuova train station to a parked black Mercedes SUV. The gunman that shot Savi and Hajjar pushed Reynolds into the back third row seat. Prescott sat in the second row next to the other gunman in jeans.

"Who are you people?" Reynolds asked.

"*Chiudi la tua fottuta bocca,*" the gunman said in Italian followed by a hard elbow blow to Reynolds' chest.

Prescott turned as she heard Reynolds grunt at the blow but she remained silent.

The well-dressed couple tied the wrists of Reynolds and Prescott with large plastic cable ties. The man then got behind the wheel with his female companion in the front passenger seat.

Except for a short cellphone call by the woman, everyone remained silent for the next ninety minutes on the drive south to Bologna.

As the SUV left the A1Autostrada entering into the suburbs of the large city of Bologna, Reynolds knew he must try some attempt at escape no matter how futile. These thugs were obviously in the employ of the Russians. Recalling Savi's terrifying comment the Russians undoubtedly intended to torture them before killing them sent a wave of panic through Reynolds.

Not the first desperate situation in his long career to test his survival instincts and ingenuity. Setting aside his rising fear, those experiences served to focus his mind to search for escape opportunities no matter how desperate.

By any assessment, he and Prescott were in a grim spot. While philosophically he possessed a certain fatalism, Victoria Prescott must be terrified. A wave of guilt passed over him. It was his idea to withhold going to the government. The Russians must have discovered Prescott's connection to Grigoryev then placed her in Paris with him before killing him. Yet the Russians might hesitate making an attempt on them in the United States. It was his journalistic arrogance and greed to pursue Savi for a bigger story that was the cause of their predicament.

Once they arrived at their destination, these Italian contract thugs would hand them over to the Russians. Having lost two of their operatives killed by Savi, he and Prescott could expect brutal treatment by the Russians' questioning. If it came to that, no reason to hold back telling them what they want to know. Avoid suffering worse under torture since they were dead anyway. But the Russians still might inflict suffering out of revenge.

This must be more instinctive than planned. Reynolds had no resources. His only advantage being their captors must avoid shooting them. Pistol-whip them perhaps, but undoubtedly delivered in sufficient condition for questioning by the Russians.

Having left the high-speed toll road, they were now traveling at fifty miles per hour down a major street in what appeared an industrial district. No other traffic visible.

Reynolds made as if to reach down with his bound wrists, a move intended to provide enough energy in the blow he intended to deliver with his elbow. The man already in a relaxed state after the drive and confident of his prisoner's incapacitation sat resting his gun on his lap. Bringing his elbow up violently Reynolds caught the man seated to his left on the nose. The blow hard enough to hear the cartilage breaking.

The unexpected attack and immediate pain caused the man to drop his weapon. As blood spurted from the man's damaged nose, Reynolds dove with his bound wrists to retrieve the gun from the floor.

Seated immediately in front of Reynolds, Prescott and the other gunman seated to her left turned at the commotion from behind. The headrest blocked a clear view for the gunman in the seat next to Prescott to see what was going on with Reynolds now hunched down attempting to get the gun.

No matter what, Reynolds knew he must succeed in getting to the gun or they were doomed. Grasping the 9mm Beretta automatic after agonizing seconds, he thumbed back the hammer. He knew what he must do.

The other gunman sitting next to Prescott in the seats ahead turned to face Reynolds between the seats pointing a Beretta automatic. An apparent standoff except Reynolds had no choice if he and Victoria were to survive this. Facing the weapon in Reynolds' hand, the startled gunman hesitated. Reynolds did not as he shot him in the face.

The woman in the front passenger seat turned firing at Reynolds with her pistol. Her hurried shot from an awkward position missed. Reynolds fired two rounds into the back of her seat.

Prescott screamed in sheer terror as the SUV swerved erratically as the driver reacted then fought to regain control.

Reynolds' next step posed a dilemma. With the driver also armed, he could threaten to shoot Victoria if he just turned back to his right. If Reynolds shot him a violent crash would result. Secured by a shoulder belt, Prescott might survive uninjured. The gunman with the damaged nose never secured Reynolds' belt making him vulnerable.

As the driver steered with his right hand, he thrust his weapon held in his left hand underneath his arm, pointing it at Prescott. Reynolds reacted immediately by firing three rounds in rapid succession into the back of the driver's seat.

The driver slumped forward held by his shoulder belt as the SUV veered wildly to the right. Decelerating as the driver's foot left the accelerator, the vehicle hit a streetlight post in the right front. The impact twisted the vehicle's forward motion causing the SUV to roll onto its left side, smashing into the curb after sliding along the pavement.

The SUV sat on its side, everything quiet. No traffic in this industrial neighborhood this time of night.

Prescott sat restrained in her seat by the seat belt with the now SUV turned on its side. The crash left her disoriented following the deafening noise of the gunshots contained inside the vehicle. The sequence of violent events lasted less than twenty seconds.

Reynolds landed on top of the gunman with the destroyed nose after the crash. Unsecured in his seat, Reynolds propelled forward into the back of Prescott's seat dropping the gun as he fell to the left on top of the man as the SUV tipped over. A short struggle ensued with the gunman as both desperately tried to find the weapon with the SUV turned on its side.

The explosion of another gunshot shattered the silence.

Reynolds won. No hesitation taking the point-blank shot to the man's heart recalling how the man murdered Savi and Hajjar.

"Mark! Mark! Are you okay?"

Reynolds groaned. "I'm not shot but something is causing a lot of pain. Can you get out?"

"I don't know. I'll try."

After disconnecting her shoulder belt, she first tried opening the door now above her. Too heavy to open in this vertical position, she opened the door window since the electrical system remained engaged. Standing on the armrest, she tried hoisting herself out through the window but with her wrists bound there was no way to lever herself up.

"I can't make it, Mark."

"Okay. Crawl to the back. I'll go first."

As he moved, he let out a yelp from a shooting pain.

"What's wrong?"

"My shoulder. Hurts like hell."

A painful maneuver but he managed to climb over the dead man, squeeze between the seats, and then navigate their luggage to open the SUV's rear door.

Prescott followed trying to ignore the blood while crawling over the bodies of the two gunmen to squeeze to the rear of the SUV.

"Let me see your shoulder."

She unbuttoned his shirt exposing his shoulder. Touching an area that appeared as a swelling, he let out a cry of pain."

"Oh my god! I think your collar bone is broken, Mark."

"Then I'll live. Got to find a way of getting to the police."

"Aren't we in some real deep legal trouble? My god you just shot four people, Mark. And then what happened on the train. I can't get my head around being this up close to such violence."

"Self-defense. They kidnapped us. But you're right, still a legal mess. Worse yet, we're in Italy. Much rather get to a U.S. consulate. Don't know if there is one in Bologna. Best bet is getting a train to Milan as planned. Ellsberg will have altered them.

"Right now let's get the hell away from here then figure out how to get to the train station. Not going to find a taxi in this industrial sector this time of night. And we sure as hell will look out of place dragging along luggage."

"What about these?" she said holding up her hands referring to the cable ties binding their wrists.

"Got anything in your purse we might use to cut them?"

"Some manicure scissors?"

"That should work. Let's get away from here first then we'll give it a try."

"Are you taking that?" She said looking at the Beretta still in Reynolds' hand.

"Yep. Until I know we're safe. Should still have a few rounds left."

Inside the SUV, the woman in the front passenger seat stirred. She leaned down at an awkward angle still restrained by her shoulder belt with the SUV on its left side. Blood dripped from her mouth. Pain brought her eyes open. Frantically she tried to unfasten the belt without success.

Realizing she was seriously wounded, she groped for her handbag. Must call for help. Finding it laying against the center console at her feet, she pulled it up with one hand then reached in with the other to find her cellphone.

Bleeding profusely, her hand smeared the phone's screen. The rush of adrenalin made concentration difficult. After a minute of frustrated fumbling and trying to clean the screen of blood, she touched the number for her brother.

"*Si*?" a male voice answered.

"Bruno. I've been shot! Help me!"

"Chiara is that you? What are you talking about?"

"The American. Somehow got Giorgio's gun. Shot everyone. All of us."

"You're shot?"

"Yes. I'm hurt real bad, Bruno. I'm bleeding! I don't want to die!" She then coughed disgorging a flood of blood from her damaged lung.

"Where are you?"

Struggling to talk while gasping to breathe, she said, "Some industrial street. Don't know the name. Not far after getting off the A1. The car is wrecked. Everyone is shot, Bruno! They look dead! Come and help me! I don't want to die!"

He and three others raced in a car to what he believed was the general area. His sister's location became obvious when they came to flashing blue lights from many police cars closing off the street ahead.

Approaching the police cars blocking the street, he asked the officer, "What happened?"

He could see the overturned SUV fifty yards away with emergency personnel peering inside.

"An accident. Fatalities unfortunately."

"Any survivors?"

"Doesn't appear to be. Now turn around and find a different route."

CHAPTER 24

BOLOGNA, ITALY

After walking out of sight of the wrecked SUV, Reynolds and Prescott cut the plastic cable ties with the manicure scissors. After walking further from the scene, they sat down to rest on their rollaway luggage out of sight behind a large industrial company sign.

"Now what, Mark? How are we going to get out of this?"

He hugged her. "We'll make it. Just hang in there."

The thought passed in his mind of how many people died while helping him in the past. Victoria Prescott must not become another.

"I'm going to call Ellsberg."

He extracted his phone noticing there was little remaining power. Once Ellsberg answered, he said, "Just listen, Phillip. Got to make this short. Things have turned to shit. Savi is dead."

"Dead? What happened?"

"Bunch of Italian thugs killed him on the train then abducted us. Drove us back south to Bologna. Must be working for the Russians. Anyway we got away but we're in a bad way."

"Can you get to the Italian police?"

"Probably, but I'd rather not. No time to explain, but our escape was messy. Some Italians got killed."

"Jesus Christ! You mean you killed them?"

"No choice. Self-defense. Anyway, I think our best bet is to make it to Milan. Get the first flight we can and make it back to New York. Did you already start the ball rolling to arrange for Savi's defection?"

"Yes, off course. Waiting for a counter-terrorism person at State to get back to me. But it's only been a few hours since your earlier call so I've not heard back yet.

"That's good. Just continue to pursue it."

"But you told me Savi's dead?"

"He is, but Victoria and I need to get out of Italy quickly. Don't need the U.S. government to turn against us which will happen once you release everything to the world press. Which I still want you to do the day after tomorrow. That might get the Russians off the hunt. And *Victoria approves*."

"Are you going to the consulate in Milan?"

"I'm thinking of going to the airport instead. I'll feel safer back in the United States. Might as well have them think the Savi defection is still on. If we can't get a flight out, we may need their help if somehow we are implicated in all these killings. Once the stuff becomes public, they'll know we played them. I think we'll need a good lawyer."

They needed to lay low until morning. With the shooting of four people there would be a heighten presence in the area. The Italian police however were the least of their concern. The thugs that murdered Savi and Hajjar were Italian, probably Mafia. Must be contract muscle for the Russians. Killing four of them meant some very bad characters seeking revenge. Best not to panic by making a risky run for it in the dark, especially not knowing Bologna.

Using back alleys, they made their way further from the crime scene. Eventually they made their way north of a main thoroughfare, the Via Nuova Bazzanese. The moonlight revealed a large expanse of undeveloped tracts of open land and a soccer club set back from the highway surrounded by stands of trees.

"We'll spend the rest of the night here," Reynolds said as they walked under a row of trees further shielded from view by a row of dense hedges. "In the morning we'll see if we can flag down a bus or taxi. Our cover story, *car broke down in the middle of the night stranding us*. We need to avoid police and get out of Bologna."

As dawn broke Prescott and Reynolds stirred, chilled after an unpleasant night. Reynolds let out a grunt of pain as he tried to ease the stiffness in his throbbing left shoulder.

He said, "Okay, let's do this. How do we look?"

"Like shit. We both have traces of blood on our clothes."

"Yeah. Probably should change. Dispose of these clothes. Then let us hope for some luck to get to the train station before being spotted. We'll get some food and coffee there. Once we are on the train to Milan, we should be home free. Nothing should connect us to what happened last night. We'll take the first flight to anywhere going west. Just hang in there a while longer."

"I can't get the images of all those dead people out of mind, Mark. I was right in the middle of it."

"Everyone feels the same when they're involved with acts of violence."

"And you? You shot those people. What do you feel?"

"Hard to put into words. Unfortunately, I've been in that position before. My life or theirs. A sickening feeling to take another life but if it's someone out to take yours the emotion is different. I image the same feeling as a soldier in combat killing an enemy. But in this situation, not just an enemy but criminals intent on doing us harm. No longer people."

"Speaking of guns, give me that," she said pointing to the 9mm pistol in his waistband. "You can't go about like that. I'll put it in my purse."

Before Major Ivan Kozlovsky boarded a train in Rome for Bologna, Boris Lebedyenko called with the news of the capture of the Americans in Verona. Savi and his woman are dead. The Italians were in route driving south to Bologna. They should arrive within two hours.

Kozlovsky breathed a sigh of relief. Not according to plan, but his mission salvaged. His career salvaged.

As Kozlovsky's train slowed for arrival at Bologna Centrale, Lebedyenko called his cellphone again alerting him to the disaster awaiting him.

"Something has happened, Major. The Americans have escaped."

Kozlovsky could not believe his misfortune. "What happened?"

"I do not know. The Italians report four of their people shot to death inside the SUV transporting the Americans. The Americans are gone."

"How is that possible, Lebedyenko?"

Lebedyenko resented Kozlovsky and wondered if he was holding back something.

"Unlikely this journalist and the woman pulled this off. Are you sure the CIA is not involved, Major?"

Not entirely sure after this, Kozlovsky declared, "Absolutely. If the CIA was involved then there was no reason for capturing the Americans."

"Well this is your show, Major. The Italians were searching the entire area. Unlikely Reynolds and Prescott could escape without help. Immediately following the shooting, they put people to watch the nearest police stations. This happened in an industrial zone at night. They assume Reynolds and Prescott found some place out of sight for the night. Come daybreak they will probably try to get to the airport or train station. The Italians have people watching both locations."

"They *assume*? Who are these stupid Italians, Lebedyenko? A bunch of petty criminals you enlisted? A real fuckup. I thought the Bratva was better than this."

"We are. The Italian Mafia apparently not so good. However, one must use available resources when faced with a contingency. Had your people not failed in Rome then it would be my Bratva people doing the abduction and we would be on the ship in Bari."

"And the Italians drew unnecessary attention shooting the Iranian and his woman on the train."

Lebedyenko said, "That will eventually blow over. We'll indirectly leak enough to the press to establish his real identity. Blame will be cast in the direction of Iran's enemies not a Mafia hit. Disinformation circulated in the right places implicating the Israeli Mossad, or perhaps even the American CIA."

"Enough wrangling, Lebedyenko. What is the plan when I arrive in Bologna?"

"You will be met by someone. An Italian. They will find you around the newspaper kiosk. Somebody will approach you and say in English, *I am a friend of Boris.*

"But there is another problem, Major. One that is out of my hands."

"What now, Lebedyenko?"

"One of those killed was the niece of the local Mafia underboss. These Americans are now a personal matter. His name is Marcello Fattore. You do not want to get on his wrong side, especially on his turf. There is also the matter of the dead woman's brother Bruno Fattore. They will be looking for revenge."

"Thanks for the warning, but I think my people are more than a match for these Italian riffraff."

Lebedyenko decided it was unproductive to argue with the arrogant Russian special forces commander. Outside of his own obligation as handed down by his superior to assist these assassins, he had no vested interest in whatever the Kremlin feared from these two Americans.

"A suggestion, Major, if Reynolds becomes a matter of vendetta with the Fattore family, point out the shootings must be his doing. The woman obviously did not do this. She is an academic. Bargain for her and give them Reynolds."

Kozlovsky and his team of five disembarked the train at Bologna Centrale at 10:35pm. An Italian dressed in a designer sport coat, introducing himself as Bruno Fattore, approached him as arranged.

"Are you aware of what happened?"

"Our common friend Boris called me a short time ago," Kozlovsky said.

"My uncle told me to take you to the scene. It happened less than an hour ago."

"I am told you have people out looking for the Americans?"

"That is correct. Including here at the train station. We have teams driving throughout the area of the crash. The Americans could not have traveled far on foot."

Kozlovsky gave his men orders in Russian, "Stay here with the Italians covering the train station. If the Americans show, make sure the Italians do not take them away. Reynolds killed the Mafia boss's niece and this guy's sister so their blood is up."

To Fattore, Kozlovsky said, "I want to see the scene and understand the search area. My men will stay here and cover the train station."

The crash scene remained a dazzling scene of flashing police lights as Fattore's Mercedes approached the street cordon barrier for a second time that night. This time his powerful uncle Marcello Fattore called in a favor from a senior police official in the local Carabinieri command to allow his nephew access to the crime scene. The body of his sister and three other dead men remained inside the vehicle awaiting daybreak for the forensic teams to process the scene.

A police officer allowed Bruno Fattore and Kozlovsky to accompany him to the SUV, admonishing them not to touch the vehicle.

Both looked into the front seat. With the SUV lying on its left side, the dead body of Fattore's sister was clearly visible through the windshield. Suspended by her shoulder harness, her long dark hair covered her face. Her blouse soaked with blood.

Staring at his dead sister, Fattore wept as Kozlovsky peered closer inside trying to determine what might have happened. No outside evidence of bullet holes. This happened from the inside.

Hard to image how Reynolds concealed a weapon or somehow got hold of one of the Italian's weapons to do this kind of damage. Were the Italians stupid enough not to restrain their captives?

Kozlovsky said to Fattore, "What next?"

"We wait till my people find them. If they found cover for the night, it will not help them come daylight. The word is out on the street. No one dare help them. We just need to make sure they cannot escape by train or air."

"What if they get to the police?" Kozlovsky said.

"Then we will know where they are. We have contacts at all levels. And people have been known to die while in police custody."

"Listen, Senore Fattore, the Americans cannot be killed until I have the chance to interrogate them."

Fattore looked at him with a menacing stare. "Understand me well, Major. This was a business matter before the Americans did this." He said while gesturing toward the SUV. "Your Russian friend Lebedyenko is just a business associate. You also are Russian. We care nothing about your political interests. Do you understand what has happened? This is now a personal matter. A family matter of honor."

"I understand your personal grief. Let us work together to satisfy both our obligations to duty."

Kozlovsky disliked relying on those outside of his control. The mission again plunged into serious jeopardy. A black mark on his otherwise outstanding record. The only redemption to this succession of operational failures was the capture of Reynolds and Prescott and determining what they know.

Lebedyenko's suggestion about sacrificing Reynolds to get at Prescott might prove the best option. Assuming he even got that chance. If these Italians found the Americans first, no telling what they might do.

"Let me propose a compromise to satisfy us both. It must be the reporter Reynolds that did this. I know his background. He is an adventurer who has killed before. He alone is responsible for the death of your sister.

"Once we find them, give me just thirty minutes with him then he is all yours. Give me the woman. She did not do this. She is a professor somehow connected to the reporter. I will pay you double the fee just for her."

Bruno Fattore replied, "I shall consider your proposition."

Kozlovsky suggested to Fattore that they maintain their vigil at the train station while waiting on word from those searching for the Americans. Essential he stays close to Fattore. Once Mafiosi locate the Americans, Fattore will be the first to know.

"Can you provide a vehicle large enough for my team? I want immediate mobility to respond when we find the Americans."

"Of course."

At the first indication of sunrise, Reynolds suggested to Prescott they carefully make their way to look for a bus stop sign.

"I think the best option is a bus. Unlikely many taxis will be out this early. Plus we look too conspicuous waving down a cab. The police must be on heightened alert."

His greater worry was the Italian criminals. If Mafia, that meant they had a wide reach including informants, and motivated now by revenge. He did not voice that concern to avoid frightening Prescott further.

"And you still think it's best not to go to the Italian police? They can't connect us with the shooting can they?" Prescott said.

"Don't think so. But how do we explain stranded out here with luggage? How did we get here? Coming from where? We have no plausible story that can stand up to scrutiny. If we go to the police then we're in for a long ordeal. Forgetting what happened in the SUV, they might also connect us to the murder of Savi and Hajjar on the train. We left a trail there. We can say we left the train in Bologna before they were killed. But why? How do we explain what we did for these last twelve hours?

"Explaining this as a Russian black operation will sound preposterous until the story breaks in the world media. At least that is in motion. No telling though when that will actually happen. Even then, no telling where we stand. We need to get back to the United States. I don't relish being defendants in the Italian legal system while sitting in an Italian jail."

Telling Prescott to stay out of sight, Reynolds reconnoitered the main street in front of the soccer club grounds while the semi-darkness still allowed seeing the lights of any approaching vehicles.

Returning to Prescott five minutes later, "We're in luck. There's a bus top about a hundred yards that way. Unfortunately, no place close to conceal ourselves. We'll wait until full daylight then I'll position myself just to end of these trees. Enough to watch for an approaching bus. I'll take the luggage but you stay hidden until I signal you."

"No way. I'm going with you."

Too tired to argue, he hugged her. "Okay. I'm so sorry. This whole mess is my doing. It's what I do, but I had no right to drag you into this. Should have just turned everything over to the government."

She shook her head no. "We've been through all that, Mark. I agreed we should instead go public."

"But going after Savi was a bridge too far."

In that, she agreed. However, she signed on for her own reasons so she offered him some solace by saying, "Perhaps, but the origins of the Russians involvement go back to when we were still in New York. They followed us to Beirut. It wasn't Savi they were after, it was us. That meant it started with me.

"It's always been about us, Mark, not Savi. I led them to you."

A stressful thirty minutes passed slowly before the first bus of the morning arrived. The driver looked at them incredulously when Reynolds asked about the fares in English. The riders at this hour were local commuters not foreigners with luggage. Unfortunately, Reynolds could not adequately understand the driver's response to his question about how to get to the central train station.

Once the bus came into a more commercial part of the city, taxis became visible. Not knowing the bus route or train station location, it was faster and less conspicuous to disembark and take a taxi to the train station.

"Should be lots of trains to Milan then we get the first flight out. We'll make it, Victoria."

Major Kozlovsky and Bruno Fattore spent an equally difficult night. While rigid discipline trained Kozlovsky for periods of interminable waiting, the well-dressed Fattore looked disheveled after too much coffee and a night of dealing with his grief. Continual cellphone calls reporting no results in finding the Americans compounded his anger and frustration.

"Where the fuck are these Americans?" Fattore remarked rhetorically.

After driving about the area with Fattore, Kozlovsky knew there were countless places to hide as long as it was dark. Obviously, Reynolds possessed survival skills. After reading his dossier, not surprising he decided to hunker down instead of running last night. He had a history of getting into dangerous circumstances then escaping. Maybe he or the woman was wounded in that bloodbath in the SUV.

"Reynolds is smart. He will make his move now that it is daylight. You have all the police stations nearby under surveillance?"

"Of course," Fattore said.

Given this violent encounter, Reynolds and Prescott should logically seek refuge with the police. Even if Fattore's Mafiosi kept the nearby police stations under surveillance, it was not certain they could prevent the subjects from entering. In any event, that meant game over for Kozlovsky's mission. However, Kozlovsky still thought they would instead try to escape Bologna.

"And hospitals?" Kozlovsky said.

"Yes."

"Unless he or the woman is wounded, I do not think our journalist will want to explain shooting four people. There is also the matter of the earlier shootings on the train outside of Verona. No, I think he will attempt to leave Italy. And quickly."

"I have people covering the airport and the regional bus station. Word is out covering all possible methods of escape with a large reward offered. If the Americans are looking to leave Bologna by train, I have people stationed throughout the station and your team is also here."

"Then there is little more to be done except wait."

CHAPTER 25

BOLOGNA, ITALY

Before disembarking the bus, Reynolds said to Prescott, "Slight change in plans. We are going to take a taxi to Modena, the next train station stop on the Bologna to Milan route. Haven't been thinking clearly. Too risky to go to the Bologna station. The Italians will undoubtedly be looking for us there."

The reverse side of his map of Rome had a map of Italy.

"How far is Modena?"

"Appears to be about a one-hour drive."

They walked a block in a commercial district of offices before waving down a taxi. Seeing they had luggage, the driver exited the taxi, saying, "*Buongiorno.*"

"Do you speak English?" Reynolds said.

"Ah, yes. Americano? Where you want to go?" the driver said in passable English.

"Modena. The train station."

The driver looked perplexed.

"There is train station here in Bologna, *Signore*. Many trains to Modena. At least every hour. Much less costly."

"Thank you, but we are to meet some friends coming from Milan. We should have left earlier. Need to get there right away. Can we get there quickly on the autostrada?

"*Si*. I shall drive at top speed, *signore*. You and your friends perhaps are visiting the Ferrari factory?"

"Yes. Exactly."

"Of course. Most famous cars in all world. *Scusami*, I shall call dispatch then we shall be off."

The driver entered the A14 getting his toll ticket and racing off on the Autostrada to merge with the A1 to Modena.

A couple of miles along, the driver said, "The car may have a problem, *signore*. The *olio* warning light came on then went out. I had problem yesterday. Believe there is *olio* leak. Added a liter yesterday. Thought everything fine."

"Can you make it to Modena?"

"There is service plaza short distance ahead. Best to stop and add *olio*. Shall only take little time. Do not worry. I shall still get you to Modena very quickly."

A frustrated Bruno Fattore and Major Kozlovsky sat drinking coffee at the Bologna train station. After Fattore continually placed calls throughout the early morning hours pressing his people about the search for the Americans, a return call eventually came through.

The exchange lasted only thirty seconds. After disconnecting, Fattore said, "We know where they are. In a taxi on the autostrada. We must hurry. You will follow me."

Kozlovsky said, "No, I will go with you. Remember our deal, Fattore."

Fattore nodded agreement as Kozlovsky called his subordinate to bring around the SUV provided for his team. They were to follow Fattore's Mercedes.

The two vehicles raced through the streets of Bologna to the closest entrance to the A14.

Sitting in the backseat of the Mercedes, Fattore placed another call. Leaving the line open, he turned toward Kozlovsky sitting next to him. "My people spread the alert to everyone last night, including the taxi companies. A driver picked up the two Americans, a man and woman, just ten minutes ago. They are headed to Modena. The train station."

"Can we beat them there?" Kozlovsky asked.

"Yes. The taxi driver will make an excuse to stop at the service plaza just before the A14 merges into the A1 north to Modena. I have other people that should arrive before they reach the service plaza."

Finally a break, Kozlovsky thought. Should be less public to seize the Americans at this service plaza than the train station. Unlikely any police will be present. Few people probably at this early morning hour. The unknown remained the issue with Fattore. The killing of his sister demanded revenge on the Americans.

The driver slowed the Mercedes as he approached the exit to the service plaza. Kozlovsky checked to insure his team was close behind. He slowed to a crawl looking for the taxi among the many fuel pumps, spotting it in the last row furthest from the highway.

Fattore placed a call, obviously to his other Mafiosi having arrived ahead of them. He gestured to his driver to pull into position behind the taxi with its engine hood raised.

"I don't like this, Mark. Something's wrong," Prescott said.

"Stay here," Reynolds said as he opened the door.

As Reynolds exited out the right side, Prescott got out on the left. They both converged at the front of the taxi to see their driver already some distance away entering the service building.

As Reynolds and Prescott looked at each other, a raging Bruno Fattore ran toward them. Instinctively Prescott reached into her purse grasping the grip of the 9mm pistol.

She watched in horror as the man in the suit closed on Reynolds holding a knife.

As Reynolds held up his hands in defense while stepping backwards, Bruno Fattore lunged with an Italian stiletto switchblade catching Reynolds in the shoulder causing him to lose balance. As Reynolds hit the pavement hard on his back, Fattore dropped to his knees and continued his attack, sinking the blade a second time into Reynolds upper chest.

Prescott gasped while extracting the 9mm. No more than ten feet from Fattore attempting to plunge the knife again into Reynolds, she pulled the trigger repeatedly in desperation. The three remaining rounds in the weapon struck Fattore in the chest in rapid succession, sending him backward then falling to the pavement on his side.

The unexpected attack on Fraser and the shooting of Fattore froze the Italians, including the two arriving before the taxi and another two arriving with Fattore.

Arriving just behind Fattore's Mercedes, the Russian Zaslon team quickly exited their SUV. With the gunshots, they immediately fanned out into a perimeter to contain the unfolding situation. By preexisting order from Kozlovsky, their mission was to capture the Americans. Should the Italians interfere, they were expendable.

For several seconds nothing happened. The Italians looked around in bewilderment trying to access what to do. The Russians went into tactical mode looking toward their commander Kozlovsky.

Adding to the chaotic scene, a Carabinieri patrol car pulling into the service area came to a screeching stop at the sound of Prescott's shots. Exiting their vehicle, both police took up defensive positions behind their opened car doors radioing for reinforcements.

The ensuing gun battle proved difficult to piece together in detail from the many differing accounts. A single shot ignited a fierce exchange between the Italians and the Russians. By the time additional police arrived on scene, most of the combatants lay dead or wounded.

According to Victoria Prescott, a well-built man with a close-cropped beard struck her on the jaw with his fist immediately after she shot the man attacking Mark. She could recall nothing further until regaining consciousness minutes later. By then the gun battle was over. Bodies lay everywhere. Her overriding thought was to get to Mark.

Screaming for help in frustration she ripped her blouse off to hold against his chest wound as blood discharged in rhythm to his heart contractions. He appeared conscious. She remembered someone in uniform relieving her and applying real bandages to Mark's wounds.

The man with the beard that hit her lay face down on the pavement unmoving and bleeding from multiple gunshot wounds.

A short time after watching a medical helicopter airlift Mark from the scene. They told her only that he was alive. Overcome by shock, her last recollection was an aerial view of the scene from a police helicopter.

Without any definitive statement from the police, the following day the Italian press could report little in the way of detail other than casualty statistics. Of the thirteen combatants involved in the raging gunfire exchange, seven were dead. Six others survived. All but one suffered wounds with two remaining in critical life threatening condition. No police or innocent bystanders suffered injury. All the dead and injured participated in the deadly confrontation. The police attribute containment of the victims to the active participants resulted from no use of assault weapons. The police recovered thirteen handguns at the scene.

The police identified several of the dead and arrested as belonging to the local Mafia in Bologna. Among the dead was Bruno Fattore, nephew to regional Mafia underboss, Marcello Fattore. Two American nationals, a man and woman, were among the survivors although the man remains hospitalized in serious condition. Their names withheld from the press. Six others involved in the incident remain unidentified. Four are among the dead and two survived their wounds.

Media speculation ranged from some sort of internecine Mafia struggle to terrorism.

Even for the Italian media, five days later the *Massacro di Bologna* shootout on the autostrada story gave way to the first headlines appearing in every major newspaper and television outlet throughout the world, *Mancano le Bombe Nucleari Russe*, in English, *Russian Nuclear Bombs Missing*.

Victoria Prescott sat in a Bologna jail cell. Her only injury a badly bruised jaw and facial swelling. She refused to answer any questions until she could talk with an American consular official and her attorney in the United States. Although the police provided no details, they did inform her that Mark Reynolds underwent surgery. The doctors categorized his condition as remaining serious but stable. However, she was not allowed to talk to him.

The New York Times front-page lead story read:

> API NEW YORK – The International Consortium of Investigative Journalists released the following story today. Most international news organizations will publish the story by freelance journalist and best-selling author, Mark Reynolds and Stanford Professor of History, Victoria Prescott.
>
> Reynolds is the author of two published books on international subjects. *Nuclear Threats for Our Time* published in 1998 dealt with the insecurity of nuclear weapons within the former Soviet Union republics. *Shell Game* published in 2015, chronicled his investigative work leading to the downfall of the large international corporation Martinelli Global. The book concluded with the startling allegation of missing Russian nuclear warheads.
>
> Professor Prescott, an expert in twentieth century Soviet Union-Russian history, published *Critical Mass* in 1999, revealing the identity of a previously undiscovered

WWII Soviet spy working at the highest level within the Manhattan Project.

Reynolds and Prescott came into possession of stolen classified files from a highly placed source in Russian intelligence known to Prescott. Lieutenant General Anton Grigoryev, First Deputy of the Russian foreign intelligence agency, the SVR, assisted Prescott twenty years earlier in her research during the Yeltsin era of Russian glasnost. Several weeks ago, Grigoryev was murdered in Paris. French police determined the murder most likely an ordered assassination by the Kremlin. Prescott claims Grigoryev intended to defect to the United States using her as a back channel while he remained in hiding in France.

After meeting Grigoryev in Paris and returning to New York, Prescott failed in attempts to reconnect with Grigoryev by telephone, soon learning of his murder after reported in the French press. Prescott decided to contact Reynolds for assistance, recalling the investigative work by Reynolds alleging stolen Russian warheads in his book four years earlier. Fluent in Russian, Prescott translated the documents given her by Grigoryev. For reasons not disclosed, Prescott and Reynolds decided not to turn over the sensitive material to U.S. government authorities, choosing instead a public release.

Prescott and Reynolds remain unavailable for comment. In a separate story, Italian police report both Prescott and Reynolds detained and placed in protective custody as material witnesses in connection with violent events in Northern Italy within the last few days. A spectacular shootout occurred on the autostrada outside Bologna, killing seven people. The Italian police declined to comment on why the two Americans were present at the scene. Seriously wounded, Reynolds is now undergoing medical treatment.

The New York Times discovered another violent crime in Italy lending further mystery to this breaking story. The day before the shootout on the Italian autostrada outside Bologna, a man and woman were discovered shot to death on a train arriving from Rome after stopping in Verona, a city north of Bologna. The woman victim, identified as Leila Hajjar, is a Lebanese national and a professor at the American University of Beirut. Sources unauthorized to release information have confirmed the male victim as Iranian but declined any further information on his identity.

However, included in the trove of released Russian documents, is a Russian FSB dossier on Colonel Farzard Savi, chief of the foreign intelligence directorate of the Ministry of Intelligence of the Islamic Republic of Iran, commonly abbreviated as the MOIS. In the Russian documents, Savi is named as the mastermind behind the theft of three operational thermonuclear Russian warheads now supposedly in the hands of Iran. The Russian dossier identifies Hajjar as the mistress of the Iranian Savi. Italian police decline to confirm if the murder victim is the Iranian Savi.

Italian police also revealed yet another layer to the expanding story. Tracing the movements of Reynolds and Prescott, another murder occurred outside their hotel in Rome just hours prior to the subsequent killings in Verona and Bologna. The victim an unidentified armed man shot by an unknown perpetrator.

Authorities further revealed Reynolds and Prescott made an overnight journey from Rome to Beirut, Lebanon before returning to Rome two days prior to this sequence of violent events. Again no official comment of a possible connection with the murder in Rome and the murder of Leila Hajjar and the Iranian on the train in Verona.

The New York Times authenticated the various original documents used as the source of this story to explain the theft of the warheads. At the center is a detailed confession by a Russian national named Yuri Antonovich Dratshev. Dratshev allegedly controlled the operational aspects of the theft under the direction of his boss Feliks Alekseev Garnitsky. Garnitsky, an executive of the now defunct Moscow Capital Partners caught up as a partner to U.S.-based Martinelli Global brought down in the international scandal uncovered by the journalist Mark Reynolds several years ago.

The whereabouts of Garnitsky and Dratshev remains unknown. Both believed dead following the death of their oligarch boss Nikolai Krasin for having done extensive harm to the Putin regime. After confessing his complicity in disposing of various Russian Army officers involved in the theft, Dratshev anticipated his own demise as the only remaining witness, and set down a detailed accounting of the nuclear warheads theft. He then gave this to his estranged brother an orthodox monk secluded in a monastery in Greece. The full translation of that original document appears at the end of this article.

When Mark Reynolds originally floated his allegations gleaned from hacked cellphone conversations between Garnitsky and Dratshev, governments around the world, including the United States, dismissed the allegations as a misreading of the limited evidence. Russia in particular was most vocal in its denial that any nuclear warheads were missing from their inventories, pointing to internationally supervised audits.

Since the alleged time of the theft in 2014, Iran has done nothing to indicate they possessed these or any nuclear weapons. They point to the 2015 agreement in which Russia was also a signatory. Even with withdrawal by the United States from the agreement, and the imposition of renewed U.S. sanctions, Iran continues to abide by the terms according to U.S. intelligence. Iran has made no shift to a new militant posture militaristically signaling any change to their continued denial of an Iranian nuclear weapons program. Sources close to Western intelligence state there is nothing that might Iran is doing anything that might suggest leveraging possession of such advanced nuclear weapons.

Every major country in the world is hurriedly issuing statements ranging from denial, guarded skepticism, various stages of incredulity, to the most strident condemnation with calls for drastic immediate countermeasures. Most of the statements from those countries with expressed views toward Iran fell along predicable lines.

Iranian President Hassan Rouhani and Foreign Minister Mohammad Zarif issued statements calling the entire story an American fabrication led by the current Trump administration.

Russian Foreign Minister Sergey Lavrov and Russian ambassador to the United States Anatoly Antonov issued separate denials stating the allegation to be ludicrous journalistic fiction, hinting at the possibility of this being a clumsy CIA attempt at disinformation.

Secretary of State Mike Pompeo, Acting Secretary of Defense Patrick Shanahan, and National Security Advisor John Bolton held a joint press conference announcing the entire United States intelligence apparatus is working hard to evaluate these new allegations. Shanahan announced that until undeniable determination of the validity of what amounts to an immediate threat to the entire world, the Defense Department is raising the defense readiness condition to DEFCON level 3. This is the same readiness level immediately following the 9/11 terrorist attacks. However, if the allegations prove correct, in effect if concluding Iran possesses functional thermonuclear warheads, Shanahan suggested the readiness level might be raised to DEFCON 2, the same level as during the Cuban Missile Crisis.

President Trump remains unusually silent in commenting on the situation while avoiding opportunities where reporters can bombard him with questions. Unnamed sources within the West Wing revealed that President Trump is in telephone communication with Russian President Putin. None of the sources claimed knowledge of the substance of these private conversations.

Israeli Prime Minister Benjamin Netanyahu, a strident accuser of the Islamic Republic of Iran as an avowed enemy of Israel, was less guarded. “Israeli Defense Forces have been placed on the highest alert status. Essentially the State of Israel is on a war footing. Iran denies the right for Israeli to exist. Now they possess thermonuclear weapons. Weapons many times over the destructive power of those nuclear bombs dropped on

Japan in World War Two. The world felt relieved with the signing of the Iranian nuclear agreement to curtail enrichment of fissionable fuels, a necessity for constructing nuclear weapons. This now shows that agreement to be nothing more than a ploy to reduce sanctions while Iran pursued an even more aggressive weapons program."

Saudi Arabia, a longtime foe of Shiite Iran, remained silent. It is uncertain how they view a nuclear-armed Iran as an actual military threat. With the downfall of Saddam Hussein's regime in Iraq, the struggle between the Saudis and the Iranians has been more about hegemony in the Middle East.

More measured responses came from the major European powers, China, and Japan. All indicating the documentation is undergoing strenuous analysis.

North Korea issued a congratulatory statement to Iran as an aspirational sister state. "Both suffer under the same relentless efforts of the United States to subjugate the national ambitions of both their countries to protect themselves from hostile foreign military aggression, including the United States and their regional surrogates."

Calling from New York, Phillip Ellsberg said, "How are you holding up, Victoria?"

"Frustrated. Now that I have refused to talk to either the Italian investigators or the assorted U.S. diplomatic functionaries, I just sit here and read. Mark is recovering which gives me comfort. They finally let me talk with him. Doctors tell him he will fully recover but it will take some time. Lot of muscle and tendon damage from the stab wounds."

"Yes, I also talked with him and some appointed Italian attorney yesterday. He did not tell me what happened. Says he can't be sure the Italians aren't recording his conversations."

"I know. We both agreed about that before everything went unexpectedly wrong. Mark said we could never adequately explain our circumstances, at least until after the story broke."

"Sound advice. As I told him, I'm working to secure you a first-rate Italian lawyer. Someone fluent in English. Going to explore pursuing a deal whereby you and Mark can be interviewed under a grant of immunity from any related prosecutions."

"Why's that even necessary? We're not guilty of anything except defending ourselves against the Italian Mafia."

"I understand, Victoria, but this is not the United States. Not sure how these things work in Italy but the Italians have two uncooperative material witnesses in multiple homicides involving various foreign nationals. Since the Iranian Savi is an intelligence official, that creates another dimension.

"Adding to all that is a New York Times related article. Seems some Middle East stringer dug further into the death of Savi's girlfriend Leila Hajjar. Apparently, a couple days before her and Savi's murder on the Italian train, there was another murder in a Beirut hotel. A body found in the stairwell with two bullet wounds. Savi was registered in a room on the same floor. Reports suggest he checked out before even spending one night. Can this become any more complicated?

"As the story plays throughout the world, you and Mark are the center of interest. Already there are speculations about the identities of two of the wounded arrestees. They are not Italian. Sources from my DOJ days say the IDs are fraudulent but so good as to suggest state-sponsored forgeries. Both men are severely wounded and not yet able to undergo questioning. I suspect we both know their nationalities."

"So why would the Italians grant us immunity?" Prescott said.

"Because you and Mark are the only ones able to explain this series of violent events. And you are likely victims rather than assailants. With the release of the Russian story to the media, the background of your involvement is circumstantially explained as the motivation for the attacks on you and Mark. May take a little time to work out an arrangement, but I think we may have a chance. With the continuing serialized release of the additional financial scandal material, the threat to the Russians will become clearer.

"That and pressure from the U.S. I've been working the phones to enlist support from the DOJ, the State Department, and even the CIA. Lots of interest in debriefing you and Mark for additional information beyond the Russian documents. That won't happen until you get immunity deals in both the U.S. and Italy."

"How long do you figure?" Prescott said.

"Hard to say. Legal systems everywhere move slowly. Italy is probably as bad as it gets. Just keep your cool and continue to make no comments. I'll keep you posted on progress."

"Okay. Thanks, Phillip."

"Unfortunately, I have some related bad news. I already told Mark. He took it badly. I'm afraid your associate Bernie Poole is dead."

"Oh my god! What happened?"

"According to police, shot as he left a Brooklyn delicatessen by a fleeing gunman just after sticking up the liquor store next door. No arrests, no suspects yet identified."

"Too much of a coincidence. It must be the Russians," Prescott said. "What about Josef Novak in Washington?"

"Thought the same thing. After reading of Poole's death, I immediately called Josef Novak. Says he is fine except worried about you and Mark. Told him to be cautious by maintaining heightened awareness when he was out and about. Consider his exposure anywhere he went. Knowing your predicament, he said I should have given you that advice. He sends his love."

"I've seen the newspapers with our story about the nuclear weapons theft. When do you think the other financial stuff will come out?"

"No idea. I just sent the material to the director of the International Consortium of Investigative Journalists, Howard Benedick. Mark included specific instructions and suggested journalists for distribution, along with a suggested sequence of time-phased content releases to maximize the impact while sustaining the drama for as long as possible.

"My guess is each editor will probably follow their own instincts as to how and when to release. They will of course want to corroborate your source material before going to press. In the meantime, do not say anything to anyone. That means Italians or American officials. My guess is you might receive a visit from someone senior out of the U.S. Embassy in Rome. Might even bring the resident FBI liaison along. Make no statements to anyone no matter what. Tell them you refuse under advice of counsel. Your American counsel. I'll find you a temporary Italian lawyer but he will be just window dressing to help me navigate the Italian legal system until I find appropriate counsel. Tell him nothing about what happened without consulting me first."

CHAPTER 26

MANHATTAN, NEW YORK

Reynolds suggested the serialized sequence of publication release of the voluminous material on the financial wrongdoing of the Putin regime for sustaining effect. Progressively stoking the scandal with each new revelation. Eventually, the material should become self-sustaining as journalists began probing details. The raw data would then take on various narrative tracks with what should become a flood of interconnected stories. The feeding frenzy should rival the unrelenting American drama associated with the investigation of Russian interference in U.S. elections.

Those allegations put forward by the entire U.S intelligence community sparked the even greater domestic crisis by the troubling affinity President Donald Trump expresses toward Russia and Vladimir Putin specifically. His consistent unwillingness to confront Russian aggression of all types remains inexplicable to allies and foes alike.

Reynolds believes these new Russian allegations should at least thwart President Trump's odd pro-Russian agenda, and possibly damage Trump directly. In boxing parlance, the nuclear warheads revelation delivers a hard right hook to the Russian jaw. The financial corruption leaked over time will act as an unrelenting series of jabs directed to the body. Since the Russian led corruption involves huge U.S. investments, the scandal should take on a life of its own domestically. Undoubtedly a cast of U.S. nationals caught up in the scandal will be paraded if not through the courts then at least in the media. Tainted investments will see asset values plummet on the order perhaps billions of dollars.

While Reynolds viewed the issue of the nuclear weapons theft and the Russian financial corruption as separate scandals, the media frenzy would likely fuse them into a single anti-Russian narrative. Following the opening summary drafted by Prescott, what followed was a dump of names. Corporations, banks, tax haven LLCs, and individuals.

The devastating exposure of the *Panama Papers* and the *Paradise Papers,* largely embarrassed thousands of individuals and corporations throughout the world. Those confidential data breaches came from within legal service firms that set up thousands of offshore entities. While not illegal, these corporations created in tax haven countries hid ownership and records of financial transactions, with no government reporting, and no compulsory sharing of information with foreign regulatory agencies.

Prescott's secret Russian documents however exposed how these offshore shell corporations served to facilitate and hide the flow of illicit money from inside records of what amounts to an international criminal enterprise. Collectively, the data trove presented a prima facie case to pursue criminal prosecutions on an unprecedented scale.

Accompanying what the media labeled as the *Russian Papers,* are explanations of some of the elaborate mechanisms the Putin regime used to launder illicit funds into legitimate investments outside Russia. As a former U.S. district attorney prosecuting white-collar crime, Phillip Ellsberg found the level of investigative and analytical work accomplished by Reynolds, Prescott, Poole, and Novak, remarkable.

Just a brief read of the lengthy New York Times, Wall Street Journal, and Washington Post stories suggested all sorts of lines for federal and state prosecutors to pursue criminal investigations. Founded on actual source documents suggested investigators could construct strong criminal cases to seek indictments on a range of charges. Targeting not only Russians, but American and European defendants. This was already ballooning into a worldwide scandal while only in its earliest phases.

Each day brought new headlines and dominated broadcast media coverage. The 24/7 news cycle became filled with endless opinion debates of the impact of the release of the Russian Papers.

The earliest releases named virtually the elite of the Russian financial world. Not only naming individuals but also citing what the documentation alleges to be their involvement in criminal activity. Criminal activity even under Russian law along with violations in other countries where Russian business or banking interests operated.

Accompanying the names were brief biographies showing the interconnected relationships. Those relations intertwined between the Russian government and private financial sectors.

Most prominent was the financial oligarch Alexei Romanovich Balakin. Principle shareholder in Rossiya Bank and Chelyabinsk Commercial, both sanctioned as was Balakin personally following the Russian annexation of Crimea. Known as a close associate of Vladimir Putin, the leaked documents repeatedly identified Balakin as the central figure managing illicit financial ventures. The characterization also suggested Balakin as the principal expert in constructing the secret financial empire to launder the flow of billions of rubles of Russian money derived from a range of illegal enterprises. Enterprises only possible with the collusion of the Russian President and ministerial-level conspirators.

Balakin rose to prominence simultaneously as Putin ascended to the presidency in 2000. They became acquainted years earlier in Saint Petersburg when both were part of the city municipal government. Balakin is a close personal associate of Putin, accompanying him on trips and appearing together at social functions.

Balakin teamed with the former oligarch Nikolai Krasin to set up Chelyabinsk Commercial specifically to finance firms engaging in government contracts. Balakin quietly assumed control of the various Krasin enterprises following Krasin's complicity in the international scandal that brought down MGI and Krasin's own Moscow Capital Partners.

One of those enterprises was a Moscow Capital Partner subsidiary. Rusatomic held government contracts to manage the two nuclear weapons reprocessing facilities cited in the details of the nuclear warheads theft.

Speculation is already openly circulating as to possible Russian collusion to deliver the warheads to Iran. Might this be another of Putin's bold provocations, this time directed at the United States? Not out of the question when considering Putin's many recent aggressive international ventures. The annexation of Crimea, active support of civil war in eastern Ukraine, cyberattacks directed at the U.S. 2016 election, and Russian military support of the Bashar al-Assad's regime in Syria's ongoing civil war.

In addition to Balakin, the documents implicated other powerful governmental financial officials as conspirators. Oleg Sochinsky, Minister of Finance, Dimitri Markarov, Chairman of the Board of Directors of the Central Bank of Russia, and Ilya Rabrenovich, Minister of Economic Development, plus a long list of deputies in the various financial institutions.

Rabrenovich also figures prominently in many of the documents suggesting his involvement in managing the source of much of the illicit money laundered outside Russia. Several documents implicate him extensively in preferential government contracting schemes. These include non-bid contracts, cost-plus contracts, non-existent engineering and consulting services, and what appears an elaborate pattern of banking fraud.

Rabrenovich, with Balakin's Chelyabinsk Commercial Bank and Markarov's complicity at the Russian Central Bank, designed a method of flowing state funds for fraudulent government contracts. This involved awarding government contracts to unqualified Russian shell companies or straw man companies. Many of these companies had no experience or even resources to deliver on the contracts, thereby subcontracting the actual work or services to other firms for enormous management fees. Chelyabinsk Commercial provided operating capital funding and loans. In turn, the Russian Central Bank secretly underwrote this unsecured debt.

The bogus recipients of these loans misuse the funds, skim profits, pay kickbacks, and eventually become insolvent or simply dissolve altogether. The Russian treasury takes the losses. The process is secret with enormous amounts of cash accruing. All is needed is the vehicle to launder it.

Additional sources of illicit funds flow in from more conventional sources of criminal enterprise. The single largest source comes from the natural resources sector. The name Sergei Leonidevich Terekov enters the cast of villains. Another oligarch within Putin's inner circle, Terekov derived his wealth from mining. He eventually branched out to engage in the next step in the supply chain involving extracting the valuable ore content then transforming it into usable form such as steel, aluminum, nickel, copper, gold, and uranium. This naturally led to expanding investments into rail, trucking, and maritime logistics.

Along his path to power, Terekov realized that the extracting of natural resources was an industrial segment of Russian enterprise particularly susceptible to corrupt practices. An environment providing the ability to falsify yield numbers to skim profits, outright theft on a large scale, avoiding taxes, and in some cases, evading western imposed sanctions on exports.

With such a ripe climate for illegal enterprise, Russian organized crime had long since infiltrated everywhere. In particular, the Solntsevskaya Bratva held tight control on much of Russian transportation infrastructure. With plenty of money at play, Terekov collaborated with the Bratva. The synergies of that partnership expanded into other lucrative endeavors. Aiding in all manner of organized crime export and import smuggling, including drugs, Terekov also charged a service fee for managing the finances and laundering the profits. The partnership proved a profitable working relationship for all parties. Solntsevskaya Bratva now enjoyed the implicit protection as a partner to the highest placed officials in government.

From the perspective of the governing regime, Putin now had at his disposal a shadowy violent force from which to intimidate or eliminate threatening opposition while maintaining plausible deniability. While the released documents included few specifics, many journalists speculated that with this known economic connection with Russian organized crime that certain past violent events might have a different origin. Could the controversial Moscow bombings of 1999 that helped propel Vladimir Putin into the Presidency be attributed to collusion with Russian organized crime rather than Chechen separatists? The many years of unsolved murders of journalists and dissidents provoked renewed speculation.

Like Balakin, Terekov's relationship with Putin began in the 1990s. Some speculate Terekov brokered an arrangement with the Solntsevskaya Bratva to provide a private unrestricted resource for furthering Putin's political ambitions?

The initial wave of world outrage pointed at the named Russians now routinely referred to as a state-sponsored criminal organization. The U.S. media soon focused on the money laundering possibly implicating American co-conspirators, and what that meant for the affected U.S. investments.

First to come under intense scrutiny was Vincent Fletcher, a New York international business attorney. A name unknown to the public but not to the FBI and DOJ. The documents did not directly reveal his name but they did reveal the name of the Panamanian-based corporate legal service firm that created the hundreds of offshore tax haven corporations specifically for the Russians.

Within days of naming the firm of Servicios Corporativos de Panamá, the Panamanian justice ministry detained the managing director, a Mexican business attorney named Arturo Calderón. The following day, the Panamanian government shutdown the firm. A spokesperson for the ministry said, "Panama is not a haven for criminals around the world. The corporate legal services and preferential tax advantages of incorporating in Panama are intended to be a legitimate service to corporations throughout the world. Corporations doing business in accordance with the laws of their respective countries. The anonymous leak of confidential information in 2015 resulting in the unfortunate label as the *Panama Papers* damaged the entire Panamanian international corporate legal services sector. Given the scale of foreign transactions, it is not possible to vet the origin of funds within these Panamanian corporations. However, the recent revelations were sufficient to suspend the operating license of Servicios Corporativos de Panamá and open a criminal investigation. Panama will not tolerate its legitimate international corporate services sector knowingly used for criminal purposes."

Investigative journalists now resurrected Vincent Fletcher's past. His ties to Russia went back years when he was a lawyer with a now defunct New York law firm. That firm discredited for their work with Martinelli Global and its affiliate Moscow Capital Partners in setting up their sophisticated scheme for laundering money from various international criminal enterprises. The managing partner of the law firm and the senior management of MGI all subsequently convicted on a range of federal and New York state criminal charges. Fletcher escaped prosecution only for lack of a strong enough case of his personal culpability.

The mountain of secret Russian documents clearly pointing to the beneficiary of billions of dollars of laundered money as the large real estate hedge fund RK Investments rocked the Wall Street investment sector.

RK experienced exponential growth during the last five years, reaching a level of $40B in managed assets. Analysts jumped all over the revelation. The obvious speculation being the dramatic growth resulted from a flow of investments originating within Russia. The perfect money laundering mechanism. Impossible to distinguish the legitimate investment from the laundered funds. Not only did the Russian crooks avoid paying fees for the laundering service, they additionally received a return on the investments.

The newsworthy footnote making the airways had to do with RK CEO Russell Koning. Not only was he a known close associate of Donald Trump, they shared a long history in real estate related businesses. For the embattled President, here was yet another connection to the ever-expanding interaction with all things Russian by so many of those in his orbit.

RK Investments represented the first tangible casualty of the Russian Papers. Overnight they became a pariah in the investment world. Inflow of new investments virtually ceased. Fund share value dropped 30% in one day resulting in suspending trading on the NYSE. Even though analysts pointed to real value in the now undervalued fund shares, buyers shunned RK. As a week passed, financial watchers anticipated that trading would not resume for the foreseeable future.

Raising the specter of where next and how far the scandal might spend within the U.S. financial sector, the markets dropped 6% over the first week of the scandal. The geopolitical uncertainty of a nuclear-armed Iran only compounded market weakness.

TEHRAN, IRAN

Within ten days of the public release of the irrefutable evidence that Iran possessed three thermonuclear warheads, the United States elevated demands into an ultimatum for Iran to give up the weapons or face an imminent military response.

During this time, Foreign Minister Mohammad Zarif continued issuing denials while condemning the United States as looking for an excuse to ignite a new Middle East war.

The day following Zarif's most recent public address, events took an unexpected turn. President Hassan Rouhani took to the airways at a news conference attended by Western news correspondents.

"After consultation with Our Supreme Leader Ali Khamenei, I am instructed to deliver the following statement. After an exhaustive investigation, a secret plot has been discovered involving a small group of senior government officials. A plot not to overthrow the current government, rather a zealous plot of misguided patriots. Unfortunately, their efforts have brought about serious consequences to the Islamic Republic of Iran. Fortunately, those efforts did not go further thereby risking Iran's very existence. The allegations appearing in the press throughout the world are regrettably accurate.

"A small number of senior officials sanctioned the theft of Russian nuclear weapons four years ago. Since that time, the weapons have remained carefully hidden in Iran. This unknown and unauthorized act runs counter to our consistent assertion that Iran has not, nor are we currently pursuing a nuclear weapons program. As I negotiated the agreement in 2015 to curtail nuclear fuels enrichment, I knew nothing of this rogue effort to undermine Iran's peaceful use of nuclear energy.

"To validate our claim, Iran not only acknowledges the weapons are in our possession, but will actively assist in restoring the warheads to the Russian Federation under international supervision. We trust this demonstration of good faith will be sufficient for the United States and its allies to withdraw their threat of military action.

"As further proof of our good intentions, the conspirators responsible for this theft have been removed from their positions of trust and imprisoned while awaiting trial on criminal charges. Among those responsible for this act of treason and now imprisoned are Major General Mohammad Ali Jafari, Commander of the Republican Guard, Major General Qasem Soleimani, Commander of the Quds Force, Hossein Taeb, Chief of Intelligence of the IRGC, Mahmoud Alavi, Minister of Intelligence, and Amir Gilani, Governor of the Central Bank of Iran. The mastermind behind the theft, Colonel Farzard Savi, Head of the Foreign Intelligence Directorate within the Intelligence Ministry, died in Italy under unknown circumstances."

While the world breathed a sigh of relief, Iranian experts around the world discounted Rouhani's official mea culpa. While possible, it was extremely unlikely that Rouhani could not have known of some hardliner faction taking matters in their own hands. Equally unlikely that Supreme Leader Khamenei did not at least give tacit approval. Such a move without Khamenei's nod would be unthinkable where the Supreme Leader is all-powerful, even legally considered inviolable. Many suggested that the named individuals were those sacrificed to extricate Iran from an inescapable fate of military strikes and isolating sanctions on the scale of North Korea. The conspirators rolled the dice and lost because of the premature disclosure.

One cynical pundit quipped, "I wonder if these misguided devils will now go willingly to the gallows as martyrs for Allah?"

CHAPTER 27

ROME, ITALY

Victoria Prescott looked up as her cell door rattled then opened. Led into a conference room, she registered surprise and relief seeing Phillip Ellsberg with two other men she did not recognize.

Enveloping Ellsberg in a hug, she could not hold back the tears. "So good to see you, Phillip."

"Very good to see you, Victoria. Considering all you've been through, you look well. Please let me introduce Signore Antonio Bertoletti. He is your Italian lawyer."

The distinguished middle-aged Bertoletti with coffered gray hair in an expensive tailored suit offered his hand to Prescott. "Signorina Prescott, a pleasure. Hopefully we can improve your accommodations very soon. Let me introduce Signore Gabrielle of the State Prosecutor's office."

The younger Gabrielle extended his hand to Prescott but merely nodded.

"Let's all be seated," Ellsberg said. Turning to face Prescott, "I've been in Rome for several days. Sorry I could not see you sooner but I wanted to have some good news when I did see you. I will let these gentlemen explain what I believe is a resolution to your predicament. The same deal applies to Mark as well."

Bertoletti said, "Mr. Ellsberg has made a persuasive case on your behalf and that of your associate Mr. Reynolds. In brief, the state prosecutor's office has agreed to your terms of immunity from prosecution in exchange for testimony at trial of those arrested in the violent incident on the autostrada. Signore Gabrielle has all the necessary paperwork defining the terms of the agreement. Reviewed of course by Senore Ellsberg."

Turning to Ellsberg, she said, "And the scope of the immunity?"

Without articulating specifics, he understood she meant what about the bloodbath in the SUV and the murder of Savi and Hajjar on the train.

"The immunity extends to any criminal exposure since you arrived in Italy. The prosecutor's office also does not feel you or Mark committed any crimes. At least crimes of any consequence. The same deal of course extends to Mark. He is doing fine by the way. I saw him this morning and discussed the particulars of the offer with him. He is in favor of signing but wants to discuss this with you before agreeing to all the prosecutor wants in return."

"And what is it you want Signore Gabrielle?" she said.

"Simply your full testimony so we can understand the background to this string of violent encounters involving you and Mr. Reynolds. The newspaper accounts attributing you as the source for the secret Russian Papers creating new headlines each day provides us a good idea of your involvement. However we would like to probe that more fully."

"Additionally, you can provide testimony to convict the four defendants surviving the shooting incident outside Bologna. We know the two Italians are Mafia. The other two are Russian. What we do not know is the connection between these groups.

"And what went wrong to cause the violent confrontation between the two groups. We believe there is also a connection to four killings the night before in a vehicle found in the industrial zone of Bologna. Known Mafiosi shot to death during that incident. Before that, a murder victim outside your hotel in Rome followed by the Iranian and the Lebanese woman shot to death on the train outside Verona only hours later. Their names revealed in all the newspapers as connect them with this Russian nuclear weapons story making world headlines. You and Mr. Reynolds obviously know more details of the story than anyone else.

"We know you and Mr. Reynolds were on that train. Therefore, likely connected in some way to the shootings of the four Mafiosi in the vehicle. Perhaps even inside the vehicle at some point. However, we have no witnesses or forensic evidence to support that. Frankly, it is difficult to believe you and Mr. Reynolds somehow overpowered these killers. That is a mystery requiring resolution. Yet we have no reason to believe either you or Mr. Reynolds committed homicide. The government is therefore willing to grant you immunity to get at the truth of what happened.

"The immunity extends to all those instances, or anything else for that matter. Does that explain our side of the agreement satisfactorily?"

"Yes. When does the trial happen?" she said.

Ellsberg answered, "Initially a preliminary hearing, Victoria. Much like in the United States."

Bertoletti said, "The hearing is scheduled for a few weeks from now. However, that is only the beginning of the process. The actual trial will follow probably months later."

"And Mark and I are expected to remain in Italy all that time?"

"Not exactly, Signorina Prescott," Bertoletti said. "Only until conclusion of your testimony at the hearing. The agreement stipulates your voluntary return for subsequent testimony at the actual trial. You and Mr. Reynolds are also consenting to fully cooperating in debriefing by investigators of everything related to any of these crimes in Italy during the period prior to the hearing."

"Very well. When can I speak with Mark?"

Ellsberg looked at the prosecutor Gabrielle. "Right now?"

Gabrielle nodded and stood up going to the door to summon the guard.

They were escorted into another room with a telephone on a table and several chairs.

Gabrielle said, "I will let you have your conversation in private. I assure you there are no listening devices."

As the call connected, Reynolds answered.

"How are you, Mark?"

"Sore as hell but medically doing fine considering a broken collar bone and two stabbing wounds. Thanks to you, I'm still here. The worse time was the first couple of days not knowing what happened to you. All I was told was you were okay but they withheld any details. Considering what happened, I still worried you might have been wounded."

"Hardly a scratch. Just a badly bruised jaw but nothing serious. We can comfort each other when I see you. So are we good with the offered deal?"

"Absolutely. Phillip did an outstanding job negotiating the terms."

"What about having to return at a later date to testify at the trial?"

"The least we can do as our part to put away the remaining guys that tried to kill us."

"Okay. I'll sign then. Do I get to see you soon?"

"Better than that. You get out of jail and I get out of the hospital. We are to be put up at a secure location under heavy guard. Remember the hours of debriefing we are agreeing to."

"Sounds romantic," she said with feigned sarcasm but relieved to see this ordeal coming to an end .

"Well, it might still be better than weathering the storm we'll face when we get back to New York. Tell you what. When we must come back for the trial, it should be during the winter. Good time to visit Rome because it is not too hot and less tourists. This time we'll enjoy the city and make it a holiday."

"What's going to happen when we return to the United States? I mean, the government will want to interview us."

"I talked to Phillip about that also. Since he can identify no U.S. laws that we violated, they will have to temper their zeal. According to Phillip, you never talk to any agent of the federal government without counsel present. Even then he says probably tell them nothing. Any mistake in recall or an opinion refuted by someone else might be construed as providing false information, or falling into some trap of some obscure violation. He usually counsels to wait for a grand jury subpoena which forces their hand if they are serious. Of course, Phillip is a bit of a hard case since he knows DOJ tactics.

"Anyway, he told me he is already negotiating blanket immunity for both of us before testifying either to the DOJ or Congress. If he does not get that, we then play hardball. He's betting they want to know the background of the leaked material more than prosecuting us, which might be difficult anyway.

"Information like what Grigoryev may have told you in Paris? Did he convey opinions as to the climate within the Kremlin? How deep did this financial conspiracy go beyond the names identified in the documents? Is this a criminal enterprise numbering in the hundreds or just select senior officials? How widely known is this within the government? What governmental institutions are compromised? Stuff the spooks want to know for strategic intelligence."

She said, "Even with immunity, this will be a never-ending ordeal. The boredom of preparing lectures and grading papers looks real attractive right now."

"Yeah, I know what you mean. I could use some downtime myself. Tell you what, since you have to return to Stanford, how about I stay in San Francisco with you until the government types have squeezed us for everything we know?"

"I'd love that, Mark.

Thirty days after the gun battle on the autostrada, the preliminary hearing commenced after changing the venue from Bologna to Rome. Two surviving Mafiosi arrested in the aftermath of the shooting and the two Russians faced an array of criminal charges. Mark Reynolds and Victoria appeared as witnesses protected under a broad immunity agreement.

Prescott and Reynolds waited in a witness holding room prior to their testimony. Reynolds was ambulatory but still in a bad way. His arm remained in a sling, and he was bandaged tightly in his upper torso from the stab wounds. Avoiding pain medication, he still suffered considerable pain. They anticipated two long days of testimony but at least the ordeal nearing an end.

Phillip Ellsberg entered the waiting room smiling.

"A real media event out there. Most of the courtroom is media including cameras. Correspondents from all over the world.

"I have some very interesting news. According to Bertoletti's sources in the prosecutor's office, both of the Russians have agreed to plea bargains. One of the two by the name of Major Ivan Kozlovsky turns out to be the commander of the mission. Kozlovsky is part of a little known Russian special forces unit within the Russian SVR. Badass guys called Zaslon.

"Their mission was to abduct and extract information from both of you. Determine specifically what you had. Who else possessed the information? Seems the Russians did not know the extent of what is now publicly coming out. The mission went into high gear when you left the United States."

Reynolds looked over to Prescott shaking his head with an expression conveying *I'm sorry*.

"Both Kozlovsky and the other Russian suffer from multiple gunshot wounds. They are appearing via closed circuit TV from their hospital beds.

"Kozlovsky used a Russian Mafioso that runs Russian organized crime smuggling operations in Italy after things went wrong in Rome. This Russian then used his connection with the Italian Mafia to intercept you and Savi. Seems Savi's girlfriend made a cellphone call. Moscow cyber experts having previously hacked her phone were monitoring. Anyway, this Russian criminal recruited these Italian Mafiosi out of Bologna to abduct and hold you until the Russians special ops guys caught up on a later train north.

"Arriving in Bologna later that night, Kozlovsky learned that you guys escaped. The female victim you shot, Mark, was the niece of the local underboss. Her brother set out on his own vendetta mission. Hence the bloodbath on the autostrada. I'm sure Kozlovsky regrets his subcontracting to common criminals."

Prescott said, "Why would a Russian special forces assassin turn state's witness?"

"I asked the same thing. He'll get some sentencing consideration but still faces life in prison. The prosecutors say the Russian expressed disillusionment once he found out that this was not about Russian state secrets. Wanted his own revenge for being deceived to shield corrupt officials stealing money from the country. Condemns Vladimir Putin as a traitor to Russia. He's a fierce nationalist with a career in a gung-ho, high risk violent world of black ops. His testimony at trial will make international headlines. A personal blow to Putin as Kozlovsky links him directly to the attempt on your lives. By association, it also reinforces the allegations of his personal involvement with the many murders of people opposing him over the years."

The door opened and a uniformed bailiff entered. "Signore Reynolds. Please follow me."

CHAPTER 28

MOSCOW, RUSSIA

While tensions cooled throughout the world following the Iranian President's public admission that his country did in fact possess Russian nuclear warheads and avowed to give them up, the firestorm against Russia only intensified. An ever-increasing outcry condemning Vladimir Putin as the head of an international criminal enterprise reached new levels with each passing week. The loss of the warheads debated intensified. Russian gross negligence or the intentional arming of Iran with nuclear weapons. The latter an arguable possibility as another strategic maneuver in Putin's imperialistic ambitions to advance the status of Russia by indirectly confronting the United States. However, massive financial wrongdoing infecting the United States economy touched off a primal American public response.

The outrage in the United States exceeded any previous scandal involving Russia. The drumbeat from both the right and left drowned out the silence from the White House. Congressional members of both parties voiced outrage. Whereas the continuing cloud hanging over the current administration over allegations of collusion with Russia relating to the 2016 elections polarized the American electorate, this galvanize into bipartisan nationalistic fervor.

Within 120 days, federal criminal indictments were occurring on a weekly basis. The circle of Americans involved in the Russian money laundering began feeding on itself. Plea agreements and cooperation agreements from lower level targets became routine as prosecutors worked up the food chain.

RK Investments became the biggest loser with ten indictments already handed down, including the Chairman and CEO Russell Koning. Announcement of several immunity deals for other RK staffers suggested probable future indictments. With RK as patient-zero, the investigation spread to an ever-widening circle of investors, investment funds, and corporations associated or doing business with RK.

Vincent Fletcher, the lawyer named as the architect of how to move illicit Russian money into U.S. investments, is currently a fugitive under an arrest warrant. The FBI believes Fletcher is no longer in the United States, probably in a safe haven not subject to U.S. extradition.

With a tightly constrained press in Russia, it was more difficult to gauge the impact of these financial wrongdoing revelations on the Russian public. The underpinning of their governmental institutions to provide for legal checks and remedies to such abuses of power proved notoriously lacking. During Putin's nineteen years of power, what safeguards might have existed became severely eroded as Putin continually steam rolled new legislation to invest increased power to the president. Any objective analysis concludes Russia as governed by an autocratic regime with a single unchallenged authority at its head. A dictator by definition.

What came about on Christmas Eve sent a new round of shockwaves throughout the world. The implications so breathtaking that experts found no consensus in predicting the outcome.

At dusk, tanks from three armored divisions sealed off the Kremlin. Elsewhere, army forces seized television and radio broadcast stations. Troops also secured communications centers and power generating stations. Throughout the city, ten thousand soldiers from elite parachute units began a systematic roundup of targeted government officials.

Well-supported military police units seized control of the Lubyanka, the notorious prison and former secret police headquarters on Lubyanka Square. The neo-baroque style building took on its dark role following the 1917 Revolution with the earliest Soviet secret police organization, the Cheka. It retained that function for one hundred years through the subsequent iterations of Soviet secret police as the NKVD then the KGB. Following the fall of the Soviet Union, it continued to function as headquarters for the Russian Federation's internal security apparatus, the FSB.

A battalion of military police displaced the entire FSB headquarters staff and relocated prisoners held in the subterranean prison levels to other locations. The Lubyanka was to be the central location for incarcerating the most important of the new arrestees. The first detainee was the head of the FSB, General Mikhalitsyn and his entire senior staff. Arrested in his office, Mikhalitsyn made an attempt to reach into a desk drawer for a handgun. The army officer in charge disabled the attempt by smashing the general's hand with his weapon.

The arrest list prioritized all those named in the published stories appearing in the West. The oligarchs Sergei Terekov and Alexei Balkan were arrested at their residences. Throughout the night, senior executive staff from their many enterprises received the dreaded knock on the door in the early morning hours and taken into custody.

The comprehensive military coup d'état demonstrated meticulous planning. Surprisingly, with so many involved in the conspiracy, the FSB never discovered the takeover plot suggesting either extraordinary security, or the lack of FSB sources within the Russian military.

All conventional forms of communication ceased with the shutdown of all radio and television broadcasting, cellular telephone service, and access to the Internet. The only available images coming out of Russia were from the rare satellite phones used by Western journalists.

The grainy poorly lit videos were however enough to shake the world.

Who was leading this coup? What were their intentions if successful? What about Vladimir Putin? Wild speculation even swirled that it was not really a coup in the conventional sense but rather a move by Putin to take over with no pretext of preserving any semblance of a democratic state. Had this scandal of personal corruption threatened his hold on power?

The following brought some answers to the Russian people and the outside world, although through the interpretation of the leaders of the military coup. The first surprise was the speaker appearing on a broadcast carried on every Russian television station and fed to the Internet.

Colonel General Levka Veselovsky, dressed in formal uniform, made a brief statement from his office:

'I am here this morning to announce that the Armed Forces of the Russian Federation have seized control of this corrupt civilian government. The ruling regime has debased its responsibility to serve the Russian people by conducting a vast criminal enterprise for personal enrichment. Since 2000, the presidency of Vladimir Vladimirovich Putin has consistently moved to alter the very structure of our government to invest increasing power to the office of the president. While those of us in positions of responsibility suspected various forms of corruption, we did not understand the breadth of this criminality until stolen official documents leaked to the West became public. Furthermore, the rule of law is now so corrupted to the extent there is no remedy under current law to correct the situation. Unfortunately, no alternative remained other than for the military to takeover. The armed forces of the Russian Federation acting as patriots beg the support of the Russian people as we see this crisis through to a better Russia.'

The speech ended there. No explanation as to who now ran Russia. General Veselovsky delivering the public message left a large unanswered question. Was he acting as merely the spokesperson for the coup or was he in de facto control? Although a high-ranking officer, Kozlovsky was largely unknown and with just three stars. What about those general officers senior to him?

He offered no proclamation that this was a temporary situation, how the country would operate under military rule, and no declaration of a return to democratic civilian rule. Was this a precursor to yet another form of Russian autocratic form of rule? A military junta? No mention of what happened to Vladimir Putin.

Days later, sketchy details emerged through unofficial sources about the fate of Vladimir Putin. Spending Christmas at his estate known as Villa Sellgren located on Lodochny Island in the Gulf of Finland was a typical holiday retreat for Putin. This remote wooded estate remained one of Putin's favorites among his many residences. Located 125 miles west of St. Petersburg, Putin saw the property years earlier as part of a national forest reserve. With his love of the outdoors, it became a favored retreat after extensive remodeling of the original 1913 building.

On Christmas Eve, a full battalion of Russian Army *spetsnaz* special forces descended in a fleet of troop helicopters supported by a dozen attack helicopters. While the first helicopters landed on the front lawn disgorging their troops then lifting away to make space for other incoming helicopters, guards around the villa's perimeter scattered attempting to set up defensive positions. A bullhorn announced them to drop their weapons. The villa was now under control of the Army. Punctuating the message was the rattle of machine gun fire from one of the attack helicopters destroying Putin's personal helicopter sitting idle some distance from the villa.

In subsequent press briefings the coup leaders eventually acknowledged the arrest of Vladimir Putin, now in custody at Lubyanka Prison along with the many others accused of criminal activity against the State. The new regime provided no information as to future legal proceedings.

The world braced itself for the endless unknowns resulting from a militarily ruled Russia.

Georgiy Alexandrovich Shevkunov, officially known as Metropolitan Tikhon, an Archimandrite, or superior abbot of the Russian Orthodox Church, and unofficially the personal confessor of President Vladimir Putin, made a brief statement after visiting Putin in the Lubyanka. Shevkunov was a hard-line ultranationalist often arguing against emerging Russian democracy. A prolific writer, his views made him a close confident of Putin.

"Vladimir Vladimirovich Putin denies these personal attacks. If any truth lies in the Western instigated allegations of financial corrupt, he disavows any knowledge, and vigorously denies any personal gains. His long and illustrious career has always been to serve Mother Russia. During his presidency, Russia has regained its position of stature in the world. In doing so, our great enemy the United States of America has perpetrated unrelenting attacks on Russian sovereignty. My good friend Vladimir Putin believes those that have seized power regrettably succumbed to yet another American conspiracy to destroy Russia."

EPILOGUE

Victoria Prescott and Mark Reynolds returned to Rome in mid-December. This time for a Roman holiday. Better yet, the Italian prosecutors did not plan to call them as witnesses during the trials, their lengthy depositions sufficing. Prescott's teaching duties did not resume until the spring semester at Stanford. An understanding university provost arranged for her leave during the fall semester. That time instead spent in continual days of grueling interviews with a host of government types from various U.S. agencies.

Prescott insisted the interviews take place at her townhouse in the Telegraph Hill neighborhood of San Francisco. Although intruding into her private space, it was preferable to some sterile conference room at the federal building.

In between those sessions with the government, she and Reynolds worked on their respective books. Her academic work in collaboration with Josef Novak, his a rousing adventure-like recounting of their harrowing journey with her as coauthor. As an expert on modern-day Russia, she was not only at the center of recent events, but part of the story.

As a conduit for the whistleblowing efforts of Grigoryev and his brother-in-law, Russia suffered its third major political convulsion in one hundred years. Regrettably a change from a kleptocracy to something unknown resulting from a military coup.

With all that meant, it left little reason to hope for a better Russia.

For Reynolds, his next book promised to be a fitting sequel to his earlier bestseller, *Shell Game*. With his celebrity status as a key figure in the continuing earthshaking events, his literary agent kept busy managing competing offers even before the manuscript was ready.

By tacit agreement, Reynolds moved in with Prescott immediately on their return from Italy. They talked like lovers, deciding to maintain San Francisco as their base while keeping his apartment in New York and spending her summer breaks and the holidays there. For Prescott, a perfect solution given her love for San Francisco and growing up in New York.

Their personal relationship now advanced to mutual thoughts of this being a long-term commitment. The intense experiences and even the long hours spent together explaining every detail to investigators served to deepen appreciation for the nature of each other. Both were sure of their mutual feelings.

"You must admit trying to do this alone was a foolish mistake, Mark. Are you always going to be this way in your work?"

"It certainly didn't turn out the way I hoped. Not a mistake though, just a professional gamble that did not play out well. However, I agree I've played long odds too often in my journalistic career. This was obviously not my first scrape with danger. But I'll admit those odds almost caught up with me this time. Unfortunately, it almost took you down with me. I deeply regret putting you in such danger by underestimating the unknowns, Victoria."

She touched his cheek and kissed him. "I'm a big girl. I agreed to go along with your plan for my own reasons. And you didn't want me to follow you to Beirut and Rome. By that time however, I had fallen in love with you. Impossible to let you go it alone while I stayed behind and worried."

"If it's any comfort, I think I can curtail my instincts to purse stories that inevitably take me into harm's way. Pursuing stories in dangerous foreign places. Plenty of opportunities to investigate bad characters here in the United States if I realign my focus. Perhaps take on a new role as an elder journalist. Work on projects in collaboration with younger colleagues risking their necks."

"Really? Doesn't sound like your style to manage from behind the desk. You like getting your hands dirty. Don't promise changing your life too radically. But if we're to be together, I cannot continually worry about you risking your life. How about sticking to white-collar bad guys and avoiding Mafia types and spies?"

He returned her kiss and smiled.

"Finding you puts a new perspective on life, Victoria. If I regress to old habits, I am sure you can use your considerable skills to temper those tendencies."

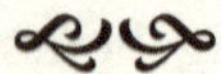

www.ingramcontent.com/pod-product-compliance
Lightning Source LLC
Chambersburg PA
CBHW020639020726
47494CB00001B/264

* 9 7 8 1 9 4 9 7 5 6 4 0 1 *